THE RAIL SPLITTER

THE RAIL SPLITTER

FIRST EDITION

This is a work of fiction. Though some characters, incidents, places, and dialogue are based on the historical record, and historical works such as speeches, letters, and reports are sometimes quoted, passim, the work as a whole is a product of the author's imagination. Any resemblance to other persons, living or dead, events, or locales is entirely coincidental.

ISBN: 9781645720645 (Hardcover)

ISBN: 9781645720652 (ebook)

For inquiries about volume orders, please contact:

Republic Book Publishers
27 West 2oth Street
Suite 1103
New York NY 10011
editor@republicbookpublishers.com

Published in the United States by Republic Book Publishers

Distributed by Independent Publishers Group

www.ipgbook.com

Cover designed by Laura Klynstra

Interior designed by Mark Karis

Young Abe photo by Carroll Foster, Hot Eye Photography

Printed in the United States of America

THE RAIL SPLITTER

A NOVEL

JOHN CRIBB

John Cribb

REPUBLIC
BOOK PUBLISHERS

To my mother and the memory of my father

CONTENTS

Author's note vii

PART 1: THE WOODS 1
Summer 1826 to March 1830

PART 2: THE PRAIRIE 81
March 1830 to Autumn 1835

PART 3: THE TOWN 175
April 1837 to November 1842

PART 4: THE PATH 245
Spring 1846 to December 1859

Acknowledgments 368

AUTHOR'S NOTE

It has been said that if you wish to understand the man, you must first know the boy. *The Rail Splitter* follows Abraham Lincoln from his youth on the frontier to his days as a prairie lawyer and politician, the years that prepared him to be America's greatest president.

I wrote this book as historical fiction so we can walk beside Lincoln, through Indiana forests and Illinois cornfields, and come to know his hopes and struggles on his winding path to greatness. Though this is a novel, I've tried to give an accurate portrayal of Lincoln in his pre-war years. I've turned to hundreds of primary and secondary sources, drawing on the words of Lincoln and his contemporaries when possible. For example, when I write that "a cross word or look" had rarely passed between Lincoln and his stepmother, it's because that's what she told us in an interview she gave after Lincoln's death. In many cases, I've taken artistic license to provide details of action and dialogue. Because this novel spans more than three decades, I've had to condense and simplify some events, occasionally I've bent the timeline for minor events, and of course I've had to leave much out. The line between history and legend is sometimes thin, and there is, no doubt, some lore mixed into any account of Lincoln. I've tried to be faithful to the spirit of his life and times.

The story of the rawboned youth who makes his way from a log cabin to the White House is, in many ways, the great American story. I hope this book brings Lincoln to life and reminds you that the country he loved is a place of wide-open dreams where extraordinary journeys unfold.

PART ONE

THE WOODS

Summer 1826 to March 1830

CHAPTER 1

SUMMER 1826

The book was soaked through.

He knew before he reached for it, knew what had happened the instant the sound of water dripping somewhere near his pallet bed jerked him from sleep. It had stormed overnight, and the rain had found its way through a chink in the cabin loft.

Abraham half rose to pull the book from the ledge beside his bed. His fingers met a heavy wet mass lying in a small pool. A groan rose into his throat.

It ain't mine to ruin, he thought.

Darkness filled the loft. The only light in the cabin came from low flames in the fireplace below, but the song of a wren fluting through a window told him the rain was almost done and, somewhere behind the thick Indiana woods, the sun was rising.

He crawled off his corn husk mattress, crouching low to avoid hitting his head on the rough-hewn rafters, pulled on his buckskin britches, and slipped into his moccasins. Three feet away, his stepbrother, John, grunted and rolled over.

Abraham picked up the soggy book and dropped his long legs through a hole in the loft floor. He grabbed a peg driven into the wall and scrambled down. His feet landed on the cabin's plank floor with a soft thud.

The light from the fireplace touched a few wavering shapes in the room—a four-post feather bed, table, chairs, spinning wheel, corner cabinet, chest of drawers. He stepped to the hearth to open the book. The pages stuck together. He tried to separate two or three, but they began to disintegrate as he peeled them apart. His stomach churned at the thought of losing the precious words.

The cabin door opened and his stepmother entered, toting a few pieces of wood in a bucket.

"'Morning, Abe."

Abraham gave her a stricken look and held out the volume.

"I borrowed it from Si Crawford. The rain came in and spoilt it. I've put books in that little cubby next to my bed lots of times. Water never got in before."

She set down her load and moved to his side.

"Oh, Abe, that's a pity." She lit a small lamp, just a wick placed in a cup of hog grease, and held it up for a closer look. "Let's set it beside the fire awhile. It'll dry."

"It won't be the same. The pages will turn all wrinkly and stained."

"Si will understand."

"Well, I'd be mighty angry if it was my book." He ran his fingers along the cover's warped edges. "I have an idea to go over to his place and talk to him about it."

She set down the lamp before answering.

"Why don't you give that book a day or two to dry? It might turn out just fine."

"I'd better go today. I've got to make it right with Si."

John's face appeared above their heads.

"Pa ain't going to like that," he called down from the loft. "He's set on pulling fodder in the big field today."

Abraham watched his stepbrother climb slowly down the ladder of pegs in the wall.

"I can't help that," he said. "I've got to go see Si about this book."

His stepmother tried him one more time.

"Can't you wait 'til tomorrow, Abe? Your father's counting on you to help pull that fodder."

"Pa won't like this," John announced again.

Abraham searched Sally Lincoln's face. Her black hair, which she always wore curled, was beginning to show tinges of gray. But the blue-gray eyes shone with the strength and sympathy he had always known in her. A cross word or look had rarely passed between them in the years since she had come into his life.

"Don't worry, Mama," he said, breaking into a grin. "There's nothing to pulling fodder, and John here knows more about nothing than any man alive. He can help Pa just fine."

He snatched a cold corn pone from a wooden bowl on the table.

"I'll go explain it to Pa."

He pecked his stepmother on the cheek and stuffed the corn pone into his mouth. Book in hand, he stepped outside to face his father.

CHAPTER 2

SUMMER 1826

The storm had already blown off, and the sun approached like a distant lantern coming into a dark place. In clear patches overhead, the stars were fading out of the sky. On a knoll beside the cabin, the silver horn of the moon nestled into the branches of a hackberry tree. The woods rustled with water dripping from leaves. It would be a hot day.

Abraham found his father behind the cabin in the carpenter's shop, a log shed stuffed with axes, saws, draw knives, and any other tool a man might need to work wood, as well as rakes, sickles, hoes, and other farm implements. He was sitting at his shaving horse, peeling layers from a stout piece of ash.

Tom Lincoln, age forty-eight, was a solid man approaching six feet in height and two hundred pounds in weight. His body was as hard as an oak barrel. Neighbors said he was so solidly built, a man poking his finger into his chest could find no space between his ribs. His dark hazel eyes surveyed Abraham from a well-rounded face beneath a high forehead and coarse, black hair.

"'Morning, Abe. Ready to pull a little fodder today? The path that leads to a loaf of bread winds through a field of toil."

Abraham sighed. This wasn't going to be easy. The day had barely started, and already his father had his mind on that field.

He sometimes felt as if his pa regarded him as just another set of arms and legs to be used for cutting hay or hauling corn to mill. There was always another row to plow, another bucket to fetch from the spring, another rabbit to skin or hide to cure. Standing in the gathering dawn, listening to a dove give its hollow, mournful cry somewhere way back in the woods, he contemplated the cycles of toil that stretched without end.

His father stopped shaving the piece of ash and looked to see what his son held half-concealed behind his back.

"Ready to pull a little fodder?" he repeated, a sudden edge on the question.

Abraham held up the soggy volume.

"Pa, I have to go over to Si Crawford's place and talk to him about this book. I can't pull that fodder just now."

The last darkness of the early morning hovered about the carpenter's shed and filled the space between them. Tom rose from the shaving horse and moved to a table where a pitchfork with a broken handle lay.

"Abe, you know I don't begrudge you reading books. I'm the first to say that a man should learn a little reading, writing, and ciphering if he can."

There was truth to that, Abraham knew. Tom Lincoln had been quite willing, even determined, to see that his son got some schooling in both Kentucky and Indiana. But his idea of a formal education didn't amount to much. Tom had grown up without setting foot inside a schoolhouse door. He could stumble his way through a page of words and write his own name, and to him that seemed enough. So he had sent Abraham to school by littles—a little here and a little there—when the rounds of plantings and harvestings allowed. All in all, the boy's snatches of schooling had amounted to less than a year. To Tom, that seemed practically enough to make a man a scholar.

"I don't begrudge you your books," he repeated. "But to every thing there is a time and a season. Today is for fodder pulling. There'll be time for books and such after." He turned his attention to the broken pitchfork.

"Pa, it's not that I want to read this book today. It's ruined. Look." He held it out in the dim light. "I put it in my cubby, and the rain came in and ran through it last night."

Tom's face clouded over. Abraham quickly decided to appeal to his father's sense of honor.

"This book is Si Crawford's property. It got damaged in my hands. I need to go make it right with him."

Tom laid down the pitchfork.

"Well, I reckon you do owe Si a visit. But not today. It's not going to hurt him to wait a day or two to find out you went and left his property in a place where it would get ruined. Today is for pulling fodder in that cornfield."

"I can pull the fodder after I go see Si. It ain't going to hurt that field to wait a bit, either."

A flash of anger showed in his father's eyes. Tom leaned on the table with both palms and waited a moment.

"Just what is that book about?" he asked.

"George Washington."

Abraham watched his father take that in. Tom Lincoln held the greatest respect for those who had fought in the Revolution, Washington most of all. In fact, Tom considered himself a child of the Revolution, born in its midst. One of Abraham's earliest memories was of a summer morning in Kentucky, when his father stepped out of their cabin's door, pointed his rifle toward the sky above Knob Creek, and let loose a volley. He told his son that it was a day to make a racket, because on the Fourth of July, the United States had declared its independence and the right to call itself a free nation.

"You already read a whole book about General Washington," Tom pointed out. "What do you need to read another for?"

"I want to know more, Pa."

His father reached across the table and took the book from Abraham's hands. He turned it over as if he could get at its contents by weighing it but did not try to open it.

"Well, if you've ruined it, you'll have to pay Si for it. How much does a book like this cost?"

Abraham had hoped his father would not ask that question. "I don't know. Maybe fifty cents. Maybe seventy-five."

"Seventy-five cents! Land o' Goshen!" Tom's jaw clenched. Seventy-five cents was three days' labor or better. They both knew that Abraham had no money. He would have to work off the price of the book—labor spent in another man's fields for which Tom Lincoln would get nothing in return.

"Land o' Goshen!" Tom said again. He handed the book back in disgust. "You're setting off down the wrong path, Abe, fooling around with more education than you need. Reading books is fine. But it don't put food in your mouth. You can't eat a book."

"There's more to living than eating."

"Not if you starve first."

"Well, fodder ain't on my diet."

His father did not smile.

"You're seventeen years old, Abe. Almost a man. Before long, you'll want to have your own farm."

Abraham shifted uncomfortably. Owning a farm was the last thing he wanted.

"If a man is willing, he can take a piece of land and turn it into something useful," his father said. "And there's still land to be had in this country, thank the Lord. But a man has to put his back into it. He can't be sitting around on a stump, messing with books and stories."

Or pieces of wood for carving and cutting, Abraham thought. He didn't dare point out that his father had never liked farming himself. Tom much preferred building bureaus or bedsteads to grubbing and hoeing. He was happiest turning thick walnut planks into a sturdy cabinet. But there was no great call for cabinetmakers in territory where people were used to making things for themselves. Farming was the only way Tom could keep food on his family's table.

"Look here, son. I want to show you something." He pointed to a beam covered with several straight charcoal marks. "These here are my accounts. I owe Gentry three dollars, so I signify it here. These marks here signify I owe Romine two dollars. And these over here signify the two bushels of corn that Barrett owes me for. There, you see? That's all I need to know. I ain't got much education, but I get along far better than if I had. That there's a heap better than fooling yourself with too much learning."

"That's all fine," Abraham shot back. "But maybe I don't want to be breaking my back in a cornfield the rest of my life. And maybe I want to learn more than a few scratches on some rafters is going to tell me."

The words hurt Tom. His voice rose. "Your britches is getting a mite tight, ain't they? Just what is it you aim to do with all this book learning?"

Abraham flinched. He felt impaled by his father's gaze, sharp as an awl. He stood a good four or five inches taller than Tom, but at moments like this, it seemed as though his father was the one who loomed over him.

"Abe, I need that fodder pulled. Now, are you going to get to it?"

Through a window in the back of the shed, Abraham watched a hog appear at the edge of the woods. It rooted at the base of a hickory tree, looking for early nuts. Not finding much in the way of breakfast there, the hog settled for scratching its side against the trunk.

The boy decided to hold his ground.

"I'll pull it, after I see Si."

Anger flashed again in his father's eyes. Tom clenched and unclenched his fists. He was still a bull of a man. I wonder if he's going to wallop me,

Abraham thought. He knew he would not try to hit him back.

"This is the last time I'll say it. Get in that field and get to work."

"No, Pa."

In the silence that throbbed between them, Abraham heard a weary sigh. This life is running him down, he thought. It's a hard life to endure, with too much scraping and pounding and breaking. He felt a pang of guilt at telling his father no.

Tom picked up the pitchfork again. He ran his hand down the broken handle, searching out the exact place where the grain of the wood had failed. After a moment he laid it down for a second time and turned back to the shaving horse.

"You've made a bad bargain, Abe. Now you'll have to hug it all the tighter. Go on. Off with you."

CHAPTER 3

SUMMER 1826

The corn pone breakfast and the talk with his father had made him thirsty, so he loped over to the spring, which lay a short walk west of the cabin. He took a long drink, then filled a pail to wash his face and neck.

In the dawn light, he glimpsed his watery reflection, and his mind's eye filled in the details. He was homely. He knew it and felt it keenly. His face was full of crags and sharp angles. The nose was too large, the cheekbones too high, the jaw too long. His skin was a leathery yellow. The heavy brow cropped out like a rocky ledge on a hill, jutting over cavernous eyes, and the ears ran out like shingles tacked onto his head. Scraggly black hair lay piled up wherever the wind or his fingers left it.

His body was all limbs and joints. His legs had gotten long when he was young, and it seemed they would never stop growing. At church meetings and corn huskings, his head stuck up above everyone else's. His britches lacked meeting the tops of his shoes by several inches, exposing his ankles and narrow shins, a display that sometimes made him shy. His father joked that he looked like he had been chopped out with an ax and still needed smoothing with a jack plane. Folks around Little Pigeon Creek laughed about it good-naturedly, and he laughed with them, but a spot deep inside him was pricked by the jests.

He thrust his hands into the bucket, past the dim reflection, and bathed his face with cool water. His washing done, he skirted the cornfield, keeping a safe distance from his father's carpentry shed, walked past the little cemetery that held his mother's grave, and ambled toward Josiah Crawford's place.

Walls of green rose around the forest path. Gnarled oaks spread their arms a hundred feet wide. Yellow poplars guarded the wilderness like sentinels, their trunks holding themselves ramrod-straight into the high green canopy. Thick grapevines, some eight inches through, circled trunks and wove nets from branch to branch.

In places the woods were so dense the sunlight could barely penetrate, and there was no sign of the sky. Southern Indiana was miles and miles of woods, broken every once in a while by a spot where someone had managed to push back the trees. Sometimes it brought on a lonesome feeling. When you stepped outside your cabin door, you could see no further than the little clearing around you, and no sign of your nearest neighbor.

He passed through one of those clearings, where the meetinghouse of the Little Pigeon Baptist Church stood, a good place for listening to the itinerant preachers who spread the faith in the Indiana woods. Their sermons were full of words like *malice*, *charity*, and *righteousness* that Abraham liked to ponder. Nearby stood the settlement's one-room schoolhouse, deserted until after the fall harvest. He lingered a moment, recalling how, during his short time there, he had devoured the ragged books the schoolmaster had put in his hands and eagerly scratched out his lessons with a buzzard-feather pen and maple-bark ink.

Several more minutes of walking brought him to the clearing where the Crawford house stood along a branch of Buckhorn Creek. It was a low, one-room cabin of unhewn logs. Beside it, under the boughs of a cottonwood tree, spread a flower garden where Elizabeth Crawford had laid out little beds of sweet pinks, marigolds, and roses.

Abraham looked at Si's book. The back cover was working loose. He grew nervous. Among some folks at Little Pigeon Creek, Si Crawford had gained the reputation of being closefisted. They groused that he drove too hard a bargain when trading a horse or selling a hog. Abraham liked both the farmer and his wife. They had always been fair with him whenever his father had hired him out to clear ground or cut fence rails on their place. But Si took great pride in his library, which consisted of a dozen or so books he had brought with him when he emigrated from Kentucky. Abraham was not sure how he would react to the news that one of his volumes was soaking wet.

He screwed his courage to the sticking place, stepped up to the cabin, and knocked. Elizabeth opened the door, a pot hook in her hand.

"Abe Lincoln, what brings you to our neck of the woods so early?"

Abraham thought Elizabeth Crawford a handsome woman, at least by the hard-life standards of Little Pigeon Creek, with an intelligent face and a mouth given to warm smiles. She was just two or three years older than he was, and he would have been shy around her had she not been married.

"Come in and sit down. I'm just putting some breakfast on the table for Si. You might as well help him lap it up."

Abraham raised his cap and made a little bow as he ducked through the doorway.

"'Morning, Elizabeth. 'Morning, Si."

Josiah sat at a table in front of the fireplace, sharpening a knife. He was a hearty-looking man in his midtwenties. His face's most prominent feature would have been probing eyes if not for a trumpet of a nose covered with purple veins. It had prompted Abraham to call him

"Bluenose" behind his back, and the nickname took hold around Little Pigeon Creek.

There was no use beating around the bush, especially since Josiah was already focusing his gaze on the book. Abraham explained what had happened.

"I reckon that by the time it dries out, it won't exactly be good as new. I want to make things right. I can't repair it. All I can do is work it off."

Josiah took the book and turned it over two or three times, inspecting the stains and bubbles on the warped cover. Abraham watched in fascinated alarm as the man's face changed color. Red spread across his cheeks, and his nose turned a deepened purple. Elizabeth remained quiet by the fire. Josiah kept turning the book in his hands, as if expecting that each rotation might suddenly fix it.

He shifted his eyes toward the fire while he considered the situation. The low flames burned in his pupils for a moment, then died when he looked back at Abraham. The red and purple drained from his face.

"Well, Abe," he said slowly, "if it was anyone but you, I suppose I would be riled. But as long it's you, we'll work it out. I'll tell you what: I could use a hand pulling fodder. You pull the blades in the lower field for me. It should take you two or three days. Then we'll be square."

Abraham cringed. It was the one job he'd been hoping to avoid. When his father found out that he was pulling fodder in Si Crawford's field instead of doing the same at home, he'd hear no end of it. But he had no room to bargain.

"All right, Si. That sounds fair."

"And as you'll be working for it, you might as well keep the book when you're done."

Abraham's mournful face brightened.

"Do you mean keep it for good?"

"Yes. If the pages don't stick together, they'll probably fall out. But I expect you'll manage to read them anyhow."

It was an unexpected twist. Abraham's spirits shot up at the thought of owning the volume, even if it was in a sorry state.

"Well, now that that's settled, you men eat," Elizabeth said. "Pulling fodder takes nearly as much strength as reading books, and there's no point doing either on an empty stomach."

Abraham sat at the table while Elizabeth busied herself at the fire. He surveyed the cabin. His father had made some furniture for the Crawfords, including a walnut cupboard. In a flourish of inspiration, Tom had set the initials *JC* and *EC* in the center of the front panels.

On a nearby shelf sat Josiah's little library. At the end of the row of books, Abraham spotted *The Kentucky Preceptor*, a volume he had recently borrowed. The title page announced that the book contained "a number of useful lessons for reading and speaking." He had spent several nights poring over stories such as "The Faithful American Dog" and "The Child Trained Up for the Gallows." He had an itch now to reach and flip through its pages, but considering the circumstances of his being there, decided against it.

He watched Elizabeth as she pulled a skillet away from the fire.

"Elizabeth, you're just about the cleverest woman I know when it comes to making johnnycakes," he drawled. "I'll bet you could take that skillet, toss them johnnycakes up the chimney, run outside, and catch them coming down."

Elizabeth smiled. "If I could do that, I'd run off and join the circus, and I wouldn't have to put up with big clumsy farm boys." She set breakfast on the table.

"Your garden looks especially fine today," Abraham kept on, determined to please her. "You surely can grow flowers like nobody else."

"Now, there's a compliment I'll accept. The good Lord created man to keep a garden. You remember that, Abe. Have some johnnycakes. My cooking's especially sweet when it's had so much flattery poured on it."

"What news on the Rialto, Abe?" Josiah asked. "Tell us what's going on in the wide world."

Abraham was Little Pigeon Creek's unofficial news boy. He read every newspaper he could get his hands on at Gentry's store or the river towns of Troy and Rockport. Copies of the Vincennes *Western*

Sun, the Washington *National Intelligencer,* and others came floating through the area, carried by steamboats or passing travelers. They were often days or weeks old, but their news was still news to folks in the backwoods. Abraham enjoyed repeating the information he gleaned to almost anyone who would listen.

"They say the Erie Canal's going gangbusters. Boats keep pouring into Buffalo—so many barges, they get all jammed up against each other waiting to use the locks. They're hauling grain, timber, cloth, coal, and anything else you could want. You can even ride a fancy passenger boat all the way across the state of New York and eat on board with silver forks. Now they're building a canal to connect Washington with the Ohio River, and another between Cincinnati and Dayton."

"Merciful God!" Josiah snorted. "There'll be man-made rivers criss-crossing this whole country before they're through."

"And over in Massachusetts, they're building a railway that'll be three miles long. They're going to use horses to pull wagons full of granite to some wharves, for building a monument at Bunker Hill. They say that before long, they'll be using steam engines to haul wagons on rails, just like engines run steamboats."

"Well, I wish they'd build one of those railways right here to my door. I'd haul my corn to those wharves and see Bunker Hill to boot."

"And the *Western Sun* says the president offered to pay Mexico a million dollars for Texas. But Mexico said no."

"A million dollars! For Texas? Good God Almighty! I wouldn't give two fleas off the hind end of a hound for Texas."

They talked over all the latest goings-on in the newspapers. A new school called Western Reserve College had started in Ohio. The people of Boston had organized an American Society for the Promotion of Temperance. A writer named James Fenimore Cooper had written a book called *The Last of the Mohicans* that was selling thousands of copies. And folks back East were still talking about how Thomas Jefferson and John Adams had both died on Independence Day, exactly fifty years after the Declaration of Independence.

They ate until they were full of news and johnnycakes. Abraham pushed his chair back, stood up, and stretched.

"Well, all this talk will never get the child a coat. I guess I'd better get to that fodder."

CHAPTER 4

SUMMER 1826

He made a little pallet of sticks to keep the book off the wet soil and placed it in the shade of a beech tree. Too much sun will make it faded and brittle, he thought, like an old autumn leaf.

Gently lifting the cover, which announced *The Life of George Washington* by David Ramsay, M.D., he turned to the water-logged dedication page and read aloud.

"To the youth of the United States, in the hope that from the example of their common father, they will learn to do and suffer whatever their country's good may require at their hands, the following life of George Washington is most affectionately inscribed by the author."

That was enough to hold him for now. He kicked off his moccasins, pitched his cap, and strode into the cornfield to get to work.

Like so many farm tasks, pulling fodder was a simple but tedious job. He moved from stalk to stalk, stripping the elongated leaves and tying them into bundles, which he hung on the stalks. After they had dried a few days, Josiah would gather the bundles and store them in his barn for his livestock.

The cornfield was full of the hot smell of late summer sun. The day grew humid, and the air lay still between the rows. Crickets trilled all around him. He watched his hands as they moved down each stalk, stripping and tying the leaves, and his thoughts drifted across the pages of other books he had read—*Aesop's Fables*, *Robinson Crusoe*, *The Pilgrim's Progress*. And *Lessons in Elocution*, full of rules for a polished speaker to follow, like, "Let your articulation be distinct and deliberate." It had pages of verses to puzzle over. There was Shakespeare saying, "All the world's a stage, and all the men and women merely players." And Alexander Pope: "Honor and shame from no condition rise; act well your part—there all the honor lies."

Every once in a while, he paused to move the book a few inches to keep it in the creeping shadows. If Pa could see me, he thought, he would shake his head and say that his son was just filling his head with fool ideas. There ain't enough time to break ground and break open books too, he would say. Well, as far as Abraham could see, there was more than enough time for plowing, hoeing, and grubbing. It was time for reading and learning he lacked. And books to read. He was always on the lookout for a new one, but they were hard to come by. Books weren't as plentiful as wildcats in that part of Indiana.

Why was Tom Lincoln suspicious of books? Abraham had spent much time pondering it. His father didn't seem to dislike the things books said. Sometimes he took down the family Bible, sat by the door, and mumbled his way through the places he liked best. And sometimes he called on his son to read aloud to the family a chapter from *The Arabian Nights* or *The Pilgrim's Progress*. Every once in a while, Abraham thought he could tell that his father was a little proud to have a son who could read so well, and tell about things in books, and write letters for neighbors who didn't know how.

He worked through the afternoon until the sun touched the tops of the cornstalks. More than a third of the field was done. That was good. He carefully picked up his *Life of George Washington* and walked toward his sister, Sarah's, cabin, a short distance west of the Crawford place.

Only a few weeks before, Sarah had married Aaron Grigsby. The wedding had taken place at the Lincoln cabin, where neighbors gathered for roast venison and corn pudding. It had been a hard day for Abraham. He felt closer to his sister than to any other soul, and he had hated to lose her.

He found Sarah outside her new home, lugging a big iron kettle to a fire pit in back of the cabin. A smile broke over her face when she saw him.

"Abe, you've grown six inches in the last six days. If you don't slow down, I'll have to put a rock on your head."

"Where's Aaron? Why is he making you haul this thing around?"

"He went to Boonville to look at some mules. I expect he'll be gone a day or two. Stay awhile. It's beginning to get lonesome around here."

He bent to help her. "Why didn't you tell me he was going? I would've come to look after you."

"Is it your notion that females get helpless soon as they're married? I guess I've slung around a few pots in my time."

"Well, Aaron should have let me know," he grumbled. "Ain't no sense in going off and leaving you all alone without telling your family."

She laughed when he told her about pulling fodder to pay for the book.

"I'd liked to have seen old Bluenose's face. I'll bet he turned three shades of purple." She said it without malice. When Josiah and Elizabeth came to Indiana, Sarah had helped them get their house established, and she'd grown fond of the Crawfords.

She rustled up some cornmeal mush-and-milk for supper, and afterwards Abraham laid the book by the fireplace to keep it drying.

He sat on the floor, his back against the log wall and his knees pulled up to his chin, watching her straighten her cabin.

Sarah was his big sister by only two years, but now that she was married, the difference in age seemed greater. Her plain, modest ways made her well-liked at Little Pigeon Creek. She was a thickset girl, a little on the short side, with dark brown hair and deep gray eyes. Abraham had heard it said that he resembled her. He could never understand how any face that looked remotely like his could light into beauty, but it happened every time she smiled.

She sat and began to spin flax, humming to herself as she fed strands onto the reel. Abraham stared into the low flames on the hearth. The soft clack of the spinning wheel and the dark glow of the embers made his thoughts wander. He imagined what his father would say when he came home with the book, and he began to feel glum. With Sarah, he felt no need to disguise his moodiness.

"What would you say if I went away?" he asked.

"Away? Where?"

"I don't know. I could hitch a ride on a flatboat down to New Orleans and sign onto a ship to California."

"California? What in the Lord's creation would make you want to go to California?"

"Well, I imagine there's lots to do there. Maybe I could hire myself out to a boat hauling things up and down the coast. Or I could sign onto a ship bound for China. It would please me to see old Kublai Khan's palace."

Sarah left her wheel, sat on the floor beside him, and rambled her fingers through his hair.

"You look as solemn as a papoose," she said.

It was an old family saying. When he was a newborn, neighbors and cousins who had come calling to see Abraham in his cradle remarked that the wrinkled little face sucking on a sugar tit looked as somber as an Indian. The expression had stayed with him. When thoughtful spells came over him, his eyes turned serious and sad.

"How are you getting along at home?" Sarah asked.

Abraham shrugged. "Seems as though every time I turn around, Pa's found something else for me to do. If we lived in a desert, that man would put me to work shoveling sand from hill to hill."

"Well, it ain't much different living with Aaron. These woods are filled with long days, that's for certain, and more than enough to get done."

She spent a few minutes studying the fire with him.

"You know Pa does the best he can for us, Abe. He always has."

"I reckon. I'm just feeling more and more hemmed in."

She rumpled his hair again in her motherly way. "You do have an itch at your heels. Had it for a while." She half smiled. "You'll be leaving us. It's in your nature. But don't leave yet, Abe. I'll tell you a secret. Aaron and I aim to start a family soon."

They both blushed.

"Wait 'til a young 'un comes along before you go. Then I'll have a playmate to pick berries and skip stones with sometimes, and it won't be so lonely without you. If it's a boy, I'll name him Abe, and he'll cause me to recollect you."

The thought pleased him, although he knew that Aaron would not likely let her name her firstborn after her brother. He grinned at her, and his gloom began to slide away.

"All right, Sis. I'll stay awhile. For you."

CHAPTER 5

SUMMER 1826

He fell asleep by the fire and had dreams of his childhood, good and bad. He dreamed of wood shavings. Brown walnut shavings piled high in his father's carpenter shop, shavings that curled from planks at the touch of Tom Lincoln's jack plane and dropped to the packed dirt floor. He and Sarah played together once again, he building little mountains with the shavings and she flinging them over her left shoulder to see what kind of letters they made where they fell, as signs of who she might marry.

He dreamed of the days he had trailed Sarah through the Kentucky woods, filling pails with wild grapes, blackberries, and pawpaws. On summer afternoons, they lay on their backs behind the cabin, making guesses about what shapes the white clouds meant to be as they came scudding over the hilltops. On school days, they walked two miles up the Old Cumberland Road to the Knob Creek schoolhouse, their dog, Honey, trotting at their side.

His mother was there, too, and he glimpsed her face: the blue eyes filled with shades of light, the high forehead, the smile both tender and melancholy. He saw her sitting beside the fire at night, running a horn comb through her soft, brown hair a few times, then taking him in her lap and letting her fingers wander through his hair. He could hear her singing one of the hymns she loved most:

When I can read my title clear to mansions in the skies,
I bid farewell to every fear, and wipe my weeping eyes.
And wipe my weeping eyes, and wipe my weeping eyes
I bid farewell to every fear, and wipe my weeping eyes.

He dreamed of the day his father had loaded the family into a wagon and left Kentucky, heading across the shining Ohio River into the Indiana wilderness. Abraham and Sarah had clutched each other to keep from tumbling out of the wagon as it jolted over rocks and roots. They had clutched each other again that first winter at Little Pigeon Creek, huddling under bearskins as wind sliced through the shed that served as their home until their cabin was built.

That spring, Tom placed an ax in Abraham's hands and showed him how to put it to work. He was only eight years old, but he was large for his age, big enough to start learning a man's work: clearing ground, cutting brush, splitting firewood. They got a nice surprise one day when their cousin Dennis Hanks arrived from Kentucky along with Aunt Betsy and Uncle Tom Sparrow. Suddenly they had family close by again. Dennis was older than Abraham by ten years, but he was full of tricks and fun, and Abraham and Sarah were glad to tag along when he went fishing in the creeks or hunting rabbits and quail.

Then the milk sick came to Little Pigeon Creek. It was the disease the settlers feared more than any other. They didn't know where it came from, only that it struck after cows got the trembles, and that anyone who had drunk milk from such a cow would likely die.

One crisp autumn morning, Sarah stepped outside to do the milking and reappeared at the cabin door a minute later, face ashen. One of their cows had the trembles. It died three days later. By that time, Uncle Tom Sparrow was stricken. It came on him fast with dizziness and vomiting. His swollen tongue was coated white, his breathing turned slow and labored. He was dead within a week.

Aunt Betsy was next. Abraham's mother did her best to make her feel comfortable, nursing her with whispers and tears. By the time Betsy Sparrow was gone, the signs were showing on Nancy Lincoln.

She knew she was going to leave them. She lay on a bed in a corner of the cabin and called her children to her side. They tiptoed in and stood beside her, looking into the tired face and the eyes growing dull with the coming long sleep. She told them to be good to their father, to one another, and to the world.

"I want you to live as I have taught you, and to love your heavenly Father," she said.

The lines of weariness about her eyes softened, the corners of the mouth lifted into the sweet smile she meant them to remember her by, and she passed out of their lives.

Tom Lincoln whipsawed a log into planks while Abraham whittled pegs for fastening the boards together into a coffin. Three neighbor women dressed the body, and Tom lowered it into the coffin and gently fastened the lid. They buried her on the little knoll where Thomas and Elizabeth Sparrow lay. Some weeks later, a preacher passing through the area gave a sermon over her grave. Abraham and Sarah clutched each other again as they stood in the hilltop cemetery and listened to the parson lift his voice in prayer.

Lonely, dirty, wretched months without a mother came upon them. There were four in the cabin then: Tom, Sarah, Abraham, and Cousin Dennis. Sarah tried her best at cooking, cleaning, churning, spinning, and all the other chores her mother had performed. But she was just eleven, and at times, she could only sit by the fire and cry. Abraham and Dennis caught a baby raccoon and a turtle to cheer her up. They tried to get her a fawn but could not trap one. What little comfort they found came in telling the Bible stories their mother had taught them. The old stories came close to bringing back her voice.

The loneliness and squalor got worse when Tom Lincoln decided to leave them while he went back to Kentucky to fetch a new wife. Dennis hunted while Sarah tried to cook and Abraham toted water from the spring. Their clothes turned threadbare, and their stomachs grew leathery from want of food. The wind shook the bearskin that hung across the cabin door and scattered the piles of dead leaves they slept on. Weeks passed. Abraham was sure his father had been killed by an outlaw or some wild animal.

Both he and Sarah cried unembarrassed tears of joy the evening they heard the rattles of an approaching wagon and ran outside to find Tom Lincoln pulling up to the cabin. Beside him sat a woman they did not know, and behind them, two girls and a boy, as well as a wagonload of furniture and household goods.

"Children, this is your new ma," Tom announced as he climbed down.

They watched the tall, handsome woman with curled black hair follow their father off the wagon. She shepherded her own children down, gently pushed them forward, and made their introductions: Elizabeth, age twelve; Matilda, called Tildy, age ten; and John, age nine.

Tom explained as gently as he knew how that he had known Sally Bush Johnston in his younger days in Kentucky. He had heard she was widowed and hunted her up in Elizabethtown.

"I have no wife, and you have no husband," he had told her. "I came apurpose to marry you. I've no time to lose. If you're willing, let it be done straight off." Several days later, on a cold December morning, a Methodist minister had performed a hasty service.

Abraham's eyes grew wide as a hoot owl's at the cascade of belongings that came pouring off the wagon. A table and set of matching chairs. A black walnut bureau. A big clothes chest. A feather mattress and feather pillows. Pots, pans, skillets, forks, and spoons. He had never dreamed that such luxury would come flowing into their cabin.

Among Sally Bush Lincoln's possessions lay a few books. He eagerly seized them and ran his fingers over their stiff covers. The tall, straight-backed woman put her hand on his shoulder and said quietly, "Abe, you can read these books all you want."

Her first act of authority had been to turn to her new husband and announce, "This place isn't fitting for pigs to live in, let alone children. We'll commence cleaning now."

She rubbed and washed Abraham and Sarah, then mended their clothes until they once again looked as human as their own good mother had left them. The cabin came next. Sally swept out the filthy leaves and cornhusks they had been sleeping on. She prodded her new husband to lay down a plank floor, hang a door in place of the bearskin flap that had covered the cabin entrance, and repair the roof to keep snow out of the loft.

It had not taken long for Sarah and Abraham to begin calling her "Mama." She took the five children, mixed them together like hasty pudding, and loved them all as her own.

Eight people bedded down in the one-room cabin the first night of Sally Bush Lincoln's arrival. Over the next seven years, half of that number moved into homes of their own. Cousin Dennis and Elizabeth courted, married, and started a family in a nearby cabin. Tildy married Dennis's half brother, Squire Hall. And Sarah married Aaron Grigsby.

The scream of a panther woke him. He sat upright and listened to the savage wail receding through the woods. Sarah slept undisturbed on a rope bed tucked into a corner of the cabin. The coals she had banked in the fireplace threw a soft glow on her face. Abraham reached for

The Life of George Washington, turned a few pages to a place that still needed airing out, and went back to sleep.

The next morning, he was back at work in Josiah Crawford's cornfield, pulling away. As the book dried, and he got closer to making a clean sweep of the field, his anticipation grew. He found it harder not to pause every ten minutes to leaf through a few pages.

On the frontispiece he found a drawing of a large stone beaten by waves in a storm. Inscribed on the stone was the name *Washington*, and beneath it the words: "Firm as the surge-repelling rock." Chapter headings like "Washington as Commander in Chief of the Armies of the United Colonies" and "Winter Quarters in Valley Forge" called to him.

Washington's address to his troops before the battle at Long Island caught his eye. He read the passage several times, repeating the words until he knew them. Mounting a stump at the edge of the field, he addressed the rows of leafless stalks, raising and dropping his arms as the plates in *Lessons in Elocution* instructed.

> *The time is now near at hand, which must probably determine whether Americans are to be freemen or slaves; whether they are to have any property they can call their own; whether their houses and farms are to be pillaged and destroyed. . . . Our cruel and unrelenting enemy leaves us only the choice of a brave resistance, or the most abject submission. We have therefore to resolve to conquer—or to die!*

Elizabeth Crawford, passing by on her way to retrieve a stray heifer, called from behind the stalks.

"Abe Lincoln! You do beat all. What's to become of you?"

Abraham grinned at the measureless, blue Indiana sky.

"Me? I'm going to be president of these United States!"

CHAPTER 6

SUMMER 1826

He arrived home the next day in high spirits, carrying his *Life of George Washington* like a poor fisherman who had hauled up a shimmering pearl. It was the first book he could claim as his very own. He snatched a piece of cornbread from the cupboard, cocked his legs up on the table, and started to read.

"Don't be getting too comfortable," his stepmother told him. "There's a whole big stretch of that field waiting for you. Your pa's going hunting with Dennis and John tomorrow. He wants you to finish it while they're gone."

Abraham sighed. More fodder to pull. Well, he didn't really mind. With his father gone, he could take the book with him and read between rows.

"And Abe, I want you boys to keep your grubby hands off my ceiling. I spent all yesterday whitewashing it."

"Where do you expect me to wipe my fingers? A fellow can't keep clean if he can't at least rub his tater-grabbers on the ceiling."

"You do your rubbing and wiping outside. And as long as you're cleaning yourself, you might as well scrub your noggin. If you do any more growing, that mop on top of your head will leave smudges all over my ceiling too."

"Yes, ma'am."

Dennis Hanks arrived, spotted Abraham reading, and grinned. He was an easygoing young man with a companionable soul and a few drops of Kentucky wildcat blood in him.

"There's that no-good cousin of mine." He winked at Sally. "I tell you, he'll never come to much."

Abraham smiled at the prophecy, as he always did. It was the punch line of a story he had heard a hundred times. On the morning of Abraham's birth in Kentucky, ten-year-old Dennis had raced two miles down the road from the cabin where he lived with Thomas and Betsy Sparrow, eager to greet the newborn babe. He had found Nancy Lincoln lying under a bearskin, the soft, pink infant in her arms.

"What you going to name him, Nancy?" the boy had asked.

"Abraham, after his grandfather."

"His skin looks like red cherry pulp squeezed dry. Can I hold him?"

"All right, but be careful. You're the first boy he's ever seen."

Dennis took the baby, rocked him in his arms, tickled his feet, and rambled on about how glad he was to have a cousin to play with. The infant wrinkled its red face into a tight wad and wailed at the top of its little lungs. The boy turned and handed the child to Betsy Sparrow.

"Here, Aunt. Take him," he said in disgust. "He'll never come to much."

Dennis stood before Abraham now, peering at the water-stained book, eyes flashing in his sun-gold face.

"Why don't you come hunting with us, Abe? If any bears or coons go scampering into the treetops, you can just reach up and pluck them down for us."

"No thanks, Denny. I'll stick around here and finish this book. But if you see any bears, you send them this way, and I'll wrestle them for you."

"I swear, Abe, there's something peculiarsome about you. If you read any more of those books, your head'll bust open like a pumpkin, it'll be so ripe with knowledge."

"The things I want to know are in books, Denny. My best friend is a man who can get me a book."

Dennis had brought his wife, Elizabeth, and their four children with him for a visit. At dinnertime, all the Lincolns and Hankses crowded up to the table. Tom rattled off his usual grace.

"Oh, Lord, fit and prepare us for life's humblest service, for Christ's sake. Amen."

They fell to eating a meal of venison stew and cornbread.

"Tom, I saw Jim Taylor last week," Dennis mentioned in an offhand way. "He was asking if you might have an interest in hiring Abe out for a while."

Abraham looked up from his plate. Jim Taylor's farm was on the Ohio River, a favorite place.

"What kind of work does he need done?" he asked quickly.

"I suppose he wants someone to maul a few rails and such. Said he could use some help at the ferry too."

"How much is he paying?" Tom asked.

"I didn't inquire."

Abraham had recently spent several days on the banks of the Ohio, cutting and stacking firewood at a wooding station that supplied fuel for steamboats. Watching the vessels churn up and down the Ohio, trading news with their crews, and hanging around the river town of Troy had turned into a grand escape. He had let it be known at the wharves and wood yards that he wouldn't mind another sip of river life.

He had to choose his words carefully now.

"Pa, if there's nothing pressing here, it might be a good idea. I could make some extra money for you. And I could always come home to give you a hand with anything that needs doing."

"I'm not inclined for you to do it."

"Why not?"

"I don't believe I can spare you."

"But cold weather'll be coming on before we know it. There won't be much for me to do around here. What there is, John can help you with."

His stepbrother put on an unhappy expression. John was not generally inclined to work without a push, and the thought of being Tom Lincoln's sole prop for a while discouraged him.

"I'm thinking of clearing a little more land," Tom said. "And putting a new roof on the barn. I'll need you both for that."

Abraham didn't want to get into another argument. His father wasn't likely to give in a second time in one week. But he tried prodding.

"Well, it just seems a shame to pass up the chance to earn good money."

"I don't want you lollygagging around the river with a bunch of keelboat ruffians. You're likely to get yourself into trouble."

Abraham surrendered. "I'm more likely to get into trouble if I don't get shut of this place," he grumbled under his breath.

The next morning before sunup, Tom, Dennis, and John headed into the woods with their rifles. When they were gone, Abraham tilted back in a chair and read while his stepmother swept the floor with a cornhusk broom.

"Abe, I'll talk to your pa about working for Jim Taylor."

The offer was unexpected.

"I sure would like to get down to the river."

"I know you would, son. I believe I can probably persuade him."

"Hallelujah!" He jumped up and slapped the ceiling. His stepmother looked up at her fresh whitewash in despair.

"Sorry, Mama." He sat back down. "What does Pa have against my going? It's a good chance to make some money."

"Your father has gotten to where he depends on you a good deal."

"I'll just be down at the river a while. It ain't like I'm going to Timbuktu."

"That's true."

They both studied the situation for a minute.

"Of course, with you down at the river, there won't be so much foolishness and jabberjawing around here."

"Well, if you miss it, I can sneak up here any old time and put hog grease on a broom handle or stick a calf up in the loft."

Sally chuckled. "That would be just fine."

She finished sweeping and propped the broom by the fireplace.

"As long as you have nothing better to do, you could make yourself useful by watching the children a few minutes. Elizabeth and I want to pick some blackberries. We won't be long."

"Yes, ma'am."

"Abe, a word to the wise. Your father might be more inclined to say yes if you get that fodder pulled by the time he gets back."

"Yes, ma'am"

"And hands off the walls and ceiling."

"Yes, ma'am."

He went outside to sit under a hackberry tree and read in the early morning light. Nearby, the Hanks children played around the horse trough. The youngsters chattered happily as they scooped handfuls of water onto the ground to make mud pies. Abraham's stepmother and Elizabeth headed down the path and out of sight, gossiping as they strolled, Sally bouncing Elizabeth's infant on her arm.

He pondered this woman who had come into his family after the milk sick took his mother away. She had found them dirty, frightened, and alone, and had folded them to her breast. When he felt like cutting up, she laughed at his jokes. When he was moody, she left him to himself. When his father grumbled about the uselessness of too much education, she made a way for him to attend a few weeks of school, patted him on the shoulder, and said, "Abe, you go and learn all you can." In many ways, their minds moved in the same channel.

The children were hopping around the horse trough, dancing barefoot in the muddy puddles. Abraham put down his book and loped over to where they were playing. A little devilishness was coming over him. He picked up the oldest.

"Come with your Uncle Abe for a minute, sweetie. We're going to do some painting."

He carried her into the cabin.

"I'm going to lift you up and flip you upside down. Now, you put your feet on the ceiling and take a few steps while I hold tight, just like you're taking a walk."

"Granny's going to be mad!" the girl squealed.

"Don't worry. I'll clean it all up."

A few minutes later, muddy footprints tracked across the ceiling, from one side of the cabin to the opposite wall.

He was back under the tree, nose in book, when the two women returned. They stepped inside the cabin, Sally holding the baby and Elizabeth carrying a basket of berries. Abraham fastened his eyes on the page while he listened to their chatter.

The talking died abruptly. Silence fell over the cabin and the yard. Even the squirrels in the branches overhead left off their clucking. At the horse trough, the children stood still in the puddles.

Abraham closed his book and leaned his head back against the trunk. He shut his eyes and saw, inside the cabin, two heads on two necks craning back and forth, one mouth gaping, the other beginning to twitch up at the corners. He let the grin that he'd been holding back break over his lank face. He crossed his arms, cocked his head, and turned his face to the warm morning sun.

In another moment, the sound he was waiting for came spilling through the cabin door—the sound of Sally Bush Lincoln laughing.

CHAPTER 7

AUTUMN 1826

"Can you kill a hog?"

"If you'll risk the hog, I'll risk myself."

Jim Taylor stroked his chin and studied Abraham's sinewy limbs.

"The pay is six dollars a month, and thirty-one cents a day extra for killing hogs."

"That sounds all right."

"Well, then, put her there."

They shook on it.

Working on Taylor's farm turned out to be the roughest work a young man could be made to do. Abraham plowed, built fences, cut hay, turned a hand mill, skinned and cured hides. He lived and ate at Taylor's home. After the day's work was done, he often read until midnight, then climbed upstairs and threw himself down to sleep in a room he shared with Taylor's son, Green.

Hog killing time began when the weather turned cool. It was a wretched business. Abraham clubbed each hog in the center of the forehead, flipped the stunned beast onto its back, and stuck a long-bladed knife in the underside of the neck to bleed it to death. He came to know the stench of opening the abdomen to remove the entrails, of splitting the carcass down the middle, and of taking it to the cutting table to carve out the jowl, the feet, the loin, the ham.

Splitting rails came more naturally to him. He knew how to measure with his eye a good chestnut or oak log, how to find the precise spot where the grain would willingly part, how to grasp the stout hickory handle of the maul and send its big, cheese-shaped head pounding against the iron wedge. After he split a log in two lengthwise, he split the halves, then the quarters, making eight rails from each log. With Green Taylor, he stacked them into zigzagging fences, bracing each place where the sections met with two poles slanting up from the ground, checking to make sure that each length was horse high, bull strong, and pig tight.

When travelers rang the ferry bell, he got to run Jim Taylor's ferry across Anderson River near its mouth on the Ohio. Taylor kept a flatboat big enough to carry a wagon and team. Abraham directed the wagons onto the boat, heaved on the rope that ran between pulleys tied to trees on the banks, and ferried them over the stream. He carried foot passengers in Taylor's rowboat, charging each a picayune, or six and a quarter cents. When the water was low, he could send the rowboat across the little Anderson River with one big sweep of the oars.

Better yet were the days he had time to loiter on the banks of the wide Ohio River itself. There the trees didn't crowd all around. The big waterway's spacious bend gave a view that swept in miles of river and sky. He liked seeing it at all times of day—in early morning, when mist hugged the water; in afternoon, when bright flecks of light danced on the currents; in evening, when swallows darted and swooped.

The steady, restless pageantry of the river highway spread before him. Clumsy flatboats taking settlers downstream, the bigger ones carrying whole cabins and farmyards cluttered with wagons, plows, children playing, mothers rocking, and the morning wash fluttering in the breeze. Broadhorns bound for New Orleans loaded with flour, cornmeal, turkeys, chickens, pork, whiskey, furs. Keelboats spreading their square sails to catch a favorable wind while their crews lolled on deck and a fiddler scraped his strings on the housetop. Proud steamboats of every size plowing the river with their V-shaped wakes, leaving trails of wood smoke in the sky.

Whenever he got the chance, he borrowed a rowboat, headed out to the middle of the river, and drifted awhile amid the procession of vessels. It seemed as if all of civilization were floating by, a human tide of immigrants and fortune seekers. Travelers, traders, and peddlers with their faces turned west. Land speculators and gamblers with gleams in their eyes. Preachers, teachers, and lawyers with books in their bags. He closed his eyes and rocked on the water while he listened to the jangling of bells and melodies of steamboat whistles. Sometimes he pulled up alongside a flatboat to swap news with its voyagers.

"Howdy, son. Where are we?"

"That town back there is Troy. Rockport's coming up soon. Where you headed?"

"Illinois. Got a claim waiting for us. What's the land like here?"

"Good as any, worse than most. Where you coming from?"

"Pennsylvania. Half the state'll be out here soon. How far to Cairo?"

"Just a whoop and a holler if a big catfish don't swallow your boat. What's the news in Pittsburgh?"

At night the rollicking keelboatmen and steamboat roustabouts came swarming up the riverbanks into Troy, looking for fun and trouble. They were a rough-talking, deck-dancing, ballad-belting, eye-gouging bunch. Abraham found himself half-repulsed, half-intrigued by their boasts and brawls. He liked loafing in the streets and listening to the rivermen shout that they could outrun any wildcat, outwrestle any bear, out-bite any rattlesnake this side of the Missouri.

He realized that if he had his own little scow, he could make some extra money ferrying travelers onto the river where the steamboats paused to take on passengers. He borrowed some tools from Jim Taylor, whipsawed some planks, and like Robinson Crusoe, set to work constructing his own boat. For once he was glad for the knowledge of fitting and shaping wood that he had picked up from his father. The day it was finished, he sculled up the Ohio a mile and back, feeling a surge of freedom with each exultant sweep of the oar.

When he pulled up to the Anderson River landing, the exuberance on his face made Green Taylor guffaw.

"I guess you'll be the river king now, Abe."

"I reckon I will!"

He jumped onto the bow, flapped his arms, and cracked his heels.

"Cock-a-doodle-do! I'm the biggest ear-biting, jaw-breaking river pirate from Pittsburgh to New Orleans! I can leap the Ohio and wade the Mississippi without getting my knees wet! I can break a full-grown alligator across my knee and carry two wildcats under each arm with nary a scratch! I sun myself in thunderstorms, scratch my back with lightning bolts, and ride to church on whirlwinds. Whoop! I'm a ring-tailed roarer, and I'll be kiln-dried and split into coffin pegs if I can't whip every chicken-livered river rat in sight! Whoop! Whoop! Whoopee!"

A laugh rang out from the riverbank. Abraham looked up to find two gentlemen dressed in tailor-made suits and top hats standing beside the road, staring down at him. The one who had laughed tipped his hat and bowed.

"I believe that is the finest speech I've heard this side of the Alleghenies," he said. "Mr. Mike Fink, I presume?"

"That's me, old Mike Fink, the almightiest man on this river, and if anyone denies it, let them make their will before I cut them up for catfish bait!"

"Well, Mr. Fink, is this mighty vessel your boat?"

"It is."

"Will you do us the service of taking us onto the river? My companion and I would like to catch the steamer."

"I surely would, but there's no steamer just now."

The short blast of a whistle came floating down the river. Abraham turned and spotted the *Pride of Cincinnati* in the distance, churning toward them.

"My mistake. Climb aboard."

He carried two trunks down the bank and set them in his boat, elated that luck had brought him passengers so quickly. The men seated themselves on the trunks. The one who had spoken to him kept up a broad, satisfied smile. A shadow clouded the other's face, and he cast dubious glances around the scow, as if he expected it to spring a leak and go to the bottom before it left shore.

Abraham pushed into the river, grasped the oar, and began sculling. He looked over his two passengers, the jovial and the melancholy. Smooth hands, clean shirts, and silk hats. Too polished up to be from around here.

"Where you coming from?"

"Oh, Baltimore, Philadelphia, New York, Buffalo," the first man replied, still smiling. "We are merely two of fortune's wanderers, wafting wherever the currents take us."

"How far you traveling?"

"As far as this steamship will take us, and then some. We are out to see what we can see."

Abraham stood, the scow rocking perilously as he rose, much to the alarm of the melancholy traveler. He waved both arms at the steamship to make sure its pilot knew he had passengers to deliver. The steamer tooted its whistle in return.

"I heard a man say he caught a catfish bigger than tomorrow on this river," the cheerful traveler remarked.

"That so?"

"Yes, indeed. That fish was so big, it took four mules to pull it out. It was too big to fry, so they threw it back. The water rose so fast, all the millwheels on all the streams for miles around turned backwards, and they unground two hundred bushels of corn."

Abraham laughed. "That's a good one. I'll pass it along if you don't mind."

"Oh, I've got a hundred more like it. A thousand more. I pull them out quite often, on account of my companion here." He winked and nodded sideways toward his friend, who looked even sadder than before.

"You mean to cheer him up?"

"Who, him? Oh, no, he don't ever cheer up, at least not for very long. Not that I haven't tried. I don't believe he really wants to be cheered up."

The jovial traveler reached over the side and trailed his fingers in the water, making careless splashes as Abraham sculled along.

"No, I tell such little stories to keep myself buoyed up. Otherwise, I might just sink to the bottom of the river with my friend here."

The dejected traveler paid no attention to his companion. He heaved a sigh and peered into the depths.

"What makes him so melancholy?"

"There's a deep question, one with no bottom. You might as well ask why some clouds turn dark and swell up with rain. He's simply made that way."

Scrutinizing his passengers more closely, Abraham realized how much they looked alike. They must have been brothers, maybe even twins. The same high brows, the same deep-green eyes and long chins. But the natural levity of one face and leaden shadows of the other obscured the resemblance.

The somber traveler gave another long sigh. He seemed to spread his own gray atmosphere about him, like a vapor hanging over a swamp. Abraham had to force his gaze away from the doleful face and back to the genial passenger.

"Well, maybe the change of scenery will do him good," he offered.

"Perhaps. But I doubt it. He has seen the sun rising out of the Atlantic and rainbows shining above the Blue Ridge. Still, he refuses happiness."

The steamboat had pulled out of the river's main current and stopped its engines.

"He likes to brood and to think deep thoughts. If he had his way, he would not travel at all. He'd rather sit in a twilight grove, or gloomy bower, or perhaps some mossy cave, and consort with his divine melancholy."

A trace of exasperation crossed the jovial passenger's face, but it quickly dissipated.

"I ask him, what is the point of brooding? Even if we *are* all bound for dust? It's not as though the world we travel is only one long vale of tears, I tell him. There are shining peaks as well. Why should a man despair when there is so much to smile at?"

The sad traveler rolled his eyes, but his companion paid no attention.

"As for me, give me mirth. I'll take laughter holding both its sides, torchlight feasts, and buxom beauties kicking up their heels to a fiddle tune. No, my friend, no lonely sulking for me. I want wide rivers and merry steamboat whistles and the busy hum of men."

The scow pulled up to the waiting steamer. The travelers clambered up a short ladder, and Abraham handed their trunks up to a roustabout.

The two faces—one smiling, one glum—peered down at him over the rail. "Goodbye, Mr. Fink, and good luck to you. Keep an eye out for snags and sandbars."

A bell signaled. The steamer made ready to get underway.

"Hold on! You forgot to pay me!"

"Oh—of course."

The affable traveler reached inside his coat. His silent companion did the same. Two coins flew over the rail of the ship and clattered into the bottom of the scow. The steamer pulled away, and the two faces disappeared with it.

Abraham picked up the money and blinked. He had hoped for one or two bits. There in the palm of his hand lay two silver half-dollars.

"Great day in the morning!" he exhaled.

He turned the two coins over in his hands. On one side shone thirteen stars and the image of a lady with flowing hair, the word *LIBERTY* inscribed on her cap. The other side showed an eagle with spread wings and a shield on his chest, the words *UNITED STATES OF AMERICA* and the motto *E PLURIBUS UNUM*. The coins gleamed up at him like two unexpected promises. He could scarcely believe that he, a poor boy, had earned a dollar in less than a day—money he did not have to turn over to his father. The world before him suddenly seemed wider and fairer than before.

"By jing!"

In a burst of exuberance, he flipped one of the coins into the air to watch it shimmer in the sun. The second it left his hand, he knew it was a foolish thing to do. A gust of wind caught the boat, swung the bow around, and left the half-dollar hanging over the water. He lunged for it as it started its downward arc, nearly upsetting the scow. It skipped off the side of his palm and tumbled into the river.

He plunged his arm into the brown water, but the coin eluded his grasping fingers. It quivered and shone as it receded before him. For an instant he saw the visage of the melancholy traveler looking up through the depths and shaking his sad head as he sank from sight.

"Damnation!"

His cry tore the air. A half-dollar. Worth a whole book. Maybe two. Down to the bottom.

He sat motionless in the scow, staring into the water and cursing himself, stunned to have lost half his fortune so quickly. After a moment he glanced around, wondering if anyone had seen or heard. There were no nearby vessels.

He looked at the one coin he still possessed. It shone with promise. On the front Lady Liberty smiled as she looked past the orb's edge, as if she recognized some bright future beyond the horizon.

Well, a half-dollar is still more than I expected, he told himself. He laid it carefully on the bottom of his boat and began to scull toward shore. The world still seemed open and wide.

CHAPTER 8

AUTUMN 1826

One late autumn day, Jim Taylor sent him to Huffman's Mill, a few miles up Anderson River. Abraham slung a two-bushel bag of corn across the back of Taylor's old sorrel and started off. As he got close to the mill, he ran into Dennis Hanks coming from Little Pigeon Creek with his own bag of corn.

"I woke up with an itch on the top of my head and told Elizabeth I'd have good luck today." Dennis grinned. "And here you are."

"Mighty poor good luck, Denny." Abraham grinned back.

They rode along together, joking and laughing, the horses' breath pluming in the chilly air, until they reached Huffman's Mill. Abraham dismounted and went immediately to admire the machinery. Creek water ran down a sluice and fell onto the paddles of a horizontal tub wheel, which turned a vertical shaft. Wooden gears and more shafts led to the millstone, which was fashioned from flinty rock and housed in a rough log structure. He liked the mathematical precision of the way the teeth on the gears moved in and out of their assigned places. The cumbersome but accurate movement, the quick spinning of some pieces and slow revolutions of others, the rhythmic grindings of the burrstones all whispered that there must be some definite order to the labors of men.

Inside the millhouse, a big fireplace welcomed anyone passing by and gave patrons a place to whittle away the time in cold weather while they waited their turn to grind. There were several here now—Henry Brooner from Little Pigeon Creek, Alfred Grass from Rockport, big Bobby McDaniel from Troy, and three or four others. As Abraham dropped his bag of corn on the floor, he felt the warm anticipation of swapping talk while the log fire crackled and the machinery clacked away.

Soon Dennis proposed a contest.

"We've got two of the biggest corn-fed fellows this side of the Wabash sitting here in this room. I wonder who can hold up an ax-head the longest, Abe Lincoln or Bobby McDaniel?"

"I'll give it a try," Abraham consented.

Someone rounded up two axes. Abraham took one and balanced it in his hand for a moment, to get a feel for the tool. He curved his fingers around the smooth hickory handle, searching for the surest grip.

"All right. Get ready," Dennis warned.

Each boy stood with his ax at his side, the heavy iron head resting on the floor beside his right foot.

"Go!" Dennis called.

Abraham closed his hand on the handle like a vise. Arm stiff, he slowly lifted the ax off the floor, swinging his arm from the shoulder, so that the head rose in an arc until he was holding the ax straight out before him, his arm and the handle one horizontal line.

He glanced to his left. Bobby had done the same.

For a few seconds the act felt effortless. His powerful muscles raised no protest, responding as surely and efficiently as the gears of the mill machinery. The head of the ax floated before him while the men called out approving oaths. Few in Indiana had the strength to accomplish the feat he and Bobby had just performed.

It didn't take long for his wrist and shoulder to feel the strain. The muscles running up his arm began twitching. The big iron head, which had seemed at rest in the air a moment ago, quivered. It wanted down.

Abraham looked at Bobby. The strain was showing in him as well. His face was burning red. Abraham could see Bobby's arm tremble and his fingers shift for a better grip.

He stared hard at the handle in his own hand. The head of the ax was bobbing up and down now. Every time it dipped, his muscles pulled back. But he could feel their strength draining away and the blood rushing to his head.

Bobby stifled a cry filled half with agony and half with joy in the contest.

Abraham felt his muscles beginning to spasm and tear. His shoulder and wrist screamed that it was time to let go. He closed his eyes. I'll count to five and be done, he thought.

A loud thud and a cheer sounded over the clatter of the machinery. Bobby had dropped his ax.

The men slapped the boys' backs and cracked jokes about hiring them to cut the National Road all the way to Missouri. Abraham and Bobby stood in their midst, shuffling their feet, rubbing their arms, and exchanging the grin of youth, confident in its own strength and potential.

The door opened, and a stranger entered the mill. The little cluster of men fell silent as they regarded his sharp, canine face. He cast a look about the room with the cautious approach of a man on the hunt. They could tell right away what he was by the hard glint in his eye and the bulge of a heavy pistol in his coat pocket.

"Mind if I sit awhile?"

"All are welcome," the miller said in a matter-of-fact way and turned back to his work.

The stranger surveyed the faces before him.

"Come to do some grinding?" Alfred Grass asked. Abraham heard the note of scorn in his voice.

"No, but I wouldn't mind having a taste. I ain't had breakfast today."

The miller nodded. The stranger went to the hopper, scooped up a double handful of corn, and put it on the hearth. He pulled a stool closer to the fire, sat, and got down to business.

"I'm looking for a couple of fiddle-footed runaways from over Lexington way. You fellows seen any around here lately?"

He took from his pocket a creased and dirty page from the *Kentucky Reporter*, which he offered for inspection. Abraham read aloud an advertisement circled with a heavy line.

> *$200 REWARD—will be paid for the apprehension and delivery of my Negroes named Charles and Eliza, who ran away from the subscriber, living in Fayette County, Kentucky, on the 17th of last month. The man Charles is about 30 years of age, 5 feet 6 inches high, light complexion, straight hair; carries scars on forehead and left arm. He is pleasant in conversation but stutters when spoken to. The woman Eliza is about 25 years of age, 5 feet 4 inches high, light hair, blue eyes and so white that she can pass herself for a white woman. All are warned against harboring or employing said Negroes, at the peril of the law. James Redding.*

Abraham handed the paper back. The stranger folded it and slipped it into his pocket.

He was by no means the first slave hunter Abraham had seen. The Ohio River, lying between Kentucky and Indiana, separated more than two states. Kentucky was slave territory. There one man could own another. Indiana's constitution outlawed that kind of servitude. If a slave could escape in Kentucky, cross the river to Indiana soil, and keep going, he had a chance at freedom. Slave hunters often prowled the Little Pigeon Creek area, hoping to catch runaways as they worked their way north.

Feelings about slavery ran mixed in southern Indiana. Most settlers, like Tom Lincoln, were glad to live on free soil. They were troubled by the idea of enslaving another human being. Besides, making a living was hard enough without having to compete with slave labor. Back in Kentucky, it had seemed like the more the land filled up with slaves, the harder it was for a poor white man to get along. But if folks down south wanted to keep slaves, that was their concern. After all, slavery had been around since the beginning of time. Half the settlers in southern Indiana had come from Kentucky. Many of them knew folks back home who owned slaves.

Slave hunters were another matter. No one liked their company. They were generally regarded as unsavory intruders, opportunists out to make money from an unfortunate situation. Some even crossed the river looking for free blacks they could kidnap and carry down south to sell into bondage.

The mill had stopped running for a moment while the miller wrestled the machinery to correct some deficiency his ear had detected. In the silence that filled the room, the stranger bent to the hearth and pulled his pan of parched corn away from the fire.

"Business been good lately?" Dennis asked.

"Good for me, bad for the runaways. When I start after one, I get him. They can hide in swamps or the hollows of trees, wade down creeks or run across the river when it freezes up. It don't matter. If I can't catch a runaway, no one can."

The man reminded Abraham of Aesop's wolf who came upon a lamb. The lamb protested again and again that he had never done the wolf any harm, but the wolf would have his dinner, and he devoured the helpless creature anyway.

"I had a peculiar case last month. I'll tell you boys about it."

The man took a couple of bites of his parched corn and chewed slowly.

"A girl named Fanny got away from over near Frankfort. She's a feisty little thing, and the overseer was talking of selling her down the river, so she made up her mind to skedaddle. You know what that girl did? She cut off her hair, stepped into some trousers, pulled an old felt hat over her head, and made out to be a man. Then she hoofed it."

He took another bite, chewed, and studied the faces around the fire.

"I got the hounds and followed her a good twenty miles. Then I lost the trail. Well, I found her the next day riding along in the back of an old wagon, heading north. An old nigger was driving the wagon. 'Where you going, Fanny?' I asks. She puts on a husky voice and says, 'Why, sir, you must be mistaken. My name is Henry.' And that old driver, he says, 'Yes, suh, that's right. Her name is Henry!'"

A couple of the men chuckled. The slave hunter took a last bite of parched corn and set the pan down. He rose, stretched his arms, and took one more look around.

"Well, I best be going. Got some traveling to do today. If you boys see any runaways that don't belong in these parts, I'd be obliged if you'd send word to my partner down in Lexington. His name's Ballenger."

The man turned to the miller, nodded, and headed out the door. The machinery started up again. The clack of turning wheels and spinning shafts filled the room.

"I wish that business would stay on the other side of the river," Dennis muttered.

CHAPTER 9

SPRING 1827

His tangle with the law started the afternoon a faint hallooing came floating across the broad Ohio River from the Kentucky shore. He was sitting on the bank at the mouth of Anderson River, watching leaves make slow spins on labyrinthine currents. The calls riffled the afternoon air like acorns dropping into glassy water.

At first Abraham ignored them. John Dill, who lived over in Kentucky, had the license to ferry passengers across the Ohio at that spot. Dill was fiercely protective of his business. There was no point in getting his hackles up.

But the halloos kept coming. Evidently someone needed to get across and couldn't find the ferryman. Might as well go see who's making so much noise, he thought. He climbed into his little scow and rowed across the river.

As he approached the far shore, he saw a man sitting on a log, head in his hands. Abraham landed the scow and stepped onto the Kentucky bank. The man sprang to his feet. It was Lin Dill, the ferryman's brother. A second figure stepped out of the bushes—the ferryman himself.

"Just what the hell do you think you're doing, boy?"

John Dill was a lean man with a hoary beard grown wild and eyes that glowered from thick brows. His brother was a younger version of the same.

"I heard somebody calling. Seemed like you weren't around, so I rowed over to see who was raising such a ruckus."

"You come over here to steal my business, that's what you done."

Abraham saw that a trap had been set and sprung. He chose his words carefully.

"I ain't stealing anything. I heard someone calling. I just came over to see if he needed help, that's all."

"I seen you carrying passengers in that little boat of yours, Lincoln," Dill insisted. "You ain't got a license to operate on this river."

That was true.

"I've done you no harm, Dill."

Abraham turned to get back into his boat. Both Dills rushed down the bank at him.

"You ain't going nowhere, Lincoln. We're going to take your thieving hide and dunk it in the river. And that damn boat's going to the bottom."

Abraham's shoulders tensed. "I don't believe you'll do any such thing."

The Dill brothers took a second look at Abraham's sinewy arms and big knuckles. He was more than a match for either one of them and could most likely handle both at one time.

"You ain't getting out of this, Lincoln," John Dill growled. "You're a lawbreaker, and we're going to see that you go before the law. You come with us to Squire Pate's right now, or we'll give you a thrashing you won't forget."

The brothers took a step closer but held back. Abraham could see they had no real hankering to fight.

"Either way's fine with me, Dill. But if you come out on the losing end, it might be easier on you in Squire Pate's court. Try thrashing me, and losing might hurt something worse."

The brothers looked at each other. An unspoken communication passed between their eyes.

"Let's go over to Pate's house. You're going to pay, Lincoln."

They followed a path along the river, Lin Dill walking in front of Abraham, John Dill guarding behind. Abraham tried making small talk to lighten the situation, but the brothers were in no mood for it. Lin made a point of informing their prisoner that Squire Pate happened to own the land from which the Dills operated their ferry, a fact that didn't bode well.

They climbed the bank through a stretch of timber and an apple orchard, then past a little cemetery dotted with markers and fieldstones to the house of Squire Samuel Pate, the justice of the peace. It was a big new double-log house with a wide porch stretching across the front and a good-sized room on the east side that Pate had built for holding court.

Some of the local magistrates viewed the application of the law the same way they plowed a row: if it swerved a little here and there, so be it. Pate wasn't one of those. He built his courtroom as a temple of justice and tried his cases with as much dignity as the backwoods would stand. But on warm days, he didn't mind presiding outside. Today he sat down at a little table in the shade of the porch, opened a law book, and let the Dill brothers state their case.

"Lincoln's been carrying passengers for hire on the river in that boat of his," John Dill said. "He ain't got a license, he's interfering with my business, and I want you to make him stop."

The squire turned to Abraham. "Well, Mr. Lincoln, what have you got to say about it?"

Abraham's chest tightened. He'd never been hauled in front of a judge before. He had no money with him to pay a fine. If he could not pay, would he end up in a Kentucky jail? His father would skin him alive.

He tried to size up the squire. Pate was two or three years over thirty, a prosperous farmer and slaveholder who had inherited land and added to it. The man was inspecting Abraham with a face that seemed to be open and fair.

"Well, Your Honor, I suppose I should tell you that I work for Jim Taylor over on the Indiana side. Sometimes Jim pays me to run his ferry across Anderson River. Jim's got a license from Indiana to operate his ferry on that stream. I reckon no one here has a problem with that."

"That's correct."

"It's also true that I built my own scow, and sometimes I make a little money taking folks from the Indiana side out to catch steamers coming up and down the river. Or sometimes, if a man wants to get off a steamer and come over to the Indiana bank, I'll go out and get him. I never took anyone to or from the Kentucky shore. Just the Indiana side."

"The fact that you launch from the Indiana bank does not matter, Mr. Lincoln," Pate said. "Kentucky owns the whole river to the low water mark on the Indiana side. Only the state of Kentucky has the right to issue a license for operating a ferry on the Ohio."

"I don't argue with the state of Kentucky's right over the river," Abraham said. "The question I want to know is: Does the law forbid anyone except John Dill to operate a ferry from the Indiana bank to steamboats in the river? If that's the case, then I suppose I'm in the wrong."

"Well, let's look at the law."

Pate read aloud from the book before him:

> *If any person whatsoever shall, for reward, set any person over any river or creek, whereupon public ferries are appointed, he or she so offending shall forfeit and pay five pounds current money, for every such offense, one moiety to the ferry-keeper nearest the place where such offense shall be committed, the other moiety to the informer; and if such ferry-keeper informs, he shall have the whole penalty, to be recovered with costs.*

Abraham searched the words the judge read, picking over them as carefully as he might scrutinize the grain of the wood in a log to be split, trying to locate the exact place where the fiber might best part.

John Dill took on the satisfied look of a man counting out in his mind the five pounds he had coming to him. Abraham and the squire locked eyes. He could tell that Pate was dissecting the words as well.

Abraham spoke slowly.

"Your Honor, that law says I cannot set any person over a river without a license. But the question I'm still looking to answer is this one: Does the law stop me from taking a person from the Indiana bank to a steamship in the middle of the river? I've done that more than once. Most of the time, John and Lin Dill are clear over on the Kentucky side."

Pate gave no sign, one way or another.

"If a man comes along on the Indiana side," Abraham went on, "and wants to catch a steamship, and there's no Dill in sight, somebody has to take that man from the Indiana shore to the steamship. The steamship ain't going to wait. It seems to me the law can't expect me to sit there and let that man miss his steamer just because the Dills are way off someplace else. Does John Dill's license say no one else can help a stranger get on his steamer, when the steamer is right there and there is no other way?"

Pate gazed at him intently.

"What I mean to say, Your Honor, is that I never set anyone clear across the Ohio River, from one shore to the other, not for hire, anyway."

"You sure crossed that river today," John Dill protested. "How else did you get here?"

"That's true, but only because you were hollering to wake the dead, and it got me curious as to what it was all about. I didn't set you over any river."

Abraham turned to the judge.

"I've only carried folks as far as the middle of the river. And I don't hear that law say anything against that."

Squire Pate looked at Abraham, then at the Dills, then down at his law book. He looked way off down toward the river, turning the matter over in his mind.

"Gentlemen, Mr. Lincoln has a point. The law says that Mr. John Dill, the holder of the ferry license, has the sole right to set passengers over the river for hire from one bank to another. But no one here has cited to me an occasion when Mr. Lincoln has set anyone over the river. He's only taken passengers to and from passing steamers in midstream. The law says nothing about that."

Pate looked squarely at John Dill.

"I find for Mr. Lincoln. This case is dismissed, and the defendant is discharged."

The judge closed his book and stood up. Abraham watched him shake hands with the Dills, then heard the brothers' grumblings ebb away toward the river. It took him a moment to grasp that he had made a complete victory of it.

"Sit down for a minute, Mr. Lincoln," the squire said in a friendly way. "As long as you're here, you might as well tell me about yourself."

Abraham found himself taking a seat in the cool of the porch, telling the squire how he lived about a dozen miles from the river as the crow flies, how he came to work for Jim Taylor and build his own little boat, how he liked books and wished he had enough education to perhaps be a clerk on a riverboat so he could see a bit of the world instead of being a plower of fields and a splitter of rails.

"Well, Abe, there aren't many around here who can do what you did a minute ago—I mean, hold a string of words up to the light of day and tell exactly what they mean. You might enjoy studying the law a little." He picked up his volume of *The Statutes of Kentucky*. "You're welcome to come here and read through this book any time you care to cross the river. Or come over on law days and watch a while. If a man knows a little law, it helps him no matter what business he's in."

Abraham pondered what the squire had said as he walked back down the hill past the cemetery and through the apple orchard. He sculled across the wide Ohio toward Indiana with the sun behind him and his thoughts skimming along beside the boat, over shades of purple, luminous water, marveling that not only had he managed to outwit the Dills, but that a justice of the peace had invited him to come sit on his porch to read a book of Kentucky laws.

CHAPTER 10

Winter and Spring 1828

His sister, Sarah, died in childbirth on a cold January night. The blow came out of nowhere and hit hard. Tom Lincoln built the box Sarah and her stillborn child rested in, just as he had built a coffin for his first wife. Abraham tried to help, but the jack plane fell from his hands, and he staggered away.

He avoided people for several weeks after her burial. When others spoke to him, he turned away or muttered something incomprehensible. Some days, he slipped away to Anderson River and tried to find peace by gazing into swirling eddies on the water's surface.

At night he wandered the forest, walking through moon shadows to the cemetery at the Little Pigeon Baptist Church to sit beside her grave.

He thought about how, when they were young and had first come to Indiana, they had huddled together under a bearskin blanket beside the fire, clutching each other and sharing what heat their little bodies provided. Now she lay cold and still under the damp earth.

After a while he would rise and walk through the dark woods to the hilltop where his mother lay. He closed his eyes and listened hard for his mother's voice reciting Bible verses. *The Lord shall give thee rest from thy sorrow, and from thy fear.*

It was his stepmother who pulled him to her, spoke words of love, and brought him back to the land of the living. That and a stern reminder from his father that there was work to be done. At first he struggled through his chores, but presently he found that the work was good for him and threw himself into it. It felt good to be behind a plow, and he drove it with vigor, as if to open the land was to dig out the hurt so the healing could begin.

Jim Gentry, the richest settler in Little Pigeon Creek, waylaid Abraham with a surprise one day when he stepped into Gentry's general store to buy a straw hat.

"Abe, can I interest you in taking a little trip for me?"

"What do you mean?"

"I'm sending Allen downriver to New Orleans with a load of pork. He'll need a deckhand to handle the sweeps and keep the boat out of trouble. I was thinking you might be interested."

"You know I would." Abraham's eyes lit up for the first time in weeks.

"I can pay you eight dollars a month plus your passage home."

"That sounds more than fine, Jim."

"Good. I figure that you and Allen can hold your own against any bushwhackers that might try to jump the boat. Besides," he said, putting a hand on Abraham's arm, "I expect a jaunt down the river might do you some good."

He was even more surprised when Tom Lincoln quickly gave the idea his blessing. His father reminded him that he, too, had made the flatboat trip to New Orleans as a young man.

"Now, twenty years ago, there were no steamships to carry us back upstream," he pointed out. "I walked back home to Kentucky."

Maybe he's willing for me to go because it's like I'm following in his path, Abraham thought. The prospect of the eight dollars a month, which Abraham would turn over to his father, pleased Tom as well.

As spring arrive, Abraham and Jim's son Allen began building their flatboat at Rockport on the bank of the Ohio. They built the hull bottom side up near the water's edge, making it sixty-five feet long and eighteen feet wide, using thick poplar and oak planks. When the hull was done, they used windlasses and levers to flip it over so it landed in the water right side up. Then they constructed a big deck house with a long steering sweep mounted on the stern of the roof and a long sweep on each side.

Once the boat was finished, they loaded it with goods to trade and sell: pork, bacon and venison hams, cornmeal, beans, and beeswax. Allen stood at the stern, holding the big steering sweep, while Abraham pushed away from the bank with a long pole. In a moment the current took hold, and they were off.

The timber-covered bluffs moved past like big oxen lumbering off to the fields. Rockport fell behind a bend, and the river opened before them. Neither boy spoke for a while. They wanted to soak up the pleasure of being on the water with the prospect of a twelve-hundred-mile trip before them.

They listened to the river and absorbed its language. Wavelets lapped against the hull while the planks groaned and creaked in the wandering currents. The water gurgled about the blades of the sweeps, and the river sighed as it slipped under the bow. Every once in a while, a faint shout came drifting across the water like a thistle's down blowing from the distant shore.

The days slid along as easily as the river. Allen had made the flatboat trip to New Orleans once before with his father, so he knew some landmarks to look for. If his memory failed, they called to passing boats and landings to find out where they were.

When they passed the mouth of the Wabash River, they knew they had reached the boundary between Indiana and Illinois. Then came Shawneetown, one of the rowdiest spots on the Ohio. And after that, Cave-In-Rock, a yawning fifty-foot-wide opening in the limestone bluffs where bandits had once run a gambling parlor and house of prostitution, luring travelers off the river and into the cave, where they were beaten, robbed, and murdered.

They floated past the infamous cave with relief and began to look for the mouth of the Cumberland River, then the Tennessee, coming one right after the other, pouring out of the south, bringing waters from the far-off Great Smoky Mountains and points beyond, fattening the Ohio with their flows.

The river started into a long, sweeping arc, carrying them first northwest and then southwest. At the end of the arc, they found the town of Cairo lying on a peninsula behind muddy banks full of rushes and reeds. There the Ohio River came to an end, and they entered the Mississippi.

They held their breaths as they glided onto the mystical, promising Father of Waters. Abraham saw at once that while the Ohio moved at an unhurried pace, the Mississippi swept along at a quick, determined rate, and that the Mississippi was muddy brown compared to the clear Ohio. Mississippi boatmen claimed that their river's water was far more wholesome to drink, there being nutrition in its murkiness.

"Gulp two or three cups, and you'll have enough mud to grow corn in your stomach," Abraham observed.

They slipped along a ribbon of light and shadow while the inscrutable forest glided past, the cottonwoods and sugarberry trees raising their limbs to the sky behind the hills. Every once in a while, a huddle of cabins appeared on a ragged bank, then fell back into the endless line of woods. Low islands floated by, curled up like bears asleep on the water.

The current ran honest and smooth here, so the boys had little to do but give occasional tugs on the long sweeps. Here and there they saw another flatboat spinning along or a steamboat coughing its way upstream. The boats were piled high with the riches of the American land: pine logs from western New York, apples from Pennsylvania, cotton and whiskey from Tennessee, cattle from Missouri, big heaps of corn from Illinois.

The river widened as they floated along, then widened some more. Abraham thought of the story of George Washington hurling a stone across the Rappahannock in Virginia.

"If it was this river, he'd-a left that stone lying where it was," he said to himself, and he noted with satisfaction that Western rivers must be big-horned bulls compared to the East's little calf streams.

The proud white steamboats ran along with grand names painted in gold on their sides: the *Independence*, the *Columbia*, the *Prairie Belle*, the *Star of the West*. They carried a human cargo hailing from every corner of the far-reaching country: sun-bronzed farmers, hawk-eyed traders, satchel-toting lawyers, Northern merchants, Southern planters, Western speculators, Eastern dandies. The Mississippi bore them all, this mysterious main artery flowing at the heart of the continent, carrying the life blood of the nation.

Often several flatboats lashed themselves into floating communities for a stretch of the downriver trip. The conjoined flotillas became little traveling cities, alive with bartering and brawling. Abraham loved to tie up and go hopping from boat to boat, querying the travelers about where they were from and where headed.

"Come in and see us," called an old woman rocking atop her deckhouse beside a painted sign that read "Island of Pleasure." Her grin showed gaps between her black teeth, and her face was as shriveled as a dried peach, but behind her lounged two river sirens with beckoning smiles.

"There's more to this river than catfish and mud flats!" she promised. Abraham grinned back and blushed.

"Abomination! Unclean! Hell-bound!" A backwoods preacher stamped his foot on the deck of a neighboring boat with a wooden cross nailed to its bow. He waved his Bible over his head. "The shoals of damnation lie waiting, ye drifting mansions of evil!"

"It's democracy afloat," Abraham told Allen when he hopped back to their boat. "Whorehouses, churches, and everything in between heading down this river."

When the sun glared on the water, or a mist hugged the river from shore to shore, Abraham had to keep a sharp lookout for hidden snags, whole trees embedded in the river that waited to snare boats.

"They'll tear the bottom out of your raft faster than a dog chewing meat off a bone," an old flatboatman told them. A day seldom passed without their seeing the skeletons of two or three boats that had killed themselves running up on a snag.

But most of the time the river gave them no trouble, and they could just float along carefree, lazing on the deck while they watched the hillsides float by, the fish jump, and big steamboats hunt easy water. In the afternoons, Abraham pulled out a tattered schoolbook that a Tennessean had swapped him for a knife. Thomas Jefferson's inaugural address, given twenty-seven years before, caught his eye. He read Jefferson's thoughts on republican government, his vision of "a rising nation, spread over a wide and fruitful land . . . advancing rapidly to destinies beyond the reach of mortal eye."

When they tied up at night, Abraham lay on the roof of the deckhouse and looked up at the stars sprinkled across the open heavens, and every once in a while, one would shoot out of the rest and fall toward the river. The dark water and deep sky brought a lonely feeling, and he would think of his sister and mother in their graves, but the next morning, when they were on the river again, with the sun on the water and the merriment of the traffic all around them, the night thoughts dissipated, and the melancholy lifted.

They passed the village of Memphis, sitting atop the Chickasaw Bluffs, a place with roads so muddy in the rainy season it was said that an oxteam once drowned in the main street. Vicksburg, perched on rugged castle-like cliffs, looked like a town built to withstand a siege. Further downriver lay Natchez, where the cotton aristocracy lived in white-columned mansions.

As the river carried them into the Deep South, the air warmed and they happily shed a layer or two of their clothes. The land was green and looked cheerful under the sun except in the places where Spanish moss hung gray and dismal, shrouding the cypress trees standing in the water. They reached the domain of the sugar barons, where the shore was lined with levees to keep the river from washing away the fields, and the voices of black slaves rich in song floated across the water as they rowed snub-nosed barges from landing to landing.

One night they tied up their boat a few miles below Baton Rouge near a sugar plantation where they had spent the afternoon trading. They lay on the roof of the deckhouse, gazed up at the stars, and dropped off to sleep.

A noise that should not have been there woke Abraham. He looked at the stars through half-opened eyes and judged that it was two thirty or three o'clock.

From the stern of the boat came the sound of someone grunting and cursing in a low, menacing voice, then scuffling and feet stumbling across the deck.

"Lincoln! Lincoln!"

He jumped to his feet, trying to shake the cobwebs from his head. Moving in the direction of Allen's cries, he made out a half dozen shadowy forms coming up over the edge of the roof. He grabbed for his hickory club and roared into their midst, swinging like a wild man.

Right away he knocked one of them into the river, and as the man tumbled backward, Abraham saw a black face grimacing up at him in surprise. Two others sprang at him together with clubs of their own. He ran at them, yelling and brandishing his club with his long arms. One of them sidestepped his rush, leaped forward, and landed a deft swing that caught him on the forehead and sent him staggering back. The blow stunned him for an instant, but more than anything else it infuriated him, and as soon as he recovered his balance, he plunged forward again, flailing with all his might. His club thudded hard against flesh, and he heard the man's ribs crack.

Ahead of him, from the dark, came more sounds of struggle, and he knew that Allen had his hands full. Abraham rushed forward and hit one of the intruders square on the side of the head. The man dropped his club, and Abraham swung and hit him again on the shoulder. The man doubled over, turned, and leapt off the boat. Abraham heard him splashing his way through the shallow water for the bank.

The two Indiana boys were still outnumbered, but the ferocity of their defense gave them the upper hand. Their assailants began to retreat across the deckhouse roof toward the stern. Abraham ran after them again, yelling at the top of his lungs. The dark figures jumped off the boat and scrambled up the bank.

Abraham and Allen leapt after them and gave chase through the woods for twenty or thirty yards, but the attackers had disappeared. The two boys leaned over, hands on knees, gasping for breath. Then they hurried back to the boat, checked the cargo until they were satisfied nothing was missing, and sat on the deckhouse, straining to hear any movement on shore.

"Damn slaves," Allen muttered. He picked up one of the clubs they had dropped and flung it into the river.

"What do you reckon they were after?" Abraham asked, still dazed.

"Anything they could make off with and hide. The whole damn load. They would've killed us and stripped the boat clean, the thieving bastards."

Abraham knew it was true. Such crimes were frequent on the river. "Are you hurt?" he asked.

"Not much. At least I don't think so." Allen peered into Abraham's face. "God Almighty, Abe! You're spouting blood."

Abraham wiped his face, found that it was wet with blood, and realized for the first time that his whole head was afire with pain. Probing gently, he located a gash over his right eye. He folded a bandana and pressed it to the cut, gritting his teeth while the throbs of pain shot down his neck through his whole body. When the blood stopped flowing, Allen inspected the wound.

"That one's going to leave a scar," he concluded.

"Hope it don't spoil my beauty."

Allen dipped the bandana into the water and cleaned the cut.

"How many of them you reckon there were?" Abraham asked.

"Six or seven, I guess. We better get out of here. I don't want to be around if they come back with more troops."

Moving quickly now, they untied the lines and pushed the boat away from the bank until the current began to pull them downstream.

"Let's just float for a couple of hours," Allen said. "I'll feel safer putting some distance between us and them bastards."

Abraham sat at the bow and nursed his wound while he kept an eye on the moonlit river for snags and shoals. It wasn't until morning, when the pain subsided and his head cleared, that he realized what a narrow escape they had had. He studied the murky brown waters and knew that he had been baptized by the river.

CHAPTER 11

Spring and Summer 1828

A few days later, the flatboat swung around a big crescent in the Mississippi, and New Orleans spread before them.

"Great day in the morning!"

A city of boats stretched as far as Abraham's eye could see, a vast floating mat of barges, keelboats, and flatboats lashed four or five deep along the levee. Beyond them, tied to a highway of wharves, a fleet of white steamboats rested with the sun gleaming on their tall black funnels. And below those, standing at anchor in the river, a sight he had never seen: oceangoing ships, their masts crowding as thick as trees amid a tangle of rigging and spars, arrived from Havana, Vera Cruz, New York, London, Gibraltar, and beyond.

"There's more boats here than corn in a crib. Think we can squeeze ours in?"

They talked a Kentuckian into letting them tie their boat to his, then hopped across three other flatboats and climbed the levee for a look around.

Along the waterfront, a stream of wagons flowed both ways at once, full of cotton bales and hogsheads of tobacco and sugar. More wagons loaded with crates and barrels pulled through yawning warehouse doors. A raucous tide of people swarmed around the cargo traffic: English sailors swaggering along, looking for trouble; French traders waving their arms; Spaniards with long knives; Italians decorated with red silk handkerchiefs; black slaves hoisting bundles on their shoulders; roustabouts with dice in their pockets; Yankees from Boston, Irishmen from Dublin, Creoles, Portuguese, planters, teamsters, squatters, horse thieves, ship captains, and fortune seekers all mixed together in this one harlequin of a city.

The two boys sold their cargo for the highest prices they could get, sold their flatboat to a man in the business of breaking up such craft for lumber, and plunged into New Orleans for a few days of sightseeing.

They wandered the narrow streets, trying hard to look as if taking a stroll through an exotic port of fifty thousand inhabitants was no more unusual for them than fetching a bucket from a spring. The white and yellow houses with flaking stucco, wrought-iron balconies, and shady courtyards seemed ancient and fine compared to roughcast Indiana. In the market, they found tables piled with bananas and nuts from the tropics, pompano from the Gulf of Mexico, crawfish and eels from the bayous. They peered through shop windows at displays of ruffled shirts, green parasols, four-layer cakes, and glistening bottles of perfume.

In the Place d'Armes, the St. Louis Cathedral sat opposite the river, flanked by the Cabildo, the seat of the old Spanish government, and the Presbytère, built to house priests and monks but used for commerce instead. An old Creole explained to Abraham that inside the Cabildo, French and American representatives had signed a document transferring the whole Louisiana Territory to President Jefferson and the United States for fifteen million dollars.

Abraham loitered in the square, gazing up at the great, whitewashed cathedral with its towers, bells, and carvings of saints, barely able to believe that any church could be so grand. When he slipped inside and stood in the flickering candlelight, he found it as quiet as the woods back home, with only the murmurs of prayers in foreign tongues to disturb the heavy silence.

At night the streets were lit by lamps suspended from chains hanging over the roadways and by the glowing windows of saloons. For a dollar apiece, the two Indiana roughnecks gained admission to a public ball, where they stood at the edge of a big room, dazzled by the crystal chandeliers and bright red paper on the walls. More dazzling were the famous New Orleans quadroons and octoroons—dusky, mysterious women of one-quarter or one-eighth Negro ancestry in low-cut silk gowns who sent promising glances while the men around them talked loudly of bullfights and horse races.

On one street the boys stumbled upon the auction store of Messrs. George W. Boyd & Co., where they saw on display an Egyptian mummy in its sarcophagus, an artifact the proprietors claimed to be more than three thousand years old.

"That fellow's as ugly as a mud fence after a hard rain," Allen commented.

In the Faubourg Sainte Marie, they found the American Theater. They paid a few pennies, found seats in the dark performance hall, and watched a romance about the Indian princess Pocahontas, who fell in love at first sight with Captain John Smith, saved the Jamestown colony from destruction, married another man, and sailed to England to meet the queen, only to die in a cold, foreign land.

Abraham was entranced by the costumed figures appearing and disappearing on the stage, the scenery that changed continents at the draw of a curtain, the fast-moving dialogue that swept the audience from the woods of Virginia to the Palace of Whitehall in London. He went back to the theater two more times, alone. Allen said he was a fool to keep paying to see the same show.

"I've sat and watched corn bread baking on the skillet a thousand times. Guess it won't harm me to watch that play another time or two."

"Yeah, but you don't have to pay to watch corn bread bake."

"Good thing, too, or I wouldn't be the rich man that I am."

On their last morning in the city, they wandered beyond the cathedral to take a look at New Orleans's famed slave market. Here the trading firms kept pens where hundreds of slaves were housed and showrooms where traders displayed the human chattel for prospective buyers. Abraham and Allen had seen their advertisements posted along the riverfront and in the roadways.

Forty-three Virginia slaves of both sexes for sale, to be bartered for sugar or to be sold for cash or on short credit, John Clay, 44 Gravier St.

Just arrived from Baltimore, about 100 Negroes, including tanners, blacksmiths, and cooks, all excellent subjects. Terms: one half cash, the other half in notes at six months. Inquire at 113 Charles St.

They turned into a block where they found dozens of slaves lined up on the street, the men outfitted in black suits with top hats, the women in calico dresses with colorful kerchiefs on their heads. Most of the slaves stood with their backs to the wall. A few sat. One played a fiddle. Some looked down at their new shoes, while others gazed at the white men strolling along the lines and tried to discern which were buyers and which merely curiosity-seekers.

The boys stepped through a doorway into one of the traders' large showrooms, where the serious buying took place. Here dozens more slaves stood on display, men along one wall and women along another, each group arranged by height, tallest to shortest, again the men in suits and women in calico.

"They get 'em all gussied up and polished for sale so they'll fetch higher prices," explained Allen, who had seen the slave market when he had made the trip to New Orleans with his father.

Traders moved about the room, encouraging the buyers.

"Dennis is just about the finest Negro in this lot. He's a mighty good cook, an experienced carpenter, and he's always in a good humor."

"Now, this is Emma, sixteen years old. A girl of unusual good sense. Speaks English and French and knows how to wait on a table. Only reason she's for sale is her owner's leaving for Europe."

Sometimes the traders made the slaves dance, jump, or run around to demonstrate their agility. The buyers walked about the room, inspecting and questioning.

"How old are you, boy?"

"Have you ever driven a carriage?"

"Fanny, can you sew a shirt?"

When buyers grew interested in particular Negroes, they ordered the slaves to roll up their sleeves or lift their dresses so they could look for wounds or disease. They ran their hands over torsos and limbs, feeling muscles and pulling back cheeks to inspect gums and teeth.

"This one's no good, Bill. Look: they've stuffed rags in her blouse where her teats ought to be. Probably full of consumption. She'll be dead before you could get her home."

"I like the looks of this one. Would make a good cane cutter."

"This one's got whipping scars on his back. More than likely a troublemaker."

Abraham marked the faces of the buyers, some hard and calculating, some joking and good-natured as they went about the business of purchasing other human beings. In the slaves' faces, he read resignation, although a few looked as though they hoped for a good master, and two or three stared back at the buyers with sullen eyes. He suddenly felt a very long way from Indiana, where life was not easy, but where a man could pretty much do as he pleased, and where everyone was on more or less equal footing with everybody else.

A group of men had gathered around a pretty young mulatto woman who was sure to fetch a high price.

"She's a delicate thing," the trader enthused, "a real beauty. Inspect her closely, gentlemen. She'll make a mighty fine house servant."

The buyers pinched her flesh, made her trot across the room, like a horse, to see how she moved, and plied her with questions about whether she had ever been sick and what kind of work she had done. At a signal from the trader, she was taken behind a screen that concealed little when she was stripped to the waist for closer examination. The men crowded around, taking turns running their hands over her limbs and patting her abdomen.

Abraham watched in fascination. When he glanced at Allen and saw his friend's grinning, gawking expression, he felt his own face blush.

"Come on. Let's go," he said. "I've seen enough of this to last me a while."

The next morning, they boarded the steamship *Daniel Boone* for the trip home. Wealthier travelers paid a small fortune for the luxury of sleeping in the boat's cabins, taking their meals in a dining room, and gaining admittance to the bar. Most of the passengers, like Abraham and Allen, paid eight dollars, still a hefty price, for the lesser privilege of jamming themselves onto the main deck, which sat two or three feet above the water and was packed with boilers, engines, stacks of firewood, and whatever cargo the captain could haul on his boat. Herded aboard like cattle into a floating pen, the two hundred deck passengers squatted wherever they could find a space.

Abraham did not mind. He enjoyed trading stories with the other passengers as the engines thumped, the wheels churned, and the mellow notes of the ship's bell floated over the water. When the *Daniel Boone*'s captain challenged the *Cumberland* to a race, he spent part of a happy afternoon helping feed wood to the ravenous boilers. He made friends with the clerk's assistant, a barrel-chested fellow with a missing ear who possessed the title of "mud clerk" because it was his job to stand on the muddy riverbank and keep track of the cargo as it left the ship or came aboard. Two or three times, when the *Daniel Boone* stopped to take on freight, Abraham went ashore to give him a hand.

At times he sat alone with his thoughts, watching the shoreline crawl by as they traveled north and thinking over the great adventure that was drawing to an end. He had been gone two months and earned sixteen dollars. For souvenirs he brought home a head full of glittering memories and a scar over his right eye. He had seen more than a thousand miles of river, and it struck him that his country was a grander and more promising place than he had dreamed.

CHAPTER 12

Summer 1828 to March 1830

Little Pigeon Creek, in contrast to New Orleans, seemed remote and discouraging upon his return. He had not realized until then just how tiny his family's cabin was. The Indiana woods, stretching lonesome and bleak, seemed thicker than ever. His wages from the flatboat trip temporarily brightened the atmosphere, but even that faded when he handed the money over to his father.

"Before I know it, I'll turn twenty-one," he told himself as he toted a bucket of water to the trough. "Then I'll be free to keep what I earn. And get clear of this place."

As he split firewood and turned earth with the plow, his thoughts ran to faraway schemes. He'd get a job on a steamboat as a roustabout, or maybe a mud clerk. From there he'd work his way up. Maybe someday he'd even be a pilot. Why not? He had seen men who held such positions. He guessed that he was just as capable.

He had to content himself with occasionally slipping down to Troy and hanging around the waterfront. When he got the chance, he rowed across the Ohio to watch Squire Pate hold court and leaf through his book of Kentucky laws. Sometimes he hiked fifteen miles and more to Boonville or Rockport to hear lawyers in county courthouses apply statutes to cases in which men had stolen hogs, sold bad beef, or conspired to defraud each other of land. He liked to watch the attorneys dressed up in their law finery, their hair pulled back in queues tied with eel skins, wrangling and speechifying to the delight of the crowds. He told himself that if he could ever speak that well, his soul would be satisfied.

Every once in a while, his father let him do a little clerking in Jim Gentry's store. He liked lounging amid the inventory of dry goods and whiskey, gossiping with folks who came in to make a purchase or to just swap talk. When no one else was around, he sat against the wall and plowed through newspapers that Jim took.

The papers were full of things to talk about. The country was moving and growing faster than ever, it seemed. Men were laying plans and tracks for a railroad in Baltimore. Back East, some folks had founded the American Society for Encouraging the Settlement of the Oregon Territory. Much of the talk in the newspapers and around Gentry's whiskey barrel was about Andy Jackson, Old Hickory, born in a log cabin on the Carolina frontier, and how he had grown up to be a fighter of Indians, a racer of horses, a gambler, a cyclone, a judge, a general, a smoker of corncob pipes, and seventh president of the United States.

Dennis Hanks stopped by Gentry's store one day with an announcement.

"I'm ripping up stakes and leaving for Illinois," he declared.

Abraham barely looked up from the *Louisville Journal*. He had heard this threat before. Their cousin John Hanks had recently moved from Kentucky to the valley of the Sangamon River in Illinois, more than one hundred and fifty miles northwest of Little Pigeon Creek. He had sent letters praising the rich, unbroken country there and urging his Indiana kin to join him.

"I tell you, Abe, I'm determined to find a place without the milk sick. I lost four good cows to it in one week. John says they ain't got it on the Sangamon."

"That so?"

"They say anything will grow in the soil out there. All you have to do is turn the sod. Sangamon—that's Injun for 'land of plenty to eat.'"

"Hills look green that are far away," Abraham said.

"That's true. That's why I'm going out there next week to take a look myself."

Tom Lincoln scowled when Abraham told him that Dennis planned a scouting trip.

"It's all a bunch of foolishness. I wish John Hanks would stop his letter writing." He took up his whittling knife and began to shave a piece of maple. "Why should I pick up and move? I've got plenty of land here free of debt, forty acres of it cleared and good for planting, and my orchard. And more than a hundred hogs. I'm getting too old to go traipsing off into the wilderness to break in new land."

"Well, nobody says you have to go," Abraham pointed out.

Tom pared the stick thoughtfully. "Dennis is hell-bent on going. I believe he's talked Squire into moving as well. And your mother says that if Elizabeth and Tildy both go . . ." His voice trailed off.

Abraham at once grasped the situation. If Dennis and Squire Hall, each married to one of Abraham's stepsisters, both moved to Illinois while Tom stayed put, it would be a devastating blow to his stepmother. With her daughters and grandchildren gone, and Abraham planning to strike out on the river, the Little Pigeon Creek settlement would feel pretty empty to her.

"It's all a bunch of foolishness," Tom said again. "It'll blow over. You'll see."

But Dennis came back from Illinois full of the moving fever.

"I tell you, there's choice land for the taking," he reported. "The tops of the cornstalks scrape the bottoms of the clouds out there. I've seen the future, boys, and it's called Illinois."

Dennis and Squire began working on Tom. To sweeten the pitch, John Hanks sent word that he'd already cut logs for a cabin.

"They're laying there all in a row, Tom, cut to size and ready to go," Dennis said. "We'll raise 'em up, pop on a roof, and you and Sally'll be snug as you could ever hope to be."

Their arguments had little effect, but that was before Sally Lincoln put her own campaign into motion. She launched her first line of attack by trying persuasion.

"Tom, we're getting along in years. It looks like the rest of the family is heading out. We don't want to end up here all alone with no one to take care of us when we get old."

When that didn't work, she simply announced that her mind was made up.

"My children are going, and I'm going too. You'll have to decide which will be the easier for you, breaking up new Illinois land, or breaking in a new Indiana wife."

When they had finally worn him down, Tom decided to take the longer view. He recalled that he came from a long line of frontiersmen, from the woods of Pennsylvania to the valleys of Virginia and wilds of Kentucky. He himself had hacked his way into untouched Indiana forests. The roving spirit was in his blood.

"The Lincolns have moved so many times, our chickens can tell the signs of another trip," he mused. "Lincoln chickens will just walk right up to you, lie down, and stick their legs up in the air to be tied for the next wagon ride."

Once swayed, he made up his mind to be determined. The urge to push civilization west gripped him.

"Sharpen your ax, boy," he told Abraham. "There'll be plenty to swing at in Illinois."

Abraham was dumbfounded. It had not occurred to him that his father expected him to go along.

"I ain't going to Illinois, Pa," he said. "My aim is to get on with a steamer. You know that."

"We'll need you on the new place."

Abraham struggled to contain his anger. "I said I ain't going."

His father ignored him.

"Pa, I'll do everything I can to help you get ready to go," Abraham said slowly. "But by the time you leave, I'll be twenty-one. Then the law says I'm free and clear, and there's not a thing you can do to make me spend the next ten years busting sod for you in some godforsaken corner of Illinois."

His father looked at him wearily, as if his boy were a hound that could not get it into its head that it was put on earth to hunt coons.

"You can yip and growl all you want," he said simply. "You're going to Illinois."

Abraham went down to the Ohio, sat on the bank, threw rocks in the water, and stormed inwardly about it for three days. He could kick John Hanks for stirring everyone up with his letters. He saw himself chained to a plow, trudging back and forth across a dull, lifeless field, row after row, day after day, for the rest of his life.

"I'll be damned if they'll make me go!" he shouted across the river. His voice floated downstream, laughing back at him as it set off for a distant shore.

It was his stepmother who changed his mind, without saying a word. One afternoon, as he sat reading with his back against a cabin wall, he looked up and found her mending a hole he'd torn in a shirt. He had meant to sew it himself but had put off the chore, and she picked it up to make a quick repair.

She's always doing for others, he thought. But she won't ask me for help if it means ruining my plans. He suddenly felt ashamed. He put down the book, went to her, and gave her a peck on the top of her head.

"I suppose it won't hurt me to take a peek at Illinois."

Sally slipped her arm around him. "Thank you, Abe. It'll be only for a little while to help us get settled. Then you can go your way."

Now that everyone's mind was made up, they brought in their last harvest with the bittersweet excitement that comes with moving on. Tom sold his land to Charles Grigsby. David Turnham purchased his hogs and corn. Jim Gentry bought a table, chairs, barrel, and other household goods not worth hauling to Illinois. He could resell them at his store. He bought them for more than he could most likely get back, and when Abraham mentioned the fact to him, he said merely that he hated to see them all go.

Abraham worked alongside his father to knock together three wagons, one for each of the departing families. With their axes and knives, they cut big blocks of wood into wheels, which they fitted with rawhide tires. Wooden pegs, hickory withes, and vine knots served to bind the contraptions together.

They were at work on the wagons the day Abraham turned twenty-one. Finally he was free to set his own course without his father's interference. As he worked, he felt at peace with his decision to go along to Illinois. At least he was getting out of southern Indiana, and he would have the opportunity to see territory he'd never seen.

Once they're settled, he told himself, I can head out on the river and see what I'm made of.

The time came to load up for the trip. A few pieces of furniture, bundles of bedclothes, spinning wheels, pots, skillets, and Dutch ovens were all piled, shoved, and tied to the wagons, which looked like three cabins turned inside out ready to lumber down the road. As Abraham stepped back and surveyed the bulging loads, he thought of their journey from Kentucky to Indiana, when he was not yet eight years old. He remembered jolting over the twisting paths and trying hard not to tumble out of the wagon while they fought their way past roots, ravines, and fallen trees.

This is the way we arrived, he mused, and this is the way we depart.

On the afternoon before their leaving, he sat alone for an hour beside Sarah's grave to tell her goodbye. A cold wind blew across the little pioneer cemetery, scraping withered brown leaves against the church door and rattling jagged branches against the sky.

A flood of images rushed through his mind. Sarah helping him learn his letters by scratching them into the dirt with a stick. Playing hide-and-seek behind thick forest trunks. Climbing together to the top of the rocky knob behind their old home in Kentucky.

He rose, followed a forest path a short distance north, and climbed the knoll where his mother lay buried. The winter afternoon was lowering into evening. In the coming dusk, he again tried to picture her face: the blue eyes filled with shadows, the high forehead, the tender, melancholy smile. He saw her leaning over the wooden tub she used on washdays, rinsing clothes and then beating them on a stump with a smooth stick before hanging them over the fence to dry. Sitting at her spinning wheel beside the fire, laughing as he and Sarah rolled on the floor, pretending to be bear cubs. Lying in the corner bed, her body racked with the milk sickness that would kill her, calling her children to her side to tell them goodbye.

For we must needs die, and are as water spilt on the ground, which cannot be gathered up again.

The next morning brought a crisp blue sky and the exhilaration of setting out on a long journey. A crowd of neighbors came to say goodbye, the men shaking hands and slapping each other on the back, the women offering long, tearful embraces.

Jim Gentry, who had trusted him to navigate a small fortune in pork and corn down twelve hundred miles of river with his son, put a hand on his shoulder.

"Take care of yourself, boy. If you ever need anything, you send word to me."

Si Crawford, in whose field he had pulled fodder for three days to pay for *The Life of George Washington*, looked solemn. Elizabeth Crawford handed him a dried rose to press between the pages of a book. He leaned down so she could kiss him on the cheek.

"God bless you, Abe—we'll miss you!"

All of these people had made up a big, rough family who leaned on each other to survive in the wilderness. Together they had cleared the forest, turned the land, raised each other's cabins, helped bury each other's dead. Here at Little Pigeon Creek, Abraham had grown to a height of six feet four inches. He had come of age here, and along the way, he had learned how to swing an ax, read a book, welcome a stranger, and make a friend. He had lived through some pretty pinching times. Yet whatever he was to make of himself in the world, he would do it with this place in his sinew and blood. He was surprised to discover that he would miss it.

When all the handshakes and hugs were done, the men lifted the women and children onto the wagons. Thirteen people made up the migrating party. Abraham; his father; his stepmother; and his stepbrother, John, made up one family. His cousin Dennis Hanks and stepsister Elizabeth, along with their four young children, made another. His stepsister Tildy; her husband, Squire Hall; and their infant son made the third.

The caravan started forward with horses and oxen snorting, wooden axles squeaking, whips cracking, and the men bawling, "Haw!" and, "Git on there!" The teams puffed little clouds of warm breath into the cold air as they tugged to get the wheels turning over the frozen red and yellow clay. Dogs ran alongside, yapping at the lumbering pioneer loads. Some of the neighbors, reluctant to let their friends go, walked with them half a mile, calling out, "Don't forget us!" and, "Send us a letter when you get there!"

Walking alongside the lead wagon, goading the sluggish oxen forward, Abraham called back his final goodbyes. The wagons climbed a slow rise and rounded a bend, and the neighbors dropped out of sight. He took one last look in the direction of the knoll where his mother lay buried, then turned west and left his Indiana home.

PART TWO

THE PRAIRIE

March 1830 to Autumn 1835

CHAPTER 13

March 1830 to February 1831

They followed a jagged ridge road that wound northwest through oaks, maples, and tall tulip trees. A skin of ice lay on the trail, which thawed every day as the sun climbed. At night it froze over again, so the teams spent the mornings slipping on the crusty ground and the afternoons slogging through cold mud. After a week of travel, the three immigrant families drove their wagons onto a ferry, crossed the Wabash River, and entered Illinois.

The little caravan crept onto the immense prairie, black and dismal in early March. The grass, which Dennis claimed stood taller than a man in the summer, lay withered and flat. Abraham had never seen such an endless horizon, not even on the wide Mississippi.

The bleak openness was exhilarating and a little unnerving. Every once in a while, as they passed a clump of trees huddled alongside a creek, they spotted a lonely column of chimney smoke rising into the sky. But as far as they could tell, the whole country was almost uninhabited wilderness.

On the fourteenth day, the wagons rattled to a halt before an unfinished log courthouse in a muddy clearing amid an oak grove. Two roads filled with tree stumps crossed the clearing, and a dozen or so cabins sat under the trees. Dennis announced that they had arrived in Decatur.

An old woman who perched on a stump, smoking a pipe with a bowl as big as a melon, directed them to John Hanks's place.

"Lord, Abe!" John laughed when he greeted them. "Don't get caught out on the prairie in a lightning storm. You'd be the tallest structure for miles around."

His cousin was a comforting sight in this unknown land. That night they all stayed up late talking of old Kentucky and Indiana days, and of prospects in Illinois. As Abraham looked into John's face, a face of honest grain with a firm jaw and steady gaze carved into it, he forgot his irritation at him for having stirred them all into a long, arduous move.

The next day they proceeded to the piece of land John had picked out for them. It lay eight miles southwest of Decatur, along a bluff overlooking the Sangamon River at a junction of timberland and prairie. Tom looked over the site, stroked his chin, glanced at Sally, and approved it.

They went straight to work hewing timber and clearing underbrush. Up went a sixteen-by-sixteen-foot cabin with a puncheon floor and oak shakes on the roof. After the cabin was up, they made a barn and smokehouse. As spring came on, the men tackled the job of breaking up fifteen acres of sod with plow and hoe. Abraham discovered that cutting into the hard-baked prairie was no easy task.

"Hercules would have worked up a sweat digging through the tangle of roots under this grass," he grunted. Yet as they slowly peeled back the tough sod, they found rich, black earth underneath.

He was relieved when John Hanks laid out a proposition.

"Sheriff Warnick says he could use some hands on his place for a while," John said. "He's paying cash. I told him I'd pitch in after we finished helping Tom. You got any interest?"

"I reckon so."

Bill Warnick, sheriff of Macon County, lived across the Sangamon River two and a half miles from Tom Lincoln's new home. They spent day after day working with maul and wedge, splitting white oak logs into halves, quarters, and eighths. They laid the rails in zigzag fences along the edges of fields until they began to wonder if the sheriff intended to turn every tree in the county into a piece of fence.

"I've lost track of how many of these durn things we've made since we started," John said one afternoon. "Must be close to two thousand."

Abraham walked along the fence lines counting segments, surveyed the piles they'd split but not yet laid, and scratched some figures in the dirt. It turned out to be more than two thousand rails, and it looked like it would be three thousand before they were through.

"He'll have enough to fence in the whole continent, and maybe a couple of oceans," John snorted.

Autumn brought the Illinois Shakes, a demoralizing affliction with fever, chills, and a trembling of the arms and legs that made a trial out of simple chores like spinning flax or swinging a maul. All the Lincolns came down with it. There was no remedy. The ague was an annual visitor on the Illinois frontier, so common that folks who had been there two or three years barely regarded it as a disease. "No need to concern yourself," they said. "You ain't sick, you've just got the shakes."

"Good God, this is awful," Tom moaned. "I wish I'd never left Indiana. I wouldn't take the whole damn state of Illinois if you gave it to me for free."

"Well, at least it ain't the milk sick," Sally pointed out. "You're not going to die from it."

"Be quiet, woman. The thought of death is the only thing that's keeping me alive just now."

The shakes passed, a golden Indian summer followed, and a gentle early December. Then winter storms came raging across the prairies. The snow piled up two feet, three feet, four feet on level open ground. Hogs, cows, and horses froze to death. The settlers, running low on food, lived on cornmeal pounded at home with mortars and pestles.

"This place has more ways to pester a man than the number of sinners in church on a Sunday," Tom grumbled.

John Hanks sent word that a business opportunity had cropped up and that Abraham should meet him at Decatur's general store and bring along his stepbrother. On the appointed morning, they tromped though the snow into town and found their cousin sitting beside the store's fireplace with a stranger who cradled a small jug of whiskey in one arm. John Hanks made the introductions.

"Abe, this is Mr. Denton Offutt. He's up from Kentucky. He's got a proposition for us."

Offutt jumped off his stool and pumped Abraham's hand.

"Ah, young Mr. Lincoln—the Samson of the Sangamon! Just the man we need to bring our mercantile ventures to remunerative success." He wore a swallowtail coat, a bit ragged at the tails, blue cloth vest, black cravat, and bright red pocket handkerchief.

"Mr. Offutt wants us to help him take a hog boat to New Orleans."

"Ahem!"

Offutt cleared his throat, apparently to signal that he wished to clarify.

"I am indeed laying plans to set forth with a shipment of provisions eagerly awaited by some contacts I have cultivated in that distant port city."

He smiled broadly, happy to have placed the matter on a more substantial footing, and planted himself back on his stool.

"My intention, my plan, my stratagem, so to speak, is to transport said supplies—which consist of the bounty of this grand state and the fruits of certain men's hard labors—to transport these goods, as I say, down that great arterial roadway known as the Mississippi River to the ancient French capital your kinsman has mentioned, where they may be sold or bartered to those who wish to further distribute them as they see fit."

He jumped up again and paced the floor, hands behind his back and gaze lifted to the ceiling so his mind's eye could take in the whole panorama of his undertaking.

"And I might add that if Fortune deigns to smile upon our endeavors, this voyage will represent but the first of a whole fleet of merchant vessels that will pour forth with cargoes bound for southern climes."

He paused for a moment, apparently overwhelmed by the sweep of this vision.

"You gentlemen appear to be the kind of men who appreciate the value of discretion. Knowing that, I have no fear in placing with you a confidence that I know you will safeguard."

He leaned close and lowered his voice, even though there was no one else in the store at that moment.

"I am in the process of establishing various commercial operations up and down the entire valley of the Sangamon. At present I have several irons in the fire, several biscuits in the oven, several eggs in the henhouse, so to speak. I expect them to hatch before long, at which time we will witness the birth of a substantial trading empire of which I hope to make you an integral part."

He sat again, leaned back, and raised his hand, a signal, they took it, that he wished to say more.

"Now, why, you may wonder, am I so willing to devote my hopes, my endeavors, my very future, so to speak, to these plans? Two words, my friends, two words—the West. In my mind, there is no doubt about it. The future of this nation lies in the West. It rests with this grand reach of country, from the Great Lakes to the Gulf, from the Alleghenies onward."

He stretched out his arms to demonstrate the region's grandeur.

"People are moving west, roads are moving west, products and markets are moving west. Fortunes are moving west! If I were a betting man—and I am not—but if I *were* a betting man, I would wager all the tea in China that the man who stakes his heart and his toil here in the West, that man shall be a wealthy man!"

He slapped Abraham on the knee, personally conferring the promise of riches on him.

"That sounds mighty fine, mister," Abraham said. "I hope it all comes true."

"It will, my boy, it will. But before embarking on any large venture, one must have the proper resources in place. That is where you come in. Not being personally acquainted with the intricacies of the Mississippi River system, I find myself in need of procuring the services of those who are. Glowing reports of Mr. Hanks's fame as a boatman have come to my ears. I am told that he has made several successful expeditions to New Orleans, and therefore I have come up the river to engage his services. He tells me that you, too, are an experienced riverman. Therefore I have asked you to this meeting to ascertain your interest in joining my crew."

Abraham needed little urging. After some talk, they came to an agreement. Offutt pledged to pay them fifty cents per day plus sixty dollars, to be split among the crew, including John Johnston, who would go with them. They planned to meet at Springfield as soon as the snow went off.

"I shall have a boat there ready for loading," Offutt promised.

He offered them a round of whiskey to celebrate their agreement. They declined since it was still early in the day.

"I myself am usually not much of a drinking man," their new employer explained. "If I were a regular drinking man—and I am not—I suppose I would have no qualms about refreshing myself with libation at this particular hour. As I am not much of a drinking man, a sip or two at this time of day does not come naturally to me. But as this is a rare occasion, and as I consider it bad luck to inaugurate such a venture without raising a small glass for good luck, I will allow myself the luxury of observing the custom of a toast.

"To Fortune, gentlemen. May she cast her benevolent smile in our direction!"

CHAPTER 14

February 1831

His father's face clouded over when he heard the plans. He was quiet for a moment. Abraham and John Johnston stood before him in calf-high snow in the lee of the barn and waited.

"Well, I suppose that will be all right," Tom said at last. "You can come up the Ohio on the trip back and meet your mother and me at Little Pigeon Creek."

"What do you mean?" Abraham asked.

"We're heading back to Indiana. If you'd stick around home a little more, you might keep up with the family news."

Abraham's jaw dropped. "But we just got here."

"And now we're going back. Never should have come in first place."

Abraham tried to grasp this turn of events. He quickly surveyed the last several months, looking for missed warning signs. He had heard his father grouse about the relentless winter storms, the bone-rattling shakes, the hard-baked prairie that took so much sweat to break—but until now had not recognized these complaints as signals that his father truly hated this place.

One thought hardened and pushed itself to the front of his mind: I gave in and let him haul me here. I'm not going to let him haul me back.

"There's nothing for me in Indiana," he told his father.

"There's sure as hell nothing for you here in this frozen desert. And it seems to me, if I remember correctly, that I practically had to drag you here. You never wanted to come in the first place."

"I guess I changed my mind. Now that I'm here, I sort of like it."

He saw no point in bringing up the fact that his father had at first not wanted anything to do with a move to Illinois either and that he had changed his mind about it as well—twice, now.

"I'm not going back," Abraham said.

Tom was quiet another moment. He looked at his stepson.

"What about you, John? Where do you stand?"

"Indiana's as good a place as any," John whined. "I suppose I'll go back. I've got no place else to go."

Tom turned back to Abraham with a brow-furrowed expression that said: He's not even my own flesh and blood, yet I can depend on him, but I can't expect as much from you.

"I need to get out on my own, Pa," Abraham said, more gently. "I can't live under your roof forever. I want to go out and earn my own way."

"I got no argument with that," his father answered, a note of hope in his voice. "It's time you had a place of your own. Come back to Indiana, and we'll find a good piece of land for you. What spare cash I have, I'll put into it. That plus what you make on your New Orleans job should be enough for a down payment. We—John and me—we'll help you get a crop in."

Abraham realized that it was a sincere offer, and a generous one.

"We've been through this before, Pa. You know I don't want to be a farmer."

"Well, maybe we need to go through it again to get it into that thick skull of yours. If you're going to make anything of yourself, you need land. That's the way it's always been, ever since the good Lord sent man out of the garden to till the ground, and the way it'll always be. Prices are going no place but up. There's more and more folks moving into this country. Before you know it, there'll be more people than acres. Get land now, while it's still there for the getting. Ask Jim Gentry. He'll tell you the same."

You've been breaking your back for land ever since I can remember, Abraham thought, and what do you have to show for it?

"I don't want to be a farmer."

His father was struggling to keep a rein on his temper.

"If you're not going back to Indiana, where will you go?"

"I don't know."

"What do you plan to do with yourself?"

"I don't know that, either."

"How are you planning on making a living?"

"However I can, I reckon. I don't know."

"I don't know. I don't know. Is that all you can say?"

"I guess so. I don't know."

"God Almighty, son!"

John roused himself, mumbled an excuse about going to look for a missing whetstone, and slipped around the corner of the barn. Evidently he saw a storm coming and had decided he wanted to get out of his stepfather's way before it broke. Abraham braced himself.

"Damn it, boy! Wake up and look at yourself. You're as big and strong as three oxen put together. Right now, you're acting dumber than four. God gave you muscles, and by God, you ought to use them to make something of yourself instead of lying around in the shade of a tree with a book in your lap. All that reading has put some notions into your head—exactly what they are, I don't know, and I doubt you do, either. But if you plan to go through life standing on tree stumps, yakking in the wind about this and that you've read, I've got news for you, son. No one wants to hear it."

Tom stopped, closed his eyes, and took a deep breath to calm himself down.

"Son, I don't want to hurt your feelings, but there's something to be said for recognizing one's lot in life. There's no point in trying be something you ain't."

Abraham winced. One of Aesop's fables flashed through his mind, the one about the bullfrog who wanted to prove he could be as big as an ox. He puffed himself out, and puffed and puffed, and swelled and swelled, until he burst.

Maybe Pa's right, he thought. Maybe I'm like that bullfrog, wanting to make myself into something I'm not and just making myself ridiculous.

But he stood his ground. "I ain't going to Indiana, Pa. That's going backwards, and I can't do it."

A cry of anguish, half sob, half roar, tore loose from Tom's throat. "I wish *I* could go backwards! I'd give anything to get back what I've lost! I was a fool to let a bunch of women and boys talk me into moving to this godforsaken place. Couldn't they see I'm getting too old to bust sod twice as hard as rock and shovel through ten feet of snow just to get to my chicken house? A hundred acres gone—a hundred acres! Everything I had! Lord, what was I thinking? Now here I am in the middle of nowhere, past fifty years old and squatting on land that ain't even mine and not half as good as what I left behind. God, what have I done?"

He heard panic in his father's voice, saw it in his eyes, and it frightened him. For the first time he could remember, Abraham felt sorry for him. He wanted to reach and grasp him, but his determination to go his own way held him in place.

"Maybe I can still get it back," Tom said, more calmly. "We've still got all the money—cash in hand. We'll go ahead and write Grigsby about it. You can write up the letter, Abe, and make it sound real nice.

He's a reasonable man. He'll see what's right and sell the land back. If he won't, we'll find other land. There's other land in Indiana. We'll get land, and we'll work it, and no harm done. Do you see?"

Abraham remained tautly silent, sick at the thought that his father needed his help and he had none to give. If he went back to Indiana now, he would never get away. He saw that clearly—saw all the years left to him toiling like a slave in a field. He could not do it.

"I'll write that letter for you, Pa. But I won't go back."

His father was quiet for what seemed like a very long time. When he spoke, his voice was hollow with defeat.

"I don't know why I even asked. It don't matter anyhow—even if you came back with us, you'd be tramping off all over the countryside every time there was any danger of hard work. A lazy traveler makes a long journey, Abe. You've got a long, tough road ahead of you if you don't knuckle down. There was a time when I thought you'd come around. But you're on the verge of turning out to be no good. I never thought I'd have to say that about a son of mine. Go where you want—I don't care."

That evening his stepmother came to him and rested her hand on his arm. She looked worn down. Whatever fight she'd put up was over, and she'd resigned herself to going back. She made no attempt to convince Abraham to accompany them.

"It's time for you to go your own way, Abe," she said softly. "Your father knows that deep down. He didn't mean to be harsh. It's just that he's feeling like he's lost his footing, and at his age, a stumble in life can mean a hard fall. Don't be bitter toward him."

He looked steadily into the kind, honest face. If he could be thankful to his father for one thing, it was for bringing his stepmother into his life. With Sarah gone, he felt more akin to her than any other. He had few regrets about parting ways with his father, but the thought of leaving his stepmother behind brought an empty feeling, like the still, snowbound prairie.

"I'm not bitter," he said slowly. "Just sad."

CHAPTER 15

MARCH TO APRIL 1831

The thick snow melted off around the first of March, sending creeks over their banks into the roads and fields. Abraham, John Johnston, and John Hanks bought a dugout canoe and paddled their way to Springfield, a booming town of nearly seven hundred, to meet Denton Offutt. They found their patron at the Buckhorn Tavern, entertaining himself with a tankard of ale and the tavern's customers with his grand designs. Offutt reported that the promised flatboat had failed to materialize.

"I am disappointed to say that despite vigorous pangs of labor, certain unexpected contingencies have for the present delayed the birth of our venture, and our mercantile vessel remains in the womb of the future."

He quickly hired the three expectant navigators to go onto government land, hew timber, and make the boat themselves. They felled the trees, sawed them into logs, floated them to a sawmill to be ripped into planks, and began the job of hammering together a flatboat.

The job took about four weeks. At night they camped in a shanty they threw together on the bank of the Sangamon River. Abraham elected himself chief cook, bottle washer, and dispenser of poetry. When they didn't feel like working, they lounged with some of the locals on a long, peeled log, where they played cards, talked politics, and told jokes that made them whoop and roll off the log until it was polished like a mirror.

Offutt appeared shortly after the work was finished and pronounced it a job well done. They slid the boat into the water, loaded it with barreled pork, corn, and live hogs, and pushed out onto the Sangamon.

The spring floods had receded, and the water moved slowly. Abraham lounged on the deckhouse roof, where he could dream as he pushed away low-hanging limbs and kept an eye half-open for snags. He was happy to be back on a river. When he looked down, he could see silvery fish darting beneath the unruffled surface. When he looked up, past the brim of his soft felt hat that had once been black but was now sunburned into a combine of colors, he saw a wandering strip of blue sky. Lines of turtles basking on logs drifted by, and a muskrat splashed off a bank on its way to an underwater hole. In dusky places, spring peepers chanted their sweet, thin chorus.

All went well until they swung around a bend where the river skirted a high bluff, and they saw the water ahead falling over a low mill dam. Abraham and John Hanks stood on the bow, studying the depth of the backwater, the river's speed flowing across the dam, the height of the ripples atop the ledge. They decided to ride over it. Securing the cargo as best they could, they steered into the part of the stream where the current ran strongest and poled hard, straight for the dam's midsection.

The bow slid across, and they braced themselves for the short drop. A low grinding of wood on stone rose through the deck. The timbers rattled beneath their feet. The flatboat shuddered, groaned, and jolted to a stop.

"Damn!" John Hanks yelled. He and Abraham both scrambled forward and peered down. They were stuck halfway across, with the front part of the flatboat hanging in the air a foot above the free water on the dam's downstream side.

"Stranded! Stranded, gentlemen, stranded!" Offutt assured them. "But no doubt it is merely one of the many small setbacks that customarily accompany any great undertaking. We shall overcome!"

Abraham looked at his cousin and stepbrother.

"Let's try shoving her off," John Hanks said.

The three crewmen pulled off their rawhide boots and lowered themselves into the cold water while Offutt sat atop the deckhouse to direct the rescue operation. They put their shoulders to the transom and heaved, but the boat would not budge.

"We're foundering, gentlemen, foundering!" Offutt cried, now with alarm in his voice.

Abraham looked over the gunwale into the boat. The water, striking the backside of the stationary vessel, was beginning to find its way through the seams between the planks. As Abraham watched, a small pool appeared on the deck. In a moment it was an inch deep, with more coming in. The stern of the boat began to ride lower, and the bow lifted. The pigs on board squealed as they tried to keep from slipping down the deck.

"We'd better lighten this load fast, or we're going to be a shipwreck," Abraham said.

He waded ashore and climbed the bank to talk over the situation with the miller, who seemed eager to get the boat off his dam and was happy to give use of his ferry if that would expedite matters. Abraham pushed the ferry out to the flatboat. The water in the stern was still rising. They loaded the ferry with as many pigs and barrels as it would hold, and John Johnston poled it back to shore while Abraham and John Hanks rolled the rest of the barrels to the forward part of the boat. With the weight of the cargo in the front, the bow gently lowered, the water on the deck sloshed forward, and the stern slowly rose, until the flatboat balanced on the dam like a seesaw on its fulcrum. Now at least they were in no danger of sinking.

A cheer broke out from the mill shore. A small crowd had gathered to watch the contest with the dam. Evidently a village of some sort nestled on the wooded hill beyond the mill, out of sight of the river. News of the stranded flatboat had reached it, and some of its citizens came out to enjoy the drama. A few shouted words of encouragement.

"Next time, you fellows be sure to grease the bottom of your raft before you start out!"

"Why don't you harness these here hogs to your boat and let them pull it off?"

Abraham grinned at John Hanks. "Let's see if we can shove her off now, before someone starts to sell tickets for the chance to see what sort of fools we are."

They splashed back into the cold water and tried pushing on the transom again. The flatboat still wouldn't budge.

They took a step back and surveyed its condition. It was riding more or less level, but the bow was still suspended above the water on the downstream side. Inside the boat, a few inches of muddy water covered the deck. Denton Offutt perched serenely on the deckhouse roof, gazing down at the flood.

"We'll have to drain that water to have a chance of shoving her off," Abraham said. "I'll go fetch an auger."

He waded ashore again. The crowd at the mill had grown to fifteen or so people, all ready to offer advice or josh him in a friendly way. They told him he would find the tool he was looking for at the cooper's shop and gave directions.

On the road up the hill to the village, he passed a girl sitting alone on a tree stump at a place overlooking the dam.

"You've gotten yourself into a fix, haven't you?" She laughed, not unkindly.

Abraham blushed when he saw that she was pretty, with blue eyes and wisps of corn-silk hair that strayed from beneath a red, wide-skirted sunbonnet. At once he realized how comical he must look in his soaked jean trousers, mud-stained blue-and-white striped cotton shirt, and ruined old buckeye chip hat.

I must look like a big gawky heron wading around in the river, he thought. He mumbled something that even he could not understand and hurried past her.

The village consisted of a few rough houses scattered along either side of a road. The cooper's shop, which he identified by the barrels stacked outside its door, sat at the far end. He found the cooper inside, plying his trade among an assortment of planks, staves, hoops, and signs advertising flour barrels for forty cents, pork barrels for a dollar, well buckets and wash tubs for a dollar fifty.

The cooper showed amused pity for the raftsman's predicament and loaned him one of his augers. Abraham thanked him and promised to return it shortly. Then he stepped into the woods to locate a green stick about as thick as the auger's screw. On the way back to the river, he rehearsed what he might say to the pretty girl if he passed her again, but when he reached the stump where she had been sitting, he was relieved to find it deserted.

The river water seemed even colder than before. He waded back out to the flatboat, climbed aboard, and bored a hole in the deck where the bow hung in the air over the edge of the dam. It took several minutes for all the water to drain out. While he waited, he sat on a gunwale and whittled the end of the stick to a taper. When the water was gone, he pounded it into the hole, making sure the plug was good and tight.

He hopped into the water again with his stepbrother and cousin, and they shoved hard on the stern. This time the lightened boat slid over the dam and into free water. The crowd on the bank sent up a cheer.

Offutt decided they would spend the night there so they could reload the flatboat and look around the village, which they discovered was called New Salem. The place had sprung up only a couple of years earlier, but already it had become the trading point for the farms and settlements scattered around the area. Offutt quickly located a saloon on the bluff just above the mill. He declared that he liked the looks of the village, offered a toast to its future, and hinted that it might find a place in his commercial empire.

"When I return from my voyage to New Orleans, I intend to commission the building of a steamboat," he announced to a knot of listeners. "I believe that your burgeoning town will make a fine port of call for the river trade."

"If your steamboat's going to navigate the Sangamon, it'll have to go on ice in the winter," the saloon keeper told him.

"And mighty puny water in the summer," another added.

"No matter, my friends. I shall build it with runners on the bottom to skate over the ice, and rollers underneath to roll right over dams and sandbars. With young Lincoln as her captain, she'll go—by thunder, she'll have to go!"

Several villagers shook Abraham's hand and congratulated him on his wit in freeing the stranded flatboat. He felt the blood rising to his cheeks when the girl with corn-silk hair smiled at him again.

"Well, you got yourself right out of that fix," she said. "That was clever of you."

"Even a blind hog occasionally finds an acorn," he said, grinning back.

Her compliment made him grateful for getting stuck on the New Salem dam.

CHAPTER 16

July to Autumn 1831

Several weeks later, on a hot July day when the sun was high, the flies were biting, and the Indian hemp was in bloom, Abraham made his way down an empty road that followed the west bank of the Sangamon River. A handkerchief bundle thrown over his shoulder held his worldly belongings—an extra shirt, a knife, a few coins, a couple of thin books—and swung at his back as he hiked along.

Rounding a curve, he heard the murmur of water falling over the New Salem mill dam. A man stood on the bank beside the mill, which was idle for the moment, with his hands clasped behind his back, gazing at the stream. He had good, square shoulders and graying hair that made him look to be about fifty. Abraham recognized him as one of the villagers.

The man turned and extended his hand.

"Well, it's our tall flatboat friend, back from New Orleans, I see, and without a flatboat this time. I'm glad to find you safe and sound. I was afraid someone might mistake you for a steamboat funnel and try to light a fire under you."

"No, once we got off this dam, those hogs and I had a pretty easy ride down the Mississippi."

Abraham clasped his hand.

"I'm back to stay for a while. Offutt plans to open a store here. I'm to be his clerk and floor scrubber."

"Offutt, eh? I heard talk that he was laying plans along those lines. Didn't think he'd follow through on it. Sort of a windy, rattling fellow, isn't he? Well, you're both welcome in New Salem. We're glad to have all comers."

Within a few minutes, Abraham learned that the man's name was Jim Rutledge, that he owned the mill with his nephew John Camron, and that he ran a tavern in the nearby village. He had been born in South Carolina and migrated to Illinois by way of Georgia and Kentucky. Just three years before, Rutledge and Camron had brought their families into the area, built the dam and mill, and hired a surveyor to lay out New Salem on the ridge above the river. They sold lots for around ten dollars apiece, and already the place boasted about a hundred residents.

Few settlements existed between there and Chicago, which also claimed about a hundred people in cabins near Fort Dearborn. New Salem perched on the edge of wide-open territory just waiting to be filled up with thousands of eager sodbusters.

"You got here just in time," Rutledge said. "Looks like we'll be a boom town."

"I guess Offutt thinks so too. He figures you could use another general store. I figure that clerking behind a counter beats pushing a plow."

His employer showed up several days later.

"Brilliant news, my young friend!" Offutt greeted him. "I am pleased to announce that I have made arrangements to secure a lot in a strategic location, one which will allow us to command both the river and highway trade. I have also procured a vast inventory of goods—tea from China, coffee from Brazil, sugar from Louisiana. I expect it to arrive from St. Louis any day now. In short, we stand on the threshold of triumph. We have only to raise the walls of our emporium, and our star shall begin its upward course."

They spent the better part of a week throwing up a small log building on the edge of the bluff just above the mill. It sat at a fork in the road near the village saloon. It was a good spot, one that would attract farmers bringing their corn to the mill.

As promised, Offutt's wagonload of goods arrived. Abraham spent an afternoon hauling barrels into the store and piling the shelves with plates, cups, bonnets, gloves, calico prints, lard, cheese, honey, lanterns, and just about everything else a settler might need. He began his career as a general store clerk with the glorious income of fifteen dollars a month and the benefit of sleeping on a narrow cot in the rear of the store.

The job suited him just fine. Traffic in and out of the store was not exactly what you would call congested. There was plenty of time to read newspapers and gab with the farmers who came up from the mill to ease themselves into a chair, spit, and raise the jug of fellowship.

"The thing I like about this work is the lack of it," he confessed to Rutledge. "I suppose that leisure never did sit heavy on me."

On Saturdays, men with nothing better to do gathered to race horses down New Salem's main street and toss feisty gamecocks into the village cock pit. Abraham eagerly joined any games that involved feats of speed and strength. His long, sinewy limbs gave him the advantage in footraces, wrestling matches, and contests to see who could make the longest jump or throw a maul the farthest. Every once in a while, he showed off his trick of grabbing an ax by the end of the handle and swinging it up with one arm straight out before him, elbow locked. Before long, he was known as the village champion.

Denton Offutt realized that such a clerk cast glory on his store. He couldn't help but polish up Abraham's reputation to give it extra shine.

"You've never seen anything like this boy," he boasted. "He's a Hercules, Billy Earthquake, and Davy Crockett all rolled into one. He can outrun, outwrestle, and throw down any man in Sangamon County—no, in all of Illinois!"

Bill Clary, who ran the saloon no more than thirty steps from Offutt's door, took umbrage.

"That's mighty big talk, but here in New Salem, such honors have to be won before they're worn," he told Offutt. "Lincoln's a fine fellow, but I say that Jack Armstrong is a better man."

"Nonsense, my friend! Abe could wrestle an oak tree to the ground. I'd wager any man five dollars—"

"Done!"

Bill Clary was a member of an extended clan that had migrated north from Tennessee to populate a patch of woods known as Clary's Grove, a few miles southwest of New Salem. The Clary's Grove Boys took part in every brawl, card game, and wedding feast within twenty miles. They were always trimming horses' tails when the owners weren't looking or putting sharp rocks under saddles to make the horses throw their riders.

"Don't let those boys fool you," Jim Rutledge told Abraham. "They're rough-and-tumble as they come, and they'll fight for the sheer love of fighting. But place before them a lame man, a defenseless woman, or an orphan child, and those fellows melt into sympathy. There never was under the sun a more generous parcel of rowdies. It's just that a stranger's introduction is likely to be the most unpleasant part of his acquaintance with them."

Jack Armstrong was the acknowledged leader and champion of the Clary's Grove Boys. He was a sturdy, square-built man, about five years older than Abraham, with a clean-shaven face and eyes that said, "I can whip you, and I just might decide to do it too." But his grin said, "Even if I do whip you, it's all in good fun."

Jack and his friends dropped by Offutt's store as soon as Bill Clary told them about the wager.

"Well, Lincoln, I hear that you and I are to be married," Armstrong drawled.

Abraham looked down at him. He was several inches shorter and a good forty pounds lighter than Abraham, but the man was all muscle, solid as a plow designed to bust through hard sod.

I'll have to fight him, Abraham thought. They want to see what I'm made of. If I say no, they'll think I'm chicken-livered, and that'll be the end of me here.

"All right, I'll fight you, Armstrong," he said slowly. "But no eye-gouging and ear-biting—I don't like that kind of fight, and I won't do it. I'll wrestle you."

One of the Clary's Grove Boys let out a groan.

"Oh, Lord, he's one of them scientific wrestlers. We might as well pick out two old women and lay bets on which'll fall asleep faster."

A chorus of mutterings backed him up. Scientific wrestling—that meant a contest with rules and prescribed grips, not the free-swinging, fist-throwing spectacle the Clary's Grove Boys had in mind. Just two fellows taking hold and straining until one managed to throw the other.

Abraham threw down the challenge again.

"How about it, Armstrong? I'll wrestle you. Muscle against muscle."

"All right," Jack said in an agreeable way. "We'll wrestle. I choose side holds."

"Good," Abraham said.

Just what he wanted.

A week later, a crowd gathered for the contest in a clearing next to Offutt's store. The Clary's Grove Boys turned out in force, laughing and jabbing each other in anticipation. All the men and boys of the village were there, as well as a good many farmers from surrounding settlements, like Sandridge and Sugar Grove.

Denton Offutt and Bill Clary sat at a rough puncheon table under a tree and recorded all bets. The wagers ran in favor of Armstrong since no one had seen him lose a fight.

"I'll stake two dollars against Onstot's one that Jack'll throw Lincoln."

"I got a twelve-cent jug of apple brandy against Kirby's best plug of tobacco that says Abe can take him."

"I'll put a good jackknife on Lincoln if one of you fellows'll stake a daughter of marrying age against it."

Jim Rutledge agreed to referee the match. He drew a ring in the dirt with a hoe and motioned the two contestants to step inside. Each stripped off his shirt and tied a bright red handkerchief around his waist for a wrestling belt.

"All right, boys," Rutledge said, "this'll be a clean fight. I'll be the sole judge of what's a true fall and what's a dog fall. No arguing with the referee, and no interference from the spectators. Wrestlers, take your holds."

The two locked hold in a half crouch, with the left sides of their chests against one another, each grasping his opponent's belt with one hand and an arm with the other. They took a moment to find a secure grip. According to the rules, once the match began, they had to maintain that grip. The object was to throw the other man so that he landed three points down—either two shoulders and one hip, or two hips and one shoulder touching the ground.

"All set?" Rutledge asked. "Have at it."

At once Abraham felt Armstrong's grip tighten like a noose. He grunted in spite of himself. Jack yanked hard on his belt, knocking him off his stance. The crowd let out a yelp. Abraham staggered backward, dragging Armstrong with him, threw out his left leg, and braced himself just in time to keep from going down.

Armstrong was every bit as strong as he looked, and then some.

This isn't going to be easy, Abraham thought.

He heaved himself back to an even keel and tightened his grip to match Armstrong's. Abraham was already breathing hard. His feet shifted in the dirt, searching for a stance that might give him an advantage.

"Push him over, Jack! We'll roll him down to the mill and saw him into planks!"

"Come on, Abe! Pick him up and set him down on his head!"

All right, now I know what I'm up against, Abraham told himself. Let's see if he knows how to defend himself.

He pulled hard on Armstrong's belt, forcing him to shift his weight. When he saw Jack begin to lift his right leg, he lunged forward, pushing hard to throw him off balance. Armstrong gave a grunt and fell backwards. Before he hit the ground, he turned to land on his side and was up again before the crowd had a chance to yell.

"Dog fall!" Rutledge cried.

"Dog fall!" the Clary's Grove Boys cheered.

Armstrong had managed to land two points down, instead of the three required to be counted as a real fall. He came up wearing a grin. Won't do any good to shove at me like that, it said, I'm way too quick at twisting and turning to go down that way.

They locked together again, tightened grips, and settled in for a siege. Each pulled the other close. They had established that they were well matched. Now it would be a matter of wearing the other man down.

Ten minutes later they were both breathing hard, grunting at every small move or shift in position.

This is like trying to wrestle a boulder, Abraham thought.

"Hey, you two! You ain't in church! Do something!"

He listened for the rhythm of Armstrong's breathing. Jack's grip didn't seem quite as ironclad.

If I can keep him in check a bit longer, he thought, I'll come out the winner.

Suddenly he heard Armstrong's voice in his ear, low but strong.

"Lincoln, there's no sense in this. I can't throw you, and you can't throw me. What do you say we both let go and call it a draw?"

What? Had he heard right?

"I mean it, Abe," Armstrong whispered. "I'm content with a draw if you are. Let go on the count of three—one, two, three!"

Armstrong broke his grip, grabbed both of Abraham's legs, and yanked. Abraham had no chance to catch himself. He went straight down.

The back of his head hit the ground with a thud amid whoops and yells of the men. He caught his breath and jumped up with shoot in his eyes, ready to lunge. Jack Armstrong was already shooting back with a friendly, Now-you-didn't-really-think-I'd-stick-to-your-silly-scientific-wrestling-rules-did-you? grin all over his face.

Abraham saw at once that it was all a frontier joke. The fellows from Clary's Grove were already moving toward him with extended hands, chuckling and snorting at the fun. No one here gave a second thought to tunking over a newcomer with a good-natured legging.

He dropped his fists, and the anger slipped from him like an old blanket.

They're watching me to see how I'll take it, a shrewd voice inside him said.

"Well, boys, I can see that I'd better stick to beauty contests."

The crowd closed around the two combatants, slapping backs and joking with Abraham about how when he hit the ground his feet had landed in Ohio and his head in Missouri.

"All right fellows, don't be shy about claiming stakes," Bill Clary called out. "Looks to me like Mr. Lincoln landed three points down. Offutt, I'll ask you to kindly pay up five dollars."

Wide grins hung on the Clary's Grove Boys.

"That's right, Lincoln went down flat as a board. Herndon owes me a sack of meal."

Three or four assenting voices chimed in, their tones lubricated by a few drops of corn whiskey.

Abraham looked at Jim Rutledge

"Now, hold up," Rutledge said, starting forward.

"Hold up, nothing," Clary answered. "A fall's a fall. No hiding behind ladies' rules. Lincoln went down, and his men ought to pay."

Denton Offutt glanced from Clary to Rutledge and back to Clary. The look on his face said it was probably better to pay up and save some trouble.

Abraham felt his blood rising. A legging was one thing, but this was taking the joke too far.

"I went down because Jack broke his grip," he said calmly.

"We thought maybe you fell over 'cause the air up there is so thin, you just finally passed out."

Laughter spilled across the broken ring, but it had an edge to it.

"All I know is, I saw you fall," Bill Clary said in a reasonable tone. "If you fall, you lose, and if you lose, you pay."

Abraham kept his voice firm. "Nobody won any wagers, Bill, and you're not going to take Offutt's money."

A few of the surrounding faces turned dark.

"If Jack wants to wrestle again, and wrestle fair, I'm ready," he said. "I told you I'm opposed to fist throwing and scuffling, but if nothing else will do you, I'll fight Jack that way. In fact, I'll fight any of you, so long as you come on one at a time."

Some of the Clary's Grove Boys were edging closer, showing expectations of a pretty good brawl. The men who had backed Lincoln began closing ranks. Jim Rutledge stood in between, urging them all to hold back. Abraham braced himself.

Jack Armstrong stepped forward.

"Hold on, fellows. There's no use kicking up a stir. Abe and I both agree to call it a draw, right, Abe? No one's paying anyone anything. Let's all step over to Bill's place—I could use a little rejuvenation."

That's all it took. Smiles replaced dark glances. Men who a moment ago had been ready to take a swing at each other remembered that they were neighbors and friends and turned as one in good humor toward Bill Clary's saloon.

Clary and Offutt shook hands, and Jack thrust his own toward Abraham.

"You've got sand in your craw, Lincoln. They say that ferocious fights make fast friends. Glad to have you in New Salem."

CHAPTER 17

AUTUMN 1831 TO MARCH 1832

The days grew shorter. The afternoon rays of the sun slanted lower, and the woods along the Sangamon River showed signs of turning into a ribbon of scarlet and gold on the summer-baked prairie. Inside Offutt's store, Abraham manned the counter amid shelves crammed with tea and molasses, socks and gloves, crockery and candle wicks. He knew the twists and turns of rivers. Now he learned the ins and outs of frontier trade, which operated mainly on the barter system, with local farmers bringing in everything from coonskins to whiskey for trade.

Offutt hired a local boy, Bill Greene, to give Abraham a hand and tip him off as to which customers were good to buy on account. Bill was a genial fellow, nineteen years old, with sharp eyebrows that lay on a smooth forehead like lean marks on a ledger. When a customer walked through the door whom Bill knew to be good for his word and able to pay top dollar, his eyebrows shot up on the credit side as he quickly calculated how far to push the bargaining. When a poor risk darkened the threshold, his forehead creased into a frown and his eyebrows plunged to the debit side. He was so good at cutting a deal, New Salem folk began calling him Slicky Bill.

"How do you do that?" Abraham asked.

"Do what?"

"How do you figure how many sacks of corn a man is worth the minute you lay eyes on him?"

Slicky Bill just shrugged.

When men gathered around the store's fireplace, the jokes and stories grew as plenty as blackberries.

"Did you hear that Jesse and Ira Rumsey had a shindig for their fortieth wedding anniversary?"

"Nope."

"She told him to go out and slaughter a hog for the feast. 'Looky here, old woman,' he told her. 'There's no cause to blame the pig for something that happened so long ago.'"

When Slicky complained that a gambler named Estep had tricked him out of some money, Abraham told him to go hunt the man up.

"Bet him that I can lift a full barrel of whiskey off the floor and hold it while I take a drink out of the bung hole."

"Can you actually do that, Abe?"

"Go bet him, and we'll see."

The gambler took the bet. Abraham squatted in front of the barrel, lifted it off the floor by rolling it up onto his knees until the bunghole got to his mouth, took a drink, put the barrel down, stood up, and spat the whiskey on the floor.

"You lose," he said. The gambler laughed and paid up.

Later that same afternoon, the girl with golden corn-silk hair appeared. Abraham was reading a two-week-old edition of the *Western*

Sun when she stepped into the little store. He put the newspaper down.

She stood about five feet four inches tall and wore a simple, blue flannel dress that showed the outlines of a slim but shapely figure. She gave both clerks a warm hello.

"I'm glad to see you survived your travels, Mr. Lincoln."

"Yes, ma'am. I'm back." He stared at her, suddenly feeling stupid.

"I just stopped in for a few sheets of writing paper," she explained. "Do you have any?"

He dredged his brain for a clever remark while he fetched the paper. He could feel her looking at his rough, sinewy hands as they fumbled with the thin sheets.

"You can put it on my father's account," she said.

"Your father?"

"Yes, Jim Rutledge."

"Oh—Jim Rutledge. Of course," he said, grateful to know who she was. "I guess his hand was the first I shook the day I got here."

She took the paper with a smile.

"Well, goodbye, Mr. Lincoln, Mr. Greene."

"Goodbye, Miss Rutledge."

He stood behind the plank counter, watching through the open doorway as she disappeared up the path.

"You and every other unmarried man in these parts," he heard Slicky laugh.

Abraham colored. "She ain't hard to look at, is she? What's her name?"

"Ann."

"I sort of met her back when Offutt's boat got stuck on the dam. Didn't get her name then, though."

"She spends a good bit of her time at her father's tavern, helping run the place."

"I reckon she's good for business."

"We won't see much of her in this store."

"Why not?"

"John McNeil's her beau."

"Oh."

John McNeil was partner with a merchant named Samuel Hill in a rival store that sat practically across the street from the Rutledge tavern. Recently arrived from New York, McNeil had quickly made a name for himself as an industrious young man with a good head for business. The word in New Salem was that he was already worth a few thousand dollars and destined to become a man of substantial wealth.

"Well, beauty is best admired from a distance, anyhow," Abraham said. "Least that's what they tell me."

He worked in a fog for the rest of the afternoon. When he closed shop and was reviewing the day's transactions, he realized he had overcharged Clarissa Hornbuckle, a regular customer, by six and a quarter cents for a few yards of cloth she'd purchased.

"I suppose I'd better go return her money," he told Slicky.

"Long way to walk to give back a picayune."

"I can use the air."

A few miles lay between Offutt's store and the Hornbuckle house. He had the climbing moon and dim, fitful shadows to accompany his thoughts. As he walked along, he brooded over his homeliness. His leathery face and long limbs seemed all bone and odd angles. Sometimes he felt as thin as a beanpole and ugly as a scarecrow.

It can't happen that a sucker like me can have a gal like Ann, he thought.

With each passing week, his doubts grew as to when the store's rivulet of customers would turn into the surging tide envisioned by his employer. It seemed to him that Offutt's inventory was stuck on the shelf side of the plank counter.

Offutt himself displayed no worries. "To climb steep hills requires a slow pace," he assured his clerks. "From little acorns mighty oaks grow!"

He said it as he filled his pocket flask from the store's big oak barrel of Kentucky rye whiskey.

Slicky Bill privately offered a different assessment.

"Offutt's winking out," he said. "He'll be gone in a couple of months. Wait and see."

Abraham's instincts told him the same.

"This much spare time takes all the fun out of lazy," he observed. "I suppose I'll have to improve myself."

He joined New Salem's debating society, which met in a room carved into the ground beneath a cabin built on a hillside. Jim Rutledge was its president. Locals whom Abraham was learning to admire were members, men like Mentor Graham, the village schoolmaster, and Bowling Green, the jolly, bighearted justice of the peace whose belly had earned him the nickname Pot. John McNeil, Ann Rutledge's beau, was there as well, and Abraham could not help but like him when he discovered that the young man was a reader of poetry and had his own library with volumes by Shakespeare, Homer, and Burns.

By the glow of hanging lanterns, they gave spirited debate to questions blowing across the prairies in the winter of 1831–32. Should Congress reduce the price of public lands? Should people join temperance societies? Is it right for one man to own another?

Abraham joined in with gusto, bringing to bear all the knowledge he had collected from his newspaper reading. His arguments earned some praise.

"There's more in Abe's head than wit and fun," he heard Jim Rutledge say.

The encouragement revived his longing to become a polished speaker like the lawyers he'd seen in court at Boonville and Rockport back in Indiana. But he needed to plane the rough edges off his backwoods drawl and carve the knots out of his phrases.

One morning he strolled over to see Mentor Graham, who had built a brick house a mile west of New Salem. He arrived as the schoolmaster and his wife, Sarah, were starting their breakfast. Sarah sat him down and pushed a big plate of flapjacks at him.

"Mentor, I have a notion of studying grammar."

A smile replaced the stern expression that usually governed the teacher's clean-shaven face.

"You need to get hold of a copy of Kirkham's *Grammar,*" he said. "I believe that John Vance has one. I bet he'll let you have it."

When Abraham finished his flapjacks, he walked the six miles to Vance's house and got the book. He walked back head down and eyes glued to the volume in his hands, *English Grammar in Familiar Lectures* by Samuel Kirkham.

For several nights he sat at the Grahams' gate-leg table, elbow to elbow with the schoolmaster, attacking the book page by page.

"All right, Abe, what is the definition of a noun?"

"A noun is the name of any person, place, or thing—like 'man,' 'Springfield,' or 'mule.'"

"Good. Now, tell me what you know about person."

"Person is a property of the noun and pronoun which varies the verb. The first person denotes the speaker. The second person denotes the person or thing spoken to, like, 'Listen, mule!' The third person denotes the person or thing spoken of, like, 'That mule never listens to me.'

"Nouns have but two persons, the second and third. The first person, that's saved for the pronouns *I* and *we*, like, 'I got an urge to shoot that damn mule.'"

One day he was stretched out on the counter at Offutt's store, head propped up on a stack of calico prints, reading aloud to himself from Kirkham's *Grammar*, when Jim Rutledge and Bowling Green dropped by and asked to have a talk. The three of them settled down before the fire, and Abraham watched in fascination as the big justice of the peace lowered his two hundred and fifty pounds onto a stool. Pot Green had the habit of hitching up his trousers with just one linen suspender, and his belly tumbled like a full sack of grain against the thin strap.

"Abe, what would you think of running for the state legislature?" Rutledge asked.

Abraham gaped at them.

"Are you joking?"

"No, not at all."

"Why in the world would you want me?"

"We think you'd make a good candidate."

"But I ain't even been here a year."

"That's true, and it will count against you," Rutledge said. "That can't be denied. But most voters in these parts haven't been here very long themselves."

"Folks around here like you, Abe, and that's worth a lot," Pot explained. "They know an honest, smart young fellow when they see one."

Abraham studied their expressions. It was clear that they were in earnest.

"Well, who all is running?" he asked.

"There'll be several. John Stuart, Ed Taylor, Peter Cartwright, Achilles Morris, among others. The county gets four representatives, so the top four vote-getters will win seats in Vandalia."

"Come on, now. The only race I could win against those fellows would be a footrace to Vandalia. And even then, I'm not too sure about beating Cartwright."

Jim Rutledge smiled. "We want to be up front with you, Abe. The truth is, you probably won't win—not this time around. Not because you can't do the job. I believe you could go down to Vandalia tomorrow and, once you learned the ropes, represent the people as well as anyone in the statehouse. You'll lose simply because it's your first time out, and your name isn't well-known across the whole county. The quickest way to change that is to go ahead and put yourself before the people. In time it will do you good—you'll see."

Abraham fought to contain the hope surging through his chest. Here were two of the most important men in New Salem sitting before him, offering votes of confidence in his future. For the first time in his life, he saw a path that might lead clear of his backwoods youth. He couldn't refuse it.

"I want to be up front with you too," he said slowly. "I won't pretend the idea doesn't please me. But do you really think I'm cut out to be a legislator? You know I've hardly had any schooling."

"That may be, but Mentor Graham tells us that you're running through that grammar book like a hound on a hare," Pot said. "You've got a sharp mind, Abe, and you're turning yourself into a fine speaker. You'll make a good account of yourself before the voters."

Both of his visitors looked hopeful.

"One other thing, Abe," Pot said. "You know that most folks around here are Jackson men."

Abraham saw what he had in mind. On the Illinois frontier in 1832, political parties were inchoate things. Voters attached their allegiance not to political organizations but rather to individuals. Andrew Jackson, the man of the people who had whipped the British, raced fast Tennessee horses, and smoked a cob pipe, was the great hero of the frontier. In friendly arguments around the fireplace at Offutt's store, Abraham had made it clear that although he saw much to admire in Jackson, he favored Henry Clay of Kentucky.

"I like what Clay and the Whigs have to say," he explained. "If this part of the country is going to amount to anything, we need to build up trade. Like Clay says, that requires more roads and canals, a strong national bank, and tariffs to help our businesses compete with goods from Europe."

"Well, that pretty much makes you a Whig," Pot said.

"But if you're worried about me antagonizing folks when it comes to Old Hickory, I think I can put your minds at ease. It's true that I favor Clay, but I've got nothing to say against President Jackson. I can't honestly claim to be a whole-hog Jackson man. But I suppose the ice wouldn't be too thin under my feet if I were to say that though I'm a Clay man, the clay is mixed with some Jacksonian grit."

Green and Rutledge looked at each other, satisfied.

"Abe, you'll do just fine."

CHAPTER 18

MARCH TO JULY 1832

He wrote an announcement of his candidacy for the *Sangamo Journal*, which published it in its March 15, 1832 edition. Good Lord, he thought when he saw the declaration in print, I've actually gone and done it.

All the villagers dropped by the store to offer congratulations, including Ann Rutledge.

"Good luck, Abe," she said, smiling. "We're proud of you."

"Andy Jackson and Henry Clay got nothing on me." He grinned back, blushing a little.

Then his streak of good luck met a snag. Several days went by without anyone seeing Denton Offutt. At first Abraham hoped his employer had gone to St. Louis to procure more goods without telling his clerks. But as time passed, he concluded that, true to Slicky Bill Greene's prediction, Offutt had winked out. Like so many frontier entrepreneurs, he had left his debts behind and struck out for parts unknown to lay the foundations of a new empire.

"Well, at least I have the steady prospect of losing an election to fall back on," Abraham told Slicky.

He did not have long to contemplate his employer's disappearance. One soggy April afternoon, a mud-spattered rider galloped down New Salem's main street and thrust an official proclamation into Slicky's hands. Abraham looked over his friend's shoulder and skimmed a message from the Illinois governor: "Fellow-Citizens: Your country requires your services. The Indians have assumed a hostile attitude, and have invaded the State, in violation of the Treaty of last summer. . . ."

It was a call to arms. The Sauk and Fox tribes had grown unhappy about being forced to move west of the Mississippi River. Black Hawk, one of their leaders, had recrossed the river with several hundred men, women, and children, claiming that he had returned to plant corn. His party included three or four hundred well-armed braves.

Black Hawk's appearance sent shivers of terror across the frontier. Jittery settlers left their bread baking on the fire and scurried toward the nearest fort. Frenzied reports of painted warriors and cabins in flames had reached the governor.

"Do you think you'll sign up?" Slicky asked.

Abraham thought it over for a minute. He could use the militiaman pay, and a stint as a soldier would no doubt be good for his prospects in the upcoming election. At any rate, he told himself, if the state has been invaded, I'm not going to sit on my haunches.

"I reckon I'll go."

"Me too."

The militia mustered on Richland Creek, nine miles southwest of New Salem. Abraham knew most of the fellows who turned out. They included Jack Armstrong and a number of the Clary's Grove Boys. Jack ambled up to Abraham and clapped him on the arm.

"Abe, we want to nominate you to be captain of our company."

Abraham was surprised. "You know I don't have any military experience."

"That's all right. Neither does anyone else around here. Hell, half these boys can shoot straight only when liquored up, and the other half couldn't hit a bull's-eye with the bow of a bass fiddle no matter what. If anyone can keep this sorry bunch from decorating their own hindquarters with a few more holes, you can."

Abraham looked the throng over. They were a hard-looking, unkempt, dirty-shirted set. Maintaining some semblance of order would be no easy task.

"All right, Jack. I'll do it if they'll have me."

Bill Kirkpatrick, who operated a nearby sawmill, also desired the post. Following frontier tradition, the two candidates stood apart in a field, facing the company, and at the command "March!" each soldier stepped forward and lined up behind the man he wanted for captain. It was no contest. Abraham's line stretched twice as long as Kirkpatrick's.

He shook Kirkpatrick's hand while everyone cheered. Then he appointed Jack Armstrong to be his first sergeant and made a brief speech.

"Well, boys, I thank you for putting your confidence in me. I'll do my best to prove myself worthy. Now, the governor wants us right away, so I suppose that the first order of business is for us all to report for duty tomorrow at Beardstown. Try not to be late."

"Aw, go to hell!" someone yelled, and his new command broke up in laughter.

He set off the next day on a horse borrowed from Bowling Green. As an officer, he felt he should bring one to the fight. At Beardstown, Indian concerns gave way to a holiday mood as men rendezvoused from all over the state, throwing their arms around old friends and clasping hands with new ones. The camp was filled with the hollering of footraces and wrestling contests, the clanging of horseshoes tossed against stakes, and tough talk about what the army would do to Black Hawk when it caught up with him.

"Those Injuns need to get on the other side of the river and stay there, like they promised. First they sell land, then they say they want it back. What's wrong with them?"

"Hell, you can't reason with a savage who'll grab a white baby by the ankles and brain it against the nearest tree. It's us or them, and that's all there is to it."

Between games, Abraham drilled his men as best he could and requisitioned guns for his company. When they broke camp, the going got rougher. Cold and drizzle set in. The troops sloshed down muddy roads and beat through briars that tore their clothing. When supplies ran low, they foraged for food, often by stealing pigs and chickens from deserted farms, or gnawed on jerky, which was like eating saddlebags.

One morning Abraham had a harder time than usual rousing his men from their blankets. Most staggered into line. A few refused to budge at all.

"You fellows are drunk as an army of fiddler's clerks!" he roared.

"Yes sir, we are," one of them giggled. "You just go on without us."

He pried out of them what had happened. With the aid of a tomahawk and four buckets, they had broken into the quartermaster's supply of liquor and made off with a good amount. He finally got them moving, but two miles into the march, most of them had to lie down and sleep off their drunk.

He knew that as the company's captain, he'd catch it for the misconduct. It didn't take long for word to come down from the regiment's commander that he would have to carry a wooden sword for two days. It was more or less the equivalent of wearing a dunce cap.

At first the punishment rankled him. He fretted that the other officers would think he couldn't handle his troops. But pretty soon he realized that no one much cared, and that his men were genuinely sorry, so he ended up laughing it off.

Word arrived that an advance detachment under Maj. Isaiah

Stillman had run into a band of Blackhawk's warriors and been whipped in battle, with several killed and the rest scampering back to the safety of the main army. The news put the militia in a sour mood, which grew even darker several days later when they passed through a deserted settlement and found the scalps of women and children the Indians had killed.

They marched south, toward the Fox River.

One evening, an old Indian, tired and helpless, ventured into camp looking for food. He pulled a crumpled paper from his coat to show the white men. It was a safe conduct pass from the army, certifying that he was friendly.

The men left off their card games to examine the pass.

"It don't look right to me," one of them muttered. "Bet it's a forgery."

"He's a damn spy, that's what. Let's shoot him."

Abraham took the pass and gave it back to the Indian.

"No one's going to shoot this man."

The circle of dark faces tightened.

"Step aside, Abe. We come out here to fight Indians, and by God, we intend to do so."

Abraham stood his ground. "I'm telling you, he has a pass. Leave him alone."

Sullen murmurs and oaths surrounded him.

"This is cowardly on your part, Lincoln."

He could feel his blood surging. He drew himself up to full height.

"If any man thinks I'm a coward, let him test it."

"That's easy for you to say, Lincoln. You're bigger and heavier than any one of us."

"You can guard against that. Choose your weapons."

The men hesitated, growling. One of them stepped forward—Jack Armstrong. He moved to Abraham's side, turned, and faced the crowd. A second later the rest of the Clary's Grove Boys were standing with him, shoulder to shoulder.

The militiamen pawed at the dirt and spat in the fire while their tempers cooled. They let the old Indian slip away.

By the time they reached Ottawa, at the mouth of the Fox River, the volunteers' term of enlistment had expired. Most of the New Salem boys decided to go home. They were tired of marching on empty stomachs and sleeping on hard ground.

"May's almost gone. I've got crops to get into the ground," Jack said, hurrying away.

Abraham thought it over. He had no one in New Salem waiting for him. The campaign for the legislature could hold off a bit longer. He decided to reenlist, this time as a private. He didn't mind shedding the duties of a captain.

At least I won't run the risk of having to drag a wooden sword around camp if any of these fellows get liquored up, he told himself.

He was grateful to strike up a friendship with John Todd Stuart, a lawyer from Springfield serving in the new company. Barely a year older than Abraham, but well connected and college educated, Stuart had come from Kentucky to Illinois a few years earlier to get into law and politics. Like Abraham, he was running for a seat in the state legislature. Unlike Abraham, he was expected to win.

As they sat beside their campfire, poking sticks into the flames, Abraham was gratified to hear the courtly Stuart praise him for the way he could handle men and tell a story better than any other in the battalion.

"I've been studying to better myself so I might rise in the world," he confessed.

"Well, you ought to think about studying law," Stuart said. "If that grammar book didn't stump you, there's no reason a law book should. You'd be good at it."

That night Abraham fell asleep with his head on a pile of leaves, wondering hard if that could really be true.

As hot weather came on, the volunteers spent a good bit of time chasing rumors of Indian sightings and battling mosquitoes. "They got so much of my blood, we're practically kin," Abraham complained, swatting.

He was delighted to find that his stepbrother, John, had also enlisted. It gave him a chance to catch up on news of his parents, now living in

Coles County, Illinois, about sixty-five miles south of Decatur. They had stopped there on their way back to Indiana and decided to stay put.

"Pa figures he'll give Illinois one more chance," John said.

"Well, I hope Illinois decides to give him another chance too," Abraham said, thinking mainly of his stepmother.

Abraham's company saw no fighting, but at the tiny settlement of Kellogg's Grove, they helped bury five men killed in a skirmish the day before. As they rode up a hill into the dead men's camp, the red light of the morning sun streamed over the bodies strewn about the ground. Each man had a round, red spot on the top of his head, about as big as a dollar, where the Indians had taken his scalp. Abraham shuddered as he stooped to move a corpse wearing buckskin britches into a grave. The scene was grotesque. The red sunlight seemed to paint everything all over. He suddenly understood why strong men sometimes turned and ran in battle.

He spent the last days of his enlistment stumbling through forests and swamps in an attempt to locate Black Hawk. His company crossed into the Michigan Territory following reports of scattered war parties. They never found any Indians.

As the hot days of July came on, the army decided it lacked provisions and had better disband the volunteer troops. The morning Abraham started for home, he woke to find that the horse Bowling Green had lent him was gone—probably stolen by another soldier. He was three hundred miles from New Salem.

"I guess one of these other fellows had a longer way go," he said mournfully.

"Hell, some of those boys would steal money off a dead man's eyes," John Stuart said. "Come on. You can ride my horse part of the way."

The company headed south, most of them walking a good bit even if they had a ride since their horses' backs were so sore. When they reached Peoria, the volunteers went their separate ways. Abraham embraced his stepbrother and shook hands with John Stuart.

"Think over what I said about studying the law," Stuart said.

A few days later, Abraham trudged into New Salem and threw

himself on the ground, bone-tired.

"Welcome back," Jack Armstrong greeted him. "How was the war?"

"It was all right," Abraham said. "No one killed me or made me kill him, so I guess we came out even."

CHAPTER 19

July to October 1832

He arrived at New Salem three weeks before the election for the state legislature and immediately wondered if he had any business being in a race he was bound to lose. Why in the world should anyone in Illinois vote for an Indiana farm boy with almost no education and little more to his name than the dingy calico shirt on his back?

He went to Bowling Green for reassurance. He found the justice of the peace outside his cabin, lounging in the shade of a butternut tree, patting a belly full of fried ham and cornbread.

"I don't think I'm up to this, Pot," he confessed. "You can't make a silk purse from a sow's ear."

"You're going to do fine. Jim and I wouldn't have asked you to run if we weren't certain you'd make a good accounting of yourself."

"I don't know."

"You just need to get out there, introduce yourself to as many people as you can, and ask them to consider you for office. The rest will take care of itself. Oh, and by the way, a candidate does need a horse to get around. You can use my old bay roan for the next couple of weeks. Try not to lose this one."

He dropped by the Rutledge tavern to get advice from Jim and another smile from Ann. She left off her sweeping to greet him.

"If women could vote, Abe, I'd vote for you," she promised.

"Miss Rutledge, that's all the encouragement I need," he said, bowing and lifting his old straw hat.

He spent the next several days going from farm to farm, introducing himself and making friends. Pot was right. Folks seemed glad to spend a while talking with him, especially if he kept the conversation light and helped shuck corn or cut wheat as he talked.

"I like the way you handle yourself, son," an oldster told him. "You ain't much to look at, but looks don't split rails."

This could be more fun than rafting down a river, he told himself. I get to chew the fat and stretch my legs all at the same time.

Wherever he found a willing crowd, he jumped onto a box or the back of a wagon and gave a quick speech. Jack Armstrong and a handful of the Clary's Grove Boys often showed up to stand beside him, arms folded, and signal their support. Their presence helped win some influence among the butcher-knife boys, the class of voters who were prone to carrying big knives in the belts of their hunting shirts.

"You can't win an election without the butcher-knife boys." Jack grinned. "And, hell, my knife is three times as long as the rest of 'em carry."

Abraham threw the crowbar and wrestled with local champions every chance he got.

"Just make sure you let 'em beat you every once in a while," Jack suggested. "Folks won't vote for a man if they think he can't ever be licked."

As election day approached, Abraham began to wonder if he might have a chance of winning one of the four open seats. He knew he shouldn't let himself think it. Bowling Green and Jim Rutledge had both warned him that he wouldn't win on his first try.

But maybe I'll surprise everyone and win after all, he thought.

It didn't turn out that way. He ran eighth out of thirteen candidates, getting 657 votes. His friend John Todd Stuart was one of the four elected to the legislature in Vandalia.

He was disappointed but not discouraged. In his own New Salem precinct, he won 277 of the 300 votes cast—a consolation prize that pleased him to no end.

"Not bad at all," Jim Rutledge told him, pumping his hand. "You gained some good experience, ran on the square, and caught the notice of some of the leading men in this part of the state. Can't complain about that."

"You'd have won a seat if you were better known outside of New Salem," Ann said. Her smile was the best consolation prize of all.

As Abraham studied his defeat, he realized they were right. He had done pretty well for a first-timer and enjoyed every bit of it. All his worries about not being cut from the right sort of cloth to run for office had turned out to be needless. He made up his mind to try again in the next election.

In the meantime, he faced the daunting question that confronts each generation of footloose young men: What was he going to do with himself? He needed a way to make a living.

He thought about his old plan of signing onto a steamboat, but he was reluctant to leave friends who had been so kind to him. He sauntered over to see Joshua Miller, the village blacksmith, a man with muscles as strong as iron bands.

"You'd be good at wrestling metal—I'll teach you how," Joshua sang out as he swung his hammer, bending a piece of hot yellow-orange iron into the shape of an ox shoe.

The roar of the bellows and clang of the sledge against the anvil were cheerful sounds, but the craft was hard physical labor, and Abraham was determined to escape that kind of work.

He pondered what John Stuart had said—that he should consider studying law. He didn't see how he could succeed at that with his little bit of education.

"I'm too poor to paint and too proud to whitewash," he told Row Herndon, who owned a half interest in a small general store. "I guess I've got to find something in between. But I don't know what."

"Well, I know of something that may interest you," Row said, and he proceeded to throw an opportunity into Abraham's lap. "Keeping a store don't suit me, but you seem to have a knack for it. I'll sell you my stock of goods, if you like, and you can take my place."

Now, here was something. Having his own store could put him at the center of the little town's life. He would have his own place to talk politics and while away empty hours with friends and strangers.

"I've got my militia pay coming to me, but beyond that no more than two bits in my pocket," he told Row. "I'd have to buy it on credit."

"That's all right, Abe. I'll take your note. I know you're good for it."

He dropped by the little store to talk over the prospect with Bill Berry, who had bought the other half of the enterprise from Row's brother. Berry, about two years younger than Abraham, was a hard-drinking, hard-gambling young man. The bridge of his nose had been broken in so many fights, it ran like a crooked staircase between his gray eyes. He'd served as a corporal in Abraham's militia unit and had caused no more trouble than any other man. Abraham liked him.

"What do you think, Berry?" he asked. "Shall we partner up?"

The young man seemed eager. "We'll be going up against Sam Hill and John McNeil's store, but if the town keeps growing, there should be plenty of demand for our business," he reasoned. "We could make a good run at success."

Abraham took a long hike beside the Sangamon River to think it over. Two yellow butterflies followed along for a while, and an old turtle poked his head out of the brown water to watch the tall, thin stranger go by. He'd have to go into debt to get started, something he'd never before done. That made him a little nervous. But just about everyone else in Illinois seemed to be taking chances to get ahead. Why shouldn't he?

He thought of an image of an ancient Greek statue he had seen in one of his schoolbooks. It depicted a vigorous young man with wings on his feet, to show that he was fleeting, and a long lock of hair on his forehead, which people might grasp when they met him. But the back of his head was bald to show that once he had passed, he could not be caught. The statue's name was *Opportunity.*

"Miss not the occasion," a poet in his schoolbook had admonished. "By the forelock take that subtle power, the never-halting time."

Abraham picked up a rock and hurled it into the river.

"I'm going to do it," he decided.

He was disappointed to see doubt on Ann's face when he told her.

"Offut's store didn't last," she pointed out. "And we already have Sam and John's store. New Salem's still mighty small. Do you think we need so many places to shop?"

I guess she don't want me competing with her sweetheart, he thought.

"We have to look to the future," he said. "People are pouring onto the prairies. Hill and McNeil can't hog them all for customers."

"Have you given more thought to studying law?"

"Yes, and I'd like the chance, but this here's a real opportunity."

The store was a small log cabin in the center of New Salem on the south side of Main Street. It wasn't much to look at—it lacked even a front porch where customers might sit and chew the fat. But when the two young merchants hung the sign that read "Berry & Lincoln" outside the door, Abraham couldn't help the surge of pride that pushed up the corners of his mouth. For the first time in his life, he was his own man, a member of the village's commercial class, ready to climb the ladder of success.

I just hope I'm climbing the right direction, he thought.

Friends stopped by to wish them luck and purchase a few things. Even Sam Hill and John McNeil stepped across the street from their store with words of encouragement. But the initial burst of interest soon wore itself out. Intervals between customers grew longer. Lincoln and Berry were left alone for long stretches to rearrange items on their shelves.

The last days of August scorched the fields, and then came cool nights that burnished the prairies with September gold. The two partners found themselves stealing glances through the open door every time someone passed up or down the street.

Slicky Bill Greene stopped by to say hello. As he entered and looked around, Abraham watched his sharp eyebrows register a discernible drop. Slicky stayed awhile to talk but left with a grim outlook on his brow. Abraham suddenly recalled the old feeling they'd had about Offutt's store—the feeling of petering out.

Neither partner said anything to the other about their slow start. Abraham put up a new hitching rail outside the door, replaced some daub that had fallen out of a wall, and found a few other little chores to keep busy. When those ran out, he made friends with Jack Kelso, the village philosopher, a man who knew how to find bee trees with the best honey and catch fish when no one else could get a bite. Abraham whiled away whole afternoons with Kelso, lounging on the edge of the Sangamon with fishing poles slanted over quiet water, talking over favorite scenes from *Macbeth* and *Hamlet.* When tired of Shakespeare, they recited Robert Burns with Scottish accents until Abraham knew "Tam O'Shanter" and "The Cotter's Saturday Night" by heart.

But pleasures are like poppies spread:
You seize the flow'r, its bloom is shed;
Or like the snow falls in the river,
A moment white—then melts for ever.

With lines set deep in the Sangamon's currents, they talked of wandering topics, like why kings often turned into tyrants and what made a woman's heart true. The golds of September ripened into the deep maroons of October. The sumac gleamed in scarlet thickets and flung bright reds along fencerows. Sugar maples flamed in yellows and oranges. But few customers came to the store of Berry & Lincoln.

CHAPTER 20

AUTUMN 1832 TO AUTUMN 1833

He took jobs splitting rails and harvesting hay to make ends meet. Bowling Green, Jim Rutledge, and a few other friends with influence recognized his struggles. They managed to get him appointed postmaster of New Salem.

"It won't make you much money," Bowling Green said, "but you'll get to know every person sending or receiving mail in these parts. That'll get you votes in the next election."

Abraham built a little cabinet with pigeonholes for storing letters and hung it on a wall in the store. On top of the cabinet, he placed a sign:

A. LINCOLN
POSTMASTER
NEW SALEM, ILL.

Harvey Ross brought the mail through New Salem on horseback twice a week, once going west and once east, if not delayed by floods, wolves, or highwaymen. People did not have envelopes. Instead, they folded their letters and sealed them. The postal fee was written on the upper right corner of the folded letter, above the delivery address. The addressee paid the postage rather than the sender. It was Abraham's job to collect money from folks receiving letters. He put the coins in an old blue sock, which he kept inside a wooden chest under the store counter.

Few letters came to New Salem, but people still enjoyed stopping by the store to inquire.

"Anything for me?"

"Nope, not this time," Abraham would reply, pretending to search the empty pigeonholes.

"Well, thank God. There's two bits of my money old Andy Jackson won't get."

When he felt like stretching his legs, he put a letter in his hat and strolled into the countryside to deliver it himself. He earned a commission on postage receipts, which usually amounted to four or five dollars a month.

The best perk of the office was the newspapers. It was an unwritten rule that the postmaster could read any periodicals that came into his hands. Often, days passed before subscribers came into town to claim them. Abraham spent long, joyful hours under a buttonwood tree outside the store, devouring reports of the latest goings-on in the world, like South Carolinians declaring the right to secede if the federal government tried to force the federal tariff of 1832 on them, and President Andy Jackson warning them, "Disunion by armed force is treason." And Col. Davy Crockett of Tennessee, serving his third term in Congress, whipping his weight in wildcats. And abolitionists in Philadelphia forming an American Anti-Slavery Society.

Word reached him that the county surveyor, who lived in Springfield, needed a deputy to survey roads and farms in the fast-filling region. It was part-time work, but it would pay well. Once again, Abraham's friends put forth his name. The job was his if he wanted it.

He hurried to see Mentor Graham and found the schoolmaster sitting beside his fireplace, Virgil's *Aeneid* in his lap.

"Can you help me learn surveying?"

"It'll take digging deep into a pile of mathematics."

"Let's get to it."

He sat at Graham's gate-leg table, elbow to elbow with the schoolmaster, Abraham tussling his black hair and Mentor knitting his red brows as they burrowed into Flint's *Treatise on Geometry, Trigonometry, and Rectangular Surveying*. They tackled sines, cosines, and tables of logarithms. He learned the proper way to hang a plumb line, the best way to read a compass bearing, and how to use the stars to obtain almost true north without instruments.

He managed to borrow enough money to make a down payment on a compass and chain. The compass was a thing of beauty, a large brass Rittenhouse compass that he polished until it gleamed like a crown. Lead plumb bobs he made himself by melting several bullets, and he made range poles from straight hickory saplings. He needed a way to transport all his equipment. He gave Tom Watkins, a Clary's Grove farmer, a note for fifty dollars for a large bay horse with a star on its forehead and promised to pay him later.

By the time the leaves were off the trees, he had mastered the instruments and was ready to begin the work. Right away he was hired to survey a big stretch of land in northern Sangamon County. He talked Jack Armstrong and Jack Kelso into going along to help carry the chain, set the range poles, and clear the lines of sight with their axes.

They fought their way over high and low ground, across streams, through marshy muck and stands of timber to locate corners and determine the bearing of lines. As they moved the chain forward, sticking red-flagged marking pins into the earth to measure the distances, they signaled to each other in rhythmic chant: "Chain! Stick! Stuck! Chain! Stick! Stuck!" Kelso recited Shakespeare while Armstrong commented on the land.

"This stuff's too thick to navigate and too thin to plow," both Jacks grumbled as they dragged the chain through a swamp.

Abraham enjoyed this kind of struggle with the earth, not a mindless work, like plowing or harrowing, but work that involved reading contours and bounding tracts with imaginary lines. It gave him the satisfaction of solving a problem.

If I can master angles of elevation and the Pythagorean theorem, he thought, maybe I can master the law.

He rode the twenty miles to Springfield to get John Todd Stuart's advice. The town was little more than an oversized collection of rough houses set on the edge of a prairie, but it was still the county seat, where important men gathered, and as Abraham climbed the stairs to Stuart's law office, he began to have second thoughts. It was one thing to march in the same militia unit and swap jokes around a campfire. But Stuart now was a member of the legislature and one of Springfield's foremost attorneys. The dark-eyed Kentuckian might not want to see him.

There was nothing fancy about the office or its furnishings—a big table, a few chairs collected from here and there, and a large bookshelf. Stacks of books and musty papers occupied the table and floor. Stuart, it turned out, was delighted to see him.

"Ready to make a leap at the law?" he asked, sticking out his hand.

"I guess I am." Abraham couldn't help but feel timid in the presence of the amiable, handsome lawyer.

"Well, she's a hard mistress to serve, but I think she'll satisfy you, all the same."

Stuart hunted through the bookshelf and came up with a spare copy of *Commentaries on the Laws of England* by Sir William Blackstone.

"You'll want to start with this. It's pretty dry, but all you have to do is memorize the damn thing from front to back."

He began his studies on way the back to New Salem, holding the reins in one hand and the book in the other, reading aloud from the swaying pages as his horse clopped down the road. In the first chapter, he read that the law divides persons into two categories, natural and artificial.

"Natural persons are such as the God of nature formed us," Blackstone explained. "Artificial are such as created and devised by human laws for the purposes of society and government, which are called corporations or bodies politic."

"This is going to be hard ground to plow," he told the horse.

He did not understand half of what he was reading. The book was full of discouraging Latin terms, like *confirmatio cartarum* and *per legem terrae*. But as he read through the first chapter again, meanings that had escaped him the first time began to come into focus. By the time he got back to New Salem, he had pushed through forty pages and determined to go at it in earnest.

The more he read of the law, the more it interested him. He had never run across a subject, with the possible exception of mathematics, that demanded such habits of logic and order. The rational framework it erected for human endeavors appealed to him. He took the book with him wherever he went, reading aloud as he walked, then closing it and reciting what he had just read. He took it on surveying jobs and when he trekked down dusty roads to deliver mail. Friends teased him when they saw him stopped in his tracks, absorbed by some passage. On hot afternoons he lay for hours under the buttonwood tree in front of his store, bare feet on the trunk, grinding around with the shade as the sun moved. When he had paper, he copied paragraphs to fix them in his memory.

He couldn't wait to tell Ann about his studies.

"You look tired, Abe," she said. "You're not wearing yourself down with that law book, are you?"

"I plan on wearing it down first. It is laborious and tedious at times. But I like it all the same. Work, work, work is the way to satisfy Mr.

Blackstone. I don't see any other way to cultivate his field."

"I believe that you'll make a good lawyer."

"Do you really think so?"

"I do. I believe you can do just about anything you set your mind to."

When he was out surveying or delivering mail, he often stayed the night with Jimmy Short, who lived a short distance north of New Salem. One of the first settlers in the region, Short was a man of no polished surfaces, but a plain and honest fellow, always ready to set an extra place at his table or light an extra lantern so Abraham could study his books late at night. Abraham enjoyed talking politics with him. When the talk ran low, they pitched quoits, iron rings tossed at stakes driven into the ground. In exchange for his hospitality, Abraham helped Short around his farm.

"You are the best hand at husking corn on the stalk I ever saw," Short said. "I consider myself pretty good, but I believe you can gather two loads to my one."

"I'd feel better if I can get the husk off this *arguendo inter alia* business."

"You will. You're also the best hand at reading books I ever saw. You're a learner."

"I am slow to learn, but I am also slow to forget," Abraham mused. "My mind is like a piece of steel, very hard to scratch anything on it but almost impossible after you get it there to rub it out."

Bowling Green's village court was a good place to see the theories of law unravel the troubles of men. On law days, Abraham dropped by Pot's cabin to watch him preside with great dignity, his fat paunch balanced on his lap. Dishonesty, jealousy, greed, deception, and all the other petty vices of Aesop's old fables paraded before the squire's bench to receive their just deserts.

He learned that the course of justice could take unpredictable turns, as in a dispute between Jack Kelso and John Ferguson over a white hog. Ferguson brought in two witnesses who swore the hog was his. Kelso had no support to offer for his claim except his own word.

"Are there any more witnesses?" the court inquired.

There were no more.

"The two witnesses have sworn to a damned lie," Pot ruled. "I know this shoat, and I know it belongs to Jack Kelso. I therefore decide the case in his favor."

After court was adjourned, Abraham stayed for hours to examine Pot's old copy of the *Statutes of Illinois* and talk over the day's cases. As they conversed, Pot's wife, Nancy, loaded the table with fried ham, creamed corn, pickled peaches, butter cookies, and sweet cider.

This is the way to study law, Abraham told himself.

CHAPTER 21

Late 1833 to Early 1834

Change had come to New Salem, change that helped take his mind off the law and the store. John McNeil had left town. He told friends he was returning to his family home in New York for a while to pay off debts his father owed. Some folks in the village said he intended to come back and marry Ann. Others were wondering aloud if they would ever see him again.

Ann started coming by the post office more often. Once a week, when the westbound mail arrived, she stepped into the store with a cheerful, "Anything for me, Abe?"

For a few weeks, letters from McNeil came regularly.

"Do us a favor and read it out loud," Abraham joshed as he handed one over. "Berry and I need a few sweet words of love to spice up our sour old lives."

She slipped the letter into her basket with a smile and hurried away.

Then suddenly, without warning, the letters stopped. Weeks passed without any word from McNeil. Finally he sent word that his father was in bad health, and that he could not return as quickly as he had hoped. After that, more weeks of silence.

Ann's queries of "Anything for me?" at the store's little post office began to sound uncertain.

"Not this time. Next time, I'm sure," Abraham would say, but he wondered if she believed it anymore.

After a while, she stopped asking.

The Rutledge tavern was New Salem's largest home, boasting two big ground floor rooms—one for cooking and dining, and the other crammed with beds for sleeping. A loft full of hay mattresses provided extra sleeping room for boarders. Abraham dropped by often, staying the night when he didn't sleep at the store or a friend's cabin.

At mealtime, family and guests pulled chairs up to a long table made smooth by the passing of many plates and the rubbing of many elbows. Kettles, jugs, and ladles crowded the hearth, where stew pots bubbled and meats sizzled. Notices tacked to the wall beside the big table gave the tavern rates—37 ½ cents for a meal and overnight lodging—as well as news about horse thieves and land sales.

It was good to be part of the maelstrom of coming and going that filled the place. Jim and his wife, Mary Ann, had nine children, most still young enough to be at home, so between Rutledges and boarders, there was always someone to talk to. Abraham helped out by splitting wood, fetching turnips and potatoes from the root cellar, or entertaining the younger children with stories while the womenfolk got food on the table.

Ann spent her days stirring pots, setting tables, making beds, and taking care of a hundred other daily tavern chores. Sometimes Abraham walked with her when she carried a basket of dinner down the clay bluff to the mill where her father was working. He often regaled her with jokes he'd picked up from friends or an old joke book, *Quin's Jests*.

"A fellow over in Springfield placed an advertisement in the *Sangamo Journal* that said 'Wife Wanted,'" he told her. "The next week he got a hundred letters, and they all said the same thing: 'You can have mine.'"

She threw a chestnut at him in mock indignation. He caught it.

"We're going to have to find someone for you to marry, just to keep you quiet," she said.

"Oh, I expect I'll die an old maid."

He stole glances as she sat at the spinning wheel or leaned over the table to serve a guest. Every movement she made seemed graceful. When she lifted her arms to take a crock off the shelf, he measured her figure. He liked the way the sunlight in the window turned the tips of her locks red and gold.

He told himself not to look at her so often and worried that one of the children might notice. But he couldn't help himself. He saw that travelers who passed through the tavern, especially young men, stole their share of glances too.

One afternoon, he walked the few paces between his store and the tavern to retrieve his copy of *Kirkham's Grammar*, which he'd left behind the night before. He found Ann alone, sitting at the long table, bent over the volume. She quickly put it down when she saw him.

"I was just doing a little studying," she said, embarrassed.

She had been attending Mentor Graham's school, and the schoolmaster counted her as one of his brightest students.

"You can have it if you want," Abraham urged, without thinking.

She looked at him in surprise, then dropped her eyes.

"I couldn't," she said, picking up a coat she had been mending.

"But I've finished with it. I ain't going to be using it anymore."

She considered it for a moment. "Abe Lincoln, are you trying to give me a present?" she laughed.

"What I mean is, you and your brothers and sisters can have it to use, all of you. Maybe your father can count it as part of the payment for my board, if he wants."

He sounded like a man trying to make excuses for a gift.

"I guess it would be sort of a present," he grinned. "It would please me if you'd take it."

She smiled and picked up the book. Abraham watched her leaf through a few pages. The offer seemed to please her too.

"Well, if you're really done with it," she said slowly. "It would come in handy with schoolwork. You'll have to help me with the hard parts, though."

"I sure will. I've been over that darned thing so many times, I know everything in there." He stopped, not wanting to sound boastful.

"I was looking at the lecture on participles. It's a slippery one."

"Participles ain't nothing but words made out of verbs, and you can use them to modify other words," he said eagerly. "Take the verb *smile.* 'I see a beautiful lady who smiles.' You can turn it into a participle. 'That beautiful smiling lady knows her grammar.'"

"Abe, you act like you are shy, but I believe you are a flirt!" She laughed.

She went to a writing desk, dipped a pen in ink, and as he stood over her, watching, wrote in neatly rounded script at the top of the title page: *Ann M. Rutledge.* She paused, dipped her pen again, and added below the impulsive words: *is now learning grammar.*

"There," she said, holding it up for him to see. "Now you can't take it back, you know."

He started bringing little gifts when he visited the tavern—a crock of honey that Jack Kelso had scooped out of a hollow place in a bee tree, some cedar boughs to brighten the Rutledges' mantel. Some days he walked with Ann along the banks of the Sangamon River. They talked about changes in the weather, stories in newspapers and books they were reading, and who was coming and going in New Salem.

At night he lay awake asking himself if a girl like Ann Rutledge could really fall for a sucker like him.

CHAPTER 22

1834

Traffic at the store refused to pick up. Abraham and Bill Berry tried everything. They offered more merchandise, moved the store to a bigger cabin with a front porch where people could sit and talk, even started selling liquor by the drink. Customers remained scarce. One partner sat at one end of the counter, sampling the inventory of whiskey. The other partner sat at the opposite end, sampling newspapers and grinding away at his law studies.

One morning Harvey Ross, the mail carrier, stopped by to look at buckskin gloves.

"Here's a pair of dogskin gloves that should do you fine," Abraham told him. "You can have them for seventy-five cents."

"Dogskin? Never heard of dogskin gloves. You sure?" Ross examined them closely. "Looks like buckskin to me."

"Well, I'll tell you just how I know. Jack Clary's dog killed Tom Watkins's sheep, and Tom Watkins's boy killed the dog. Old John Mounts tanned the dogskin, and Sally Spears made the gloves. That's the way I know they're dogskin."

"It's nice to do business with an honest man," Harvey said as he paid six bits.

Honest don't put soup in the pot like paying customers do, Abraham thought ruefully.

Berry & Lincoln was a goner. He knew that. How in the world would he pay all his debts? There was the money he owed for his stake in the store, money owed for inventory, money owed for his horse, money owed for his compass and chain. It added up to hundreds of dollars, a crushing sum for a young man of little means.

He stood by helplessly one rainy afternoon as the Sangamon County sheriff auctioned off saws, axes, cotton cloth, a barrel of whiskey, and the rest of the stock that had not yet been seized by creditors. The humiliation cut deep.

The thought of disappearing into the night crossed his mind. He could strike out for the territories and finally get that job on a steamboat. But he quickly tossed the idea aside. He could not simply walk away from a wreck he had helped to make, as Offutt had done. He made up his mind that he would pay it all back, no matter how long it took.

"If I learned one thing from my father, it's that the only way to get a stump out of the ground is to keep tugging," he told Ann.

He still had his job as postmaster. He carried the little cabinet with pigeonholes to Sam Hill's store, and Sam let him keep the mail there. When he was in the countryside surveying, Sam looked after the post office for him. In return, he helped look after Sam's store. Otherwise, he scrounged for any odd job he could find—chopping wood, sowing crops, tending stills—to earn his keep and whittle away at the enormous sum he owed.

"I've got my own national debt," he told Sam. "That makes me as smart as the United States Congress."

He was sitting beside the fire in Sam's store, feet on the hearth, deep into Blackstone's chapter on title by occupancy, when Harvey Ross stepped through the door. Abraham had been waiting for him to arrive with the westbound mail. Harvey wasn't alone. Andrew Yates, a deputy sheriff for Sangamon County, followed him. The draft of cold they let into the room made Abraham shudder.

Yates came straight toward him.

"I hate to tell you this, Abe," he said, looking into the fire, "but the sheriff's got to levy your personal possessions. Berry's too. On account of the unpaid debts."

The blood drained from Abraham's face. He immediately rose but said nothing.

"I'm real sorry," Yates offered, embarrassed by the silence.

"I ain't got anything that anyone would be much interested in."

Yates looked back into the fireplace.

"Well, there's your horse. And your saddle and bridle." He fumbled for an official document he had somewhere on him. "And your surveying equipment."

Abraham was horrified. "You mean my compass?"

"I'll have to take it. And anything else of value you got."

"Do you have to take it now?"

"I'm afraid so. I'm real sorry."

Harvey was staring at him. So was Sam Hill, as if he were watching a steamboat that had just hit its last snag settle to the bottom of the river.

"Harvey, my horse is out back," Abraham said huskily. "Can you saddle him and bring him for me?"

He handed the volume of Blackstone's *Commentaries* to Sam Hill. The deputy looked at the book but did not ask whose it was.

The surveying equipment was in the back room of the failed store. He quietly retrieved it, pausing a moment to collect himself when he was alone in the dark, empty cabin. Harvey brought the horse, and

Abraham packed the saddlebags with the beautiful Rittenhouse compass, the surveying chain, marking pins, chip ax, and plumb bob.

"Anything else?" Yates asked.

Abraham considered his copy of Blackstone.

"No, that's all. What will happen to my things?"

"They'll auction them off in Springfield next week. If you can come up with the money to satisfy your debt before then, you can have 'em back."

The deputy mounted his own horse and rode away, the bay horse following. Abraham stood in the hoof-printed road, watching his worldly possessions round a bend. And just like that, he was a man worth nothing.

He knew that word of his debacle was already trickling from cabin to cabin. He had to get away. He walked north, away from the village, hurrying his long strides as if they might outpace his troubles.

I knew this was coming, he told himself. I pretended it wasn't coming. All this time I've been sitting around studying law, the law's been coiling about my feet, getting ready to bite.

He could imagine what friends would say. They had voted for Abe Lincoln for legislature, and he couldn't even keep his own horse.

He reached Jimmy Short's cabin and found him at home. By that time, he was choking with mortification.

"I'll have to walk over to the land office and announce that I can't take any more jobs," he said bitterly. "All that time I spent learning to make a survey was for nothing."

"Let's go pitch a few quoits," Jimmy suggested.

Abraham gave him a harsh look.

"I don't believe I feel up to it," he said curtly.

"The best thing you can do is do something. Pitching quoits is as good as anything else. Come on."

He handed Abraham the iron rings, and they pitched quoits beside Short's cornfield. Abraham tossed hard. His quoits landed nowhere near the stake.

"How am I supposed to pay off my debts if they take what I need to make the money to pay off those debts? Surveying was the best money I ever earned. It makes no sense."

"No, it don't. Not in that respect."

"If they'll leave me alone, I'll pay all I owe, every penny."

"Maybe you can get the compass and chain back. A horse you can borrow if you have to."

"It'll all go up for auction next week. That compass will be long gone before I have a chance."

"Well, there's more than one compass in the world."

"Rich people taking other people's things before they have a chance to stand on their own two feet. If that's all the law is, I don't want nothing to do with it."

Abraham picked up his quoits and looked at them in disgust.

"This is what I get for trying to be high-and-mighty, thinking I might be a lawyer and politician. I might as well let the whole thing go by the board."

He tossed again. The ring landed two feet wide of the stake.

"I can't even pitch quoits."

He was embarrassed to tell Ann what had happened, but he knew she would hear about it soon enough, and he wanted her sympathy.

"I'll never borrow money again," he told her. "A pig bought on credit is always grunting."

She refused to see the situation as anywhere near hopeless.

"You'll just have to earn money to buy a new compass. You can do that."

"Suppose I do. What's to stop them from taking that compass too?"

"Then you'll get another one. You can always borrow a horse for a survey and use a grapevine for a chain."

"You sound like Jimmy Short."

"Well, if two people with your best interest at heart are telling you the same thing, maybe you ought to listen."

"It's not just losing my scalp that hurts. If I try to run for office again, every voter will know I've had the sheriff after me."

"I doubt that. And anyway, why should they care?"

"It makes me want to chuck the whole thing. I ought to get on a riverboat. There's nothing to hold me here. No one will miss me."

"You know that's not true."

"If I can get out on a river, I can make money without anyone harassing me while I save up, and then I can come back and pay it all off in one chunk."

"How are you going to run for the legislature again if you're on a river?"

"You don't know what it's like drifting down the Mississippi, Ann. You lie on your back, looking up at the clouds or the stars, and everything's still and quiet, except when you want to tell a story or a jest, and there's nobody in the world to tell you what to do. You can't ask for anything better than that."

"If that's the way you feel, go on, then," she said, exasperated. "But I don't believe for a second that you'll go, and neither do you."

He knew she was right. There was nothing to do but get hold of a new compass and chain, however he could as soon as he could. And to keep whittling away at that debt.

Every man has to skin his own skunk, he told himself, and this one is mine. He winced when he realized it was one of his father's sayings.

Several days later, he was back at Sam Hill's store, sitting by the fire again, clawing his way through Blackstone's chapter on title by prescription, when Jimmy Short stopped by. The farmer grinned and jabbed his thumb over his shoulder, pointing outside. Abraham stepped to the door and squinted into the sunshine. His bay horse stood tied to the hitching rail.

He moved quickly across the porch to open the saddlebags. The compass, chain, and everything else was there.

"If the sheriff comes bothering you again, you just remind him that this is all my property," Jimmy drawled. "Of course, I don't know anything about surveying, so you're welcome to borrow it as long as you want."

Abraham stood motionless. "Where did you get it?"

"I was over in Springfield and just happened to pass by an auction."

"You bought it?"

"They were practically giving it away."

Abraham knew that could not be true. It had to have cost more than one hundred dollars. The gesture stunned him.

"I don't know what to say, Jimmy." His voice came up from his chest unnaturally deep and halting. "I'll do as much for you sometime."

Jimmy waved him off.

"I'll pay back every cent," Abraham insisted.

"Pay when you can. No need to say any more."

He stood beside the horse for a long time after Jimmy had gone, stroking its flank, feeling ashamed for having complained with such indulgence about a misfortune he had brought on himself, and wondering at his friend's generosity.

CHAPTER 23

1834

Jack Armstrong had the great fortune to be married to a woman who could handle him. When out carousing with the Clary's Grove Boys, he was not above nailing a drunkard inside a barrel and rolling him down a hill to the river for fun. His wife might laugh when he told her about it, but she might also keep her own barrel and nails handy in case Jack came home once too often with too much whiskey in him.

"She can harness and bridle me when she wants, no doubt about it," he told Abraham. "If it weren't for Hannah, I'd be one of those fellows always breaking the reins and running off into a ditch."

Hannah Armstrong was a fine-looking woman who chopped her own firewood and could lift the heavy end of a log. She was only twenty-three, but marriage to Jack had brought patience and wisdom beyond her years. She enjoyed mothering Abraham, gladly taking him under her roof whenever he showed up, patching his clothes and fixing him corn bread with butter while he rolled on the floor with her baby boy, Duff.

Abraham showed her two buckskins that Russell Godfrey had given him for surveying work. She knew just what to do with them.

"Let me have the trousers you wear when you go surveying," she told him. "I'll fox 'em for you."

She sat beside the fire and foxed a pair of his pants, sewing the buckskins onto the legs between the ankles and knees for protection from heavy brush. Abraham lay on his back and tossed Duff into the air while Hannah worked.

"You need a woman to do this sort of thing for you," she observed.

"I've got you, Hannah. Besides, I can sew as well as any woman."

"I doubt that. I hear you've been spending a good deal of time at the Rutledges' place."

The remark caught him off guard. He sat up and pulled Duff into his lap.

"Well, Jim's been mighty good to me. I like to pitch in with chores to help repay his kindness."

"Uh-huh. Why don't you walk over there and tell her how you feel? Not that she doesn't know already."

He could feel his face redden. "I'm not sure what you're getting at."

"Good Lord, Abe, anyone who ain't blind can see how you feel, and last time I checked, Ann's eyes are working fine."

Her words pierced him like the needle she pushed through the buckskin. He had been careful to tell no one of his feelings for Ann. The realization that Hannah could read them so easily came as a shock. He let go of Duff, and the child squirmed away.

"What good would it do? There's no such luck for me to have a girl like Ann."

"Why not?"

His face reddened deeper.

"Every fellow who comes into that tavern has eyes for her," he said. "That girl has more admirers than grass on the prairie. Besides, how do I know John McNeil won't show up again?"

"And where is John McNeil?"

"How should I know?"

"He's hundreds of miles away, that's where, and showing no signs of coming back."

"So you think he's gone for good?"

"Long gone. Don't you?"

"I don't know."

"Well, I suppose only the good Lord above knows where John McNeil is or what he's up to. But she is here, and you are here, and he is not."

"Why should she be interested in me? I've got nothing except a load of debt."

"And a pair of foxed pants. Is that your excuse for giving up on her?"

"It ain't an excuse. It's just that she can have any bachelor she wants in these parts. No reason to choose a poor one."

"Pshaw. A little poverty means nothing around here. Ann has feelings for you. If you don't act soon, you'll lose your chance."

She tossed the finished pants to him.

"Here. And remember, you can't catch trout with dry britches."

Jack arrived home from a trip to the mill and insisted that Abraham bed down for the night on the floor beside the fireplace. Abraham got no sleep. Jack's snoring kept him awake. He rolled and tossed until finally, before dawn, he rose quietly, pulled on his boots and old hat, and slipped out of the cabin.

He headed east, moving past black outlines of hills where bare limbs held on to dark spaces. Beyond lay the sleeping prairie, with no trace of moonlight on it.

His mind churned as he walked. Was Hannah right? Did Ann have feelings for him? He had kept that hope secret even from himself.

The thought that he might actually win her made his heart race. But the thought of telling her how he felt—that was something else. He was not sure he had the courage. Hannah might easily be wrong.

All his doubts about his homeliness, his lack of education, his crushing debt came welling up. How could any woman be interested in a man who couldn't even keep a store or win an election?

Dawn arrived, and the blackness cloaking the prairies turned gray. The hills took on shadowy substance. A fox crossed his path, pausing to look at him with its yellow eyes, then disappeared into the brush.

If Hannah was right that Ann knew how he felt, then he had nothing to lose in confessing his feelings. Except for the humiliation of hearing her say she could not return his affection. What then? Well, then maybe he really would strike out for the Mississippi and look for a job on a steamboat.

If he said nothing now, he might lose his chance. McNeil might come back or write her another letter. Or she might develop an interest in somebody else. Sam Hill had always been sweet on her. So had Bill Berry. If he stood by while someone else with more nerve won her, he could never forgive himself.

Full daylight came. The dome of the sky flashed silver and blue over the prairie. A bright yellow bird he had never seen before warbled at him from a limb, but he did not stop to take note of its markings.

He walked with more determination. If Ann could not love him, it was better to find out. Why was he wandering all over the countryside? He knew what he needed to do.

If I don't go talk to her, I'll be alone my whole life, he thought.

He strode up the road toward the Rutledge place, forcing his legs into long, hurried steps. The *whack-whack* of a loom reached his ears, coming from a shed in back of the tavern. He knew he would find Ann there, and she would likely be working alone.

She looked up from her work as he stepped into the loom house.

"You must have been reading my mind." She smiled. "I was just wishing somebody would come by to keep me company. I'm glad it's you."

She sat at the loom, a clumsy-looking contraption of wooden beams and crisscrossing threads, deftly passing the shuttle back and forth through the warp. With each pass, she pulled the heavy beater toward her and knocked it against the weft with a double *whack-whack* to pack the thread in place.

Abraham stood beside the machine, head nearly bumping against the shed's low ceiling, watching her work and trying to decide what to say. His silence made her look up at him again. She saw the agitation on his face.

"What's wrong, Abe?"

"I need a few words with you," he stammered.

He took off his hat to give his hands something to do, fumbling with it as he spoke. She stopped her work, brows knit.

"I know I look like a mangy old scarecrow," he blurted.

She flinched. The surprise on her face jolted him.

"Don't say that, Abe. I've never thought so."

"It's true. I know I ain't much to look at. And that I come from humble beginnings."

Ann laid down the shuttle and rested her hands in her lap. "We're all pretty humble around here," she said quietly.

He plowed his fingers over the top of his head, through the course hair.

"I've always thought the world of you, Ann. You're the most wonderful girl I've ever met."

She lowered her head and said nothing. His hands went back to wrestling with his hat.

"You're clever and kindhearted," he pressed on, "and everyone says you're the best-looking girl in a hundred miles of here."

"You're embarrassing me."

"It's true," he insisted. "Any fellow in the world would be lucky to call you his own. The luckiest fellow in Sangamon County, maybe the whole state of Illinois."

The shade of a smile crossed her face.

"What is it you're trying to tell me, Abe?"

There was no turning back now.

"Ann, you know I care for you."

Her hands took up the shuttle and pulled it slowly across the warp. She swung the beater toward her, then laid down the shuttle again.

"Yes, I know." She kept her eyes on the threads before her.

He tugged hard at the hat, which he held at his waist, turning it round and round.

"Do you think you could care for me?" he pleaded.

She was quiet for another moment.

"I do care for you, Abe."

"But could you care for me in the way I care for you? That's what I need to know." The words came out half-whispered.

She looked up at him. Color pulsed in her cheeks.

"Yes, Abe, I could," she said simply.

"Good, good. That's good." Immense relief swept over him. "That's all I really needed to know."

He stretched a hand toward her shoulder. He did not know if he should embrace her or what to say next. Part of him thought that if he touched the scene before him, it might shatter. He pulled back his hand.

"You can go on with your weaving if you want."

He hurried out, exhaling as though he had been holding his breath the whole time. His feet carried him quickly down the road. The *whack-whack* of the loom grew faint behind him, absorbed into the light that hung over the prairies. He could not remember ever feeling so happy. His hands were trembling. Looking down at them, he saw that he had torn his hat to pieces.

CHAPTER 24

1834 TO SPRING 1835

Before he knew it, the next election to the statehouse was approaching.

"Pot, do you think my debt problems will hurt my chances with the voters?" he asked.

"Hell, half the people in this county owe money to the other half, and it's the creditors who are praying for the debtors' success if they want their money back," Pot said. "I wouldn't worry about that. The fact that you intend to pay your debts will win you votes."

The big justice of the peace was sitting on the porch of Sam Hill's store, trying on a pair of boots he'd had sent over from Springfield. His single linen suspender did its best to keep his midsection in check as he leaned over his feet and tugged.

"You don't need to make a lot of speeches this time around," he advised. "Folks know who you are now. If I were you, I'd spend the next few weeks paying a visit to every farmer in this neck of the woods and ask for their support."

"Most of those farmers are Democrats," Abraham reminded him. "They know I still lean Whig."

"There's no presidential contest this year, so people won't care so much about what party you favor. Personality will trump politics."

A few days later, the *Sangamo Journal* carried a simple announcement: "We are authorized to state that A. Lincoln, of New Salem, is a candidate for Representative for this County." There were thirteen candidates in all. As before, the top four vote-getters would win Sangamon County's four seats in the legislature.

Abraham spent the spring and summer on a handshaking campaign, drumming up support for his candidacy as he surveyed land and delivered mail. He dropped by every cabin he passed to crack jokes with the men and pay his respects to their wives. Wherever he stopped, he split wood, carried water, and joggled babies on his knee. Jack Armstrong and his Clary's Grove Boys took him along to horse races and cockfights. He threw horseshoes, wrestled local champions, and asked for votes.

As he traveled the county, he scribbled down names of voters he thought he could count on. Every evening, before going to bed, he ran his finger down the growing list.

By election day, the prairie grass stood higher than a man on a pony. Abraham voted quickly, stepping up to a table in the shade of an oak to call out his choices for the clerk to record. As custom dictated, he refrained from voting for himself. He left the poll as soon as he'd voted and went looking for Ann. He found her sewing a dress.

"I'm as jumpy as spit on a hot skillet," he confessed.

"You don't need to be. Papa has been out talking to folks. He says you'll do fine."

"I wish I was sure. No one expected me to win last time. If I lose again, my friends may conclude I'm not cut out to hold office."

He pulled his list of supporters out of a new hat.

"I've been keeping track of who's for me. With the names I've got, and from what Pot and John Stuart tell me, I think I can count on at least a thousand votes."

"Well, that's a lot."

"Maybe more," he said hopefully. He shuffled the pages, folded them, then unfolded them again. "But some people don't always vote the way they promise."

"Most do," she said.

"Sometimes they decide a trip to the poll ain't worth the effort."

He took his finger to the list, reading names softly as he scrutinized. "I'm not sure I can count on George Lacey. He seemed somewhat reluctant."

"Abe, you're too fidgety! You need to go walk off all this nervousness."

Two days later, he was sitting on the porch of Sam Hill's store, whittling on a stick, when Bowling Green rode up and shoved a handwritten list of names and vote totals under his nose.

"Looky here, Abe. Election returns, straight from Springfield."

At first, he could not find his name on the page. Confused, he glanced up at Pot, then looked down to search the list again.

There it was. He had placed second out of the field of thirteen candidates, with 1,376 votes.

"You got 250 of 288 votes cast in New Salem," Pot told him. "And 667 votes in Springfield. Hell, even John Stuart barely beat that, and he lives there."

He heard Pot congratulating him, felt him pumping his hand. The next thing he knew, a small crowd had formed around him, slapping his back and cheering. He saw Ann's face among them, lit up with pleasure. She stepped forward and gave him a hug. Someone called on Sam Hill to open a jug of corn whiskey.

He was going to Vandalia.

The Illinois capital turned out to be little more than a ramshackle village of eight or nine hundred people on the bank of the Kaskaskia River where the great National Road, stretching all the way from Cumberland, Maryland, came to its western terminus. Other than the two-story statehouse, one other brick building, and a small church house without a steeple, the place had little to recommend it at first glance. Just several dozen cabins and frame buildings clustered around a town square.

Vandalia may have been small and rough around the edges, but when the legislature met, it became the social cynosure of the state. Lobbyists, lawyers, and favor-seekers thronged the streets.

"Stick close to me," John Stuart told him. "I'll introduce you around."

Abraham tried hard to keep track of all the faces and names. Half the fellows he met carried the title of captain, major, or even colonel, though who knew exactly when or where they had ever waged a campaign. They were all men of affairs, full of the fiery, lustful blood of the frontier. More than one grinned and asked, "How's the weather up there?" when shaking Abraham's hand. It made him feel self-conscious, but he realized that standing a head taller than most everyone else brought a certain advantage. It caused important people to remember his name.

On the opening day of the session, the legislators filed into the statehouse. Abraham followed along wearing a new suit of butternut jeans. The building, though only ten years old, was so poorly constructed that already it had fallen into decay. Its brick walls bulged in places, and plaster fell from the ceilings.

The sparsely furnished House chamber occupied most of the first floor. Members sat three to a long table, each place bearing a cork inkstand, quill, and a few sheets of stationery. The Speaker sat at the front of the room behind his own elevated table, distinguished by a pewter inkstand. Sandboxes for blotting ink and spitting tobacco lay scattered about the room. A fireplace and stove offered a little warmth, and tall candlestands provided dim light for evening sessions. Those who got thirsty could make use of a water pail with three tin cups in the back of the room.

"The House will come to order!" a stern voice bellowed, and the session got underway.

A bewildering array of legislation moved in fits and starts through the House. Acts to build turnpikes, regulate mills, and establish schools. Acts to encourage the killing of wolves and fixing the stoves in the statehouse. Abraham was amazed at the easy trading of votes, and at first a little offended by the self-serving nature of the system. "You vote for my measure, and I'll vote for yours" was the motto of every legislator. They called it logrolling, after the time-honored custom of neighbors helping each other roll big logs into place to build cabins.

"Logrolling in Vandalia ain't pretty," Stuart admitted, "but it's the only way to get a law through."

On some days, floor debates turned to matters of statewide or even national significance. Enthusiasm ran high for building a canal between the Illinois River and Lake Michigan, thus connecting the West with the Atlantic by way of the Great Lakes and Erie Canal. There was talk of constructing railroads. And much arguing over the National Bank, with the Jackson men saying the Bank was a cesspool of corruption while many Whigs defended the idea and said that Illinois should have state banks of its own. Abraham listened in fascination to the wrangling, which signified civilization spreading over the prairies.

Much valuable work took place after hours, when the House had adjourned for the day, and small groups met in tavern rooms to draft bills and work out compromises. Talking politics around a hearth came naturally. It was like being back home in New Salem or in Jim Gentry's store at Little Pigeon Creek. Everyone was welcome to throw in their two cents' worth. It dawned on him that most of his fellow legislators had no more experience at making laws than he did. Of the fifty-five House members, all but nineteen were serving their first terms.

With John Stuart's help, he waded into the lawmaking. He introduced a bill to authorize a toll bridge across Salt Creek and offered a resolution calling for Illinois to receive a portion of the proceeds when the federal government sold public lands in the state. He found himself appointed to special committees to consider education bills and the duties of the attorney general. His colleagues recruited him to help write legislation on laying out roads and handling stray horses.

Ten weeks passed quickly, and the first session of the Ninth General Assembly came to a close. He hurried back to New Salem to tell Ann all about it.

"I must prepare myself to be the wife of a senator or governor," she laughed as he described his success.

"You'll be the prettiest woman in the capital city."

"Now you really have become a smooth-talking politician."

"There ain't much smooth about me."

"Then you are a diamond in the rough. You just need a little polishing."

"And a good bit of cutting, carving, and filing down."

When the Indian paintbrush and bird's foot violets appeared, the two young people followed a path to a bluff above the Sangamon River, where they sat and talked of their future.

"I do need more polishing if I'm ever going to shine," Abraham told her. "I know that. The only way is to keep up my studies."

"You'll make yourself crazy with so much study, Abe."

"Then you'll have to spend all your time with me," he said, "because the only thing that'll keep me away from those law books is you."

He knew that despite her protests, she approved of the relentless way he drove at mastering the law.

"I've been thinking about when we might be married," he said.

She looked away out of modesty—or uncertainty. He could not tell which.

"That is, if you still want me."

"I do, Abe," she said softly.

"Well, I was thinking, if you agree, that perhaps we should wait a while. You know my financial state. If we wait a year or so, I'll have time to pay off some of my debt."

He tried to read her face and thought he saw encouragement.

"In the meantime," he went on quickly, "I'll finish my law studies. Once I'm a member of the bar, I can establish myself in a practice. Then we can marry right away."

Her smile showed relief.

"I was thinking the same thing," she confessed. "But I wasn't sure how you would take it. I was worried you'd think I was hesitant."

"And I was afraid you'd think I was stalling."

She took his hand.

"While you're finishing your studies, I'd like to do some studying of my own. I've been thinking of going to school at the Jacksonville Female Academy." She grinned. "That way I can polish myself up and be a proper governor's wife."

Her plan struck him as prudent. He felt proud to be engaged to a woman interested in learning. They sat all afternoon on the bluff, hurling rocks into the river below, talking of the coming year and all the years ahead.

CHAPTER 25

SUMMER 1835

The weather turned merciless that summer. The windows of heaven opened, and rain fell in torrents. Mold spread across the walls of soggy cabins. Wagon wheels sank deep in mud. Abraham sloshed through knee-high floods with his compass and chain, trying to complete surveys.

Then came weeks of scorching drought, with horseflies as big as bats. The earth turned brown and crusty. Fields of wheat died. A tornado ripped through the county, laying fences flat, uprooting trees, blowing down corn.

It was the kind of weather that brought sickness. Abraham was plagued by aches and chills. Hannah Armstrong advised him to swallow Peruvian bark and boneset tea. He rallied, felt bad again, swallowed more herbs, rallied once more.

He tromped through the heat and dust to see Ann and was alarmed by her appearance. She had lost weight, and she grew short of breath over simple chores like fetching a bucket of well water.

"You look sort of puny."

"I'm a bit fatigued, but I'm all right."

"Do your arms and legs ache?"

"They ached somewhat yesterday, but not so much now."

"Did you take anything?"

"A little calomel."

"Well, I think you ought to stay off your feet for a day or two. They say brain fever is going around in Springfield."

"I've just got the slows, Abe, that's all. I'll be fine. Don't you worry about me."

But the next morning, she could not get out of bed and had difficulty raising her arms. She burned all over, except for her feet, which were cold as stones. Her mother sent one of her brothers to fetch Dr. John Allen, the village physician. He bled her a little, prescribed more calomel and some jalap, and told her she must have absolute quiet.

Abraham stuck close for a couple of days, hoping to see her, until Ann's mother gently shooed him away.

"Dr. Allen says no visitors, Abe," she told him. "She needs her rest. We'll send word as soon as she's on her feet again."

He did not want to be a bother, so he collected Jack Armstrong and Jack Kelso for a surveying job on Rock Creek. The fierce heat made the work unbearable. Their skin blistered under the sun. Sweat ran down their backs and faces, soaking their shirts and stinging their eyes. The flies would not leave them alone. No amount of swatting could stop them from slicing into flesh and leaving bloody wounds that first burned and then itched.

They pushed through the rising waves of heat in slow motion, calling "Chain! Stick! Stuck!" to each other in weak voices. By early morning, the chain had grown hot to the touch. Little clouds of dust floated up around their waists when they hammered the red-flagged marking pins into the ground. They spent half the time lying in shade or in the shrunken creek, trying to cool off.

"My God, it's hotter than the hinges of Hades," Kelso panted.

Abraham could not stop worrying about Ann, could not get out of his mind the thought of her lying in bed in the stifling heat. They talked to a farmer just back from Springfield who said death had claimed some fever patients there. The report made him nervous. More than once he discovered that he had erred in his calculations of angles and distances.

They were laboring up a hillside when Jack Armstrong stepped in a ground nest of bees. The enraged insects swarmed and chased him to the bottom of the hill. He ran flapping and cursing and ended by jumping into Rock Creek to roll in the water. Abraham and Kelso laughed at first, then grimaced when they saw the welts where the bees had got under his shirt. They chewed some tobacco and packed it onto the swollen places to draw out the sting. Armstrong said that whiskey absorbed internally was the only proven treatment, and they gave up the surveying so he could go take the cure.

As they approached New Salem, they met Bowling Green, who was riding out to find them.

"Ann is asking for you, Abe," Pot said.

"Is she recovered?"

"I'm afraid not. You need to go quickly."

Abraham felt the ground caving in beneath him.

"What's her condition?"

"I don't know. They sent word to come as soon as you can."

With trembling hands, he unloaded his saddlebags, left his surveying equipment with his friends, and set off for the Rutledges' place at a fast trot. He no longer noticed the heat and dust. He sat rigid in the saddle, not allowing himself to think the worst.

Ann's family wore defeated looks. They sat quietly in the cabin's main room, solitary with their own thoughts. Ann's mother moved about the hearth, preparing some tea the doctor had prescribed. Her father looked feverish himself.

"Is she in danger?" Abraham asked.

"Dr. Allen says she is," he heard someone answer. He was not sure who.

They motioned him to the room where she lay in bed, her head resting on a big feather pillow. He was shocked by her decline in the few days since he had seen her. Her sunken cheeks and listless eyes burned with the fever. Her arms had thinned down to candlesticks. One of her sisters, Nancy, was sitting with her but rose with a sad smile and left them alone as he entered.

Ann brightened when she saw him.

"I was hoping you would come." Her voice sounded distant and small.

"I've wanted to see you, but they wouldn't let me." Abraham sat and took her fragile hand. It was hot with fever. "How do you feel?"

It took her a moment to answer.

"Still a little on the puny side." She closed her eyes and smiled faintly. "Do you remember the first time we met?" she asked.

"You were sitting on a tree stump."

"You were barefoot and soaked from toes to waist from splashing around in the river when you got stuck on the dam."

"You looked pretty as a picture."

"And you looked like a piece of driftwood washed up on the bank."

She opened her eyes and looked at him.

"Some of the girls said you were strange, the way you were always reading and studying. I never thought you were strange. I've always believed you will make something of yourself."

"I'm going to try."

He took a cloth, dipped it in a bowl of water set beside the bed, and gently wiped her brow.

"I believe I'm going to die, Abe."

"You're not going to die. You're going to be fine."

"Perhaps. But I'm not afraid. I know our Savior is waiting for me on the other side of the river."

A fit of coughing shook her emaciated frame. Her face turned ashen, and she fell back on the pillow exhausted. Abraham strangled a cry of grief. He wiped her brow again, but she gave no sign of feeling the damp cloth on her skin.

"Don't be bitter over my going, Abe."

"I'm not bitter, because you're not going anywhere except to school in Jacksonville, and I'm going to finish my law studies, and then we'll be married."

"I wish it were so. They say we are all pilgrims traveling through this wearisome land. I believe my journey is almost over."

"I don't want you talking that way. You're going to get better. I won't let anything happen to you."

Ann scrutinized his face, as if committing its details to memory.

"I would have made a good wife, and you would have made a good husband and father."

"You're feeling bad right now because of the fever. Dr. Allen will get you fixed up. You'll see."

"Sit with me while I rest a bit. I do feel stronger with you here."

She closed her eyes again and held on to his hand. The furrows of pain on her face softened.

"You must always live an honest and upright life," she said.

In a few minutes, she fell asleep. Abraham sat beside her a long time, wiping her brow and holding her hand until her mother came and led him away. He stumbled out of the room with tears on his cheeks.

Two days later, she was dead.

CHAPTER 26

Summer and Autumn 1835

They laid her to rest in a little hilltop cemetery where a handful of gravestones looked over the prairies. Sheep grazed on a nearby slope, and in the distance below, green woods followed the path of a creek. A half dozen oaks stood over the plot. In summer they offered shade, and in winter the bones of their limbs reached across the sky.

Everyone in New Salem and the surrounding settlements, from Clary's Gove to Sandridge, came for the graveside service. They gathered, heads bowed, while the prayers for the dead settled over them. *Unto Almighty God we commend the soul of our sister departed, and we commit her body to the ground, earth to earth, ashes to ashes, dust to dust.*

The leaden clang of a distant cowbell floated up the hillside on the still air. Beyond the thick oak trunks, clouds stood like mountains on the rim of the prairies.

When the funeral ended, Abraham sat alone by her grave. Rain began to fall and work on the fresh mound of earth. Rivulets carried away loose particles of soil, carving tiny valleys into its flanks. He thought of a poem he had run across a few months earlier. Its melancholy nature had appealed to him so much that he had committed it to memory.

O why should the spirit of mortal be proud!
Like a swift fleeting meteor, a fast flying cloud,
A flash of the lightning, a break of the wave—
He passes from life to his rest in the grave.

It seemed to him that he ought to go to Ann's house and say something to her family. But when he arrived, he could not bring himself to knock on the door. He stood outside the window of her death room, tears mixing with rain. The touch of a hand on his shoulder gave him a start. It was Ann's mother.

"Don't let your grief destroy you, Abe," she said kindly.

He did not know what to say, so he turned and walked away.

He made his way to the river, where he could be alone in the woods along the banks. In Indiana he had complained that the forests hemmed him in, but they had always offered solitude, and now he sought them.

The leaves of the oak and the willow shall fade,
Be scattered around, and together be laid;
And the young and the old, the low and the high,
Shall molder to dust, and together shall lie.

He slept in the woods, exhausted, then rose and resumed his wandering. When hungry, he foraged for food, though he did not want much. If he caught sight of anyone nearby, he slipped behind a tree and waited for them to pass.

More than once he went back to Ann's grave to sit by her side. How was it that she could grow so pale and weak in a matter of days? His mother had also gone quickly. So had his sister, Sarah, and her stillborn child.

The maid on whose cheek, on whose brow, in whose eye,
Shone beauty and pleasure—her triumphs are by;
And the memory of those who loved her and praised,
Are alike from the minds of the living erased.

Bowling Green found him in the cemetery, brooding beside the mound.

"Here you are. What have you been doing with yourself?"

Abraham gave him a haggard stare.

"We've been searching half the county for you."

"Who?"

"Me, Armstrong, Kelso, Jimmy Short, everyone. For three or four days now."

"I didn't realize it had been that long," he said.

"Well, you can't stay out here forever. Come home with me for a while. Nancy will put some food in your stomach." He patted his own belly. "That woman can cook."

He followed Pot to his cabin. He was shocked when he glimpsed himself in a looking glass and saw his gaunt face with dark hollows under the eyes. Nancy Green filled him with hot biscuits dripping with honey, let him sleep as much as he wanted for a day or two, then filled him with more biscuits, pan-fried ham, snap beans, and creamed turnips. Dr. Allen stopped by to have a look.

"Rest is good," he advised, "but give him something to keep him occupied."

Nancy set him to work digging potatoes and holding yarn while she spun. Friends stopped by with cakes and pies. Jack Kelso came to spend an afternoon reciting poems of Robert Burns. Slicky Bill Greene brought his law books, which Abraham had left at Sam Hill's store, and told him that Sam was looking after the post office.

Nights were hardest, especially when thunderstorms rolled across the prairies with winds that tumbled over the cabin roof. He stood at the door, clenching his fists, looking at flames of lightning on the black horizon.

"I can't bear the thought of her out there all alone with the rain falling on her grave," he told Nancy.

He looked for comfort in the Bible but found none.

"I feel like old Job," he told Mentor Graham, who came to sit with him for a while.

"Everyone feels like Job at some point in his life," the schoolteacher said philosophically.

"Well, maybe so, but what kind of God piles calamity heavier than the sand of the sea on a man? And crushes the life out of a girl who never did anyone harm?"

"I have no doubt that she has passed from death unto life."

"You don't know that," Abraham said bitterly. "If this is God's plan, he's no God of justice and mercy."

"God has a higher purpose."

"Well, I don't see it."

"We're not supposed to see it, except perhaps through a glass darkly. That is where faith comes in."

"You may be right, but I still feel like all the poison arrows of the Almighty are in me."

Summer waned and cool mornings arrived with the first hints of autumn in the valley of the Sangamon. The rays of the sun slanted to the earth in softer angles. Light filtered down from a crystalline blue sky and hung over the prairies, settling between rows of corn, signaling change. The old heat of the summer burned itself out as the chirps of the crickets slowed.

Gradually, with the turn of the seasons, he pulled himself together. He was like a wounded fox that had crawled into a hole. He had guarded its entrance and licked his wounds while they had a chance to heal. The time of danger had passed, the hurt had begun to ease a little, and he could poke his nose out of the hole to see which direction the wind was blowing.

After two weeks with Pot and Nancy, he began to laugh at jokes and take an interest in his law books. Friends told him they were glad to have him back, that New Salem had not been the same without him. He was relieved to be moving with a purpose again, delivering letters and surveying his way across unmeasured tracts with compass and chain. But there were days when gray moods came over him, and he could not help slipping away to be alone. At times he found himself sitting beside Ann's grave, brooding over dark mysteries.

'Tis the wink of an eye—'tis the draught of a breath—
From the blossom of health to the paleness of death,
From the gilded saloon to the bier and the shroud
Oh, why should the spirit of mortal be proud?

PART THREE

THE TOWN

April 1837 to November 1842

CHAPTER 27

April 15, 1837

He turned his horse onto Fifth Street and rode slowly toward Springfield's town square, keeping an eye out for hogs wallowing in his path. Spring rains had changed dusty roads into stagnant rivers of mud. Wagons struggled axle-deep through oozing ruts. At street crossings, pedestrians hopped from plank to plank, trying to keep their shoe tops from disappearing into the mire. New wood-frame buildings, some still under construction, perched on the edge of the muck. The grunts of porkers and squawks of chickens mixed with the pounding of hammers in the cool afternoon air.

On the west side of the square, he dismounted and tied to a hitching post. He eyed his saddlebags for a moment and decided he'd better keep them with him since they held most of his possessions—a couple of law books, a few clothes, seven dollars in cash. Slinging the bags over his arm, he stepped into the general store of A.Y. Ellis & Company.

It was a good-sized place, well stocked with dry goods and groceries. Abraham dropped his saddlebags on the counter. A slim young man with blue eyes and dark, curly hair who was leaning over a newspaper looked up at him.

"'Afternoon. I'm Abraham Lincoln."

"I'm Joshua Speed. I've seen you give a speech or two. Liked what I heard. Good to make your acquaintance."

They shook hands.

"I've just arrived from New Salem. John Stuart and I are going to practice law together."

"I read the announcement in the *Sangamo Journal.*"

Abraham smiled. News of the partnership had spread. That was good.

"I hope to find a place to set up my sleeping quarters. I'll need to purchase bedding supplies."

The young proprietor walked with him around the store, helping him choose a mattress, a blanket, sheets, and a pillow. Speed made a few calculations with a pencil and slate.

"It'll amount to seventeen dollars in all."

Abraham's face fell. His confidence drained out of him.

"It's probably cheap enough," he said, "but cheap as it is, I don't have the money to pay."

The thought of contracting more debt, even seventeen dollars, brought a spasm of pain in his stomach. Still, there was no other course.

"If you'll credit me until Christmas, and my experiment as a lawyer is a success, I'll pay you then."

He paused. I might as well tell him the whole truth, he thought.

"If I fail, I don't know if I can ever pay you."

The storekeeper looked as though he had never met a gloomier face. Speed thought for a moment as he rubbed out the figures on the slate.

"I think I can suggest a plan," he said. "I've got a large room with a large double bed. You're welcome to share it."

"Where's the room?"

"Up there," Speed said, pointing to some winding stairs.

Abraham picked up his saddlebags and climbed to the second floor. The room was sparsely furnished, with a couple of chairs and a rough chest of drawers, but it was spacious, and the wide bed offered more than enough room for two to lie without disturbing each other. A small bookshelf held a few volumes of Lord Byron, Milton, and Shakespeare. He set the saddlebags on the floor and clattered back down the stairs, beaming with pleasure.

"Well, Speed, I'm moved," he announced.

That evening, as he sat with Josh Speed beside the big fireplace in the back of the store, his thoughts ranged over the last several months. More than a year and a half had passed since Ann died, and he had spent the time hurling himself at politics, work, and study.

He had run for reelection to the legislature and to his immense satisfaction had won with more votes than any other candidate in Sangamon County. The Sangamon delegation had earned the nickname the "Long Nine" because its seven representatives and two state senators stood unusually tall, with a collective height of fifty-four feet. During his second term at Vandalia, Abraham had emerged as the gang's floor leader. He promoted legislation to finance internal improvements—roads, bridges, canals, and even the railroads that would someday reach Illinois. Opponents warned that the projects would cost too much, that there was no way to repay the debt, that the state would face financial ruin. But how else could Illinois turn empty prairies and thick forests into civilization? With much logrolling and back-scratching, he had helped guide the bills through the House.

More logs had rolled when the Long Nine led a fight to move the state capital from Vandalia to Springfield, which was, they argued, more centrally located for a government. A ferocious tug-of-war had erupted between towns across Illinois, from Alton to Quincy to Jacksonville, each full of boosters eager to make their city the seat of power, while Vandalia partisans clutched their crown in a death grip. Abraham used every trick he had learned in his short legislative career to help snatch away the prize for Springfield, which won the contest, earning him the gratitude of the new capital's citizens.

All the while, between campaign speeches, committee work, and traversing the county with compass and chain to run survey lines, he had kept at his law studies, digging at Blackstone's *Commentaries* until finally the day came when the State of Illinois saw fit to grant him a license to practice law. John Stuart had pulled him aside, laid an arm around his shoulder, and invited him to be his new partner. It was an offer much too good to pass up.

"Stuart has connections as good as any man in the state," Speed observed. "You'll have a successful practice before you know it."

"I'm not so sure. There are already eleven lawyers in this town, all with more education than I'll ever get. I don't know that I can measure up. An ape is still an ape though you clothe him in velvet."

"Nonsense! I've heard people say you're already one of the smartest parliamentarians in Illinois. You're like a young eagle. You merely need scope for your wings. You'll soar to the top."

Abraham studied his new friend, not without some envy. Joshua Fry Speed, five years his junior, had been born to a prominent Kentucky family on a plantation near Louisville. He had attended the best private schools before moving to Springfield and purchasing a part ownership in Abner Ellis's store. His fine manners and complexion marked him as a gentleman, and his natural optimism made him easily likable. On top of that, he was a devoted Whig.

"I don't see how we can fail in Illinois," Speed declared. "Commerce will naturally pour into the West if we give it aid. What we need is men with vision. Men willing to do what Governor DeWitt Clinton did for

New York—make dirt fly to dig canals and build roads."

"I tell you, Speed, my highest ambition is to become the DeWitt Clinton of Illinois," Abraham vowed. "I'd give anything to make a name like that for myself."

He paused, suddenly feeling sheepish.

"First I need to earn a few dollars to pay for some bedsheets," he admitted.

That night as he lay in the big double bed above the store, hopes and regrets tossed in his head. He thought of the village on the banks of the Sangamon and of Ann lying under the ground. The shock of losing her still cut deep, but with each day, the pain shrank a little.

He hated to leave New Salem, but it held no promise for a legal or political career, not like Springfield did. Bowling Green, Jimmy Short, Jack Armstrong, and all his other friends had understood. They laid no claims on him and had sent him on his way with their love and blessings, twenty miles down the road to the new state capital to seek his fortune. He fell asleep remembering their kindness and promising himself that he would not forget them.

CHAPTER 28

Spring and Summer 1837

The firm of Stuart & Lincoln, Attorneys and Counselors at Law, occupied a small second-floor room in Hoffman's Row, a set of six adjoining brick buildings just up the street from Josh Speed's store. The location was good, off the northwest corner of the town square, although the furnishings were less than impressive: an old table that claimed to be a desk, a chair containing a buffalo robe, a hard wooden bench, a small dirty bed, and a rickety bookcase where the partners might consult a few law books and volumes of legislative proceedings.

"You're going to make a fine attorney, Lincoln," John Stuart said on their first day at work together. "I'm proud to be associated with you."

The Kentucky-born Stuart had earned a reputation for courtly manners. Around Springfield, folks said he always had as fine and gallant a bow for his laundress as for a duchess. He took a seat on the wooden bench and motioned for Abraham to make himself comfortable in the chair.

"There's no sense tiptoeing around in the shallows with those long legs," he said. "We'll throw you into the deep water and let you handle some cases right away."

"I hope it's not over my head."

"Don't worry about that. You'll float like a cork."

Stuart looked out the window toward the square.

"Abe, it's no secret that I'd like to make a run for Congress," he said.

"I'll do all in my power to help you get there."

"Thank you. I can use your aid. The best way you can help me, and help yourself, is to turn yourself into an able attorney. Campaigning will take a considerable portion of my time. We'll need you to carry a load for our practice, a bigger load than most greenhorns might expect to haul."

"That sounds fine. I'm anxious to learn the ropes."

"Good. Then let's go at it."

Later that day, while investigating the bookcase, Abraham found a copy of *Webster's Dictionary*. He opened it and wrote on the flyleaf: "A. Lincoln, Esq., Attorney and Counselor-at-Law." The sight of the words filled him with pride.

John Todd Stuart's contacts and experience brought a steady flow of clients. Much of the work had to do with debt, since everyone in Illinois owed somebody something, and who owed what to whom was often a mystery to be unraveled. Abraham saw every kind of complaint of neighbor against neighbor: libel, slander, trespass, larceny, assault and battery, horse thievery, backwoods knavery.

He looked into the matter of who really owned a certain litter of pigs, and the case of whether David Woolridge "assaulted, struck, beat, bruised and knocked down" James Hawthorn and "plucked, pulled, and tore divers quantities of hair" from his scalp. George Stockton dropped by one day to explain that James Tolly had spoiled a cooking stove while hauling it between Beardstown and Springfield, so Abraham filed suit against Tolly for damages amounting to one hundred dollars. When a boat full of corn struck a fish-trap dam on the Sangamon River and sprang a leak, he filed suit against the dam's owners for obstruction of river navigation.

He spent long afternoons in the office carefully writing out pleadings stuffed with words like *whereas*, *heretofore*, and *aforesaid*. If he found himself stumped, and Stuart was not there to help, he flopped down in the chair with the buffalo robe and mumbled his way through the law books until he found an answer. When his head throbbed from too much reading and writing, he went outside and sawed wood.

The fees charged by Stuart & Lincoln, which the two partners split equally, were not large. They generally ran about five or ten dollars. But they added up. For the first time in his life, Abraham had a dependable income, about a thousand dollars a year, and he could envision the day when he would pay off his debt.

He discovered that he did not enjoy keeping track of the business's finances, and he often forgot to record receipts and expenditures in a timely manner. But he tried to be scrupulous, especially with other people's money. An agent of the Post Office Department appeared one day to collect eighteen dollars owed to the government by the old post office at New Salem. Abraham dug around in a corner and produced the blue sock he had used to keep money when postmaster. He untied the sock, poured a little mound of silver and copper coins onto the table, and counted out the exact amount the agent was expecting.

There were times when he felt like a bumpkin. Stuart sent him to defend John Baddeley, a haughty English-born merchant, in a lawsuit that had been filed against him. Abraham found Baddeley putting up his team at a livery stable and proceeded to introduce himself. Baddeley took one look at the ungainly young man in ill-fitting clothes, declared that he looked like a country rustic on his way to a circus, and stalked off to find another lawyer.

Abraham was mortified.

"He gave me no chance," he complained to Josh Speed. "I suppose he expected a barrister in a wig and black gown."

"I wouldn't worry about him," Speed said.

"He abused me so viciously, even the stable boys blushed."

"Well, stable boys know a jackass when they see one, and I guess they know that the man Baddeley hires to be his attorney will have a jackass for a client."

He decided to take Speed's advice and put the incident out of his mind. He was too busy to worry about it.

Harvey Ross, the mail carrier, appeared in his office on a summer morning along with a fellow named Hagerty. Harvey explained that he owned a quarter section of land near Macomb but that there was a defect in the title and that Hagerty could swear to some facts that would fix the problem.

"We'll need the court to amend it, and it's adjourned until the next session," Abraham said. "Judge Thomas lives about a mile east of town. Let's go see if there's anything he can do for you."

It was going to be a hot afternoon. He took off his coat, and they struck off across the square, Abraham carrying a bundle of papers in one hand and a big red handkerchief for mopping sweat in the other. When they reached Judge Thomas's house, his wife came to the door.

"He's over at our tenants' place, helping 'em build a corncrib," she said. "It's about half a mile from here by the road, but you can take a shortcut through the cornfield."

She walked them to the barn and showed them where to pick up the path. They set off Indian file through the stalks of corn, brushing past green leaves and swelling ears with pale yellow silks. The air between the thick rows smelled of ripening corn. Insects clicked and buzzed in their hiding places. The sun sharpened its rays, and Abraham wiped his brow with the big red bandana.

They found Judge Thomas and his men raising logs for a structure about twelve by twenty feet. Thomas shook hands with his visitors, explaining that the cabin would serve as a corncrib and hog house.

Abraham told him why they had come, and the judge took a recess from his work to look over the title papers. He said he thought they could fix up the matter and sent to the tenant house for pen and ink.

"We're all in our shirtsleeves," Abraham observed while they waited. "I reckon we're holding a kind of shirtsleeve court."

"Yes." The judge laughed. "A shirtsleeve court in a cornfield."

When the pen and ink arrived, Thomas swore in the witness and fixed the title. Their business done, Abraham asked the judge if he needed some help rolling up the logs.

"A couple are pretty heavy," Thomas said. "We could stand a little help."

They all pitched in to roll the notched logs up two stout poles that slanted from the ground to the top of the cabin wall. Abraham steered one end and the judge the other. When they had heaved each log to the top, they trimmed the saddle-shaped notches for a tight fit and banged the log into place.

After they finished, Harvey offered to pay Judge Thomas for his services.

"I guess raising logs is payment enough," the judge said. "No need to pay any more."

They walked back to Springfield in the heat and dust, thin shadows trailing them on the road. They could see thunderheads piling up over the prairies, and they walked quickly to get to town before the clouds exploded. Harvey talked of hailstorms and barn raisings while Abraham kept his thoughts to himself, measuring hopes against accomplishments. He walked with the satisfaction of knowing that he had been able to help his friend and the judge to boot.

Well, I'm finally a lawyer, he realized, yet somehow, I'm still stuck in a cornfield. He couldn't help but chuckle at himself.

CHAPTER 29

SUMMER 1837

His work in the Illinois House took a good chunk of his time. A massive new statehouse made of yellow-brown limestone began to rise on Springfield's town square. He watched it take form as he drafted bills, talked with constituents, and did battle with Democrats. Politics put him in touch with the most important men in the state and allowed him to measure himself against them.

When he wasn't practicing law or politics, he joined a group of young men who used Joshua Speed's store as a headquarters for discussing politics, poetry, and every subject in between.

"We're a society for the encouragement of debate and literary efforts,"

Speed said. "It's not a formal association. Fellows drop by in the evening, and we chew the fat."

The gatherings took place around the big fireplace in the rear of the store, where the cigar smoke grew so thick that whiskey glasses floated toward shining faces unattached to arms and bodies. Abraham declined the whiskey but imbibed the camaraderie with zest. Before long he'd formed a ring of friends—fellows such as the English-born Edward Baker, handsome and eloquent, who had recently been elected to the state legislature; Dr. Anson Henry, a broad-shouldered physician who loved to mix Whig politics and medicine in his practice of life; and young Billy Herndon, son of a local merchant, who was studying to be a lawyer.

When these men and others pulled their chairs up to Speed's hearth, the place nearly burst with energy. They were strong men of strong opinions who loved the tumult of friendly argument. A room ten times larger than Speed's store could not have contained their enthusiasm.

When passions grew thick, they counted on Abraham to stir the pot until wit and humor boiled over.

"Did you fellows hear that Doc Henry made a house call on Lizzy Bliss last week?" he drawled.

"Nope. Tell us about it."

"'Have you ever been bedridden?' Dr. Henry asked her. 'I surely have,' Lizzy said eagerly, 'many times, including twice in the back of Jim Matheny's buggy.'"

Matheny, who worked in the court clerk's office, accepted the tribute with a guffaw.

"Now, boys, I don't mean to impugn Lizzy's good character," Abraham said. "You know I'm the first to defend the fairer sex. In fact, I've made up a little verse of my own to show how I feel about the ladies."

"Let's hear it!"

"Don't be shy, Lincoln."

> *"Whatever spiteful fools may say,*
> *Each jealous, ranting yelper,*
> *No woman ever went astray*
> *Without a man to help her."*

When the poetry was finished, the discussion turned to issues working their way through the statehouse or Congress, including the heated topic of slavery.

"Those damned abolitionists are at it again. They'll tear the country apart with their antics."

"Damn straight. This business of calling Southerners desperadoes and the Constitution an agreement with hell has got to stop."

Every man in the room harbored some degree of sympathy for slaves tilling American soil. They were all against human bondage in principle. But their feelings about abolitionists ranged from distrust to anger. Like many in Illinois, they viewed the reformers as firebrands who were determined to stir up trouble.

The abolitionists were growing bold. They had flooded Congress with petitions demanding an immediate end of slavery. Southern planters were outraged. John C. Calhoun of South Carolina roared that the petitions were a "foul slander" on the South, and the US House of Representatives declared that it would take up no discussions of the slavery issue.

"I agree with you about the abolitionists," Abraham told his friends. "I don't like the insults they hurl at the South. But they are right about one thing. The institution of slavery is founded on both injustice and bad policy."

He said it carefully, and the others nodded carefully. He was treading on thin ice. Expressing any shade of agreement with abolitionists could be political suicide. Besides, they all knew that Josh Speed's family owned dozens of slaves on their Kentucky plantation.

"It's wicked to agitate this subject," Ned Baker declared. "The abolitionist societies are nothing more than organized zealots determined to inflame the Negroes. They'd love to see a slave insurrection leave two hundred whites with their throats cut."

"They're forging new chains for the black man," Speed said. "Every time they spread their abolitionist gospel, they force Southerners to use more severity in their fields."

"What would they have the planters do, turn every damned slave loose on the world? They'll deluge the country in blood."

They all grew silent, as if straining to hear distant thunder.

Near Hoffman's Row lived a shoemaker who loved the bottle. A man of sour temperament, he grew meaner the more he drank, and his sprees invariably ended in his beating his wife. She was a delicate Irish woman with high cheekbones and fine reddish-brown hair pulled back from her ears. When Abraham took a pair of shoes to the cobbler and she crept out of the shadows to take them, he saw purple bruises down the left side of her face. He left the shop with a hollow feeling in his stomach.

"Last spring he fractured one of her ribs," Dr. Henry said. "He's savage as a meat ax when he gets a jug of whiskey in him."

Abraham passed the shoemaker on the street one afternoon, and his anger got the better of him. He stopped the man.

"If I get word that you've laid a hand on her again, I'll thrash you myself," he promised.

The cobbler snarled and moved on.

It did not take the man long to forget the warning. A few nights later, Abraham was sitting outside on the square with Josh Speed and Jim Matheny, shooting the breeze under the stars, when a commotion started. They heard shouting and crashing in the cobbler's shop and a woman's sobs.

"We're putting an end to this now. Come on."

The three men strode across the street and beat on the cobbler's door. All was quiet for a moment. The door opened, and the shoemaker stuck his head out.

"You're coming with us, friend," Abraham growled.

He grabbed the man by the neck and pulled him out of the shop. The drunkard stumbled forward, protesting mildly, confused about what was happening.

"Closed . . . closed," he tried to explain. "Shop not open. You come back 'morrow."

They dragged him to a yard in back of a store building, stripped off his shirt, and tied him to a post near a well.

Abraham issued instructions. "Speed, get his wife. Matheny, go fetch a stout switch. Try the woodpile in back of my office."

He stood waiting, arms folded. The shoemaker, realizing that he was in some trouble, began to sober up. He blinked at his bound wrists and at Abraham.

Josh reappeared with the wife. Her face showed fresh bruises and a black eye.

"Light in," Abraham told her, offering the switch Matheny had found.

She took a step back. "I can't," she wailed.

"Yes, you can. You've got to if you want him to stop hitting you. He needs a taste of what he's been dishing out."

He put the switch in her hand. She stood still, unsure, looking from Abraham to her husband and back. The cobbler saw the disaster that was about to strike him. He tried to jerk his hands free.

"You ain't going to do it, are you, Martha?" he cried.

"She is."

The wife stepped forward, eyes fixed on Abraham, and raised the switch above her head.

It trembled in the air for an instant. She swung and brought it down on her husband's bare back.

The cobbler gave a little yelp, then laughed.

"You'll have to give him better than that," Abraham advised.

She raised the switch again and brought it down with more determination. This time it cracked like a drover's whip across the shoulders.

The cobbler bellowed in pain.

"God damn you!"

"That's it," Matheny encouraged her. "Give it to him good. Don't baby him."

The woman nodded. She reared back and laid it on as hard as she could. With each blow, the cobbler screamed new obscenities.

Abraham and his friends settled onto their haunches to watch. The wife, emboldened now, pitched into the job lustily. The shoemaker's curses became whimpers of pain and humiliation.

They let her whale at him until the man's back was rough with welts. When it looked raw enough, Abraham took the switch from her.

"You go on back home. He'll be along shortly."

They untied the man and handed him his shirt. All the drunkenness had been beat out of him.

"You'll pay for this! You'll pay, by God!" he hissed.

"We let you off easy this time," Abraham said. "The next time you abuse her, I'll be the one swinging the limb, and it won't feel so good."

The cobbler shambled toward his home, throwing back venomous looks.

"Do you think he'll try to get vengeance?" Speed asked.

"No. I reckon we fixed his flint."

They heard no more reports of the shoemaker beating his wife.

CHAPTER 30

AUTUMN 1837 TO AUTUMN 1839

"You can't wait for business to come to you," John Stuart advised. "If you want to make a decent living, you have to go looking for lawsuits. We'll do some circuit riding this fall."

Twice a year, in spring and fall, a small battalion of Springfield attorneys rode with a judge from county seat to county seat on a circuit that covered a big chunk of Illinois. At each stop, the lawyers signed up clients and tried cases before the traveling judge. It took about ten weeks to complete the whole circuit.

They traveled by horseback in weather fair and foul, a couple of clean shirts stuffed into their saddlebags, following prairie trails across land as wide and empty as the dawn of creation. There were places where they could ride nearly all day without laying eyes on another human being. Sometimes they stopped at remote cabins, where they gorged on ham and eggs, fried chicken, and hot biscuits.

"I've never tasted so much good pork," Stuart told a grizzled farmer. "You must have slaughtered a whole critter to feed us."

"That's right," the man said. "We never kill less than a whole critter."

When they arrived at a courthouse, litigious villagers gathered to shop for lawyers. Plaintiffs and defendants explained their sides of land squabbles, or why they were owed three dollars for a hog, or who had been the first to slander a neighbor. The attorneys set up makeshift law offices under trees or in taverns, where they hastily prepared for trial. The next afternoon the bailiff stuck his head out the courtroom window to bellow: "Oyez! Oyez! The circuit court is now open for the dispatch of business!"

Most of the courthouses were glorified cabins with rough floors used by small boys to play marbles when court was not in session. The judge sat at the front of the chamber on a raised platform. Nearby stood a small table for the clerk, and sometimes a larger table where the lawyers could rest their papers and the heels of their boots. In one or two places, hogs lounged in the space beneath the floorboards, grunting throughout the proceedings.

Illinois lawyers riding the circuit saw every shade of human action and dispute.

In Tremont, Manly Floyd hired Stuart & Lincoln to seek two hundred dollars from Henry Turlock in a suit claiming that Turlock seized, took, and carried away Floyd's sorrel horse for his own use.

In Bloomington, the firm filed suit for Margaret Steed against her husband for divorce on the grounds of desertion and habitual drunkenness, charging that Peter Steed left Margaret in a helpless condition with a newborn infant and never furnished child support.

In Decatur, an old farmer came to Abraham to explain that he had leased a flock of sheep with the promise to pay the owner a portion of next year's wool. He had pastured the sheep, fed them, and cared for them, but when spring arrived, they had all died of a mysterious ailment, and now the sheep's owner was suing for damages. Abraham did his best to help, but the court declared that the old man must turn over his farm.

Afterwards they stood outside the courthouse, the farmer trying to hold himself straight against the shock of the blow.

"I'll go west and hope for cheap land," he told Abraham. "I'm nearly seventy, but I guess it ain't too late to make a fresh start."

In the evenings, after court adjourned, the lawyers and judge put aside business to sit before a tavern fire and talk politics, wisdom, and fun with the locals.

"Mighty cold night," Abraham said to a wheelwright as they warmed themselves at the flames.

"Cold as hell," the man agreed.

"You've been there, too, have you?"

"Yup, and it's the same as here—all the lawyers are nearest the fire."

Jurors, judge, witnesses, litigants, and attorneys all ate together at the same long table. The tavern food was usually bad.

"If this is coffee, please bring me some tea," Abraham told a waiter, "but if this is tea, please bring me some coffee."

They slept two or three to a bed, with eight or more men piled into a dingy tavern room. Abraham often slept on the floor with a straw or two beneath him. Sometimes he woke to find miniature snow drifts on his blankets and ice in the tin wash basin. They all shared the same hand towel, and a man was lucky if it wasn't sopping wet by the time he got to it.

When they finished in one town, they rode on to the next courthouse. Cold autumn winds swept the prairies. Abraham lowered his head, hunched his shoulders, and pulled his coat collar tight as his horse pushed into the blasts. He had a feeling that despite the flea-ridden beds and long rides through desolate country, he was going to like these nomadic turns on the circuit.

In 1838, John Stuart's campaign for Congress moved into high gear.

"You'll have to handle most of the firm's business while I beat the bushes for votes," he told Abraham. "I've got a lot of ground to cover."

Stuart's opponent was Stephen Douglas, a bantam rooster of a man who stood barely five feet four inches high.

"He's the least man I have ever seen," Abraham cracked.

But Little Dug, as some called him, was a steam engine in britches. What he lacked in height, he made up for with a full chest, powerful shoulders, square jaw, and penetrating eyes. A thick mane of dark brown hair adorned his massive head. Born in Vermont, he had arrived in Illinois at age twenty with five dollars in his pocket, a keen devotion to Andrew Jackson, and a determination to make something of himself.

"I have become a *Western* man," he wrote in exuberance to his family back home, "have imbibed Western feelings, principles, and interests, and have selected Illinois as the favorite place of my adoption."

Blessed with a knack for making friends, he had lost no time in forging his way ahead. He studied enough law to get a license and hung out his shingle as an attorney in Jacksonville. People noticed that he was good at arguing and debating. In particular they noticed the voice that resonated like an organ from his deep chest. Douglas jumped into politics with the Democratic Party. He had got himself appointed state's attorney and won election to the state legislature. Now he was running against Stuart for Congress.

The two candidates stumped across the congressional district, thirty-four counties in all, often traveling together in search of votes, speaking from the same platform, eating at the same table, even sleeping in the same bed in out-of-the-way farmhouses. Tempers erupted as election day approached. Angered by some words Douglas tossed his way, Stuart picked up his opponent and carried him around a Springfield grocery like a naughty pup. Douglas counterattacked by biting Stuart's thumb. They took the brawl to a local tavern, where they fought until they were both exhausted and the floor was covered with slop. Afterwards, Stuart had the good sense to order up a barrel of whiskey for the crowd.

Their race for Congress went down to the wire. The tall, handsome Stuart defeated the stumpy, combative Western man from Vermont by thirty-six votes out of thirty-six thousand cast.

Abraham, poring over columns of election results, told himself that they had not heard the last of Douglas by a long shot. Already some who had called him Little Dug were referring to him, with respect, as the Little Giant.

This one is worth watching, he thought.

On the day John Stuart left Springfield to take his seat in Congress, the two partners stood in their office, shook hands, and wished each other good luck.

"Write me all the political news from hereabouts whenever you get a chance," Stuart said.

"I will. And you send me every piece of information you think will be a good war club to use against Douglas and his cronies."

"You're making yourself into a fine attorney, Lincoln." Stuart smiled. "You'll have no problem running things while I'm gone. I'm confident of that."

After his partner left, Abraham opened the firm's fee book, turned to a fresh page, and wrote across the top: "Commencement of Lincoln's Administration."

The office of Stuart & Lincoln sat above a courtroom that was sometimes used for public lectures and debates. A trapdoor in the office's floor, used to lift heavy items from the first to the second story, made it easy to hear what was going on in the room below. One chilly evening in 1839, as Abraham was working late, angry voices rose through the floor.

"Some of the Democrats in this state would cross hell on a rotten log to get their hands on the public funds!"

Ned Baker was delivering a fiery address on behalf of the Whigs. He was a brilliant orator, but he could also be hotheaded, and he pulled no punches. Abraham grinned as the attacks flowed. The crowded room below contained many Whigs but also a good many Democrats, including Stephen Douglas.

"Putting Democrats in office is the surest way to plant the seeds of corruption!" Baker declared.

Boos and hisses broke in.

"Knock him off the platform!" someone shouted.

"And the longer Democrats stay in office, the more those seeds of corruption ripen into a wicked harvest!" Baker shouted back.

The room erupted in a scraping of benches and scuffling of feet.

"Knock him down!"

"Get him!"

"Kick his sorry rear end!"

Abraham looked through the hole in the floor. Baker stood on a platform almost directly below, his face pale with excitement, squaring himself for a fight. Stephen Douglas was on his feet. Several other Democrats had begun to advance. Some of the Whigs jumped out of their seats and pushed forward to protect their friend.

Abraham locked his fingers onto the trapdoor's frame, swung his legs into the hole, and dropped to the platform below, landing beside Baker.

"Hold on, gentlemen!" he shouted.

The Democrats kept pushing closer. Abraham grabbed a stone water pitcher sitting on the edge of the platform and raised it high, threatening to break the head of the first man who laid hands on his friend.

That quieted the crowd.

"Hold on, gentlemen!" he shouted again. "This is the land of free speech. Baker has a right to be heard, and no one is going to take him from this stage if I can prevent it."

The men looked at each other, gauging whether the situation warranted a fight. Stephen Douglas broke the silence.

"All right, gentlemen. Let's sit down and let Baker have his say.

We're all friends here. He'll surely tone down his rhetoric."

The men settled back onto the benches. Abraham sat on the edge of the platform and wrapped his arms around his knees, feeling pleased. He made a survey of the room to see who was there to appreciate his performance.

A pretty young woman he did not recognize, one of the few ladies in attendance, sat in front beside Stephen Douglas. She wore a black woolen scarf over her shoulders and purple satin ribbons in her bonnet. Her round face was turned in Abraham's direction. He looked away quickly.

He listened as Baker resumed his speech, feigning interest in what his friend had to say. He looked down at his shoes, inspected his knuckles, examined the buttons on his shirtsleeves. After a decent interval, he casually surveyed the room again. The pretty young woman was gazing at him with a startled expression, as if she were meeting an exotic circus animal for the first time.

He realized, with sudden clarity, that he had made a spectacle of himself. Through her blue-gray eyes, he saw his long skinny legs dangling from the ceiling, his scrawny torso hanging in midair, his long, ungainly arms threatening the room with a water pitcher.

"My God, I'm a fool," he groaned. He blushed from ear to ear through the end of Baker's speech.

CHAPTER 31

DECEMBER 1839

"Ninian and Elizabeth Edwards are having a soiree this evening," Josh said a few days later. "I'm going. Come with me."

"I don't know," Abraham said. "Their place is a little fine for me."

"Don't be ridiculous. You'll have a good time. There will be girls."

"Speed, I could count on one hand the number of women who've spoken to me since I moved to this town."

"That's because you don't try. You can't get an egg without a trip to the henhouse. Let's go."

Abraham put on the best clothes he owned—patched baggy trousers, boiled shirt, too-short swallowtail coat, and black stovepipe hat. The two young men clomped down the stairs from their room above the store and headed southwest through groves of bare oaks to Ninian Edwards's two-story brick house, standing on a gentle rise dubbed Aristocracy Hill. Tall windows, a spacious front veranda, and a balustrade rimming an upper porch made it one of Springfield's most imposing homes.

Edwards, whose father had been governor and one of the first US senators from Illinois, was a fellow Whig in the legislature. His wife, Elizabeth, a tall, striking woman, had gained renown as Springfield's most energetic hostess. The ladies of the town agreed that her pound cakes were the cornerstones of the Episcopal Church.

Elizabeth met them at the door. She extended her hand to Abraham.

"Mr. Lincoln, I am so glad you came. We were hoping you might join us."

She led them into the big parlor, where astral lamps and a blaze in the marble fireplace cast a glow onto polished walnut columns. Most of the guests were already there, including Ned Baker and a cluster of other fellows Abraham knew.

"Have you met my sister, Mary Todd?" Elizabeth asked. "She has come to us from Lexington."

Before him stood the pretty young lady who had been looking at him after he dropped through the trapdoor. Abraham immediately colored.

She was shorter than her sister and a good foot shorter than Abraham. He noticed again her vivid blue-gray eyes. She wore her light chestnut hair pulled back from a high forehead. A finely rounded chin gave way to a long, graceful neck that disappeared into a white dress with black stripes.

"I am so glad to see you again, Mr. Lincoln," she said, offering her hand. "I've never met anyone who comes in through the ceiling."

"I occasionally use a door."

"Well, I hope I did not stare too hard, but that is the first time I've witnessed a real *deus ex machina* in action."

He blinked at her, embarrassed to admit he did not understand.

"I hear you are a rising star of Illinois's Whig Party," she said.

"Who told you that?"

"Ninian. He speaks very highly of you. So does Cousin John."

"Cousin John?"

"Your partner, John Todd Stuart. His mother was my father's sister."

"Of course," he said vaguely.

"Some people in Springfield say you deserve more credit than any other man in the legislature for moving the capital here. Is that true?"

"No, but I played a part." He thought of a question he could ask. "Are you a Whig, Miss Todd?"

"Oh yes, I'm a violent little Whig. Henry Clay says I can talk politics as well as any man."

"Do you know Henry Clay?"

"He's an old friend of my father. When I was a little girl in Lexington, I used to sit on his knee and promise to marry him when he becomes president—which he will do some day, of course."

This was an astounding piece of information.

"You are from Kentucky as well, Mr. Lincoln?"

"Yes, but I did a good bit of my growing up in Indiana."

"I believe that a Kentuckian remains a Kentuckian, however far he may roam. Don't you agree?"

"I believe anything you say, Miss Todd."

"In that case, we shall be very good friends, Mr. Lincoln," she laughed.

Abraham peppered Josh with questions as they walked home in the moonlight.

"What is she doing here?"

"Looking for a husband, I imagine."

"What do you mean?"

"These Todd women have a habit of coming to Springfield for their men. After Elizabeth moved here with Ninian, she brought her sister Frances up from Lexington and married her off to Bill Wallace. Now I suppose it's Mary's turn."

Josh told him all he knew. Mary Todd was the daughter of a prosperous banker, the offspring of one of the most distinguished families in the Bluegrass State. Her grandfather, General Levi Todd, had been among the first settlers to cross the Appalachians and became a founding father of Lexington. Mary grew up in luxury, attending the best private academies. She even knew how to speak French. Now she was in Springfield, paying her sister an extended visit.

"Are you interested in her?" Josh asked.

The question pained Abraham. He thought of Ann in her grave.

"No, just curious. Anyway, a girl like her could never be interested in me."

"I don't know about that. She seemed plenty willing to talk to you."

They climbed the stairs to their room, tossed off their good clothes, and slung themselves into bed.

"I hear she's a real Kentucky wildcat," Josh said as he blew out the lamp.

He saw her again at a party the political class of Springfield threw to celebrate the legislature's first session in town. An orchestra composed of three fiddlers perched on stools at the front of the columned ballroom in the new American House hotel, the grandest in town. They lashed at the strings like drovers encouraging stubborn beasts and prodded the dancers into wide swings, sashays, and do-si-dos.

Abraham stood in a corner with a knot of men, joking and keeping one eye on a pink organdy-and-lace gown whirling across the floor. Mary Todd was without a doubt the belle of the ball. Stephen Douglas, Josh Speed, and Billy Herndon took turns dancing with her. Half the men in the room, and three-quarters of the women, watched her glide past.

"Mary could make a bishop forget his prayers," Ninian Edwards said.

Abraham got up his nerve and pushed himself forward.

"Miss Todd," he said, bending low, "I want to dance with you in the worst way."

"Mr. Lincoln, I have been hoping that you could pull yourself away from your cronies to dance with me."

The orchestra heaved into "Leather Breeches," and the dancers lined up for the Virginia Reel, men on one side and women on the other, partners opposite each other. Each couple curtseyed and bowed, joined hands to whirl around, then took turns reeling down the center between the two lines. Abraham loped through the figures as best he could, worrying that he was being too rough as he swung Mary about. He was glad when the thing was over.

Mary, exhilarated by the spinning and reeling, gave him a jaunty curtsey.

"Well, Mr. Lincoln, you have certainly achieved your ambition. You have danced with me in the worst way."

She said it without malice, so he laughed.

"I've never danced much except behind a plow," he admitted.

"I've always believed that dancing is poetry in motion. We did not make a very good poem, but I enjoy doggerel as much as Shakespeare, don't you?"

He nodded and took the plunge.

"Miss Todd, may I pay you a visit tomorrow?"

"I wish you would. I would like to know you better, Mr. Lincoln."

Another dance started up, and she was gone with another partner.

He retreated to his corner, shocked at his success. Billy Herndon sidled up to him, looking unhappy.

"Did you come out in one piece?" he asked Abraham.

"What do you mean?"

"After I danced with Miss Todd, I told her that she could glide through a waltz with the ease of a serpent. I meant it as a compliment. She didn't take it that way, and she let me know it."

Abraham laughed. "Billy, that is an unfortunate turn of phrase to use on any female. As the good Lord said to the serpent, 'Because thou hast done this, thou art cursed above every beast of the field.'"

"I reckon I am. That woman's tongue is as sharp as a serpent's tooth."

The next afternoon he walked to the Edwards house, alone this time. A housemaid met him at the door and showed him into the big parlor, where he sat on a black horsehair sofa for thirty minutes, then forty-five. He was beginning to wonder if he was welcome when Mary breezed into the room, apologizing and looking glad to see him.

"I hope we did not wear you out at the cotillion last night," Abraham said. It was a line he had planned on the way over.

"I don't look worn out, do I?"

"No ma'am, you look as fresh as a Sunday morning."

She sat on the sofa, hands resting easily in her lap. He noticed that her nose turned up a bit, just enough to be appealing.

"How do you like Springfield, Miss Todd?"

"It's a charming place. I've never encountered more kindness. Almost all the ladies have called and extended an invitation to spend an evening with them."

He looked down at his big, raw-boned hands.

"And what about you Mr. Lincoln? How do you like practicing law with my cousin?"

"I like it very much. I'm lucky he took me as his partner."

"Has he sent any news from Washington?"

"Only that he has arrived and is finding his sea legs on the ship of state. I expect we'll correspond regularly about business and politics while he's there."

He put his hands under his knees.

"What do you think about Mr. Harrison's chances to become president?" she asked.

"I believe he has as good a chance as Mr. Van Buren."

He was not used to talking politics with women and did not know how far he should take it.

"Henry Clay deserved the nomination!" she exclaimed with genuine passion.

"Perhaps his day will come. I hope so."

"I am quite devastated that the Whigs did not nominate him. If more southern states had bothered to send delegates to the convention in Harrisburg, he would be our nominee."

"You have been reading the *Register*, Miss Todd."

"I read all the newspapers. I was raised on politics in Lexington."

A curtain of silence fell between them, but she brushed it aside.

"And what are your plans, Mr. Lincoln?"

"My plans?"

"Will you run for Congress after John Stuart has had his turn?"

"I don't think I'm fit for such high office."

"Of course you are. You've already made a name for yourself as a legislator."

"There's a far distance between the Illinois House and the United States Congress."

"What does that matter?"

"I'm of humble origins, Miss Todd."

"You're talking nonsense, Mr. Lincoln. Those things might matter back East, but not here in the West."

"I hope that's true."

"Look at Steve Douglas. He arrived in Illinois with almost nothing and came within thirty-six votes of going to Congress. He has no intention of letting one loss sink him into obscurity."

"That is surely true."

"Well, there you have it. You should go as far, or farther. I'm sure you'll be elected to Washington. If I can believe it, can you?"

"Miss Todd, I believe that you could charm the husk right off the corn."

They sat on the black horsehair sofa and talked for the rest of the afternoon. Mary led the conversation, hopping cheerfully from subject to subject like a sparrow on a crisp spring morning. When Abraham rose to leave, she gave him her hand and a warm smile.

"Promise to pay me another visit soon."

"I will."

"Good. I will be on the wing of expectation."

He stepped from the glow of the parlor into the dusk of a still December evening. Overhead, the first star of the night hung out its lantern. A flock of geese, roused by distant urgings, took flight across silver-black prairies. The world again looked as wide and open as a night on a big river.

CHAPTER 32

December 1839 to November 1840

Abraham was drawn into a social set that included Springfield's most promising young men and prettiest young women. They called themselves the Coterie, and the Edwardses' hilltop mansion served as their headquarters for evening gatherings. From there they moved along a circuit of the best parties, dances, and dinners in the capital city. Abraham realized that Mary's influence had gained him admission into this clique. The others readily accepted him, partly because of his rise as a Whig leader and partly because they genuinely liked him.

A troupe of actors came through Springfield, and several of the young people went to see *The First Part of King Henry IV*. Abraham and Mary sat next to each other, and afterwards, they spent a long time laughing over Sir John Falstaff's charades.

When the first snows of winter arrived on the prairies, the Coterie took a moonlight sleigh ride. The Edwards horses kicked up bursts of frozen spray, and the sleigh left long white tracks like the wake of a sailing ship. Abraham, sitting next to Mary, pulled a blanket over her shoulders and cupped her gloved hands in his.

Warmer weather brought a circus to town, with an elephant, a giraffe, and a Bengal tiger. A horseman caught an orange on the tip of his sword while he stood on his saddle and rode around a ring. A learned pig told time, and a clown showed off a parrot that sang "Yankee Doodle" and pulled a string to fire a miniature cannon that shot paper flowers into the air.

Before long, Abraham was skipping the gatherings with the fellows at Speed's store to go sit on the horsehair sofa in the Edwards parlor.

They told each other about their pasts. Mary's mother had died when she was only six years old, and her father had quickly remarried. When she was eight, the age at which Abraham's father had first put an ax in his hands, she had entered Ward's Female Academy in Lexington. Later she attended Madame Mentelle's boarding school, where French was spoken and young ladies learned proper etiquette. About the time Abraham had arrived in New Salem like a piece of floating driftwood, Mary was visiting Henry Clay's mansion, Ashland, to show him her new white pony.

He discovered that she was an ardent admirer of Robert Burns. They recited his verses to each other in Scottish brogue.

Flow gently, sweet Afton, among thy green braes!
Flow gently, I'll sing thee a song in thy praise!
My Mary's asleep by thy murmuring stream—
Flow gently, sweet Afton, disturb not her dream!

The year 1840 brought a rip-roaring presidential campaign. The Democrats ran Martin Van Buren for a second term in the White

House. The Whigs put up William Henry Harrison, hero of the Battle of Tippecanoe, which had brought the defeat of the Shawnee chief Tecumseh. The old general's running mate was John Tyler of Virginia, an ex-Democrat who had broken away from Andy Jackson and his gang.

The Whigs proclaimed that Van Buren was a low-down, corrupt rascal responsible for every ill the country had known. Harrison Reform Clubs handed out pins that read "Tippecanoe and Tyler too!" They pushed a huge tin-and-paper ball covered with Harrison slogans from town to town and told each other to "keep the ball rolling."

Acres of men marched, marched, marched, shouting, "Without a why or a wherefore, we'll go for Harrison therefore!" Whig ladies rode floats, waving handkerchiefs and wearing sashes that read "Whig Husbands or None" across their breasts.

A convention of Illinois Whigs placed Abraham on a committee to organize campaign activities. He plunged into the fray, drawing up a plan to get out the vote.

"We're going to make sure we get every last Whig in this state to the polls," he told Mary.

He stumped for Harrison throughout the summer and fall, riding through swamp and prairie to speak at barbecues and log raisings. In some places he spoke alone; in others he debated a Democrat, often Stephen Douglas. At times he stuck to issues, but often he just slung mud.

"A great volcano at Washington, aroused and directed by the evil spirit that reigns there, is belching forth the lava of political corruption!" he told Whig crowds. "It is sweeping with frightful velocity over the whole length and breadth of the land, leaving unscathed no green spot or living thing!"

"Lincoln for Congress!" some shouted. "Abe for governor!"

"Laying it on a bit thick, ain't you?" a farmer asked him.

"We must fight the devil with fire," Abraham said, grinning.

When he spoke near Springfield, Mary came to listen and offer encouragement. In his rare free moments, he walked to the Edwards mansion to sit with her on the horsehair sofa.

"I see in the newspapers that you've become one of the leading Whig spokesmen in Illinois," she said.

"Where did you read that?"

"In the Democrats' papers. They're calling you a long-legged rascal. They wouldn't bother to insult you if you weren't having success."

It pleased him to know that she was following his political career.

"I'm heading out again tomorrow," he said.

"Where to this time?"

"Tremont. Another barbecue. I swear that half the hogs in this state have given their lives in the cause of electing a president."

"And I suppose that every town and hamlet rounds up a bevy of young Whig maidens in white dresses to welcome the speaker?"

"No matter how large the crowd, Miss Todd, it is still lonely without you."

"Good," she laughed. "A girl likes to hear that all is gloom and darkness without her."

Northwest of Springfield, some of Abraham's old friends from New Salem came out to hear him speak. Jack Armstrong and several of the Clary's Grove Boys were there.

"Mighty fine speechifying, Abe," Jack told him afterwards. "But what we want to know is, can you throw this cannonball further than we can? If you can, maybe we'll vote for your man."

Abraham hefted the ball. "Well, boys, if that's all I have to do, I'll get your votes."

He swung it around and gave it a good pitch. It landed six feet farther than any other throw.

"That's a foot for every foot of me," he said. "That should be worth a half dozen votes."

"We'll see what we can do."

William Henry Harrison rolled to victory in November 1840. Mary was as exhilarated as Abraham. They sat on the porch at the Edwards house, gloating over the Whig victory while an orange moon sat like a fat pumpkin atop the prairie.

"Did you miss me while you were on the stump, Mr. Lincoln?"

"I did. Talking with you is a whole lot nicer than arguing politics in a cornfield with Steve Douglas while a bunch of farmers spit tobacco juice at our boots."

"Mr. Douglas would probably agree with you about that. He says I am one of his favorite conversationalists."

"Douglas and I agree on little."

"But on that point, at least?"

"Yes, though he is not here to be agreeable, and I'm glad of that."

"Glad to be rid of his company?"

"Glad to have you to myself."

She smiled.

"What about you, Mary? Did you miss me?"

"Women do not miss men. We collect them like pearls on a string. When one falls away, we look for another to replace it."

"What happens if a fallen bead comes rolling back?"

"It depends on its luster. We might pick it up again, just to keep it dangling on our string."

"Well, I reckon dangling on a string still beats dodging tobacco spit with Douglas."

She pulled her cloak tight against the chilly autumn air.

"Tell me, Abraham, what kind of pearl do you think I prize most?"

"I can't say."

"Can you not draw some conclusions?"

"I suppose you want someone who can give you the things you are accustomed to having," he said evasively.

"You surely don't think I would marry for money!"

"I didn't mean that."

"I hope not. I can tell you this: my hand will never be given where my heart is not."

He wondered if she could give her heart to the plainest-looking man in Springfield.

"Besides," she went on, "I would rather marry a man who has a good mind and bright prospects ahead than marry all the gold in the world." She met his gaze. "What about you, Mr. Lincoln? What sort of woman are you hoping to find?"

"I don't know," he stumbled. "I guess one who possesses a congenial mind."

"That does not tell me much. Do you want a woman who is tall, like you? A redhead, or one with light hair and fair skin? Do you prefer girls from the North, or the South? You must give me particulars."

He squirmed, unable to find a place for his long arms and legs.

"Mary, I would give anything to have a woman like you!" he blurted.

"Now, that is the kind of answer a girl likes to hear. For a moment you had me wondering why we are sitting here on my sister's porch, talking pearls and politics by moonlight."

That night he talked it over with Josh.

"She as good as said she would have me if I made an offer. At least, I believe she did."

"You're not sure?"

"Yes, I'm sure," he said, pacing the bedroom. "I'm sure."

"Then the question is: Would you be happy with her?"

"Why wouldn't I be? I'd be lucky to have a woman like her."

"Lucky is one thing, happy another," Josh said. "Let's approach it another way. What elements of your character are compatible with hers?"

"We both prize learning, to begin with."

"That's true."

"We share a passion for poetry and politics."

"Yes, she's one of those women always crowding into the *Journal* office to get the latest campaign news."

"We're both Kentuckians by birth."

"Are there any differences in your characters, ones that would cause unhappiness?"

"She comes from a more refined background and has more education. But that doesn't seem to bother her."

"Anything else?"

Abraham seized a poker and jabbed at the logs in the fireplace. "She can dance well. I cannot," he said finally.

"If your prospects depend on your ability to dance, you'll never be married."

"That's true."

Abraham put down the poker and wrestled with his hair.

"Speed, she has wit, beauty, and charm. She has ambitions for me to succeed in life. She comes from one of Kentucky's great families and is connected to one of the first families of Illinois. It's difficult for me to believe that marriage to such a woman could do me anything but good."

"It would be a good match, provided you love her."

He thought about her as the autumn days passed while he drafted pleadings in his office and whacked a handball with friends against a brick wall in an alley near the public square. He tried to imagine life with Mary Todd. With her at his side, he would surely prosper. Maybe he would serve a term or two in Congress, and they would go to Washington together.

He thought about what life with Ann might have been like. Perhaps they would have stayed in New Salem and built a cabin there. Part of him felt guilty that another had come along to replace her, but he knew it was time to let her go. Marriage to Ann was not meant to be, and this was.

It's more than a good match for me, he told himself. It's an opportunity I can't afford to turn down.

One evening, as shadows crept onto the square, he closed his office, walked to the Edwards house, and told Mary he could not be happy without her. He would devote himself to taking care of her and never cease as long as he lived.

Before he finished, she threw herself into his arms, burying her face in his chest. He pulled her close, astonished to discover she could want him so much.

CHAPTER 33

December 1840 to January 1841

Almost immediately, he wondered if he had made a terrible mistake. The doubts began as he escorted Mary to a party at the home of Virgil Hickox, a prosperous businessman who lived in a fashionable neighborhood south of the public square.

"Someday we'll have a home like this, perhaps on this very street," Mary whispered as they climbed the front steps.

The absurdity of the idea hit him like a log in a flooding stream. He spent the evening wandering the parlor, taking note of the fine carpet and chairs from Philadelphia. The clock on the mantel looked like it might cost a whole month of his income. Mary stood with a cluster of friends, showing off a new party frock her father had sent from

Lexington. How was he going to afford this kind of pampered lifestyle?

The next morning he sat in his office, brooding over the problem. His income was respectable now, more than a thousand dollars a year. But he couldn't count on it. Who knew how long his partnership with Stuart would last? His salary as a state legislator was even more uncertain. There was no telling when a man might be voted out of office. And he still hadn't paid off all his debt from the New Salem store.

She had said she would never marry for money. But how would she react when she realized that it would be her doom to see others throwing parties in fancy houses and flourishing about in carriages that her husband couldn't afford? Even if he could afford it, he would never feel at ease in refined surroundings.

Another thought worried him, a darker one. From the beginning, he had been impressed with the Todd name and Mary's connection to the Edwardses. Marriage into such clans brought obvious political and business advantages. Was that why he had pursued the match?

His doubts multiplied over the next few days when he looked at other women. Beautiful girls seemed to flock to Springfield, especially during the social season, when the legislature went into session. Mary Todd was pretty in her own way, but next to some of them, she seemed almost plain. For the first time, he asked himself what she would look like in a dozen years.

If I'm going to be in love, he wondered, shouldn't I love a woman who strikes my heart the instant I lay eyes on her?

He decided to get Josh's advice.

"I'm feeling like a treed coon," he confessed. "I don't think I love her as I should."

"Now's a fine time to think of that. If you don't love her, why did you commit yourself to her?"

"Maybe I reasoned myself into it. I'm beginning to think my affection for her is the work of my head, not my heart."

"Are you sure you're not reasoning yourself *out* of it?"

"No, I'm not sure."

Panic set in.

"Speed, it would just kill me to marry her. I think I should call it off."

He began dropping hints when he was with her. He mentioned his worries about supporting her, but she cheerfully turned them aside.

"Mary, I can't support you, or any woman, the way I'd like," he warned. "Not for a long time."

"Oh, I don't care about that." She smiled.

"But you grew up with silver and servants and fine furnishings. You're not used to hardship."

"You are forgetting that, like you, I come from Kentucky pioneer stock. I'm not a delicate blossom that's going to shatter if you expose me to the rays of the prairie sun for a while."

"I'm not very good at growing things."

"Think of me as a thistle," she said gaily. "I will flourish wherever I land."

The more she brushed off his concerns, the more convinced he became that their engagement was a disaster in the making. He decided to explain it in a letter. He spent three days agonizing over it, writing and rewriting that his shortcomings would only make her miserable, that he wasn't certain of his own feelings, and that he wished to release her from any understanding they had reached. He gave the letter to Josh.

"Speed, I'd like you to deliver this to Mary," he said.

Josh read it and shook his head.

"I'm not giving her that."

"Why not?"

"It's not the right way to handle the matter."

Josh crumpled the paper and threw it into the fire. Abraham made no effort to save it.

"Go see her yourself. Tell her what you said in the letter. You can do that. Be careful not to say too much, and then leave at the first opportunity."

He buttoned his coat and headed through cold winds to the Edwards mansion. A servant ushered him into the parlor, fragrant with greens and spiced candles. Mary's face clouded over when she saw him.

"Abraham, you look terrible! Sit down and tell me what's troubling you."

They sat on the horsehair sofa. Dead silence for a moment while he gathered his courage. He ran his fingers through his hair.

"I've thought this over carefully," he said. "I don't see how we can be married."

For an instant she looked frightened.

"What on earth are you talking about? Are you still worried about money?"

"I just want to protect you from a fate you don't deserve."

She gazed full into his face, searching.

"Do you regret courting me?"

"No, of course not."

She smiled but looked unsure.

"Abraham, do you love me?"

He flinched and looked away.

"Do you love me?" she repeated.

"I don't know if I love you as I should," he stammered.

She looked at him in terror.

"Do you mean you don't love me at all?"

She jumped up, wringing her hands.

"Mary," he said softly.

She turned her back. Her small frame shook with quiet sobs. He reached to touch her, but she shivered and drew away.

"Mary, I didn't mean . . ."

She clutched herself, rocking back and forth and moaning faintly. Her head drooped, and her shoulders trembled. It was unbearable.

He reached again and drew her to him. The next thing he knew, he was calling her name and covering her face with kisses.

He walked back to Speed's store full of chagrin and told his friend what had happened.

"You kissed her?" Josh asked incredulously. "That's your idea of breaking it off?"

"I didn't know what else to do. I thought she was going to collapse on the floor like a sack of broken sticks." He shoved his feet toward the fireplace and regarded them ruefully.

"It sounds like you did nothing but renew the engagement."

"Well, if I'm in again, so be it," Abraham muttered. "It's done, and I'll abide by it."

The next morning he arrived at his office and found a note from Mary on his desk. He took it to the window to read in clear light. In neat, fine script, she told him she realized he had experienced a change of heart. Her own feelings had not changed, yet she would not hold him against his will. Although he was in honor bound to marry her, she would release him from their engagement with all the fullness of her heart.

He leaned against the windowsill. Relief surged over him. His first thought was to run and find Speed to tell him the news. He went to his desk to read it a second time, to make sure he understood her right. There was no doubt about it. She was granting the release he wanted.

His eyes stumbled on a phrase near the end.

"Although you are in honor bound to marry me . . ."

That bothered him. He frowned, leaned forward, and read the words again: *in honor bound.*

He never fully understood what happened next, though afterwards he told himself it must have had something to do with the weather. The thermometer plunged to twelve degrees below zero, and his spirits dropped with the temperature. Piercing winds swept the prairies. Gray clouds hung in every direction.

He brooded over Mary, worried that he would meet her on the street, wondered what he should say. Word reached him that Elizabeth and Ninian Edwards were furious at the way he had treated her. Perhaps they were right. The memory of her sobbing filled him with agony.

He did not want to be around people, did not want to hear them ask about her. The legislature went into session, but he could not bring himself to be interested in politics. For several days he did nothing but go to his office, sink exhausted into a chair, and sit alone with his thoughts. When he imagined the Coterie making the rounds of parties, whispering over parlor tables about the demise of his courtship, he burned with shame.

Had he acted dishonorably? The thought tormented him as much as the knowledge that he had hurt her. But how could he marry someone who wasn't right for him? He was beginning to think he would never be satisfied with anyone blockheaded enough to have him.

His head ached. He threw on his coat, stomped outside, and wandered restlessly for hours in the cold. The exercise of walking helped ease the pain in his temples, but the snow-clad prairies filled him with dread. Blue shadows on drifts troubled him, and ice caked on black fence rails hinted of sorrow. The muteness of the landscape seemed unfriendly. When he returned to town, looking grizzled and half-frozen, his friends peered at him like something was wrong.

He was horrified when thoughts of death came to him. As he was whetting a knife, he paused to examine its edge, and it occurred to him that it was sharp enough to slice an artery with one effortless stroke.

Dreams came to him in the night. He had visions of a white moth flying into a cabin, of muddy waters covering the deck of a flatboat. Each image undoubtedly carried a message, and he spent long hours trying to search out their meanings.

The dreams turned into nightmares. He dreamed that he was insane, raving in the forest. His arms were caught in burning chains, and he thrashed to get loose. He leapt from a high brink and wallowed in the Sangamon, weeping and laughing. In his dream Speed came to force him down and hold him under the water. He woke to find Josh standing over him, putting a damp cloth on his forehead.

"What happened?" Abraham gasped. His voice came out barely a whisper.

"You've been crazy as a loon the last couple of days."

"Two days?"

"Three, actually. Tossing around and babbling with no sense at all. Anson Henry has been looking in on you. He said to get him when you came out of it."

He lay in bed, listening to sleet and freezing rain pelt the window while Josh went to get the doctor. Someone, he noticed, had taken all the knives and razors out of the room.

Dr. Henry arrived to look him over.

"I was worried about you," he said. "You came within an inch of being a perfect lunatic for life."

He made a diagnosis of hypochondriasis, which his medical textbook described as "a disease attacking men of melancholy temperament."

"We'll have to plumb your system. Clean out your liver, gallbladder, and such. We'll start by bleeding you."

For the next week, Abraham spent several hours a day in the doctor's office, undergoing the treatment's assault. After the bleeding, Dr. Henry gave him foul-tasting medicines to induce vomiting and diarrhea. Next came fasting, along with warm baths to induce sweat. Once the body was emptied of poisonous contents, the doctor prescribed large doses of ginger, mustard rubs, and cold baths.

"What are my friends saying about me?" Abraham asked Speed.

"They're saying you had two cat fits and a duck fit, and they're asking if you've gone crazy."

Abraham winced.

"To be honest, I'm worried that if you don't rally, you'll die," Josh warned.

"I'd be more than willing to die if I'd done something to make any human being remember me."

"I'm not likely to forget the sight of your big ugly feet sticking over the end of Anson Henry's sickbed. I hope that doesn't count."

He lay in the bed above Josh's store, staring out the window and plumbing his insides farther than Dr. Henry's remedies could reach, searching for a deep spot of resilience.

"Don't worry, Speed," he grumbled. "I plan to be around until I know the world is a little better off for my having lived in it."

CHAPTER 34

Early 1841 to Latter 1841

He emerged from Dr. Henry's treatment looking emaciated and spent. The worst of his depression was over, but the world seemed tinged with sadness. Some days he thought he must be the most miserable man living.

"If what I feel were equally distributed to the whole human family, there would not be one cheerful face on the earth," he grumbled to Josh.

He threw himself into work. The chance came along to start a new practice with Stephen T. Logan, one of Illinois's most prominent attorneys. He hated to leave John Stuart. After all, the chivalrous Kentuckian had given him his start. But Stuart was gone politicking half the time, and this was an opportunity too good to pass up. The office of Stuart

& Lincoln closed its doors, and the firm of Logan & Lincoln took up residence in a room on the other side of Fifth Street.

Nine years Abraham's senior, Logan was a man of careless and even shabby appearance. He wore a rumpled coat and baggy pants, and tobacco juice streaked his chin. But he possessed a superb legal mind. Exactitude and thorough preparation were his standards.

"Diligence is what you want," he advised. "Diligence is the leading rule for the lawyer, as it is for every man in every calling."

He whittled as he spoke, each stroke of the knife precise and controlled.

"Learn all there is to know about a case at hand before you stand before a judge. Study it out until you've mastered its every aspect and see clearly every principle involved."

The Illinois Supreme Court kept a treasure trove of legal reports and reference books in its library at the new statehouse building. Abraham kept the lamps burning there, searching for precedents, learning to dissect each case to find the strongest point for his client and the weakest point in his opponent's argument. It was slow going, but he liked it.

"I like to dig up a question by the roots and hold it up to dry before the fires of my mind," he told Speed.

The work made a plaster for his melancholy, though there were still times when he sank into gloom. The state's economy took a nosedive, and he realized with mortification that it was caused in no small part by too much spending on all the roads and canals that he and his fellow politicians had promised. Bad news came from Washington. President Harrison, the great hope of the Whigs, assumed office by standing in a cold wind outside the United States Capitol to deliver a two-hour inaugural address. A month later, he was dead of pneumonia. His successor, John Tyler, abandoned the agenda the Whigs had worked so hard for.

Josh added to Abraham's woes when he confessed that he had been contemplating a move.

"I'm thinking of going back home to Louisville," he said.

"What?"

"Mother wants me at home to help manage affairs."

Speed's father had died the previous spring, and his mother was struggling to run the family plantation.

"When would you go?"

"As soon as I can sell my interest in the store."

Abraham sank into a chair.

"You're my closest friend. How am I going to get along without you?"

"I wouldn't go if I could avoid it."

"This is how miserably things are arranged in this world," Abraham groaned. "If we have no friends, we have no pleasure. If we have them, we're sure to lose them and be doubly pained by the loss."

Spring arrived in central Illinois, and Josh departed for Louisville. The two friends stood on Fifth Street, clasped hands, and said their goodbyes.

"Write often," Josh said.

"I will."

"Promise you won't let your spirits get low."

"I reckon I'll just have to make up my mind to be cheerful."

Abraham headed onto the prairies for the spring round of circuit courts. Untangling knotty legal disputes was a good distraction. His practice was growing, and the farmers, millers, and shopkeepers who engaged his services treated him like a friend. In the falling-out of neighbors over the sale of a diseased horse, or the case of a widow who refused to pay a debt her husband left behind, he began to learn the hearts of a stubborn, spirited people.

As he rode from courthouse to courthouse under a fine clear sky, he counted his blessings and resolved not to sink into depression again. But whenever he thought of Mary, he couldn't help feeling regret over the way he had treated her.

Troubling news came from his stepbrother, John, who wrote to inform him that Tom Lincoln had fallen into financial difficulty. Debts were pressing on him, and he could use help. Abraham sighed as he read the letter.

I'm not yet out of debt myself, he thought. Must I now provide a patrimony for my father?

A few weeks later, while he was in Coles County on legal business, he went to see his family. The Lincoln farm crouched on the edge of Goosenest Prairie, about eight miles south of Charleston. The saddlebag cabin, its hewn logs gray-bitten by hard sun, boasted two rooms joined by a double fireplace and chimney, each room with its own ladder rising to a loft above the ceiling. A log barn, smokehouse, and root cellar huddled like ovenbirds beneath oaks and hickories, as if worried that a storm blowing off the prairie would come and sweep them away. Chickens and geese wandered the yard, pecking at the dirt.

He's no better off than he was thirty years ago back in Kentucky, Abraham thought as he rode up to the place.

He found his stepmother alone in the cabin, stirring a pot. Her face lit up when he ducked through the door.

"Abe! My boy!"

She pulled him down to look into his face, her blue-gray eyes as strong and clear as ever. It was good to feel her arms around his shoulders again. He was glad he had come.

"I brought a few things," he said, pulling three store-bought handkerchiefs and a breastpin from his bag. She welcomed them with the pleasure that only a son's gift to a mother can bring.

"What have you been eating?" she asked. "If you get much leaner, you'll have to put on a coat to make a shadow."

"I've been subsisting on savory remembrances of your corn pones."

"Then sit down and let me fatten you up." She heaped ham, potatoes, and corn bread onto a plate.

"How are you faring?" he asked as he chewed.

"Tolerably comfortable. We've got a legion of mouths to feed, but hands to help with the feeding, thank the Lord."

Besides Tom and Sally Lincoln, twelve people called the cabin home, including Sally's son, John Johnston; his wife, Mary; Sally's daughter, Tildy; her husband, Squire Hall; and eight children between them, with more on the way. Sally did not seem to mind the cramped quarters.

"I never want to move again," she said. "We moved so much, I began to think we were the children of Israel trying to find the Promised Land." She went back to stirring her pot. "What about you, Abe? How are you getting along?"

"Happy as a hog in slop," he lied.

"Does your work go well?"

"Tolerably well."

"And your politicking?"

"It ain't got me hung yet."

"How are those Springfield ladies treating you?"

Color flooded his cheeks. "I'm not ready to tie myself to the hitching post, if that's what you mean."

"Well, you'll know when you're ready," she said, and let the subject drop.

Tildy and Mary appeared with the younger children, back from hunting nuts in the woods. The little ones crawled into Abraham's lap and onto his shoulders, calling him Uncle Abe. He pulled out some rock candy he had brought. His father, John, and Squire came in from the fields with the older boys, all of them sweaty and dirty. One by one they clasped his hand, offering hearty, open-face smiles. Only his father seemed awkward and quiet, his eyes wandering the cabin walls as if vexed over something he had misplaced.

Abraham had a second helping of ham and potatoes with them. Nothing is changed at all, he thought as he listened to the talk of stray cows and sick sheep. It's no different than it was back at Little Pigeon Creek. Same food, same cooking, same blessing—"Oh Lord, fit and prepare us for life's humblest service, for Christ's sake, Amen." Same butter churn near the door. Spinning wheel, corner cabinet, chest of drawers with lantern and wash basin on top. Same chair where Sally liked to sit while she knitted and sewed. Same whitewashed walls and yawning hole in the ceiling with dark loft above—all unchanging as the endless prairie.

After dinner, the men went outside to squat on stools and discuss Tom's debt problem. There was no careless spending or rash misstep behind it, just a gradual failing to keep up with the demands of daily subsistence.

"Everything I ever touched either died, got killed, or was lost," Tom complained. "I'm unlucky at picking land. This soil's too poor to even raise a fuss."

Abraham knew it wasn't true. His father worked hard enough, and the land was fine. But he was trying to farm the way men farmed two decades ago. He wanted nothing to do with the latest methods, like deep plowing and applying the right kinds of manure. No wonder he couldn't keep up. There was no use trying to tell him. It would just start a row.

"It's the hand of Providence laid upon me," Tom lamented. "The hand of Providence."

Well, that much may be true, Abraham thought.

The next morning, he rode with his parents to see David Dryden, the justice of the peace, who lived about a mile north of the Lincolns. There Abraham purchased, for two hundred dollars, forty acres of Tom's 120-acre farm. Tom signed the document Abraham had written, and Sally made her mark. The terms of sale stated his parents would have use and control of the land for the rest of their lives. They all knew the two hundred dollars was really a gift, money Tom could use to pay off his debts.

Abraham spent the afternoon splitting new rails for his stepmother's vegetable garden. Dennis Hanks, who had given up farming to become a cobbler in Charleston, came by to say hello. It was good to hear his laugh.

"How does it feel to be working at your old chores?" his cousin ribbed him.

"It feels good to know I don't have to do them if I don't want."

"Still reading your books, Abe?"

"The things I want to know are in books, Denny. My best friend is a man who can get me a book."

"I swear there's something peculiarsome about you, Abe," Dennis laughed. "Mighty peculiarsome."

He rose early the next morning to set out for Springfield. Sally pulled him aside and gave him a big slice of apple honey cake she'd wrapped for the trip home.

"We're grateful to you, Abe," she said, tears in her eyes.

"He could make more of a go of this place," he said, trying not to sound grudging. "I know farms in Sangamon County that get twice the yield with half the acres."

"Your father has gotten pretty set in his ways."

"Always has been."

"Tom Lincoln's a good man. He's never turned a dog from his door."

"I suppose that's true."

"Take care of yourself, son."

"I will, Mama."

The sun climbed the rim of the prairie, pushing back the dark folds of the predawn hours. Gray light washed over the ungainly barn and cabin. It all looked so remote and squalid. A shudder of loneliness passed over him. He knew that a gulf had opened between him and his family in just a few short years, a divide of his own making, and that it would never be bridged. No doubt they sensed it too. He made up his mind that neither his father nor mother should ever want for anything. He would see to that. But as he turned his horse onto the road, he was relieved to make his escape.

CHAPTER 35

Latter 1841 to September 1842

He stayed busy with work as the months flowed along, sometimes passing quickly, sometimes barely trickling forward.

He went out of his way to avoid Mary, but every once in a while, he heard someone mention that she had attended a party or joined a group of friends on an excursion and had enjoyed herself. That was good. The thought that he had made her unhappy still troubled him. Once he saw her walking down Fifth Street arm in arm with Stephen Douglas, and he ducked into his office to get out of their way. Douglas was overly ambitious, and Abraham didn't like to see him flirting with her.

He took some time off to visit Josh at his family home in Kentucky, near Louisville. For three weeks he marveled at the Speeds' white-columned mansion.

"I have my own room?" he asked, incredulous, when Josh set his bag beside a large feather bed.

"All yours. Get yourself settled, and we'll get something to eat."

"Speed, our whole cabin at Little Pigeon Creek could fit into this one room, with acreage to spare."

A small army of house slaves waited on him, including his own personal servant, who brought him coffee and emptied his chamber pot every morning. The idea of someone hovering at the edge of the room, waiting to take care of his every need, made him uneasy. More slaves toiled in the plantation's hemp field, getting ready for the fall harvest. It brought back unpleasant memories of the slave market in New Orleans and slave hunters in Indiana.

Josh introduced him to a girl he was falling in love with, a spirited beauty named Fanny Henning, who lived nearby. Seeing them together made Abraham envious. Josh's mother, sensing his melancholy, gave him an Oxford Bible and said it could help him obtain release from his troubles. He promised to read it often, but he found little time for it when he got back to Springfield.

Bowling Green died. The bighearted, potbellied justice of the peace who had urged Abraham to run for the statehouse and encouraged his study of the law collapsed at a game of quoits. He lingered for a few hours, unconscious, then was gone.

Abraham rode out to New Salem for the funeral. It made him sad to see that the village by the Sangamon was dying as well, condemned by the failure of the little river to carry steamboat traffic. One by one, its residents had moved away to more promising towns. Only a handful remained, near-ghosts haunting deserted cabins.

Later that year, he got himself into a political brawl by insulting the state auditor, a hotheaded Democrat named James Shields, in letters to the *Sangamo Journal*. He wrote the letters anonymously—a tactic politicians sometimes used to take shots at each other in print.

It was the most fun he had had in months. "Shields is a fool as well as a liar," he wrote. "With him the truth is out of the question, and as for getting a good bright passable lie out of him, you might as well try to strike fire from a cake of tallow."

He was in Tremont on legal business a few days later when his friends Ned Baker and Simeon Francis, editor of the *Journal*, showed up at the courthouse. They both looked like they had come a long way in a hurry.

"Hello, boys. What brings you out to the wilds of Tazewell County?"

"Jimmie Shields is right behind us," Francis panted. "He's mad as a hornet about those letters." Baker nodded in confirmation.

"What does he want from me?"

"He says he knows you wrote them, and he wants satisfaction."

Abraham winced. Shields has hot Irish blood in his veins, he thought. I should have expected him to blow up.

"Where is he?"

"Just up the road. He's got General Whiteside with him to do his talking. We thought you ought to know."

"What do you think I should do?"

"Don't do anything until you know his demands," Baker said.

John Whiteside, the state fund commissioner, arrived and exchanged polite greetings. He handed Abraham a note from Shields and then promptly withdrew.

"It says I've made him the object of slander, vituperation, and personal abuse," Abraham read. "He's demanding an apology. If he doesn't get it, he says there'll be consequences."

Baker and Francis pored over the note. "He's quick to make threats, ain't he?" Francis snorted.

"How should I respond?"

"I sure as hell wouldn't give him the satisfaction of an apology," Baker said. "Tell him he can damn well apologize first for being a fool and a menace."

Abraham paced the courthouse floor. Shields meant to force him into public humiliation. An apology would give the Democrats an excuse to crow that Abraham Lincoln was in the cowardly habit of inflicting personal abuse in anonymous letters to newspapers.

"Do you think Shields wants a duel?" he asked.

"Probably."

"I'm wholly opposed to that," Abraham said. "I'll do just about anything to avoid it. But if the choice is degradation or a fight, I'll fight him."

"The worst thing you can do is let him insult your honor," Baker agreed.

"Jimmie Shields rattles worse than an empty wagon," Francis said. "Write him back and tell him you're not going to put up with his claptrap. At least make him treat you like a gentleman."

Abraham sat at a table and wrote a brief reply, stating that he could not in good conscience discuss the matter if Shields insisted on hurling threats.

Francis read the note with approval. "That should take him down a peg or two."

At sunset Whiteside called again, secured the reply, and went off to give it to Shields.

The next several hours were a blur. Whiteside returned with another note. Baker studied it, debated it with Francis, and advised not answering. A series of hurried conferences followed. The representatives shuttled back and forth according to the protocols demanded by an affair of honor. Appeals were offered in low, strained tones, conditions presented and questioned.

At the final meeting, General Whiteside's face looked weary. He announced that his friend was left with no option but to challenge Mr. Lincoln.

"I still don't believe it will come to violence," Baker said when Whiteside was gone. "But if it does, I'm willing to counsel you as your second."

"That would be helpful," Abraham said weakly.

He rode back to Springfield stunned by the way events had so quickly spun out of control. It looked like it might really come to a duel, despite what Baker said. As soon as he got to town, he went to see John Stuart at his old partner's office.

"Those fool letters I wrote for the *Journal* made Jimmie Shields mad, and he's challenged me. If I have to fight, I'll fight. But I don't want to."

"Has it gone as far as choosing weapons?"

"I'm to choose today. I was thinking about cow dung at five paces." Abraham smiled glumly. "I hear Shields is a good shot with a pistol."

Stuart leaned back, brow creased.

"I know Shields well," he said after a moment, "and his courage is not of the truest stamp. There's too much bluster about the man. You can make him back out if you choose broadswords."

"Broadswords?" That sounded even worse than pistols.

"He'll never fight you with broadswords. You're at least seven inches taller than he is, and your arms are three or four inches longer. You could cut him down before he got near enough to touch you."

"Can he handle a sword?"

"No, not particularly well."

"You think he won't fight?"

"Not with broadswords. He'll show the white feather first."

With Stuart's guidance, he wrote out the stipulations for weapons: cavalry broadswords of the largest size, precisely equal in all respects. The field of honor was to be divided by a plank ten feet long, fixed on its edge on the ground. Neither man was to pass his foot over the plank while dueling. Two parallel lines were to be drawn on the ground, six feet from either side of the plank. If either man retreated behind his line, it would be deemed a surrender.

Dueling was illegal in Illinois, so the contest would take place on Missouri soil, across the Mississippi River from the town of Alton, seventy miles southeast of Springfield.

"Will you come with us?" Abraham asked.

"Yes, and when this is over, I'm going to toss you in the river for being a damned fool."

They set out on the two-day trip to Alton with Ned Baker, going by way of Jacksonville. In the afternoon, the weather was warm and fine for traveling. The prairies rolled gently under the equinox sun and high open sky.

"This reminds me of the Kentuckian who signed up to fight in the War of 1812," Abraham said, trying to sound unconcerned. "When he left home, his sweetheart gave him a bullet pouch and belt to wear in battle. She'd stitched the words *Victory or Death* into the belt. He asked her, 'Ain't that rather strong? Suppose you put *Victory or Be Crippled* instead.'"

When dusk came, a chilly, penetrating wind blew. The men pulled up their collars and lowered their heads. Somewhere down by a creek bottom, a dog wailed, and everything seemed cheerless and empty.

In a short time, if this duel goes forward, I could be dead or mortally wounded, Abraham thought. I'll go out of this world forever. Or perhaps I'll give Shields a mortal wound. If I had to, I could split him open from the crown of his head to the end of his backbone with one of those swords. Then I will have killed a man.

They arrived at Alton to find Shields and his party already there. The state auditor glared at them over a dashing moustache and pugnacious chin. Word of the duel had spread, and an excited crowd gathered along the riverfront.

They boarded a ferry, the two duelists and their retinues sitting at opposite ends of the boat, and started for the Missouri side of the river. Mist hung thick on the water. A solitary crow labored through the air above their heads and disappeared into a fog bank.

On such a day, Abraham thought, Aaron Burr and Alexander Hamilton crossed the Hudson River from New York to New Jersey. Burr shot Hamilton in the abdomen, and Hamilton's friends hurried him back over the river to Manhattan, desperate to save him. He died after thirty hours of pain.

They reached Bloody Island, a low, desolate place named for the many duels fought there, separated from the Missouri shore by a narrow channel. The men climbed a muddy bank to a clearing set among cottonwood and willow trees. Three of them carried a plank ashore and began staking it into place. Baker took the broadswords out of burlap wrapping and presented them to the duelists.

Abraham rolled up his sleeves, pulled his sword from its scabbard, and gently ran his thumb along the blade's edges. He took a few swings to loosen up his arms.

It's not much different from swinging an ax, he told himself. Out of the corner of his eye, he could see Shields, coat off but wearing a bright green vest, rolling up his sleeves as well.

The representatives huddled on the field of honor, deep in negotiation. At this point, both men's friends would do everything they could to patch up the quarrel. Shields was strutting and flashing his sword like he'd rather butt his brains out against a brick wall than give an inch.

This is insane, Abraham thought. I don't want to kill this damned fellow, and I sure as hell don't want him to kill me.

He put the tip of his sword in the ground and watched the arbitrators as they parleyed. A few phrases reached his ears—*satisfactory explanation . . . prevail on Mr. Shields . . . useless to talk*—but for the most part it was impossible to tell what they were saying. Every once in a while, his friends looked over their shoulders at him.

If it comes down to hacking away at each other, maybe it would be better to back down, he thought. The easiest way to end it would be to step behind my line. Then they would say I am a coward.

Nothing about the scene before him seemed real—not the low island shrouded in mist, the long plank staked to the ground, or the shadowy faces gathered around it. Stuart and Baker broke away from the conference and began discussing something in low tones. After a moment they rejoined the group. Stuart stroked the air with his hands as he talked, like a man trying to put a baby to sleep.

Abraham stepped under a willow tree and, stretching as high as he could with his sword, lopped off the end of a branch. It fell beside his right foot, and he stooped to examine the cut. The twig was as thick as his index finger. His father never had much use for willow, though his mother had used its shoots to make baskets. He pushed the cut end of the twig into the moist ground. With luck it will take root and grow a new tree, he thought.

Suddenly the conference was over. Baker came and took the sword out of his hands, and Whiteside disarmed Shields. The parties had reached an agreement. Shields would withdraw his challenge, and Abraham would admit that he wrote the letters solely for political effect with no intention of injuring personal character. The men pushed the antagonists toward each other to shake hands. They all clambered aboard the ferry, and almost before Abraham knew it, they were heading back across the river.

His brow was wet with perspiration. He dipped a handkerchief into the water and wiped his face. I can't believe this went as far as it did, he thought. Now that it was over, he began to feel mortified that he had caused such a hullaballoo.

The mood of the others in the boat turned giddy with relief. One of them laid a log on a bench and draped a cloak over it as if it were an injured man. As the ferry approached the crowd on the Alton waterfront, he made a show of fanning it with his hat.

"That log must be Shields," someone on shore yelled. "It ain't long enough or woodenheaded enough to be Lincoln."

The crowd on the riverbank laughed. Abraham, sitting alone with his thoughts, silently vowed that he would never again hurl insults in newspapers.

CHAPTER 36

SEPTEMBER TO NOVEMBER 1842

The Illinois newspapers lambasted him for his part in the Shields affair. Editors gleefully pointed out that men charged with a duty to uphold the law had run off to a Missouri sandbar to evade laws against dueling. When an invitation to a party came from Simeon Francis and his wife, Eliza, he gratefully accepted. At least he could count on the editor of the *Sangamo Journal* to stick up for him.

He arrived early at the Francis home at the corner of Sixth and Jefferson. Eliza opened the door, threw her arms around him, and steered him into the parlor—and there stood Mary Todd.

"I didn't realize you would be here," Abraham stammered, reddening. She clearly had not expected him either.

"Blame me!" Eliza cried triumphantly. "You can both blame me. I'm tired of seeing you two go out of your way to avoid each other. It's perfectly ridiculous."

She was one of those shrewd grand dames whose task is to civilize the affairs of men, who know by instinct and upbringing what is best for society and force their will upon it with ingenious maneuvers.

"A man of brilliant political promise and woman of brilliant social ability should at least be friends," she decreed. "Now, be friends again."

She hurried away to welcome other guests.

Abraham's first thought was to get away. "If you want me to make an excuse to leave—"

"Don't be silly. I'm happy to see you."

They stood in painful silence, except for the pounding of his heart in his ears. Mary recovered first.

"You look well, Abraham."

"At least I have no sword holes to show you."

"I was worried sick when I heard you were going to fight Shields."

"It was a stupid thing to do."

She realized the topic embarrassed him and dropped it.

"How is your work going?"

"I keep pegging away. I seem to have a habit of going into partnership with your cousins." Stephen Logan was another distant relation of the remarkably connected Todd family.

A second strained pause hung in the air between them.

"Eliza can be a crafty old fox," he offered.

"Oh, I'm glad she did it. This town is too small to keep out of each other's way. At any rate, we're both here. Let's have a good time."

They sat opposite each other at dinner. The conversation whirled around the table, moving from Henry Clay's preparations to challenge President Tyler for the White House to a new treaty with Britain adjusting the Canadian border. Mary did her part and more to keep the discussion lively. He had nearly forgotten how brilliant and charming she could be and how much he enjoyed her company.

After dinner they all retired to the parlor for more talk. He watched the clock on the mantel, waiting with Mary for the other guests to begin gathering their things and head for the door. They both knew that Eliza would give them a few minutes alone.

"I'm sorry for the pain I caused you," he said in earnest.

"I have nothing but fond memories of our time together."

"Not all fond, I'm afraid."

She said nothing to that.

"I've been miserable over the way I behaved," he confessed.

"There's no need to talk of it."

"I've blamed myself for even wanting to be happy when I've made you unhappy."

She put up her hand to stop him and held it there for an instant, balancing on her fingertips all the dashed hopes of their courtship.

"Abraham, do you still have feelings for me?" she asked humbly.

The question took him by surprise.

"I don't know what my feelings are," he stammered.

She thought for a moment, then placed her hand on his.

"Well, no matter what, Eliza is right about one thing," she said. "There is no reason we can't be friends."

"I don't think Ninian and Elizabeth would welcome me in their house, not after the way I acted."

They heard a rustling on the other side of the wall, and Eliza swept around the corner.

"You shall be friends here!" she cried, nodding vigorously to show that the matter was settled. "Our parlor is your parlor! You shall have it all to yourselves, any time you want. I'll have it no other way."

They began meeting regularly at Eliza and Simeon's house. At first their conversations were halting and awkward, but it did not take long for them to slip back into their old familiarity. They talked politics, gossiped, and read poetry to each other. He told her some of the jokes he'd heard lately out on the circuit, the ones clean enough to tell in mixed company, and they both laughed until they fell off Eliza's sofa. Sometimes they sat quietly perusing the newspapers, occasionally breaking the easy silence to read something interesting aloud.

Mary insisted they meet in private. "The world is a slippery place," she said soberly. "I think it best that we keep our new friendship from other eyes and ears, at least for now."

She means she doesn't want to be humiliated again, Abraham thought. I can't blame her for that.

He knew from the outset that this second courtship could not last long. To be fair to her, he would have to express his intentions quickly. There was no doubt she still had strong feelings for him.

From their first meeting in Eliza's parlor, he realized how lonely he had been without her. But marrying her—he still doubted whether he could support her, and whether he loved her as he should. The finality of the commitment frightened him. His irresolution troubled him even more. He promised himself that this time he would not go into a tailspin over the question.

He went often to play handball with Jim Matheny and some of the other boys in the ball alley near the square. Part of him believed that if he could pound a handball against a wall long enough, he might pound an answer out of himself. Frequently the talk in the alley turned to women and marriage.

"A wife is like a gun," Matheny drawled. "Keep one around long enough, and you're going to want to shoot it."

"I don't see how you'd know, considering that you're a bachelor," Abraham commented.

"I know more about women than any married man. If I didn't, I'd be married too."

Abraham wished Josh were there to give advice. His friend had taken the plunge and married Fanny Henning. Abraham sent a letter to Kentucky, hoping for direction.

"Are you now, in feeling as well as judgment, glad you are married?" he wrote. "From anybody but me, this would be an impudent question not to be tolerated, but I know you will pardon me in it. Please answer it quickly, as I feel impatient to know."

If he's happy in marriage, I'll propose to Mary, he vowed.

Sometimes they met in Anson Henry's office, where Abraham had undergone treatment for his depression. The doctor was fond of Mary and convinced that his two friends would make a good match.

"Now, there's the cure for your hypo," he told Abraham. "When a man has a wife and young ones to look after, he's got no time to feel down in the dumps."

He spent several days on the circuit, riding from courthouse to courthouse, eyes on the horizon as half-formed thoughts darted through his mind. One day he talked himself into marriage, the next day out of it, until his head ached. In courtrooms he sat with feet propped on tables, partly listening to what the judge said, trying to reason his way through the problem as if it were any other difficult case.

More than anything else, this time, I want to do right by her, he told himself.

Josh's reply to his letter was waiting when he got back to Springfield. "I am even happier now than on the day I married," he wrote. "Don't hesitate or doubt any longer. Risk your happiness in each other's keeping."

That's it, then, Abraham thought. I'll ask her to marry me.

He rehearsed a hundred ways to propose a second time. In the end it came out short and clumsy.

"If you still want me, I want you for my wife," he said, taking her hands in his.

She dropped her head for a minute. When she looked up, her eyes were shining. She pressed her cheek to his chest.

"Is it safe for me to accept this invitation, Mr. Lincoln?" she asked. "I've no desire to get kicked twice by the same mule."

"I'm sometimes slow as a mule, but eventually I get around to doing the right thing."

"And exactly how long is it going to take this stubborn mule to plod his way to the altar?"

"I'm ready. Name the day."

She pursed her lips. "I think we should get married right away."

"All right."

"We can do it tomorrow."

"Tomorrow?" The suddenness of it shocked him.

"Yes." Her voice was determined. "I don't want to give Elizabeth or anyone else time to argue with me about it."

"All right. If that's what you want, that's what we'll do."

He smiled gently and leaned down to kiss her. Her face, radiant with happiness, had never looked prettier. With an inward sigh, he yielded to her love.

The next morning, when the shops surrounding the square opened, he paid a visit to Chatterton's Jewelry Store. Charles Chatterton, a native New Yorker who ran the shop with his brother George, helped him pick out a wide-band ring of Etruscan gold.

"We can engrave it, if you want," he offered.

"That would be nice."

"What do you want it to say?"

"How about 'A.L. to Mary, November 4, 1842.'"

The jeweler looked dissatisfied. "There's room to add a little more if you like. It's customary to include a brief personal statement."

Abraham thought for a minute.

"Love is eternal," he suggested.

Chatterton brightened. "Yes, that should fit. Come back this afternoon. I'll have it ready."

He wrote it down in precise letters before Abraham left the store:

A.L. to Mary, Nov. 4, 1842. Love Is Eternal.

PART FOUR

THE PATH

Spring 1846 to December 1859

CHAPTER 37

Spring and Summer 1846

He lay on the sitting room floor, shoes off, head and shoulders propped on a cushion placed against the back of a chair he had turned over, running his finger down a list of Whig voters in Sangamon County. Bobbie pushed a toy steamboat across the floor beside him. The child made little screeches like a steam whistle and steered the boat into Abraham's foot.

"Are you a pirate, Papa?"

Abraham put down the list.

"I'm the biggest, meanest river pirate from here to New Orleans!" he growled. "I scratch my back with smokestacks and stir my soup with paddle wheels! When I get thirsty, I drink up rivers and leave steamboats high and dry! When I get hungry, I swallow a passel of red-hot snapping turtles, and if I can't get those, I gulp down boys—and I see one now!"

He made a swipe at Bobbie, who squealed with delight and scampered away.

Mary entered the room, carrying Eddie and her sewing basket.

"You would think that a man getting ready to run for Congress would know better than to lie around on the floor, where any stranger who comes to the door might see him," she commented.

"A man getting ready for Congress needs practice lying around doing nothing."

She put Eddie in his cradle, settled into a chair, and pulled a shirt from her sewing box. Abraham watched her thread a needle, thinking how one minute a fellow can be on a flatboat drifting down a river, and the next married with two children, planning a run for the United States Congress. Time is a winged chariot hurrying along. One of the books he had borrowed from Si Crawford twenty years ago said so. It looked like that book was right.

"What are our chances?"

"Good." Abraham looked back at his list. "This is the only safe Whig seat in the state. Baker's done a good job of keeping it that way for me."

"You'll be the finest congressman since Henry Clay was Speaker of the House."

"That's aiming pretty high, don't you think?"

"And after that, the finest senator this state has ever seen."

"They say your old friend Steve Douglas will be in the Senate soon. I know I should envy no man, but I can't help but feel jealous."

"That's all right, Mr. Lincoln. A little green wood makes good steam for our engine."

"We are an engine, are we?"

"You are going to be president someday. You may not know it yet, but I do."

She took up another shirt and threaded the needle again.

"I can't wait to see Washington," she went on. "I'm going to need two or three nice new dresses. And you, Mr. Lincoln, you'll need a new suit."

He said nothing to that.

"The first thing we'll do is ask John Quincy Adams to dinner."

"Why in the world would John Quincy Adams want to eat with us?"

"I don't see why he wouldn't. You're both Whigs, and you'll both be members of the House."

Abraham stretched and put on his shoes.

"Well, if this Whig is going to get to Congress, he'd better hitch himself to the plow and start pulling."

He kissed his wife and sons goodbye, put on his jacket, and set out for his office.

He walked two blocks west on Jackson Street, past frame houses, gardens, and little backyard barns, then three blocks north on Sixth. The smell of loam was in the air, blowing across freshly planted fields of corn. The dome of the statehouse towered above the town square.

He studied the building's massive columns and yellow-brown limestone walls as he neared his office on the southeast corner of the square. When he had moved to Springfield nine years earlier, the new state capital was a rough-edged town of two thousand inhabitants on the edge of wilderness. Since then, it had swelled to about four thousand people, a city growing in shops, offices, churches, schools, hotels, theaters, and pork-packing houses.

It had been three and a half years since the rainy November evening he and Mary had said their wedding vows in Ninian and Elizabeth Edwards's big parlor. During the ceremony, he had the queer sensation that it was all happening to someone else, that he was one of the thirty guests come to see another fellow get married. They had begun their life together as boarders at the Globe Tavern on Adams Street. Their second-floor room measured eight feet by fourteen feet, barely enough space for their bed, a walnut wardrobe, a chair, and a washstand. Nine months later, Bobbie came along. Abraham had hoped to name him Joshua Speed Lincoln, but Mary had insisted on Robert Todd Lincoln, for her father.

With Bobbie's arrival, the room at the Globe was suddenly way too small and noisy. Abraham had finally paid off most of the debt on the New Salem store, and with some help from Mary's father, they bought a cottage on the corner of Eighth and Jackson Streets for fifteen hundred dollars. Soon Bobbie had a little brother named Edward Baker Lincoln, named for their friend Ned Baker, who was serving a term in Congress.

After four terms in the state legislature, Abraham had decided not to run again. There was little more he could learn from wrangling with Illinois Democrats over the state bank and road bills. It was time to take the next step. Ned promised that when he finished his stint in Congress, he would back Abraham to succeed him for a term. It was the same seat John Stuart had held. A good seat for a man to occupy for a short while on his way up the political ladder.

He climbed the narrow staircase leading to his third-floor office, above a dry goods store, and sprawled out on the firm's old sofa to peruse a couple of newspapers. Billy Herndon sat at his desk, bent over a book.

"'Morning, Billy. What news on the Rialto?"

"'Morning, Mr. Lincoln. Emmet Pace stole another bucket out of Jim Hipp's barn. The sheriff is threatening him with jail this time."

"I'm afraid Emmet's got the can't-help-its. I'll talk to him. What else?"

"Mr. Floyd sent you a check for twenty-five dollars."

"Floyd must think I'm a high-priced man. That's too much for the job. I'll send him back ten dollars. Anything else?"

"Martin Spriggs ran off to fight in Mexico and left a bunch of unpaid notes."

"I guess Martin's creditors can wait until he whips the Mexicans to get paid."

"I guess so, Mr. Lincoln."

Abraham had taken on Billy as a junior partner when Stephen Logan, his old partner, decided to go into practice with his son. From the day they hung a shingle announcing *Lincoln & Herndon* over the sidewalk, it had proven to be a good partnership. Billy was a skilled researcher of precedents and citations. Abraham had few equals at interviewing clients and talking to juries. They were both lousy at keeping a tidy office, which consisted of a couple of small desks, a big table, the sofa Abraham liked for reading newspapers, a half dozen plain wooden chairs, and a bookcase for law books—all purchased for a total of $168.65. Dust bunnies gathered in corners, and copies of pleadings lay stacked on the floor. Rummaging through piles for lost letters was an office sport.

"I guess we need a better system," Billy had admitted one day early in the partnership.

"Well, we can always use my system of last resort."

Abraham tied some of the mess into a bundle, wrote, "When you can't find it anywhere else, look in this," on top, and plunked it down in a corner.

In his spare moments, Billy loved to share some new bit of knowledge he had discovered. Abraham had never met such an insatiable reader. The fellow was a walking library, bubbling over with ideas he had come across in volumes of history, literature, theology, and science. His personal bookshelves were crammed with writers and philosophers barely recognizable to prairie-educated men—Immanuel Kant, John Locke, Thomas Carlyle, and Ralph Waldo Emerson.

"Listen to this, Mr. Lincoln," he cried, trembling over one of Emerson's pamphlets. "'The lover of nature is he whose inward and outward senses are still truly adjusted to each other; who has retained the spirit of infancy even into the era of manhood.' I believe that, don't you?"

"Billy, you believe everything you read, until you get hold of the next book that tells you something different."

"That's because every book brings dawning inspiration. A good book is like a new rose fresh from the garden of the Almighty!"

"You are a seeker of truth, my friend."

"I like to think that I can see to the gizzard of questions," Billy allowed.

"And how do you do that?"

"Plain old mud instinct. I know truth when I feel it. I can feel it in my bones."

"A kind of backwoods bones philosophy, eh?"

"That's right," Billy said. "That's how I leap forward in life. By feeling things in my bones."

"Well, I guess leaping is as good a way as any other to get someplace."

"What about you, Mr. Lincoln? Don't your bones tell you the truth of a matter?"

Abraham thought for a moment. "No, I move at a slower pace. Hand me your little knife with its short twin blades and that old jackknife lying over there."

Billy gave him the knives.

"See here, the short-bladed knife opens quickly, and the point travels through a small portion of space. But this long-bladed knife, it opens slowly and its point travels through a greater distance. It moves slower than your little knife, but it can do more execution."

He ran his finger down the length of the jackknife.

"It's the same with these long convolutions of my brain. They have to act slowly and pass, as it were, through a greater space than shorter convolutions. I commence way back like boys do when they want to get a good running start. Eventually my weight and my speed get up enough momentum to jump far."

He pulled himself off the sofa and sat on the edge of the firm's big worktable. His thoughts wandered back nearly a decade to his early days as a lawyer when John Stuart was campaigning for Congress. Yes, time was definitely a winged chariot.

"Politicking will take up a good portion of my time for the next few months," he told Billy. "You'll have to carry a load for the practice."

"I'm anxious to help any way I can."

"Thank you. I'll need it."

He picked up the jackknife and let it drop a half dozen times onto the worktable, point down, studying the pattern of tiny indentations as if to discern a sign.

"What do you think? Will I make it to Washington?"

"No doubt about it."

"How're you so sure, Billy?" Abraham asked, smiling.

"I can feel it in my bones, Mr. Lincoln. Feel it in my bones."

The Democrats nominated Peter Cartwright, a popular circuit-riding Methodist preacher, to run against Abraham for Congress in the general election of 1846. Cartwright had come to Illinois when it was barely a state, riding through the high grasses from cabin to cabin with the trumpet of God at his lips, singing and shouting the message of salvation.

"He can roar and fulminate with the best of them," Abraham told Billy. "It will pay to take no chances with Cartwright."

He campaigned hard, riding from town to town like a Methodist preacher himself, offering a shake of the hand and a "how d'ye do" at every farmhouse he passed. Everyone wanted to talk about the war that had broken out with Mexico, a fight over disputed territory, but he stuck mainly to his old themes of tariffs, banks, and improved transportation.

A story that Abraham heard more than once circulated during the campaign. It made him laugh and half wish it were true. The story went that he had dropped in on a revival meeting where Cartwright was preaching. Cartwright, it was said, had looked out over the congregation and invited all who expected to go to heaven to stand. Next he exhorted all who feared they might go to hell to stand.

He saw that Abraham remained seated both times and called out a question: "Mr. Lincoln, just where do you plan to go?"

His Whig opponent rose to his full height.

"Brother Cartwright, I am going to Congress."

CHAPTER 38

December 1847 and January 1848

The wooden dome of the United States Capitol floated above the Potomac mist, graceful and solemn, like the Pantheon of Rome above the ancient Tiber. At first sight, Abraham pulled Mary close and squeezed her hand.

They had arranged to take a room at the boardinghouse of Mrs. Ann Sprigg, a Virginian with a reputation for being especially gracious to Whigs. They had no problem finding the place, one of five row houses on First Street just east of the Capitol. Mrs. Sprigg showed them to their room, up two flights of stairs on the back side of the house.

"I do believe that your friends Mr. Stuart and Mr. Baker found everything to their satisfaction while they boarded here," she assured them. "They were both good Whigs. I'll have no Democrats in my house, Mrs. Lincoln, unless they have good manners. And Democrats with good manners are hard to find."

The room contained two beds with a screen between them, a table, chairs, bureau, clothes press, fireplace, and plenty of wood to burn. It looked pleasant enough, though on the small side.

"Breakfast is at eight, supper at five thirty," Mrs. Sprigg announced. "I can assure you there will be no Democrats at my table, Mrs. Lincoln. The last Democrat I had at my table left tobacco juice all over my floor."

She left them to settle in.

"It's bigger than our old room at the Globe Tavern," Abraham observed.

"We'll make it work," Mary vowed, a little tight-lipped.

"We can unpack later. Let's go look around."

On their way out, they met Congressman Joshua Giddings, another of Mrs. Sprigg's boarders. Broad-chested and thick-necked, he stood nearly as tall as Abraham. His mane of white hair and violent antislavery views had earned him the nickname "the Lion of Ashtabula" in the Ohio county he represented. Giddings was no stranger to dustups. When a Georgia congressman had menaced him with a pistol and sword cane, he had jeered: "Come on! The people of Ohio don't send cowards here!" He offered Mary his respects and Abraham a firm handshake.

"Ned Baker said he'd be sending a good man to take his place. Are you ready to do battle with tyranny and injustice?"

"I believe I am."

"Good! Stick with me. I always make the fur fly."

Mrs. Sprigg had an old baby carriage that previous lodgers had left behind, and she put it at their disposal with the admonition that it was for Whig babies only. They headed straight for the Capitol, Mary wheeling little Eddie and Abraham leading Bobbie by the hand.

The iron railing that surrounded the Capitol grounds stood only fifty feet from the boardinghouse door. The Capitol itself towered before them with its huge thirty-foot Corinthian columns and lofty dome, dwarfing the statehouse in Springfield. High atop the east entrance perched a sculpture of a woman representing the *Genius of America*, flanked by figures of Hope and Justice. At the south entrance stood marble statues of a triumphant Christopher Columbus, newly arrived on unknown shores, and an Indian maiden awed by his sudden appearance.

Abraham took Eddie out of the carriage, and they climbed a massive flight of stone steps to a wide terrace. They turned to look west over the Capitol Park. Again Abraham pulled Mary close and squeezed her hand.

The city of forty thousand inhabitants sprawled before them, still in transformation from wilderness to grand metropolis. Pennsylvania Avenue, broad and tree-lined, reached from Capitol Hill to the President's House. A fine brick promenade ran alongside, and bustling shops tempted pedestrians with imported luxuries, but some of the big cobblestones in the road were so poorly laid, carriages swerved to avoid them. Mansions and marble temples dotted the landscape amid smaller wood-frame houses. Here and there, boys chased pigs out of gardens, and cows roamed the streets. A narrow canal cut through the city toward the swampy banks of the Potomac River.

"It's a magnificent city, isn't it?" a voice behind them cried. "Or perhaps, as Mr. Dickens wrote, a city of magnificent intentions."

Stephen Douglas rounded a stone balustrade to greet them. Abraham was happy to see a familiar face, even if it was one from the other side of the aisle. Douglas had succeeded in getting himself elected to the United States Senate. He stood beside them on the terrace and pointed to distant sights: the stately marble Post Office, which rose three stories high and covered an entire block; the Patent Office, with sixteen massive granite columns along a front portico that brought to mind the Parthenon; the mammoth colonnade of the Treasury Department, still under construction; and the foundations of a castle that would house the Smithsonian Institution, a gift from Englishman James Smithson "for the increase and diffusion of knowledge among men."

"Just think, Lincoln, this country is little more than a half century old, and already we've accomplished all this." He swept his arm across the scene before them, and Abraham knew he meant much more than the rambling capital city. Douglas's eyes took in the Blue Ridge of Virginia, the Ohio River Valley, the prairies of Illinois, and beyond.

"We're lucky men," the Little Giant said softly. "We have an opportunity to make the boundaries of liberty as broad as the continent itself."

They looked west as the sun declined toward the hills of Arlington, flooding the broad Potomac with red and gold.

"Before we're done, we'll extend the limits of this republic from Atlantic to Pacific," Douglas rhapsodized. "You'll see. We'll make this an ocean-bound republic. That's what we're meant to be, by God, an ocean-bound republic!"

The disc of the sun quivered like a Spanish doubloon as it dropped into a cloudbank, and in its light, they could see over the peaks of the Rocky Mountains to waiting frontiers.

Three days later, Abraham took his place in the House chamber. He had never been inside a room so grand. Two dozen marble columns surrounded the semicircular hall, which was built in the form of an ancient Greek amphitheater crowned by a sixty-foot-high dome. His sturdy mahogany desk, No. 191, sat in the last row on the Whig side of the floor. Like his chair, it was on the small side. He was glad to be in the back. It left him free to push back a little and stretch out his legs.

He took a quick look around to locate other Whigs he'd met or knew by reputation. Joshua Giddings, his fellow lodger at Mrs. Sprigg's, sat in the row in front of him. There was Alexander Stephens of Georgia, a little pale-faced man with a boyish smile whom Abraham immediately liked when they first shook hands. Next to Stephens sat Robert Toombs, another Georgian, as hardy and robust as Stephens was slim and consumptive.

Over on the Democrats' side of the room, he spotted David Wilmot of Pennsylvania, who had recently caused a stir with a bill to keep slavery out of any territories gained from the war with Mexico. And there was Robert Barnwell Rhett of South Carolina, firebrand defender of Southern rights, and Andrew Johnson of Tennessee, champion of small farmers and mountaineers.

But the man who held his attention was John Quincy Adams, the old Whig from Massachusetts, who sat near the front of the room. Eighty years old, former president of the United States, son of the second president, dogged foe of slavery, scholar of the first rank, he had served in the House for almost seventeen years.

Adams swore in the Speaker, who in turn administered the oath of office to everyone else. The entire chamber rose. Abraham felt his heart thump as he repeated the words: "I, Abraham Lincoln, do solemnly swear that I will support and defend the Constitution of the United States."

He was surprised at how noisy the place was. Every sound bounced off the high, coffered ceiling and ricocheted around the hall a few times before falling back into the general din. It did not help that all two hundred and thirty-two members were in the habit of talking, laughing, rustling their newspapers, or rapping their desks for messenger boys while one of their own was trying to address them.

"I'd rather give a speech to a pen of five hundred squealing hogs," Joshua Giddings commented. "The real work is done in the committees, anyway."

Abraham found himself assigned to the Committee on Post Offices and Post Roads as well as the Committee on Expenditures of the War Department. Both met in corners of the House chamber or sometimes in one of the Capitol's basement rooms. The Post Office Committee stayed busy. Every village in the nation clamored for a new mail route. Petitions arrived by the bagful, and the committee responded by churning out reports that no one read.

"The boys in New Salem would hardly believe it if they could see their old postmaster now," he told Mary.

The legislative session opened with a flurry of parties and balls. The lone Whig from Illinois received few invitations, but there was still much to see and do in Washington. Occasionally they hired Mrs.

Sprigg to watch the boys while they stepped out for a concert or lecture. At Carusi's Saloon, which was not really a saloon but one of the best ballrooms in town, they paid twenty-five cents apiece to see the famous Ethiopian Serenaders, just returned from entertaining Queen Victoria and other royals of Europe. Six blackface minstrels vaulted onto the stage clapping and strumming like there was no tomorrow while Abraham slapped his knees with the rest of the crowd to the flash of banjos and tambourines.

Each New Year's Day, by custom, the White House threw open its doors so that anyone who wanted could shake the president's hand. On the first day of 1848, Congressman Lincoln and his wife put on their best clothes, climbed into a hired carriage, and rolled down Pennsylvania Avenue to join the masses at the reception.

They drove under the White House's lofty north portico, climbed out, and made their way into a crowded room that shimmered with pearl-white wallpaper. Generals stood erect in gold braid. European diplomats strutted in fancy lace. They joined a long receiving line that eventually reached another room where French mirrors basked in the glory of three giant chandeliers. A stiff-backed man in a polished jacket took their names and presented them to President and Mrs. Polk.

"Thank you for coming, Mrs. Lincoln," the president said. "Good to see you, Mr. Lincoln."

A colonel charged with moving the line forward gently propelled them toward a door.

"If he has to keep shaking hands like that all day, his paw will swell up to the size of a melon," Abraham commented.

They wandered the White House grounds for a while, then rode back to the boardinghouse in awe of starting the New Year with a greeting from the president of the United States.

On Sunday afternoons, he took Bobbie by the hand, walked up Seventh Street past the mammoth white marble Post Office building, and climbed a tall flight of granite steps to the Patent Office, where they wandered among glass cases exhibiting toy-sized models of American inventions: reapers, plows, firearms, steam engines, cotton gins, even a machine that sewed cloth. There were so many ingenious devices, there was surely nothing in the world left to invent. He explained to Bobbie as best he could how each worked. Both father and son would have given anything to break the glass cases so they could take the models apart and put them back together again.

Upstairs they found a vast exhibit hall stuffed with national treasures: specimens from the Pacific Islands brought back by an exploring expedition, portraits of Indian chiefs, the camp chest used by General Washington during the Revolutionary War, and, best of all, the original Declaration of Independence.

Abraham stood before the precious charter of freedom, softly reading aloud the hallowed words. It seemed to him that no finer thoughts had ever been conceived by the mind of man.

> *When in the Course of human events, it becomes necessary for one people to dissolve the political bands which have connected them with another . . .*

CHAPTER 39

JANUARY AND FEBRUARY 1848

The war with Mexico was ending. American troops, led by General Winfield Scott, had stormed the Halls of Montezuma in Mexico City. Now that the fighting was all but over, Whigs in Congress felt free to criticize the Democratic administration's conduct. They charged that the war was an act of aggression fought to enlarge the country's borders.

Alexander Stephens, the slim, consumptive Whig whom Senator Jefferson Davis once called "the little pale star from Georgia," assailed President Polk's motives.

"Waging war against a neighboring people to force them to sell large parts of their country is disgraceful!" he protested. "Does American honor aim at nothing higher than land?"

"I'm with you," Abraham told Stephens, "and I'm happy to say so out loud."

"Good. It's time to train our artillery on Polk."

"Suppose I get up a speech to deliver in the House?"

"The more who are willing to speak up, the better."

He labored over his remarks for several nights beside the fire in the boardinghouse room. Polk insisted that the conflict began when Mexican soldiers invaded Texas and spilled American blood. Whigs suspected that Polk had sent American troops into disputed territory to provoke an attack.

"If we can force him to answer a few questions about the particular spot where the fighting broke out, we can expose his deception," Abraham told Mary.

"Be careful of how far you go," she cautioned. "A lot of brave men fought and died. No one wants to be told their heroes were in the wrong."

"Most people want to be told the truth, I reckon."

He took to the floor of the House to demand that the president answer questions about exactly where the war had begun.

"Let him answer fully, fairly, and candidly. Let him answer with *facts*, and not with arguments," he railed. "If he *can* not or *will* not do this ... then I shall be fully convinced of what I more than suspect already, that he is deeply conscious of being in the wrong—that he feels the blood of this war, like the blood of Abel, is crying to heaven against him!"

The reaction was not what he hoped for. The Polk administration ignored his speech. So did almost everyone else in Washington. Back home in Illinois, Democratic papers lambasted him for mounting a "base, dastardly, and treasonable assault" while American soldiers lay fresh in their graves. Illinoisans who had taken up arms denounced him as a second Benedict Arnold. Even Billy Herndon wrote him a chiding letter, arguing that the president was right to send troops into the territory of another country if he judged it necessary to head off an invasion.

"Can't Billy see that this is exactly why the Constitution gives the war-making power to Congress?" Abraham moaned to Mary. "His view puts the president where kings have always stood, with the power to make war on a whim."

He grabbed his pen to answer his law partner, but as he scribbled, he wondered how much damage he had done to his political career.

He stayed so busy with politics, he was caught by surprise one evening when Mary signaled her discontent.

"It's not at all as I imagined it would be here," she said, almost to herself, as she undressed the children.

"What do you mean?"

"Well, for one thing, I have no one to talk to all day long."

"There's a whole city full of people to talk to!"

"For you, yes. You're in meetings and caucuses half the day. I'm cooped up in this room with the boys."

"Why don't you take them downstairs to the parlor?"

"They bother the other guests with their noise."

"Take them outside to the park. There's plenty of room for them there."

"It's cold, Abraham. I can't keep them outside for long. And Eddie's had a cough for nearly two weeks. He's not thriving here. I don't think the air agrees with him."

He picked up the child and held him on his lap. It was true that he looked sickly. When the coughing fits came, his little face screwed up and turned bright red. Abraham felt a pang of guilt for not paying the child more attention.

"Maybe you'd better take him to a doctor. I'm sure Mrs. Sprigg can give us the name of a good one."

"She gave me two names this afternoon. I'll take him tomorrow. He'll be fine. Don't worry."

He put Eddie on the bed. "I've tried my best to arrange outings for us, whenever I can."

"I know you have, and I appreciate that. But it's still lonely most of the time. I've made no friends here. Hardly any of the other Congressmen brought their wives. I can see why."

We should have thought about all this before we came, he thought. It should have been easy for us to imagine that living here would be difficult for a mother with two young children.

"They tell me that when the weather warms up, the Marine Band gives concerts on the Capitol grounds," he offered. "We can take the boys with us."

"Yes, that will be nice." She turned her back and continued undressing Bobbie. "Perhaps it was a mistake to come with you," she said softly.

The anguish in the words broke over him. She had wanted so badly to share in his triumph. He reached to draw her close, but she made herself busy with the child, and he could only put a hand on her shoulder.

"We've been here just a few weeks, Mary. Give it time. You'll make friends before long, and then you'll feel better."

She wiped her eyes and pulled Bobbie's nightshirt over his head. "You're right. It's too soon to be discouraged. It will get better, I'm sure."

Her disappointment hung between them, opaque and still, in the cramped air of the boardinghouse room.

In the District of Columbia, the seat of liberty, the rising sun touched marble columns and friezes that announced the glories of the young republic. But the stone was flawed, quarried from a vein that carried a blemish. Fractures lay just beneath the surface, easy to overlook but capable of bringing down the colossal temples of freedom.

Forty thousand people inhabited the federal district, including two thousand slaves and eight thousand free blacks. The resident population of slaves marked the capital as a Southern town. It was the transient bondsmen, human chattel en route to distant fields, that made Washington a center of slave trade.

A short walk east of the Capitol brought any congressman to an auction block, where he could hear the chant of auctioneers offering up Negroes to buyers who squatted and spat tobacco juice in the dirt while they kept their eyes open for bargains. A short distance west of the Capitol, in view of the windows of Congress itself, stood large holding pens surrounded by high wooden palings, Negro livery stables where slaves were kept until taken to Southern markets. Slave drivers routinely herded captives through the streets, the men chained in double file, young women following, with old women, mothers, and children huddled in carts bringing up the rear. Out on the Potomac, schooners loaded with slaves weighed anchor for Southern ports.

Mrs. Sprigg, though a Virginian, refused to own slaves. She employed eight black servants, five free and three in the process of buying their freedom from their masters. One of the latter, the husband of the cook, acted as waiter at mealtimes. A man of wide-ranging abilities, he could shoe a horse, turn a lathe, train a dog, or pickle an oyster. He could add and subtract much faster than most white folks. He had paid off all but sixty of the three hundred dollars his master had agreed to take as his purchase price, and Mrs. Sprigg's guests often gave him small tips to help him along toward his goal. His dream was to become a blacksmith.

One evening, just as the boarders were sitting down for supper, three men with hawkish faces appeared at the dining room door.

"We're looking for a man named Hannibal," the one with the sharpest glint in his eyes announced.

The room froze. There was nothing good about the declaration, not the way he said it.

Joshua Giddings rose. "What do you want with him?"

"What I want with him is *him*." The man laughed and drew back his coat to show a pistol in its holster. Mary clutched Abraham.

"Like I said, his name is Hannibal."

One of the boarders rose and drew back his jacket to show that he, too, carried a pistol. "We don't want any trouble here," he advised in a tone that suggested he might welcome it.

"Neither do we. We just want our man," the slave trader said. He stared hard at the only black face in the room.

"I'm Hannibal," the waiter said, fear in his voice. His eyes sought out the boarders.

"You have no right to barge in here making this sort of demand," Giddings said.

"In fact, I do. This paper gives me the right. You can look it over if you want."

He handed it to Giddings, who read it and passed it to Abraham. The warrant gave the bearer authority to arrest the slave Hannibal for return to his lawful master.

"It looks to be in order," Abraham admitted.

"Master knows I'm here!" Hannibal cried. "He hired me out to Mrs. Sprigg."

"That's between you and your master," the slave trader shrugged. "What's between you and me is this piece of paper, and it says you've got to come with me."

Mrs. Sprigg appeared from the kitchen with Hannibal's terrified wife, the cook, close behind. "How dare you set foot in my house this way!" she cried. "You're nothing but low-down, common Democrats! I can tell just by looking at you!"

The slave trader laughed again. "Everything in this town is politics through and through," he said to his companions. They grinned nonchalantly, the sort of men who are used to all kinds of insults. "Ma'am, I won't linger to discuss the latest elections with you. We'll just take this fellow and be on our way."

"But master says I can buy my freedom!" Hannibal explained in desperation.

"I guess your master changed his mind. Let's go."

Giddings exchanged glances with his fellow boarders.

"I understand that some of you gentlemen are distinguished members of the United States Congress," the slave trader said. "I'm sure that, being men of law, you don't want to stand in the way of the law."

Silence for a moment. Hopelessness thickened in the room with the evening light.

"Hannibal, you'll have to go with them," Giddings conceded. "But by God, we'll do everything in our power to bring you back. I promise you that."

The three men moved quickly toward the servant and forced his wrists into irons. His wife, begging for mercy, threw her arms around his legs. They pulled her off, and one of the slave traders held her back as the other two gagged the prisoner. By then he had stopped resisting. The waiter looked back at his wife, his face contorted, as they shoved him out the door.

"Villains! Scoundrels!" Mrs. Sprigg shouted after them. "You tell that hateful Mr. Polk he isn't fit to be called president of these United States!"

"I'll do that, ma'am, if I ever meet him," one of them sneered over his shoulder.

The next morning, Abraham and Giddings set out to find the captive, walking from slave pen to slave pen, searching the wretched faces and calling out his name.

My God, Abraham thought, this is evil.

By the time they located the jail where Hannibal had been taken, it was too late. He had already been sent down the river, bound for the slave market in New Orleans.

CHAPTER 40

February to July 1848

His work in Congress consumed him. The cold months slipped by like a fog moving down the Potomac, thick with committee meetings, debates over western territories, and petitions from constituents looking for help getting government contracts and jobs.

In late February 1848, John Quincy Adams collapsed at his desk as he rose to address the House. Abraham, stunned, watched a congressman jump up and catch him as he fell.

"Mr. Adams is dying!" someone cried.

The old man's colleagues gently carried him to the Speaker's Room. Two days later, he departed life with the words, "This is the last of

Earth. I am content." He had served his country for most of his eighty years, since the time of the country's founding, as a diplomat, senator, congressman, and sixth president of the United States. Everyone felt that his passing brought the end of an era.

The coming of warmer weather brought new chances for outings with Mary. They took the boys to a Marine Band concert on the Capitol grounds and enjoyed a stirring rendition of "Columbia, Gem of the Ocean," though they left early when Eddie broke into a spasm of coughing. One night they left the children with Mrs. Sprigg and went to see Julia Dean, young star of the American stage, in *Romeo and Juliet* at the new Adelphi Theatre. They were both excited to see the actress, and she did not disappoint. From its opening lines, the story transported them to an Italy of hidden daggers and walled city-states.

Two households, both alike in dignity,
In fair Verona, where we lay our scene,
From ancient grudge break to new mutiny,
Where civil blood makes civil hands unclean.

When the curtain fell, they stepped out of the theater into a warm spring night full of buds swelling on the tips of elm branches and a big moon hanging over the Capitol dome. Oil lamps on Pennsylvania Avenue, the only streetlights in the city, floated above the promenade.

"It's hard to believe Miss Dean is only seventeen," Mary said. "She's a prodigy, no doubt about it."

"I'd like to see her tackle *King Lear*. She'd make a fine Cordelia."

A sweet, thin chorus of spring peepers rose from somewhere off near the river. The sidewalk filled with the dark shapes of other couples drifting home.

"Abraham, I've been thinking it over, and I think the boys and I should go visit my family in Lexington while you finish the session."

"What?"

"I realize it's not what we planned, but it makes the most sense."

He stopped and looked down into her face. It was set with pained determination.

"It's going to get hot soon," she said. "I hear Washington summers are unbearable. I don't even want to think about what the room at the boardinghouse will be like."

"You think it will be that bad?"

"I think it would be very hard on the boys. There's much more room for them to spread out and play in Lexington."

"There's plenty of space for them to run around outside here now that it's warmer."

"It's not the same. They'll be much more comfortable in Kentucky. And they'll be around family. That makes all the difference."

It took him a moment to digest the idea.

"I'm worried about Eddie's cough," she went on. "I can take better care of him in Lexington." She touched her forehead. "I think this city is beginning to make my head hurt."

"It will be lonely without you," he said. He was used to being away from her while out on the circuit, but this separation would be something else, longer and more distant.

"The session will be over before you know it," she said. "With us out of the way, you'll be able to concentrate on your work, and that's the most important thing right now."

"If you think it's best, then that's what we'll do."

"It's not what I want, but I do think it's for the best."

What she said made sense. He could attend to his work in Congress better without having to worry about his family. But her retreat from the city she had seemed so determined to reach was puzzling. What had gone wrong? Without his noticing, something undefined had slipped between them. What? Ambition? Duty? Work? Or the mere fact that a stint in Congress was hard on family life?

There were times when the empty boardinghouse room made him lonely. He scoured the rambling, gossipy letters Mary sent from Lexington for news. Eddie's coughing was better, thank goodness. Bobbie had found a kitten and brought it home in triumph, but Mary's stepmother ordered it put out of the house, which made Eddie weep in despair. When Mary wrote to ask that he buy a pair of little plaid socks for Eddie that she'd seen in a shop on Pennsylvania Avenue, he spent the better part of an afternoon hunting through the city for them with no luck.

In the evenings, he often haunted the Library of Congress on the second and third floors of the Capitol and the Supreme Court library in the basement. Both were as quiet as the Indiana woods under snow. He spent long, glorious hours with more books than he had ever seen in his life. When the librarian whispered it was time to close, he pulled a bandana from his pocket, tied it around the volumes he wanted, pushed a stick through the knot, and walked across First Street with the stick over his shoulder for more reading at the boardinghouse.

One day a steamboat caught on a sandbar in the Potomac River piqued his interest. It took him back to the spring day he had gotten stuck on New Salem's dam. As he stood on the bank, watching the crew force empty barrels under the vessel's sides to help it float free, inspiration dawned. He hurried back to Mrs. Sprigg's boardinghouse and began sketching.

Joshua Giddings came into his room and looked over his shoulder. "What are you doing?"

"It's an idea I have. As of today, this Honorable Member from Illinois is an inventor."

"What is it?"

"A device that lets steamboats lift themselves off shoals when they run aground. Look here. These are collapsible air chambers. They'll be made of India rubber cloth or some other waterproof fabric. They're attached to each side of the boat, here and here. If the boat runs aground, the engine turns this shaft. That expands the chambers, fills them with air, and the vessel floats free. Do you see?"

"What are all these poles and ropes for?"

"To expand and contract the chambers and govern the depth of immersion."

"You think it would actually work?"

"Better than unloading half a ship's cargo and trying to wrench her off a sandbar."

"Looks pretty complicated."

"When it makes me rich, I'll buy my own steamboat and show you just how it works," Abraham grinned.

He borrowed a few tools and turned a corner of his room into a shop for making a model. During free moments, he whittled away on a miniature hull and lost himself in the problems of making the system work.

But his duties as a congressman and Whig politician occupied most of his time. The capital, always obsessed with politics, turned rabid with it during the hot months of 1848, a presidential election year. He threw himself into General Zachary Taylor's presidential campaign, helping to mail out thousands of Whig pamphlets and correspond with Whig officials in key states. He went to the Whig National Convention in Philadelphia, where he stood awestruck before Independence Hall. He stumped for Taylor as far north as Boston, riding trains that hurried through a rising industrial landscape of great cities where factories spouted shirts, guns, plows, and belt buckles for markets all over the world. He was struck by how different it all was from rustic Illinois prairie towns, where dried corn stalks rustled outside parlor windows.

Back in Washington, he sat and listened as arguments about slavery roiled Congress. Debate over whether territories won from Mexico should be open to slave labor turned vehement. Congressmen traded insults, knocked each other down, clinched fists in each other's faces. Men like Joshua Giddings of Ohio berated Southern traders in humanity who bred a foul contagion on the land. The proslavery men argued back that the North was full of factories where men, women, and children were treated worse than slaves, that Northern meddlers would bring social and economic disaster on the South. Over in the Senate, John C. Calhoun of South Carolina was preparing to warn fellow Southerners that if the two regions could not resolve their differences, "nothing would remain for you but to stand up immovably in defense of rights, involving your all—your property, prosperity, equality, liberty, and safety."

The Fourth of July dawned with bells pealing and cannons booming. By midmorning, a flood of humanity surged through the streets: laborers in their Sunday finest, vendors lugging baskets of fruit, boys with firecrackers stuffed in their pockets. A grand parade stretching a mile and a half long made its way to a hilltop west of the Capitol. There officials dedicated the cornerstone of a monument to be built in memory of George Washington. When finished, the white marble obelisk would rise more than five hundred and fifty feet, the tallest man-made structure on earth.

Later, as evening approached, Abraham ambled down to the river to get away from the crowds. He liked the Potomac. It was a good river, much wider than the little Sangamon back home, but not as muscular and jaunty as the broad Ohio. Here at Washington, it fell from rocky heights and spread among gentle hills on its way to the Chesapeake Bay. As he walked, a rowboat slid toward him in the gathering dusk, the figure of a large man at the oars and another, smaller one perched in the bow.

"Lincoln!"

He chuckled when he saw who it was. Bob Toombs turned the boat, and with one good heave at the sweeps, sent it to shore. Aleck Stephens's elfin face grinned up at him.

"What are you two ruffians up to?" Abraham asked.

"Going fishing!" Toombs snorted.

"You don't have any poles."

"By God, man, don't stand on technicalities. Going to watch the fireworks, then. Come aboard!"

He climbed in, and Toombs pulled toward the middle of the river. They were an odd pair, these two fellow Whigs from Georgia—Stephens frail, stooped, and thoughtful, Toombs ruddy and broad-shouldered, with dark eyes full of spirit. Abraham liked them both.

The sun dropped below the Virginia shore, leaving streaks of pink and gold in the sky. Tall oaks climbed the hills of Arlington, where eight massive columns of a grand portico stared over the Potomac. It was one of Virginia's most famous plantation homes, built by George Washington Parke Custis, George Washington's adopted son and father-in-law of Captain Robert E. Lee, an Army engineer who had fought with distinction in Mexico.

Bonfires emerged from the twilight along the District shore until the bank was a stream of flickering lights. When full darkness arrived, the fireworks began. Rockets hissed into the air, broke open like shattered flowers, and spilled bright petals of red, silver, and blue over the city. The three in the boat sat quietly, reflecting on events seventy-two years before.

"Those men who staked their lives, fortunes, and sacred honor on the outcome of the Revolution, they were a different sort from what we have today, weren't they?" Stephens remarked.

"They were iron men," Abraham said.

"There are days when I think the capital has turned into nothing more than a place where men come to protect what is theirs and take what is not," the little Georgian mused. "Days when I see so much bickering and fighting, so much sectionalism, I fear the whole country will fly apart like an old wagon hitting a rut. And then there are days like today when this nation seems nothing less than the design of God himself. On those days I think it must surely work."

A giant rocket exploded against the stars. Fiery trails arced over the Capitol dome, the White House, the whole city.

"What do you think, Lincoln?" Stephens asked. "Will it hold together?"

Hold together? He could barely conceive of it *not* holding together.

"Yes, as long as we have good men from the South like Aleck Stephens and Bob Toombs to help us resolve our differences, it will hold together," he said after a minute. "It will hold."

CHAPTER 41

MARCH 1849

The Thirtieth Congress of the United States finished its business on the first Sunday in March 1849. The Speaker of the House wished his colleagues farewell and expressed hope that they would "be bound together forever in a firm, cordial, and indissoluble union." His gavel came down and a cheer went up. With that, Abraham was no longer a congressman.

His plan had always been to serve only one term in Congress, as Ned Baker had done, to give other Whigs in Illinois a chance at the seat. But things had not turned out the way he hoped. A Democrat had captured the seat in the 1848 elections, and some of the Whigs back home were grumbling that Abraham's criticisms of the war with Mexico had cost them the race. He would be going back to

Springfield with a cloud over his head.

Zachary Taylor, on the other hand, won his bid for the White House. Suddenly Washington was full of speculation about the incoming Whig administration—who would run what department and who would be left out in the cold. Office hunters scurried from patron to patron, pleading and cajoling. It was said that if an office was brought to slaughter in the morning, it would be quartered, roasted, and consumed by noon.

March 5, 1849, brought a cold, gusty inauguration day. Church bells greeted the dawn. By midmorning, a river of humanity flowed along Pennsylvania Avenue between the White House and Capitol Hill. Boys hung out of second-floor windows and climbed onto rooftops to see the sights. Hundreds of Stars and Stripes floated on the breeze.

The throng of well-wishers made its way toward a platform on the Capitol's eastern portico. People stomped their feet and hugged themselves to keep warm while they waited for the president-elect. Shortly after twelve thirty, Old Zack appeared with President Polk, the justices of the Supreme Court, and a swarm of dignitaries. The crowd let loose a shout. Taylor gave a short speech no one could hear, then placed his hand on a Bible and took the oath. Another grand shout, and hats flew into the air. For the twelfth time in sixty years, American democracy had presented the world with a miracle: the peaceful transfer of power.

The new president and old president climbed into a carriage and started down Pennsylvania Avenue. Along the road, folks hurrahed and waved. Cannons fired and trumpets blared. President Polk got out at the Irving Hotel, and President Taylor rode on to the White House, where thousands lined up to shake his hand.

For the first time, Abraham realized how much he was going to miss the pomp and power of Washington.

"I guess I'll never witness anything like this again," he told Joshua Giddings.

"We'll miss you, Lincoln. I hope the people of Illinois see fit to send you back soon."

"It's not likely."

"Well, we need our best men back in the states anyway. That's where the truly important work goes on."

Easy for you to say, Abraham thought. You're coming back for another term.

The weather deteriorated as the day wore on. By night, ladies and gents arriving at the grand inaugural ball wore snow on their hats and cloaks. Abraham, due to his work for the Taylor campaign, had the pleasure of seeing his name listed as one of the gala's two hundred and thirty managers. Some of his co-managers, like George Ashmun and Caleb Smith, were prominent Whigs. Others, like Robert E. Lee and Jefferson Davis, were men who had served with General Taylor in the campaigns against Mexico.

The ballroom, a temporary wooden structure next to city hall, was so crowded there was no space for dancing, which suited Abraham fine. He stood near the back of the room with Bob Toombs, looking over everyone else's heads. There was Horace Greeley, founder of the *New York Tribune*, dispensing advice on how to run the country to anyone willing to listen. And General Winfield Scott, deep in talk with several officers, no doubt recounting exploits at Chapultepec. Across the room, a lady swooned from the effects of a tight corset, or the packed room, or both.

A young, pretty French woman wearing a green, satin gown and diamond tiara squeezed her way up to Abraham.

"Monsieur! You are the tallest man in the room!" she cried. "You must be a member of the president's cabinet."

"No, ma'am, I'm afraid not."

"Then perhaps you are a senator?"

"No, ma'am."

"A congressman, then?"

"I was a congressman. Now I'm going home."

"Ah, and where is home?" she asked with less zeal.

"I live in Illinois."

"Illinois? I have never heard of it. Too bad. Au revoir, Monsieur!" She moved on in search of better prospects.

Word circulated that President Taylor and Vice President Fillmore were arriving. The band struck up "Hail Columbia" as the crowd broke into applause. Taylor appeared with his daughter, the charming Betty Bliss, dressed in an elegant white gown with a single blossom in her hair. The crowd parted as the new president crossed the room. Ladies waved handkerchiefs. Politicians and generals maneuvered to offer congratulations.

The announcement that supper was available set off a general stampede. There was not enough food, and celebrants jammed up to the sideboards to grab a share of the feast. Diplomats battled over drumsticks. Gentlemen bribed waiters to find bottles of anything to drink. Three more ladies fainted and had to be carried out.

Abraham and his friends lingered until four in the morning, taking it all in. By the time they went to the cloak room, the attendants had already gone home. Coats and hats lay heaped on the floor. There was nothing to do but wade in and look for something that fit.

"I can't find my hat, boys," Abraham said.

They dug around in the pile. He found his cloak, but no sign of his silk top hat.

"There's a letter from Mary in it. I'd sure hate to lose it."

"Someone's taken it by mistake," Toombs said. "Just take another one. They all look the same."

"No, I don't want to compound the error. I'll have to go without."

They stepped outside onto Judiciary Square. The snow had let up, but the air was biting cold. The city lay dark and quiet, awaiting a muffled dawn. He threw his cloak over his shoulders and trudged bareheaded up Capitol Hill to his lodgings.

Mrs. Sprigg was just getting up when he came in.

"I hear they are sending a Democrat to take your seat in Congress!" she cried indignantly. "It's a travesty, Mr. Lincoln, that's what it is. Well, he won't find a room in my house, I can promise you that!"

He went to bed wondering if he would ever see his hat again.

There were a couple more things to do before he left Washington. For one, he was scheduled to represent an Illinois client in the Supreme Court of the United States.

It was a complex appeal involving the statute of limitations on a faulty sale of land. The leather-bound volumes in the Supreme Court library became his companions for days while he studied precedents and reasoned his way through arguments.

On the appointed day, he took a stack of books under his arm and followed a dim, narrow passageway to a semicircular chamber in the Capitol basement. Its vaulted ceiling made him feel like he was stepping inside a pumpkin shell. A big clock hung over a mantel, set five minutes fast to encourage those with business before the Court to arrive on time. Above the clock, a plaster frieze showed the seated figure of Justice with a pair of scales in her left hand, her right hand resting on a sword. On the opposite side of the room, behind a mahogany rail, nine desks and nine chairs sat in a straight line, raised slightly above the floor.

A gavel rapped lawyers and spectators to their feet. A tallow-faced marshal intoned the traditional chant: "Oyez! Oyez! Oyez! All persons having business before the Honorable, the Supreme Court of the United States, are admonished to draw near and give their attention, for the Court is now sitting. God save the United States and this Honorable Court!"

The justices filed into the room. They took nine black robes from nine pegs on a wall, attired themselves, and sat staring from their desks like a line of old crows on a fence. Chief Justice Roger B. Taney peered down from his center high-backed chair with eyes as grim as Poe's raven perched on its marble bust.

Abraham launched into his argument. He stated the questions to be resolved and described the statutes in question. He cited precedents, discussed the nature of limitations laws. The justices broke in with questions.

"When did Illinois law first limit the time to bring an action?"

"Did not the act of 1837 subject the claim to limitations?"

"What if the plaintiff had come into the state the day before that law was passed?"

Taney looked at the big clock on the wall. With a wave of his hand, oral argument ended. Justice had been satisfied. The nine old crows molted their black robes and left Abraham to carry his stack of books back to the library.

A few days later, the Court ruled against his client. He sat in his boardinghouse room, scouring the chief justice's opinion. He was disappointed, but he took consolation in seeing that Justice McLean had dissented. Well, at least he could say he had argued a case before the highest court in the land. Few lawyers back home could make the same claim.

"Not bad, considering I learned my law on a tree stump in New Salem," he told Aleck Stephens.

With his legal work out of the way, he had time to complete his invention. The model of the vessel with inflatable chambers had turned out well. A few hours of finishing touches were all it needed. That done, he wrote an application with diagrams showing a boat outfitted with his system.

He carried the model and paperwork to the Patent Office, climbed its granite steps, and passed through the line of massive Greek columns to the offices of the commissioner of patents. A lone clerk hunched over a desk, driving a quill pen across an open ledger.

"I've come to file an application," Abraham announced. "It's an improved method for lifting vessels over shoals."

No answer. The hand with the pen labored across the page as if it were the only part of the clerk that was alive.

"Pardon me, friend, but I'm here to file an application."

The man held up his other hand to signify quiet. Abraham waited. The hand with the pen advanced until it had filled a column, then paused.

"Have you the necessary papers?"

The clerk looked over the application. He nodded, grunted, made a swift notation in a second ledger.

"The filing fee is thirty dollars."

He gave Abraham a receipt and placed the application on a stack of papers at the far end of his desk.

"Please put your model over there," he said, pointing.

Abraham carried his model to a table crowded with other devices in need of processing. He moved two aside to make room for his own. When he turned around, the clerk had gone back to writing. He lingered a moment.

"I'll be leaving town soon," he explained. "If there's anything else I must do, I'd like to know now."

"No, that will be all. You may go."

He took a final backward look at his creation. Beyond it, through an open door, he glimpsed dusty shelves crammed with models of pumps, looms, cooking stoves, and devices unrecognizable, each one the incarnation of some poor devil's fondest dreams.

The scratching of the clerk's pen followed him across the vestibule. As he descended the wide steps to F Street, he had the feeling that his career as an inventor, like his days in Congress, had come to an end.

CHAPTER 42

December 1849 to February 1850

Two weeks before Christmas 1849, Eddie came down with a cough that rattled deep inside his little chest.

"I don't like the sound of that," Mary fretted.

"It's probably just a cold," Abraham said. "He'll get over it."

He glanced past his copy of the *Illinois Journal* at their two boys, playing on the sitting room floor. They had dragged three chairs together to make a train.

"We're running out of steam," Bobbie announced. "We need more wood for the firebox."

"More wood!" Eddie rasped. He clambered past the newspaper into Abraham's lap. "More wood, please, Papa!"

"You'll have to cut your own. Here's an ax."

"Thank you!" The boy pretended to swing an ax at a table leg. Each chop brought a short, high-pitched wheeze.

"I think I'll ask Bill to come look him over," Mary said. "I don't want to take any chances."

"I don't know if that's really necessary." Abraham slid out of his chair onto all fours and crawled toward the boys.

"There's a bear on the tracks!" Bobbie yelled.

"A big bear!" Eddie cried. "I shoot him with my gun!" He pulled out a rifle and took aim.

"I'm the biggest, meanest bear from here to New Orleans!" Abraham growled, lumbering forward. "I scratch my back with telegraph poles and pick my teeth with railroad ties! When I get hungry, I swallow locomotives. If I can't get those, I gulp down boys—and I see two now!"

The boys scrambled away gleefully. Eddie rolled behind the chair-train in a spasm of coughs.

"That's enough, Mr. Lincoln," Mary ordered. "You'll make him sicker than he already is. I'm putting him to bed."

"All right, Mother," Abraham surrendered.

"Bobbie, run over to Aunt Frances's house and tell her Eddie is sick. Tell her I'd like Uncle Bill to come as soon as he can."

Bill Wallace, husband of Mary's sister Frances, made a house call that evening. Trained in Philadelphia, he ranked high among Springfield physicians. His ready smile put his patients at ease, especially the young ones.

"How's my very best patient?" he asked Eddie.

"Am I really your bestest patient?"

"You surely are."

"Better than Bobbie?"

"Just as good as Bobbie."

"Bobbie is my bestest brother."

The doctor peered into the boy's mouth and listened to his lungs with a stethoscope, which resembled a small wooden trumpet.

"I'm going to swab his throat. Let's keep him nice and warm. You can give him some Wistar's Balsam of Wild Cherry to help the cough."

Abraham pulled on a gray woolen shawl and set out for Corneau & Diller, an apothecary five blocks away on the public square. Bobbie went with him, scampering to keep up with his father's long, even strides. The last of the autumn leaves skittered over the ground, and the sharp, pleasant smell of chimney smoke rose from the clapboard homes lining Eighth Street. The yellow-brown columns of the Illinois statehouse filled the center of the town square. It was the grandest building in Springfield, but compared to the gleaming white Capitol in Washington, it looked rustic.

It looks like a great big cabin with a flubdub of a little dome stuck on top, Abraham thought.

Corneau & Diller's shelves were crowded with powders and oils to treat various ailments—opium elixir for toothaches, vermifuge for worms, Wright's Indian Vegetable Pills for everything from headaches to lung disorders. A warm stove and a circle of chairs made the drugstore a good place to swap wit and wisdom. Abraham purchased a bottle of Wistar's Balsam and then stopped by Robert Irwin's general store to buy a small box of tin soldiers painted to look like patriots and redcoats from the Revolutionary War.

"This will probably do your brother more good than the medicine," he told Bobbie.

The gift delighted the boys. They spent hours staging battles across the patchwork terrain of the quilt on Eddie's bed. Abraham stretched out with his legs dangling over the bed's foot and helped them defeat the king's men at the Battle of Trenton. Mary attacked Eddie's sore throat with her own remedies. She boiled oatmeal gruel and coaxed the boy into eating it. A day later, when he came down with a fever, she set a bag of pounded slippery elm over his eyes to draw it out.

The ministrations did no good. One afternoon Abraham was at his law office, working on the defense of a man accused of burning a neighbor's barn, when Bobbie came running to say he must come home at once. He found Mary in Eddie's room, stripping the bed. The boy had coughed up blood.

Abraham went rigid. The sight of the dark-stained sheets lying in a heap on the floor hollowed out his chest.

"It's nothing to worry about," Mary kept saying. "We'll get you all better."

They summoned Bill Wallace again. This time he shooed the family out of the room while he examined the patient. When he came out, he looked grave.

"I think it would be wise to bleed him, to reduce his temperature," he said.

The color drained from Mary's face. When the bloodletting was done, Abraham stood outside the front door and conferred with Bill.

"He's showing all the signs of consumption," the doctor said quietly.

The word came as a blow to the gut. Abraham steadied himself against the doorframe.

"What's the best course?" he asked.

"For now, let him rest. I'll be back tomorrow to look him over again. When his fever subsides, we'll administer an emetic to purge the system."

Mary spent every waking minute tending to her boy. Spoon-feeding him panada and rice jelly. Reading aloud from *The Arabian Nights* until he could fall asleep. By force of her will, he rallied. His strength came back, and the coughing let up. They all breathed a sigh of relief. Eddie opened the box of tin soldiers and fought another campaign against the redcoats. Mary celebrated by making a batch of molasses cookies and decorating the parlor with Christmas greenery.

The next day the fever returned, and Eddie began coughing up blood again. The setback crushed them. As Abraham helped Mary clean the bed, he felt himself falling out of the world he had known into a gray, hopeless place. He knew that they must distrust any signs that the boy was getting better.

They took turns sitting beside the sickbed at night, watching him sleep. Abraham spent the hours gathering memories from the nearly four years since his birth—carrying him on his shoulders to see a circus parade, pulling him in a little cart around the town square, pushing him in a carriage across the Capitol grounds in Washington.

"How long will I be sick?" Eddie asked.

"Not much longer. Uncle Bill is taking good care of you."

"When I get better, will you pull me in the wagon?"

"As soon as you get better, you can harness me up, and I'll pull you around the square as many times as you want and buy you a fistful of candy sticks."

Christmas and New Year's Day passed barely noticed. Abraham took down the holiday trimmings Mary had placed on the mantels and burned them in a fireplace.

Bobbie came to him with tears on his cheeks. "Why won't Eddie get better?" he whimpered.

"We'll get him better. It's just taking a while."

"I'm scared he won't be able to play with me again."

"He will. You'll be playing together before you know it."

"Why is it taking so long for him to get better?"

"Sometimes when people don't feel good, it takes a while for the sick places inside them to heal."

"Maybe if we get him a pony he'll feel better."

"I don't think he could ride a pony just now."

"He could look out the window and see it."

"Don't you think it might make him feel bad to see a pony he couldn't ride?"

Bobbie thought for a minute, then brightened. "I could find a new kitten for him to play with. He could pet a kitten in bed."

"That's a fine idea," Abraham said.

Mary's face grew thin. Her blue-gray eyes, so vivid when they had first begun courting ten years earlier, looked haggard and dull.

"You have to get some rest," he urged her.

"I don't want to rest."

"You can't do him any good if you're exhausted."

"I can't sleep while he's so sick."

They entered a cycle of hope and despair that alternated between days when Eddie seemed to be getting stronger and days of rapid decline. Abraham made trip after trip to Corneau & Diller for more medicine. His attention to his law practice dwindled. There were cases that needed work, but he could not stomach sitting in the office. He was thankful Billy was there to hold business affairs together.

Eddie was wasting away. With each bout of fever, he grew thinner and more pallid. The life was slowly draining out of him. Bill Wallace came every day with his black bag, often two times, even when it became evident that his remedies were doing no good.

"Will he recover?" Abraham asked. He could hardly get the question out.

"I don't know. I'm doing everything in my power to help him."

"I know you are. But is there any hope?"

"You need to prepare yourself, just in case."

Something inside him folded in on itself at the words.

"It will kill Mary," he rasped.

He began to dread going out in public. Roland Diller greeted him from behind the pharmacy counter with a sadness in his voice. News that Eddie was very ill traveled through Springfield. People stopped Abraham on the street to ask about him and offer their prayers. It was painful to respond to their inquiries.

Eddie slept more and more. The long nights of sitting beside his bed were filled with frightening moments when he lay so still, Abraham bent over him to make sure he was still breathing.

One night he overheard Mary in tearful prayer: "Oh Lord, if it be your will, remove this cup from him." He leaned against a wall in the dark hallway outside their bedroom, listening to her plea.

This can't happen, he thought. Children die all the time. But surely this can't happen to our little Eddie. He offered his own silent prayer: God, please take me instead of my boy.

A numb resignation set it. The house was very quiet. Bobbie hardly said anything. Outside, the entire neighborhood lay still as if in waiting.

"Does it hurt to die?" Eddie asked.

"Let's not talk about such things. Let's talk about what we'll do when you're all better."

"All right. I'm very tired."

By the end of January, he was too weak to raise his head. Surely there must be a reprieve, Abraham kept thinking, a miracle that will bring back his health.

An unspoken fear, the shadow of death, lay over the house.

Their vigil ended at six o'clock in the morning on the first of February 1850. They sat beside his bed, holding his hands as he fell asleep for the last time. A cold rain was falling. It tapped on the roof and dripped from the eaves in a steady, soft requiem for their boy.

CHAPTER 43

1850 AND 1851

Walking helped ease the grief. He took long, quiet walks through town and ambled across fields where the frozen stubble of last year's corn lay. He walked head down, hands sometimes at his chest, clutching his gray shawl, sometimes clasped behind his back when he wore a long overcoat to keep off the prairie winds.

Images from the days following Eddie's death crowded his mind.

Mary's sisters gently washing the little face and limbs, dressing the corpse in Sunday clothes, placing coins on the eyes.

Bobbie sobbing, "Did Eddie fly away to heaven?"

James Smith, pastor of Springfield's First Presbyterian Church, giving words of assurance as he stood in the parlor beside the coffin:

"The things which are seen are temporal, but the things which are not seen are eternal."

Mary lying in bed for days, refusing all food, wailing into her pillow while Abraham bent over her, whispering softly, "Eat, Mary, for we must live."

He was determined not to slide into depression. Determined not to lose control. He knew from experience that with enough time and distance traveled, the despair would fade. He would get through it. But afterwards the world would be tinged with melancholy.

Work helped ease the grief too. It was good to be in the office, surrounded by dusty books and documents, discussing cases with Billy and listening to him enthuse about something he'd read in the newspapers.

"Mr. Lincoln, this woman Sojourner Truth has more wisdom in her than all the king's philosophers. Listen to what she said: 'I am a woman's rights. I have as much muscle as any man, and can do as much work as any man. I have plowed and reaped and husked and chopped and mowed, and can any man do more than that? I can't read, but I can hear. I have heard the Bible and have learned that Eve caused man to sin. Well, if woman upset the world, do give her a chance to set it right side up again.' By God, she is an original!"

"Billy, if I gave you a lance and a suit of armor, you'd gallop off every day to fight for a cause you found in a newspaper, and I'd never get a lick of work out of you again."

"I won't deny it," Billy said happily. "I want a betterment of conditions for all classes and all climes—here and everywhere."

There was more than enough business to attend to. Abraham could have spent every hour of every day writing motions and taking depositions if he wanted. In addition to widows, debtors, and shopkeepers, a new kind of client had appeared—railroads.

Roping the iron horse. That was the way for a lawyer to make some real money. Infant railroads were spreading across Illinois, connecting market towns to river ports and steamboat routes. Engines were beginning to chug across the prairies on roads like the Chicago & Rock Island

and the Illinois Central. Wherever they steamed, lawyers followed in their tracks, chasing cases both for and against the railroads. Farmers brought suit for negligence when locomotives hit their cows, or when their hogs lost weight while being shipped to market on trains that broke down and sat for days on the track. The railroads sued merchants who failed to pay freight costs and squatters who refused to move out of the way. There was plenty of legal business to be had, and the firm of Lincoln & Herndon got its share.

"Thank the Lord for the Illinois Central," Abraham said as he counted out half a big fee and shoved it across the table for Billy.

"You're right, Mr. Lincoln." Billy grinned, reaching for the money. He liked to complain about the avarice of large corporations, but he liked getting paid by them more. "Thank the Lord for the Illinois Central."

Traveling the Eighth Judicial Circuit was the best tonic of all. It was good to be riding across the prairies behind his horse, Old Bob, in a one-horse buggy, or behind a puffing locomotive on one of the new tracks. Good to sit in the back of a courtroom, whittling on a stick between cases, contemplating the throng of bankers, slanderers, and thieves who came before the bench. On slow days, he could waste a few hours playing billiards with other attorneys in some out-of-the-way place. Or get down on his knees beside a circle scratched in the dirt to shoot marbles with a half dozen village boys and, after he had won all their marbles, hand them back.

David Davis was the new judge of the Eighth Circuit. A bear of a man weighing nearly three hundred pounds, he needed two horses to pull his buggy from courthouse to courthouse, and it was said that he had to be surveyed every time he wanted a new pair of trousers. His beard, which extended from ear to ear under his fat chin, was trimmed short and neat. Friends declared that he had a big head and a big body, a big brain and a big heart.

"Davis is as good a man as any at keeping a swarm of lawyers within the bounds of reason," attorneys who knew him agreed.

Abraham knew he could count on Judge Davis to laugh if he cracked a joke in court. He knew that if he wanted to cut up in the back of the courtroom while whittling with some of the other lawyers, he could count on Davis to call out, "Mr. Lincoln, you are going to have to adjourn your court, or I shall have to adjourn mine—one or the other." Knew that between witnesses, the judge would summon the bailiff to ask in a whisper what sort of stories Lincoln was telling back there to make sure he did not miss any good ones.

Telling a joke or a story helped drive away the melancholy. Sometimes it helped drive home a legal point in court, like the time a man was brought to the law for selling a tonic he said cured a body of warts and itches. He had papers that called his tonic a miracle cure, but several men who had bought and drank it signed affidavits swearing it did no good.

"Tell me, friend," Abraham said when he had the fellow on the stand, "how many legs will a sheep have if you call its tail a leg?"

"Five, I suppose."

"Wrong," Abraham said, giving the jury wink. "Just four. Calling a tail a leg don't make it so. And calling that drink a miracle cure don't make it so, either."

He carried a book of Euclid's geometry on the circuit. It was a good distraction on days he felt melancholy, and he figured it would sharpen his mind. He studied by firelight after the other lawyers had gone to bed, or in his buggy as Old Bob plodded across thc prairies, until he had mastered and could demonstrate with ease propositions such as, "In equal circles, equal angles stand on equal arcs, whether they be at the centers or circumferences."

Sometimes he would slip away from his friends and spend an entire evening at a magic lantern show or a minstrel show that happened to be passing through town. When the others teased him about it, he smiled and said, "I didn't have the opportunity to see much of that sort of thing in my youth. I suppose I am just catching up."

There were nights on the circuit when he could not sleep, nights filled with too much snoring of eight or nine men crammed into a dusty tavern room. Then he would poke at the logs in the fireplace, sit with his legs drawn up, hands clasping his knees, and stare into the flames.

Sometimes he thought of failed political ambitions. True, newspaper editors acknowledged him as one of Illinois's leading Whigs. Yes, there was his one term in Congress. But many men had done one or two terms in the House and then gone back home to live on the remembrance of glory days and repeat a thousand times the words, "I used to serve in Washington." It looked now as though he would be one of those men.

Washington. Stephen Douglas was there, scaling the peaks of fame in the United States Senate. And Ned Baker, Eddie's namesake, was back in Congress, his brilliant career running at full steam. Abraham tried hard not to be jealous. He did not want to envy anyone, especially the shifty, brash Douglas. But when he thought about how his own political career had stalled while others moved forward, he could not help but feel glum.

We all started out as ambitious young men, he thought. With me, the race of ambition has been a failure—a flat failure.

Sometimes he stayed up late reading newspapers by firelight. The year of Eddie's death, 1850, brought events that threatened to pull the country apart. Passions were boiling over the slavery issue and what to do about it. From Charleston to Mobile, there was growing talk that the time had come when the Southern states must exercise their right to withdraw from the Union. "We do not intend to stand still and have our throats cut," Southern planters warned.

In the US House of Representatives, Bob Toombs of Georgia roared that he would rather see the Union dissolved than see the South submit to degradation. Ned Baker, representing Illinois's Sixth District, stood up to declare that "a dissolution of this Union is, must be, shall be, impossible, as long as an American heart beats in an American bosom!" Little Aleck Stephens of Georgia shot back: "I would rather that the

Southern country should perish—that all her statesmen and all her gallant spirits should be buried in honorable graves, than submit for one instant to degradation."

Over in the Senate, titans struggled in a dispute over whether it would be legal to own slaves in new states formed from western territories. The great Henry Clay pleaded for an end to the talk of secession.

"I conjure gentlemen—whether from the South or the North, by all they hold dear in this world," he cried, "I implore them to pause—solemnly to pause—at the edge of the precipice before the fearful and disastrous leap is taken into the yawning abyss below, which will inevitably lead to certain and irretrievable destruction!"

Senator John C. Calhoun of South Carolina, too old and ill to walk but vigorous enough to hold fire in his eyes, replied: "The South asks for justice, simple justice, and less she ought not to take. She has no compromise to offer but the Constitution, and no concession or surrender to make."

Stephen Douglas somehow pushed through legislation that quieted talk of secession with promises that the New Mexico and Utah territories could decide for themselves whether to allow slavery, as well as promises that federal officials would enforce a new Fugitive Slave Law. Bands played while the Little Giant announced, "We are united from shore to shore."

Tensions eased. Perhaps North and South could go forward, prospering within the Union as they had before. "Civil war is nipped in the bud," the *New Orleans Picayune* rejoiced. "Rebellion is quelled before it had time to show its monster head."

In the months after Eddie's death, Abraham followed the turmoil in Washington. He read about it in newspapers and journals, in his office and beside tavern hearths. He studied the debates, critiqued the speeches, and joined in the arguments with Billy Herndon and other friends. Part of him, the part mourning for his lost son, resisted focusing on weighty, distant issues. But another part, the part attuned to the deepening mysteries of events, hungered to be in the fray.

CHAPTER 44

1850 AND 1851

Mary was pregnant again. The stirrings inside her gave them hope. Not only would life go on, but new life would go on.

Getting ready for the baby restored her vigor. Suddenly she was all over the house washing floors, dusting tables, ordering Abraham to split more firewood or walk up to Irwin's store to buy a few yards of gingham.

"Mother, you're going six ways to Sunday," he said. "If you don't slow down, you'll run us both into the grave, and that child will be born an orphan."

One evening he was in the sitting room, head buried in the *New York Tribune*, bare feet stretched toward the fire, when she came in with a pile of clothes that needed mending. She settled into her chair and rummaged through her sewing box until he finally had to look up.

"I'm worried about Bobbie," she announced.

"What about him?"

"His eye is getting worse."

He winced. They boy's left eye had recently begun to drift inward. It sometimes gave him a cross-eyed look. Bill Wallace said it might be cured if he peeped through a keyhole for several minutes a day to strengthen the eye muscles, but so far that had done no good.

"Some of his friends are beginning to tease him," she said. "They're calling him cockeyed."

"Who's saying that?" He put down his paper.

"They all are, Abraham." She fought back tears. "I'm going to ask Bill to look at him again."

"All right," he said uncertainly, "but I don't know what else he can suggest."

"I don't either, but I'm going to ask. Surely there's a way to fix it."

Bill Wallace recommended an operation to alter the eye muscles. Abraham returned from three days of court in Petersburg to find Bobbie with a patch on his eye and the face around the socket purple from bleeding under the skin. Mary was pale.

"It was horrible," she whispered, out of the boy's earshot. "I don't know if I'll ever be able to get it out of my mind."

Bill and another doctor had strapped Bobbie into a chair and held him still while they forced the eyelids apart with terrible-looking hooks, sliced through a membrane, and cut the muscle with scissors.

"The blood spurted down his face and all over his shirt. He kept screaming and struggling." She buried her face in Abraham's chest. "The only thing that kept me from fainting was Bobbie calling for me. If I had known it was going to be like that, I never would have taken him there."

He wrapped her in a hug and kissed the top of her head, marveling at her courage. Her belly pressed against him, swollen and warm.

She's a strong little woman in many ways, he thought.

The new baby arrived a week after Mary's thirty-second birthday, just in time for Christmas of 1850. Bill Wallace oversaw the birth to make certain everything went smoothly. The gorgeous baby boy came into the world with a serene look on his tiny face. Both parents wept tears mixed with heartache and joy.

"I'd like to name him William Wallace," Mary said. "I think we owe Bill that after all he's done for us in the last year."

They enjoyed a peaceful Yuletide, in stark contrast with the year before. Willie proved to be a good sleeper for a newborn. In every way, he was a godsend. A group of carolers came down Eighth Street singing "The First Noel" and "Hark the Herald Angels Sing." Abraham showed off the baby on the doorstep, and they remarked what a blessing it was that he had come to them during the same time of year as the Babe for whom the season was named.

Mary came down with a mild childbed fever. Bill gave assurances that it was nothing dangerous. He ordered bed rest and stopped by the house every day to check on her. Abraham happily tended to wife and children. Cradling the baby in his arms, he promised himself that he would do everything in his power to keep his little family safe.

January 1851 brought somber tidings. Abraham's father was dead. The news came on an afternoon that was busy with meetings and courtroom appearances, so it was evening before he had a chance to reflect on this great change in his life. He felt guilty that he could muster only a numb melancholy.

"I've spent all my sorrow," he told Mary. "I don't have any left to give."

Tom Lincoln had been strong as an ox in his day, but a life of plowing and hoeing had slowly worn him down. Abraham pictured in his mind's eye the bleak country funeral, the preacher standing in an open door of the gray saddlebag cabin, the women and children inside, huddled around the coffin, the men standing pensive and stiff faced just outside. Afterwards they would load the coffin onto a wagon for the slow ride to the cemetery, where they would shiver in the cold beside the dark, open grave.

He realized with a pang of remorse that his father had never laid eyes on his Springfield grandchildren, had never even met Mary.

He went to see his stepmother that spring when work took him to Coles County, joggling in his buggy behind Old Bob across Goosenest Prairie, through clusters of pink shooting stars and wide stretches of grass beginning to push to the sky. Sally's joy at having him there moved him. She was happy to make a fuss over him, to cook for him, to stuff him full of corn bread while she asked about Mary and his children.

She looked old and tired. For the first time he could remember, there was more gray than black in the hair she always wore curled. Taking care of Tom in his last days had drained her, just as watching Eddie die had drained Mary and Abraham.

"What will you do now?" he asked.

"Go on living, like everyone else."

"I'm worried about who will look after you."

"I've got plenty of kinfolk around here to do that."

"It's a lot of work to keep a place like this going."

"Now, where did you ever get an idea like that?"

He sat by the fireplace and watched her bank coals with a shovel to give a skillet just enough heat. Her cabin looked neat and clean, with a fresh spring coat of whitewash to brighten it up. He felt a sudden urge to bring her back with him.

"Why don't you come live in Springfield?" he asked.

"I've been living in the country so long, I wouldn't know how to live in town."

"You could live with us," he suggested. The instant he said it, he realized Mary would not take kindly to the idea. "Or we could get you your own little place near us. You'd be much more comfortable."

"I'm comfortable enough here. Don't you worry about me."

"Well, I do."

She swung the crane away from the flames, hung a pot full of chicken stew on one of its hooks, and swung it back.

"Abe, I'm done with moving. When you get to be my age, you're set in your ways and just want to stay put."

Her voice retained its old strength. He knew she was not budging.

"I do love it when you stop by to visit," she went on. "It gives me comfort knowing you're not too far away."

She paused in her work to give him a smile. Her face, like her hands, was brown from decades of leaning close to the fire.

"I'll always look after you," he said.

"I know that, son. I've always known it."

He rode out to the Shiloh Cemetery with his stepbrother, John, to visit his father's grave. It was a peaceful spot beside a grove of oaks and hickories, with views of rolling green prairies and fields where the spring warmth would soon raise wheat and corn. It felt like the middle of nowhere, and it struck him that Tom Lincoln must have been destined to end up in just such a place.

The grave lay unmarked beneath a mound of black soil where little dandelions and violets had started to flower. Abraham stood in silence for a few moments, paying his respects. Long ago, his sister, Sarah, had told him that their father did the best he could for them, the best he knew how. That was no doubt true. It had been mighty hard to appreciate that while growing up, but Sarah was right.

I need to get a proper tombstone when I have a chance, he thought.

"Well, his labors are at an end," John remarked. "He'll have to bust sod and harrow fields no more."

Before Abraham left the next morning, he recorded his father's passing in the family Bible: "Thomas Lincoln, died, January 17, 1851, aged 73 years & 11 days." As he handed the book back to his stepmother, he pressed ten dollars into her hand.

"I'll send you the same every month," he told her. "If you need more for any reason, you let me know."

Her blue-gray eyes looked up at him through tears.

"No one could ask for a better son," she murmured. "I love you dearly, Abe."

"If you won't come live with us, I'll bring you to Springfield for a visit soon, to meet Mary and your grandchildren."

"I'd like that. I truly would."

He set out for court in Shelbyville, thinking as he crossed the prairie about the day his father had brought Sally to the Indiana woods to be his new wife and mother to his children. It struck him that Tom had been a younger man that day than he, Abraham, was now.

For the first time in his life, he felt old.

CHAPTER 45

April 1853

Before he knew it, yet another baby was on its way. At least I ain't old in that respect, he told himself with satisfaction.

"I hope this one will be a girl," Mary said. "I've grown fond of paper soldiers, but it would be nice to see a few paper dolls around here and to curl a little girl's hair."

"If a mother drops a knife, it's a sign the baby will be a boy," Abraham told her. "If she drops scissors, it will be a girl."

"Well, hand me my scissors."

"I think Bobbie is using them to form a new regiment of paper soldiers."

The pregnancy was a difficult one. Mary experienced a good bit of discomfort. Bill Wallace and a second doctor attended the birth with a small array of surgical instruments at the ready just in case. The delivery turned painful. The baby's head was larger than normal, and they had a hard time coaxing it out.

It was a boy. Mary let her disappointment show for only a minute.

"I should have known that any child giving me that much trouble would be the male of the species," she commented, then proceeded to shower his little cheeks with kisses.

He was another beautiful baby, with perfect features and his mother's blue-gray eyes. Looking down at him filled Abraham with contentment.

"I'd like to name him Thomas, in memory of my father," he suggested. His stepmother would like that.

"Yes, that would be good," Mary said, exhausted and happy.

He was a wiggly little thing. His large head and slight body earned him a nickname. "He looks like a tadpole squirming around in his cradle," Abraham joked, and he promptly became Tad.

The first sign that something was not right with the child came when Mary tried to nurse him. Abraham heard her weeping and rushed into the bedroom.

"He keeps choking when he tries to suck," she cried. Her voice trembled. "Oh, Abraham, the milk is coming back out of his nose!"

A thin stream of liquid flowed from his nostrils. He kept rooting for the breast, but each attempt to nurse ended in a hollow little cry. His tiny face was red from coughing. Mary tried shifting him to another position and offering the other breast, but that brought only wails of frustration.

Abraham sent Bobbie to fetch Bill Wallace. It took the doctor only a few seconds to locate a small hole in the roof of the baby's mouth.

"It's a slight cleft in his palate," he said gently. "It's nothing life-threatening. The aperture connects to the nasal cavity, so when he drinks, some of the milk goes into his nose."

"How did it happen?" Mary cried. "Is it my fault?"

"You've done nothing wrong. These things simply happen sometimes."

"What can we do?"

"I don't want you to worry about it, Mary," Bill said. "It's not a severe case. He should have no problem eating solid food when he's ready. Until then, you'll need to take extra time nursing him."

"But he's struggling to feed!"

"Try holding his head up as you nurse. You'll find the best position to help him get enough milk."

"If it's a slight case, is there a chance it will heal?" Mary pressed.

"We'll have to wait and see," Bill said evasively.

She cried for hours after he was gone. Abraham did his best to console her, but they were both crushed. There was something wrong with this frail bundle of life, and there was nothing they could do to make it right for him. The faint choking sounds that came from his throat as he tried to get milk terrified them. What if Bill was wrong, and he could not get enough nourishment into his little body? Would their baby waste away?

"Why has God done this to us?" Mary sobbed.

"God won't forget our little Taddie. We must trust in him."

"When I was a girl, I knew a boy who had a cleft palate. It was awful to hear him speak. All the children were so cruel to him. Oh, Abraham, our baby will grow up being teased and scorned."

The next day was busy with work he could not put off—pleadings to write and clients to interview in preparation for upcoming trials. He left Mary and the baby in the hands of neighbor women, who could help them far better than he could. He worried about her all day, but when he got home that evening, she was in a much calmer state of mind.

"The nursing went better," she reported. She had propped herself up on some pillows in her bed. "I think we're getting the hang of it. Bill came by, and he thinks so too."

The child was asleep on her shoulder, and together they made a picture of serenity. Color had returned to her cheeks.

"Children are a heritage of the Lord," she murmured.

Abraham reached, and she gently placed Tad in his arms. He sat in a rocking chair at the foot of the bed and stroked the soft sheen of hair that barely covered the infant's scalp.

"Abraham," she said softly after a while, "Bill told me that Harriet Dallman had her baby."

"Yes, I heard." Harriet and Charles Dallman lived a couple of blocks away. Mrs. Dallman had just given birth to a baby boy.

"Bill says Harriet isn't doing well," she said.

"Yes, I heard that too."

"She's too ill to nurse the child."

He looked up at her. She gazed back at him steadily. All the grief and pain of the last two days had disappeared from her eyes.

"They haven't been able to find a wet nurse," she said.

The hair on her forehead was still matted from the sweat of the hard delivery. Dark half circles were faintly visible under her eyes.

"Bill says their baby is growing weak," she said. "He needs to eat."

The early evening filtered through the windows, softening all the edges in the room. An amber glow hovered over the bed, touched Mary's arms and hands where they lay on a blanket. She was no longer young. How had that happened so quickly? On the day they had married, she'd looked a bride in the bloom of maidenhood. Giving birth to four children and burying one had broadened her girlish features into matronly lines.

She smiled and nodded assurance.

Abraham rose, carefully placed Tad in the black walnut cradle, so as not to wake him, and slipped out the door. Dusk was falling, and with it a fine, nacreous light. The sky was perfectly still. Through the luminous silver over the prairies ran long streaks of crimson almost too bright to look at.

He knocked softly on the door of the Dallmans' brick bungalow. No one answered, so he let himself in.

The house was quiet except for the ticking of a mantel clock. He moved silently along a shadowy hallway; through an open door he saw Harriet asleep in her bedroom. Charles, equally exhausted, dozed in a chair in the sitting room, a cradle at his feet. The infant was sleeping as well, but his pinched little face told of a fitful rest. Abraham found pen and ink on a writing table, scratched out a quick note, and left it beside the cradle where the father would be sure to see it. Bending low, he gathered the newborn in his arms, which he formed into a basket, and gently carried him to Mary.

CHAPTER 46

Winter and Spring 1854

Stephen Douglas was causing trouble in Washington. The Little Giant, serving his second term in the Senate, was determined to organize a big chunk of the West into territories that could someday become states. The region was filling up with people and needed government. Southern politicians, fearful of Northern clout, declared that they would see the region sink in hell before they would see any of it admitted as states that outlawed slavery.

Douglas cut a deal to win Southern support. He crafted legislation to set up two territories, Kansas and Nebraska, and repeal the Missouri Compromise of 1820, which had banned slavery in the region. The residents of Kansas and Nebraska would vote on the question of whether they wanted slavery. Let the people decide, Douglas said. What could be more American than that?

Billy Herndon howled at the newspaper reports.

"Has Douglas lost his mind?"

"He's acting like it," Abraham said. "He had to know this would raise a storm. I can't figure out what he's up to."

"I'll tell you what. He wants a railroad from Chicago to San Francisco, and he needs to make Nebraska a territory before he can lay tracks. He's bought thousands of acres near the route. That bill and those tracks will make him as rich as Croesus."

"Perhaps."

"He'll stop at nothing to forge an American empire from Atlantic to Pacific."

That's Douglas through and through, Abraham thought. Headstrong to the point of foolhardiness. Like Aesop's frog, ready to leap into a well without stopping to consider how he'll get out.

"He'll spread slavery across the whole country," Billy fumed.

Court business took Abraham to Urbana the day the telegraph wires flashed the news that Douglas had succeeded in pushing his Kansas-Nebraska Act through both houses of Congress. Stunned lawyers gathered in Judge Davis's tavern room to digest the report.

"This will ruin good feelings between North and South," Davis growled. "All hell will break loose."

"Gutting the Missouri Compromise is a monstrous crime. He's set the Slave Power loose in the land."

"If slavery goes into Kansas and Nebraska, we'll see human bondage in every last state."

Abraham studied the arguments in Northern and Southern papers, pored over the speeches of antislavery men like Salmon Chase and William Henry Seward. In Springfield, he sat quietly by the stove in Corneau & Diller's drugstore, listening to Whigs and Democrats fume.

"The last thing we need is a bunch of Kentuckians dragging their slave labor into the territories. There'll be no place left for white farmers."

"No slaveholders and no Negroes in the territories, I say. It ought to be white men's land."

"We ought to ship all the Negroes back to Africa so we don't have to hear no more about them."

"Slaves are bad enough, but hell, if it was up to the abolitionists, this whole country would be overrun with free niggers."

At home, he stretched out on the sitting room floor with his shoulders against an overturned chair, scoured the newspapers, and stared at the ashes on the hearth left from the last fire of the spring. Mary came into the room, opened her sewing box, and threaded a needle.

"Big doings in Congress these days," she said.

"Yes."

"Steve Douglas has kicked a hornet's nest."

"Yes, kicked it hard, I'd say."

"If he's not careful, he'll get stung."

She took up a pair of Bobbie's pants and set to work mending a hole.

"Abraham, do you realize it's been four years now since you came home from Washington?"

"Yes."

"More than four, in fact."

"Yes, that's right."

"Maybe it's time you went back."

They gazed at each other, reading the other's thoughts.

"You think so?"

"I do. Douglas has miscalculated. Whatever his reasons for pushing this bill through Congress, he's triggered a furor he was not expecting."

"That is true."

She made three deliberate stitches. "That furor can be made to help the Whigs gain seats in the legislature," she said.

"Yes, that thought has crossed a few minds around here."

"And the legislature will be choosing a United States senator during the next session."

She put down her sewing.

"My father used to say that it's not an opportunity that makes a man, but the man who makes the opportunity," she said.

"Yes."

"Perhaps this is an opportunity worth making."

Abraham wandered the outskirts of town at dusk, on paths where cottage yards met freshly planted rows of corn, walking head down with long measured thoughts and strides. Off to the west, clouds of blackbirds darkened a patch of sky. A windmill squeaked low somber notes, like a man standing alone in a field whistling to himself.

Mary was right. Here was an opportunity. But there was something deeper here as well, and out on the edge of the prairie, he went searching for it.

He thought of days when he had walked miles to get his hands on books about men like Washington and Jefferson. Days reading on tree stumps about sacrifices at places like Valley Forge and Cowpens. Grappling to understand the meaning of words like *liberty* and *equality*. Now it seemed as if those words and sacrifices were in danger of meaning nothing at all.

The nation's founders had envisioned a day when slavery would perish, when the stain of human bondage would be removed from the land, and the promise of the Declaration of Independence would extend to all. Douglas and his Kansas-Nebraska Act would wreck that vision. He would open the way for slavery to follow the railroads across plains and deserts until it was left for the oceans alone to stop its advance. The country would never rid itself of the grotesque contradiction of human chattel in a nation supposedly dedicated to the inalienable rights of men.

The tensions between slavery and freedom were becoming more marked. Two opposing ideas had been kept apart like wild beasts chained in sight of each other. Eventually one of the deadly antagonists would break its bonds, and then the question would be settled. One must overcome the other. Postponing the struggle would only make it more deadly.

Out on the verge of the prairie, alone, he saw something worth fighting for, something that left no choice but to fight.

CHAPTER 47

FALL 1854 TO SPRING 1855

The winds of political change were blowing. Maybe he really did have a chance to go back to Washington, this time as a senator.

In the 1854 fall elections, Illinois voters signaled their discontent with the Kansas-Nebraska Act by sending men who opposed the law to the statehouse. Anti-Nebraska men, they were called. They would hold a majority in the next General Assembly. One of their first duties would be to choose a new senator to serve alongside Stephen Douglas.

"They'll choose you if you put yourself forward," Mary said.

"Perhaps. But there are a dozen men willing to be known as candidates. And probably fifty secretly watching for a chance."

"Let them watch. We will act."

"The next legislature will be a disjointed bunch. The anti-Nebraska men will barely hold an edge. I'll need the support of nearly every one."

"First you'll be senator, then president!" she insisted.

"I have as much chance of rising to the presidency as I do of lifting myself over a fence with the straps of my boots," he said. "Anyway, I'd rather have a full term in the Senate than four years in the presidency. There's more chance to make a reputation, and less danger of losing it."

Letters went out to legislators, asking for support.

"It has come round that a Whig may, by possibility, be elected to the US Senate, and I want the chance of being the man," he wrote. "Think it over and see whether you can do better than to go for me."

He wrote to allies around the state with influence in the legislature.

"Some friends here are really for me for the US Senate, and I should be very grateful if you could make a mark for me among your members."

He spoke wherever he could, explaining the wrong of slavery and the Kansas-Nebraska Act in terms plain enough for prairie farmers.

"When the white man governs himself, that is self-government; but when he governs himself, and also governs another man, that is more than self-government—that is despotism," he told audiences. "If the Negro is a man, why then my ancient faith teaches me that 'all men are created equal,' and that there can be no moral right in connection with one man's making a slave of another. No man is good enough to govern another man without that other's consent. I say this is the leading principle—the sheet anchor of American republicanism."

The furor over the slavery question strained political allegiances. Party ties began to snap. Many predicted the old Whig Party would fall apart. Some of the antislavery men were joining the new Republican Party, which had sworn itself to oppose the expansion of slavery.

"More than a few of our Republican friends would be pleased to see you join their ranks," Billy Herndon told Abraham.

"Yes, and more than a few would just as quickly try to drive me out. Some of those fellows are radical in the way they assail the South."

"But there are Republicans who see eye to eye with you. Why not join them?"

"That would cost me Whig supporters."

"And if the Whig Party comes to an end?"

"Billy, I've been a Whig all my political life. I suppose I'll stay a Whig as long as I can. In the meantime, it won't hurt to stay friendly with the Republicans."

Friends pitched in to help him round up commitments. Mary helped him fill small notebooks listing members of the legislature and their political dispositions. They pored over the columns, gauging the depths and shallows of his support. The signs looked hopeful if they could pick up a few more votes, though where he was to find them, he could not tell.

For weeks he thought of little else. He was a man on a vigil. Billy noticed that even when he lay down for a catnap on the office sofa, he slept, like Napoleon, with one eye open.

A visit from Mary's sister Emilie came as a welcome distraction. She arrived from Lexington just in time for the holiday season. Eighteen years old, pretty and petite, with a doe-eyed smile, she had no trouble winning hearts.

She plunged into a whirl of yuletide festivities, pulling Mary and Abraham along with her. Laughter and the energy of youth filled the house. Mary was lighthearted whenever Emilie was around. They shared a girlish interest in gowns and lace.

"How do you like this one, Mr. Lincoln?" Mary asked. She wore a new white silk dress she had just finished brocading with garlands of little blue flowers.

"Fine feathers enough on you to make fine birds of both of us," he said. "Mrs. Lincoln, those posies on your dress are the color of your eyes."

She dimpled with pleasure. "You see, Emilie, I'm training him to see color. He didn't know pink from blue when I married him."

She took Emilie window-shopping around the square and bought her a velvet bonnet smothered in white plumes. The sisters recited poetry and took turns reading the novels of Sir Walter Scott aloud to Bobbie. On cold afternoons, they whispered in the parlor about young men who had called on Emilie. It was all good to see. It reminded Abraham of younger days.

"We must find her a Springfield husband, so she'll move here," Mary told him.

"If any more Todds move to Illinois, we'll have to give you your own congressional district."

"Give us the vote, and the Todd women will send you straight to the Senate."

January 1855 brought heavy snows with strong winds that pushed drifts up to windowsills. Shops around the square closed. Pastors, surrendering to the will of the Almighty, cancelled church services. Trains were marooned on the prairies for days, like oxen frozen in their tracks, forcing passengers to make bonfires of engine fuel and wade to nearby farmhouses for food. Telegraph lines went down, and mail service stopped. The *Illinois State Register* reported that "Springfield is now entirely cut off from all communication with the rest of the world."

Abraham shoveled paths to the woodpile, the privy, the barn. The pump froze up, so he hauled buckets of snow to the kitchen to melt on the stove. He helped Bobbie, Willie, and some neighborhood boys build a snowman on Eighth Street. They gave him a stumpy body, a huge head, and a scowl made of broken corn cobs, then hung a placard that read "The Little Giant" on it.

The blizzards kept legislators out of town, delaying the Senate election. Abraham and Mary spent late nights scrutinizing the notebooks they had put together. He had picked up supporters in recent weeks but still lacked enough for victory.

"I count fifty-seven anti-Nebraska votes," he said, "and forty-three Nebraska men. I think most of those fifty-seven will go for me."

"Then your chances are good."

"I've got more committals than any other man. The Whigs, I'm sure of. The Democrats are another matter."

The incumbent, Democrat Jimmie Shields, the man he had come close to dueling, would surely lose his Senate seat. His support of Douglas's Kansas-Nebraska Act had infuriated antislavery men. Some independent Democrats were supporting Judge Lyman Trumbull of Alton, a lifelong Democrat who hated slavery. If Abraham could peel away a handful of Trumbull supporters, he might have enough votes to go over the top. The question was, could those Democrats bring themselves to vote for a Whig?

Then there was Governor Joel Matteson. Rumors that he was maneuvering for the Senate had been swirling across the frozen drifts. Matteson was rich, popular, and not above offering a bribe or two. His operatives had been busy whispering in legislators' ears. Abraham did not trust him.

"Elizabeth and Ninian want to give us a victory party at their house," Mary told him. "We'll invite everyone on both sides of the aisle."

"Don't you think we ought to pick the apples before we bake the pie?"

"The best way to get what you want is to act like you'll get it."

The weather finally improved. Locomotives outfitted with plows bullied their way through snowbanks to free stranded trains. Weary legislators straggled into town, and the day for the vote arrived. A crowd made its way to the statehouse, some by sleigh, others by foot along slippery paths.

The rotunda was crammed with sightseers. Mary and Emilie, dressed to be seen, climbed the stairs to the gallery overlooking Representatives Hall, where the members of the General Assembly gathered in joint session. Lyman Trumbull's wife, Julia, one of Mary's oldest Springfield friends, was already there. Governor Matteson's wife looked on as well, smiling in her role as the first lady of Illinois.

Abraham stood to the side on the House floor, leaning slightly against one of the Corinthian columns rimming the chamber, as nervous as he had ever been. Stephen Logan, his former law partner, was acting as his floor manager. Logan outlined last-minute strategies in excited tones, but Abraham barely listened. He could hardly believe he was on the verge of a Senate seat. He never would have admitted to anyone, except perhaps Mary, that more than once he had whispered the words "Senator Lincoln" to himself to hear how they sounded.

A huge portrait of George Washington gazed from the wall at the front of the room. The rap of a gavel drew legislators to tightly packed rows of chairs. Abraham scrutinized faces, trying to guess from smiles and handshakes who he could count on.

The joint session came to order. The Speaker called for names to be placed into nomination. Voices wielding high-minded phrases nominated James Shields and Lyman Trumbull. Logan's shrill voice called out the nomination of his good friend and patriot Abraham Lincoln. The balloting started. Members stood one by one to announce their votes.

At the end of the first round, Abraham had forty-five votes, Shields forty-one, and Trumbull five. Eight votes were scattered among other candidates, including one for Governor Matteson.

Abraham looked up at Mary and smiled. So far it was what they expected. All the men committed to vote for him had come through. He was only five votes short of the fifty required for victory. If the handful of anti-Nebraska Democrats supporting Trumbull came to his side now, it would be over. With some luck and persuasion, that would happen on the next ballot or two.

The proceedings came to a pause while the candidates huddled with their supporters. Logan moved among allies with a hopeful look on his face. Outside the door in the great hall under the dome, the crowd droned. The Speaker rapped his gavel again and called for the second ballot.

Looking back, when it was all over, it was difficult to pinpoint the moment it should have been clear that fortune had cast her dice against him. Perhaps as soon as the second ballot, when a handful of his men deserted him. Or the fifth round, when his total slipped to thirty-four.

Certainly by the seventh ballot, when the Democrats launched their surprise attack, and the party regulars all at once abandoned Shields to break for Matteson.

With each ballot Abraham tallied his losses, the numbness of defeat creeping over him. He watched John Strunk of Kankakee, who had said he would walk a hundred miles to elect his friend Lincoln, rise and change his vote to Matteson. Men who had pledged to stand beside him looked any direction but his way. The anti-Nebraska men, seeing his votes crumble, panicked and fled to Trumbull in hopes of repelling the Matteson assault. He felt like a man standing alone at a hitching post, watching his mount trot out of sight with someone else in the saddle.

The moment came when Matteson lay just a few votes short of election. Abraham was down to fifteen loyal supporters.

"What do we do?" Logan asked. He had tears in his eyes.

Abraham looked up at the gallery. Mary sat with a frozen smile, clutching Emilie's hand.

"It's no good," he said softly. "There are too many Democrats here to elect anyone but a Democrat."

"Matteson has bought and bribed half his votes!" Logan cried bitterly.

"Yes, and if we give him any more time, he'll bribe the last few he needs."

Lyman Trumbull sat across the room scribbling a note at a desk, spectacles perched at the end of his nose, looking like the schoolmaster he had once been. His coat hung loosely on his narrow frame. Trumbull was a good man. He would make a good senator. If it had to be a Democrat, they had to make sure it would be an anti-Nebraska man.

"We can't win, but we can beat Matteson. Tell our men to go for Trumbull."

The end came on the tenth ballot, with Trumbull barely going over the top. The crowd sent a roar into the dome. Well-wishers thronged in Trumbull's direction. Abraham pushed his way toward the door, accepting condolences. It was one of those times he wished his head did not stick up above everyone else's.

Mary came down the stairs with Emilie, bristling with indignation. He steered her away from the throng as quickly as possible.

"I don't understand why the forty-five who started with you should surrender to Trumbull's five!" she cried.

"There was no other way. I couldn't let the whole result go to ruin for my own sake."

"Trumbull robbed you!"

"Lyman Trumbull is an honest man. I wish we had more like him in office."

They both knew he was practicing his game face. The thought that so many allies had ended up voting for another man stung hard. It was one thing to be beaten by your enemies, much harder to be wounded in the house of your friends.

"At least the Nebraska men are whipped worse than I am," he said. "Trumbull will make life thorny for Douglas when he gets to Washington."

The victory party that Ninian and Elizabeth had planned for them turned into a reception for the Trumbulls. Abraham and Mary bridled their humiliation and went to offer good wishes. Elizabeth hugged them both and said she knew how disappointed they must be.

"Not too disappointed to congratulate my friend Trumbull," Abraham smiled, shaking the senator-elect's hand.

Mary could not bring herself to be a good loser. In this same parlor a dozen years before, on the evening she and Abraham were married, Julia Jayne Trumbull had stood beside her as a bridesmaid. Now Mary was an attendant, and Julia stood in the place of honor. It was too much. Mary offered her old friend terse greetings, then turned her back.

They went home as soon as possible. Emilie went straight to bed. Abraham asked Mary to heat some water for coffee, mainly to give her something to do. Her hands trembled as she filled the pot. They retreated to the sitting room to lick their wounds while the water boiled.

"I've never been so mortified." Mary spat the words out. "How could Elizabeth and Ninian host a party for that man?"

"There was no point in wasting all that food and drink."

"My own sister! Imagine my indignation."

"Better to be as graceful as possible in defeat," he said gently.

"You're taking this whipping very easily."

"I'm as disappointed as you."

"You don't act like it."

"Mary, I may never run for office again. Of course I'm disappointed. I'm devastated."

"You should never have surrendered. You certainly should not have delivered your support to Trumbull."

"There was no choice. I had to make the best of a bad situation."

"He should have given his measly five votes to you after the first ballot. Lyman Trumbull is a treacherous sneak."

"Shh, shh—it does no good to talk about our friends that way."

"He swindled us out of office!"

"He has as much right to that office as I do."

He stepped into the kitchen, fixed the coffee, and brought her a cup.

"We must look on the bright side," he said. "If I do run for office again someday, Trumbull will owe me his support."

"Don't expect to get it!"

He poured himself a cup.

"I promise you this," she said. "I will never forgive Julia. Never. A true friend would have influenced her husband to deliver his votes to you."

"Perhaps her husband does not follow her advice."

"She's a cold, selfish, unpopular woman."

"We mustn't speak that way. You and Julia have been friends for a long time."

"I will never speak to her again. She's dead to me. She's nothing but a whited sepulcher."

"She doesn't deserve that."

Mary bristled. "Why are you taking that woman's side?"

"I'm not taking her side."

Rage flashed across her face. For an instant, he thought she might hurl her coffee at him.

"Perhaps you think Mrs. Trumbull is better suited than I to be a senator's wife."

"Of course not. But you're being too harsh. She's done nothing wrong."

"I see—then I'm the one in the wrong, I suppose!"

She slammed her cup down, spilling all over the carpet, and stormed off to the bedroom, banging the door behind her.

He sat alone for a long time, well into the night, staring into the flames on the hearth, trying to subdue his own frustration.

My God, he thought, she really can be a hellcat.

Emilie's Springfield visit lasted several more weeks. She refused to let either one of them brood. She dragged Mary out to plays, concerts, and parties. On Sunday afternoons, she played checkers with Abraham and laughed with Mary over old family stories. When the weather warmed, they piled into the carriage with the children for long drives in the countryside. Bobbie, who was just beginning to notice girls, gathered flowers by the armful for his pretty young aunt.

They were all sad when the day came for her to go back to Lexington. A small crowd of Todd relations showed up at the depot to see her off. Abraham hoisted her trunks onto the baggage car. When the goodbyes had been said and promises to write had been made, the train lurched out of sight with Emilie's handkerchief fluttering from a window.

They loaded the boys into the carriage and turned for home, riding in silence as gloom thickened on a morning haze. Mary slumped against Abraham. He took her little white hand in his big, bony, brown one.

"Don't worry, my girl, it will come out right in the end," he promised.

CHAPTER 48

June to September 1855

Another opportunity was not long in coming. He was lying on the floor upstairs one late afternoon, screwing a headboard to a bed frame, when someone's knuckles rapped on the front door. Mary stuck her head out the window and looked down.

"Who's there?"

A moment of silence, as if no one were there at all, followed by a voice that sounded a little surprised.

"My name is Watson. I'm looking for Mr. Lincoln."

"Business or politics?"

Another brief silence, as if Mr. Watson might have decided to go away, followed by a clearing of a throat.

"Business," the voice called up, a little louder. "I went to his office, but he wasn't there. I was told I might find him here."

Mary pulled her head back inside. "Mr. Lincoln! Here is a man who wants to see you on business."

Abraham clomped downstairs. On his doorstep stood a young fellow in a new suit that had the shine of an expensive clothier. He introduced himself as Mr. Peter Watson, a patent attorney from Washington, D.C. Abraham brought him inside.

"My associate, Mr. George Harding of Philadelphia, sent me here to see if we might retain you," Watson explained. "We're representing the Manny Company in the action brought by McCormick. I assume you're aware of it?"

Abraham's pulse quickened. News of the suit had been rippling through legal circles. Cyrus McCormick, inventor of the famous mechanical reaper, was bringing action against John H. Manny, inventor of a similar machine, charging that Manny's reaper infringed on McCormick's patents. It would be a huge case. Several other reaper companies were pouring funds into Manny's defense with the aim of breaking McCormick's dominance. The outcome of the trial would affect manufacturing and wheat cultivation across the West.

"Mr. Harding will lead the defense team," Watson said. "Edward Dickerson of New York and Reverdy Johnson of Baltimore will represent McCormick."

All three were renowned attorneys. It was hard to believe they would be interested in associating themselves with Abraham Lincoln of Illinois.

"Why do you want me?" Abraham asked.

"The case is likely to go before Judge Drummond, in Chicago." Watson glanced around the parlor as if still not quite sure he had found the right house. "We want someone on our side who knows the judge and has his confidence. Your name was recommended."

He offered a retainer of four hundred dollars and a total fee of a thousand dollars at the close of litigation. Abraham jumped at the chance. Watson promised that his firm would send copies of depositions and other legal papers needed to prepare for trial. They shook hands, and the young man hurried away.

It was an astounding piece of luck. The generous fee would go a long way toward replacing income missed while running for the Senate.

"It'll give me the chance to pick up some of my lost crumbs," he told Billy. "And measure swords with the best legal minds in the country."

The first chance he got, he went up to Rockford to look over the Manny factory. A patient mechanic went over every inch of the Manny reaper with him, explaining how each part worked from dividing iron to sickles to reel. It was better than wandering the Patent Office in Washington. The mechanic turned him loose on one of the machines and invited him to tinker to his heart's content. Abraham spent half a day taking pieces apart and putting them back together.

Back in Springfield, he dove into case law and agricultural journals, collecting facts for arguments in court. It excited him to think that, in a small way, he was contributing to the revolution in industry that was sweeping the advanced parts of the world, and that his work might help move Illinois farmers a bit further along the road of human progress. It helped take the sting out of the Senate defeat.

Weeks passed, and no word came from Peter Watson. The depositions and other papers he had promised to forward did not arrive. While in Chicago on court business, Abraham managed to get copies of some of the documents he needed. He wrote to Watson but got no response.

"It's beginning to look like these Eastern lawyers are no more organized than we are," he told Billy.

One day he picked up the *Tribune* and read that the reaper suit would be tried in Cincinnati, instead of Chicago, before Justice John McLean. It was disappointing news. Perhaps his services were no longer needed since the hearing would not be in Illinois. But there had been no communication from Harding's firm one way or the other. He could not simply fail to show up if they were expecting him. He wrote out his argument and finished preparing his notes for court. When the time came, he boarded a train and steamed to Cincinnati.

A ticket agent at the station directed him to the Burnet House, on the corner of Third and Vine, where George Harding was said to be staying. The hotel proprietor pointed out the attorney as he came walking through the lobby with another gentleman. Abraham hailed him. Harding shook hands and introduced his associate, Edwin M. Stanton, a short, balding man with thick black brows and sharp black eyes glaring through steel-rimmed glasses. Abraham recognized the name—a well-known trial lawyer from Pittsburgh.

"We're just leaving to walk up to the court," Harding told him.

"Well, let's go up in a gang," Abraham suggested.

Stanton put on a scowl. Harding looked uncomfortable.

"Why don't you get yourself settled," Harding offered. "We'll go on ahead."

They turned and left him standing alone.

"Why did you bring that damned long-armed ape here?" Stanton muttered, loud enough to be overheard. "He can do you no good. Let him go with his own gang."

The humiliation burned. Abraham closed his eyes and took a deep breath to steady himself. When he opened them, he found himself staring down at the front of his dirty linen duster, his ill-fitting trousers hardly reaching his ankles, his faded cotton umbrella clasped in both hands. He should have been more careful about the way he dressed to meet them. If he'd been smart about it, he would have asked Mary to pick out clothes for the trip. They'd been expecting a raw-boned Western bumpkin lawyer, and that's what they'd seen.

With effort, he threw off the initial shock of rejection. It wasn't the first time he'd met up with an arrogant, pugnacious lawyer. Or the first time he'd been taken for a country rube. He would just have to show them that he knew a thing or two about the law.

They had no intention of giving him a chance. The next day, when he opened his mouth to make a small suggestion, Stanton gave him a sharp, biting look. It was obvious they did not need or want him. He could stick around and observe the courtroom proceedings, if he must, but was not to take part. They refused to confer with him or let him sit with them in court. They never invited him to their table when they ate, or asked him to come to their hotel rooms, or walk to and from court with them. He tried giving them a copy of the argument he'd written, in case it might prove useful, but Harding returned it unopened. When Justice McLean asked counsel on both sides of the case to dinner in his fine home, Abraham was not invited.

As far as he could tell, Edwin Stanton was the chief source of his problems. The man was dogmatic, impatient, and rude. Granted, there were some traits to admire in him: industry, efficiency, a strict sense of duty, an iron will. There was something sad about him. Death had taken his wife and a young daughter. It was rumored that he kept the child's remains in a metal box at his bedside for more than a year and buried his grief with work. Abraham had never seen a more ferocious litigator. It was said that he once swallowed poison so he could detail its effects at trial and save a client from hanging. Now he had apparently made up his mind that no rough-edged Illinois lawyer would stand in the way of the best defense he could give Mr. Manny.

One afternoon Abraham was in the courtroom with the other attorneys, looking over a model of a reaper, when he heard a growl behind him.

"Step aside, sir!"

He glanced over his shoulder. Stanton was glaring at him, shaking his head.

"Step aside!"

I'll be damned if I'll let him treat me that way, Abraham thought. He turned his back and went on examining the model.

"I'll make you move!"

Stanton grabbed Abraham's coattails and gave two emphatic jerks. Mortified, Abraham retreated.

"If that giraffe appears in this case, I'll throw up my brief and leave," Stanton grumbled to Harding.

Abraham thought about going home but decided that running away would be even more demoralizing than staying. In the days before the trial, he spent a good bit of time wandering Cincinnati, feeling low. He remembered that his father used to say that the path that leads to a loaf of bread winds through a field of toil.

I wish my path would do a little less winding, he thought. I don't even know if I'm on a path anymore.

Indiana had been full of paths surrounded by woods so thick the light barely came through. The paths in Illinois, which cut through tall prairie grass and cornstalks, could feel just as hemmed in.

I can't see where I'm going, he thought. Maybe my path is just a dead end.

He distracted himself by taking in the sights that had brought Cincinnati the moniker Queen City of the West. The gardens at Spring Grove Cemetery, where leaves tinged with red and yellow hung over marble stones, were a good place to lose himself. Along the riverfront, a fleet of steamboats with names like *Ohio Belle* and *Cincinnatus* crowded the wharves. More than once he met droves of pigs in the streets, hundreds at a time, squealing their way to the slaughterhouses. The city's other nickname was Porkopolis.

Someone told him that it was worth viewing the estate of Mr. Nicholas Longworth. He entered the yard of the grand columned house and came upon a little old gardener weeding the shrubbery beside a pebbled walkway. The man rose as he approached. He was dressed in old baggy clothes and untied shoes.

"Does your master allow strangers to walk the grounds?" Abraham asked.

The gardener hesitated, sizing him up. "My master's a queer duck," he said. "He doesn't allow strangers to come in, but he makes an exception every time a stranger does come. I believe he'd be happy to make the same exception for you."

Abraham realized the little gardener was the owner himself. He apologized profusely.

"Not at all. I'm quite used to it." Longworth chuckled. "In fact, you realized it quicker than most. My loss. I usually get ten cents to give a tour of my grounds before they find me out. You might call it the only honest money I've ever made. I was a lawyer by profession."

"In that case, we're fellow rogues," Abraham said.

"In town for business or pleasure?"

"Business, I thought. On the reaper case, until a fellow named Stanton cut me out."

"Stanton, eh? I've run up against him a time or two. Well, it's an excellent precept to retire when a skunk is in the path."

"You think so?"

"Yes, but only long enough to let him get out of your way."

The time came for the attorneys to argue the case. Abraham buried his pride and went to see what these high-powered lawyers could really do. He wasn't prepared for the courtroom duel he witnessed. They came at each other with logic keen as polished steel, jabbing and thrusting like beings who had shed all trace of humanity. Stanton and Harding knew every last piece of the machines in question. Dickerson and Johnson, for McCormick, knew the same. They had mastered all past rulings that had a bearing on the case. Every theory of law lay at their command. They spoke with elegant precision, and when they talked to the judge directly, it was on equal terms, one refined mind to another.

He realized, as he watched with bruised ego, that he could not possibly match his legal skills and experience against these men. He would have made a fine presentation in his own way, but not a dazzling one like they could. It would have been a mistake for him to speak in this case. He did not understand it as well as they did. They were right to exclude him after all. Stanton may have been brusque, but he knew what he was doing. And from the looks of the way things were going, he would probably carry the day for the Manny Company.

When the proceedings were over, Abraham went back to Springfield, sat in his office with his feet stuck up on a windowsill, and stared through the dirty pane at the sky.

"How did it go, Mr. Lincoln?" Billy asked.

"That man Stanton handled me pretty roughly."

He stared out the window a while longer to finish subduing his mortification.

"I'll tell you something, Billy," he said. "For any rough-and-tumble case, and a pretty good one, too, I'm enough for any man around here. But these college-trained men are coming west. They've had all the advantages of a lifelong education and plenty of time to study. Soon they'll be in Illinois, and I must meet them."

He leaned back a little further and looked up at the ceiling.

"I'm going to do more studying and learning. And when they appear, I'll be ready."

CHAPTER 49

SPRING 1856

Peter Watson sent him a check for the promised fee. At first Abraham refused it, but Watson insisted. So at least the Manny case wasn't a financial setback. In fact, his money situation was good for a lawyer who kept dabbling in politics. He could safely count on about three thousand dollars a year in income—enough for Mary to decide it was time to add onto their house.

Several weeks of banging and sawing by Springfield carpenters turned their quaint old one-and-a-half story cottage into a handsome two-story residence with a new parlor, dining room, and upstairs bedrooms. Outside, Greek revival pilasters and an iron grillwork balustrade gave it the look of a home where a prosperous attorney lived, one with railroads and reaper companies for clients.

With three growing boys, they needed the extra space. Bobbie shot up like a weed. It seemed like only yesterday that he was pushing a toy steamboat across the floor, and now he was suddenly a teenager, a good-looking young fellow who resembled his mother more than his father, thank goodness. He wanted to be called Bob now and talked of going to law school someday. Sweet, gentle Willie would soon start grade school. Already he was interested in books. Tad was a bundle of energy, a happy little fellow, though his cleft palate gave him a hard time with his speech, as Mary had feared. He had trouble saying his *r*'s. Words like "drum" came out as "d'um," and "Papa dear" came out "Papa-day."

"This chai-uh is my d'um, Papa-day, and this stick is my d'umstick."

"Do you think Mother likes you to beat on her chair with a stick, Taddie?"

"When I gwoh up, I'm going to be a soldiuh, and I'll have a d'um and a wifle and a swo'd."

"If you don't stop hitting her chair, Mother will court-martial you and throw you into the stockade."

"What's a stockade?"

"It's the place where they put bad boys."

"I'm th'ohwing Willie into the stockade and hitting him with my d'umstick, Papa-day!"

Time was passing with as much stealth as the shadows that crept over the sundial behind Chatterton's jewelry store, where the citizens of Springfield paused to set their watches. Abraham was pushing fifty, and his eyes weren't what they used to be. Words in newspapers and legal papers had been looking fuzzy lately. One day, while he was in Bloomington, he passed a shop window with a display of reading glasses. He stepped inside, found some that cleared things up, and walked out with his first pair of spectacles.

Mary was getting more high-strung with age. More likely to fly off the handle when Abraham came to the table late for dinner or when she didn't like the cut of meat he'd bought at the butcher's shop. She got headaches more often. Sometimes he tried to figure out a cause. Maybe it was Eddie's death, or Tad's hard birth. Or something in the Todd blood. It was hard to tell.

Thunderstorms terrified her—left her whimpering so badly that he hurried home from the office whenever he saw one approaching. Noises were beginning to keep her up at night. Creaking and scraping downstairs. It was thieves trying to break into the house when he was away, she said.

"Now, Mother, it's nothing to worry about," he assured her.

"How do you know? You're not here when they come."

"It's just boards contracting and expanding. All houses do it."

He took to paying neighborhood boys five cents a night to help Bob defend the house when he was traveling. If it made her feel more secure, it was worth the trouble.

He came home from a week of court business in Champaign County and got an earful about the bad day she was having. Terrible headaches had plagued her since morning. Tad had dumped ink powder into a bottle of lamp oil and spilled it all over a carpet. While her hands were slippery with soap, she'd dropped a trivet on her foot—no, it was fine, though her toe was sore—and then burned herself on the iron while pressing a shirt.

"A man came to the door not thirty minutes ago asking if I had any pots to mend," she said. "He was acting very strange. Probably a robber looking things over."

"Don't you think he was probably just a tinker looking for work?"

"This is a likely house for thieves to target. Anyone watching is sure to know you're gone most of the time."

A beefsteak frying on the stove began to smoke.

"There, you see?" she cried. "You might as well get used to burnt food. That's what you get when your wife has only two hands and three children and not enough hours in the day for all the chores around here."

"Well, Mother, a few ashes are good for the system," he said cheerily. "They remind the body of the dust from which we come." He gave her a peck on the cheek.

She pushed him away and reached for the skillet.

"Now that you're making more money, is there a need to be away on the circuit so much?"

"That's where I make most of my income. If I cut back on the circuit, we'll have less money, not more."

"Can't you let Mr. Herndon take half the out-of-town cases?"

"Billy's not a courtroom lawyer. He's better at handling office business."

"Well, that's nice for him. He gets half the money you make, and I get to live half the year without a husband."

So that's what this is about, he thought. The neglected wife.

"Why don't we invest our savings?" she asked. "Buy land. The other lawyers get rich doing it. Then you won't need to be on the circuit."

"Land isn't my business. The law is."

She tossed a lid onto an iron pot with a loud, deliberate bang.

"Have I done something wrong in particular?" he asked.

"Is it wrong to wish my husband were here with his family more?"

"No."

"What about skipping one week of each term, so you're not gone so long at a stretch? Skip court at Urbana or Danville. Would the halls of justice come crashing down?"

"I have clients in Urbana and Danville who depend on me. I can't just not show up."

"Perhaps you could get home for a weekend to see your children, if not your wife?"

The tone of her voice made him dig in.

"I work weekends when I'm on the circuit. That's when I write most of my briefs."

He went to the sitting room and sat in his rocker to read the *Chicago Tribune*. By God, what was wrong with that woman? Sometimes she was enough to make a man stay out on the circuit twelve months a year. One minute full of wit and laughter, and the next meaner than a skilletful of snakes. She acted as though traveling the circuit was nothing but one long excuse for a bunch of men to get away from their wives. Well, let her try riding twenty miles a day across frozen prairies and sleeping on mattresses crawling with lice. Or choking down half-cooked tavern food. She had no idea how much pressure it meant to write pleadings on the fly and deal with clients who lied to your face half the time and then got ornery when things didn't turn out well. Let her try it herself and see how she liked it.

Mary came into the room.

"Mr. Lincoln, the fire is getting low," she said, pointing to the hearth. "Please put some wood on it."

She hustled back into the kitchen.

That was another thing. Every time he came home, she demanded he tend to some chore or another before he could take a breath. Stoke the fires or bring in some wood or carry out ashes. As if he didn't tend a fire all day long, every cold day of the year. Was she under the impression that he and Billy kept a manservant to put on more wood at the office? Every law office and courthouse in the state had a woodpile out back. Did the attorneys send for their wives to come stoke their fires whenever the flames got low?

When a man came home, he needed to be at peace for a minute. Couldn't Mary see that? No, she couldn't. She was always pestering him about something these days, even down to the way he dressed. If he came to the dinner table in his shirtsleeves, she objected. If he lay on the floor in the parlor to read, she scowled and said it wasn't dignified. Who cared? A man should be able to read on the floor in the privacy of his own home if he wanted. That was the problem with all the Todds. They worried too much about their own dignity. Even God spelled his name with only one *d*, but that wasn't enough for the mighty Todds.

She appeared at the door again and made a face.

"Mr. Lincoln, did you hear me? The fire needs mending. Please don't make me do it myself!"

She turned and disappeared.

He studied the fire. It was perfectly fine. Plenty of time to bank the coals and throw in a couple of sticks when needed. He believed he knew enough about tending fires to get along without her direction. Let her tend her own fire in the kitchen.

He took up his paper and tried to read. It was impossible to concentrate with her popping in and out of the room like that. He'd give all the wealth of the Illinois Central to be left alone long enough to get through a single page.

The smell of burned meat filled the house. Lately there was always something overcooked or underdone on the table. Potato soup without seasoning or milk gone sour. He wondered if it was deliberate. Was that her way of sending the message she was unhappy about something, by ruining meals? He wouldn't put it past her. Women were always using indirection to make a point—an offhand remark or whispered slight behind someone's back. Why couldn't they be direct about things, like men? If you've got something to say, state it face-to-face.

Here she was, at the door again.

"Mr. Lincoln! Mend up the fire!" Her voice quivered with fury. He made a show of staring into the columns of his newspaper.

"Don't pretend you don't hear me!" she cried.

Her anger blazed like flames on dry kindling. Well, let her be mad.

"I asked you three times! I'll make you hear me!"

She ran to the wood box and grabbed a stick. He looked up from his paper in time to see her waving it over her head. Before he had time to react, she brought it down with a smack across the bridge of his nose.

"Good God, woman!"

He jumped out of the rocker, stunned more by the shock than the blow itself. Mary gaped at him.

"Damn you!" he roared.

She took a step back, dropped the stick, and let out a cry. He turned and stomped out of the house, clutching his nose. The door banged shut on her sobs.

He headed east on Jackson Street, away from town. His nose was bleeding. He touched it gently, probing to see how bad it was. It wasn't much of a cut. Nothing broken but a little skin. Still, there was a good bit of blood. He pressed his handkerchief to it to stem the flow.

He walked fast to get away from neighboring houses and out in the country. Good Lord, that woman was terrible when she was mad, just terrible. She had worked herself into a rage over practically nothing. Shakespeare was right. Hell had nothing on this woman's fury. He was scheduled to argue a case in the Illinois Supreme Court tomorrow. What would the other lawyers think when they saw his nose? They wouldn't say anything, but they could make a good guess about it.

The pain subsided as he stalked along. It had really been more of a tap than a blow. Well, there was nothing indirect about taking a piece of wood to a man's nose. He almost had to chuckle about that. But really, it was just a fire, for goodness' sake. No reason in the world to get so worked up over a fire. Though admittedly he was ignoring her about it. He felt a little bad about that.

That was the thing about women. They couldn't stand being ignored. At least this one couldn't. She was probably mad because he hadn't made more of a fuss over the tragedy of dropping a trivet on her toe. She'd had a bad day—he understood that—but it didn't mean she had to take it out on him. He had plenty of bad days, and they didn't end with him taking a piece of wood to anyone's noggin. Well, there was no use wandering around the countryside all evening. He might as well go home and make up with her. But he'd be damned if he'd put up with that kind of behavior.

It wasn't as if she had no point at all. She did raise the children practically by herself for a good portion of each year. That couldn't be easy, though there was no helping his being out on the circuit, and she would just have to understand that. Maybe he'd talk to her about finding an Irish girl to help around the house. And maybe he could make it home more on weekends now that trains were connecting the courthouse towns. They would see.

She was waiting for him by the time he finished making a big circle and reached home. She met him at the front gate, full of remorse, wanting to see his nose. He told her it was not so bad, that it barely hurt at all. She could put a little plaster on it, and it would be good as new in a day or two.

"Can you forgive me?" she pleaded. "You know how I get sometimes."

"Yes, Mother, I *nose* how you get," he said, and they both laughed.

She had kept the food warm for him. They walked inside holding hands, as if nothing had happened.

What was it his friends had called her, back in their courtship days? A Kentucky wildcat.

CHAPTER 50

Spring 1856 to Summer 1857

In 1856, while the Lincolns were adding onto their house, blood was flowing across the prairies of Kansas. In the wake of the Kansas-Nebraska Act, slave owners and Free Soilers poured into the region, each side eager to fight. Proslavery border ruffians from Missouri rode into Lawrence, Kansas, smashed anti-slavery presses, burned the Free State Hotel, and plundered the town. Abolitionist fanatic John Brown, a man who had fathered twenty children, brought a midnight raid against a proslavery settlement on Pottawatomie Creek. Brown and his followers banged on cabin doors, dragged five unarmed men outside, and hacked them to pieces with broadswords before their families' eyes. A reign of terror had come to Kansas.

Across the North, men repulsed by events were leaving the old

Whig and Democratic parties to join the infant Republican Party. Their common bond was an abhorrence of slavery, though they differed in strategies, timetables, and passions about how to end it.

"I reckon it's time I join them," Abraham told Billy. "If there's going to be a Republican Party in Illinois, I want to make sure it's not too radical. Some of those boys would rather see the Union dissolved than a single runaway returned to his master. That kind of talk only makes things worse."

He went to work helping organize the young party, stumping hard across Illinois for John C. Frémont, the Republican nominee for president, telling voters in more than fifty speeches that they must stand by principle, freedom, and Union together. Democrat James Buchanan of Pennsylvania won the election to become the fifteenth president. But afterwards, as Abraham and other Republican leaders scoured returns, they saw that if they could pick up just two or three more states, in another four years, the White House might be theirs.

Two days after Buchanan was inaugurated, the United States Supreme Court handed slave owners a stunning victory. In the case of a Missouri slave named Dred Scott, who was suing for his freedom, the Court ruled that Negroes were not citizens under the Constitution and not included in the "all men" whom the Declaration of Independence said were created equal. Grim-faced, black-robed Chief Justice Roger Taney wrote that when the Constitution was adopted, blacks were considered inferior beings who were "altogether unfit to associate with the white race" and "had no rights which the white man was bound to respect."

The Court went even further. It ruled that since slaves were legal property, Congress had no power to keep them out of new territories. The decision unleashed torrents of condemnation from antislavery men across the North.

"It undoes everything we've been working for," Abraham stormed.

"Do they mean to force slavery on the free states?" Mary asked.

"I'm not sure. I don't think anyone knows."

"I hope to God we never see those poor creatures standing at an auction block in Springfield. It's one thing to see the slave market in Lexington. It's always been there. But I don't think I could bear it here."

Stephen Douglas came to Springfield, stood in Representatives Hall in the statehouse, and gave a speech defending the high court's decision. Abraham sat in the audience pondering and dissecting. Two weeks later, in the same hall, he stood and gave a reply. He reminded his audience that there was a time when the Declaration of Independence was held sacred by all. Now it was being sneered at and torn apart by great powers of the land to make bondage of the Negro universal.

"They have him in his prison house," he said, "they have searched his person, and left no prying instrument with him. One after another they have closed the heavy iron doors upon him, and now they have him, as it were, bolted in with a lock of a hundred keys, which can never be unlocked without the concurrence of every key; the keys in the hands of a hundred different men, and they scattered to a hundred different and distant places; and they stand musing as to what invention, in all the dominions of mind and matter, can be produced to make the impossibility of his escape more complete than it is."

It could not be true that the Declaration of Independence applied only to some men and not to others, Abraham insisted. Obviously, its authors did not mean to say all men were equal in every way. But they "did consider all men created equal—equal in 'certain inalienable rights, among which are life, liberty, and the pursuit of happiness.' This they said, and this meant."

An old black woman came to his office to see him. Her name was Polly Shelby, though everyone called her Aunt Polly. She had once been the slave of a man named Henkle, who had freed her after moving from Kentucky to Illinois. Early in his career, Abraham had represented her in a divorce case. She earned her living by washing clothes and selling eggs out of a little wagon she pulled from door to door. Every so often, she sold a dozen to Mary. Her skin was stretched tight over her face and shone with the luster of black pearl—a face that might have been anywhere between forty and a hundred years old. High cheekbones suggested Cherokee or Shawnee blood in her veins.

She let herself in and walked slowly past Billy and a couple of young law clerks who looked up from their scribbling to watch her approach Abraham's desk.

"I need help, Mr. Lincoln," she said.

"I'll help if I can. Won't you sit down?"

"I will. Thank you."

Her words were stiff with the self-consciousness of being in a white man's office on a matter of urgency to her. She wore a royal blue church dress for the visit.

"They have my boy down in New Orleans. They say they going to sell him."

"Who has him?"

"The men who locked him in the calaboose."

"How did he get to New Orleans?"

"On a steamboat. I told him not to go there. I told him bad men would get him. He would not listen."

Ten minutes later he had the whole story. She lived with her son, John Shelby, and his family. Shelby had signed on with a steamship out of St. Louis to work as a cabin waiter on a voyage down the Mississippi. In New Orleans he had gone ashore without his free papers and was promptly thrown into jail by the police. He had no money to pay a fine, so there he languished until the steamship left port without him. If not rescued soon, the local authorities would sell him into slavery to recover the costs of imprisoning him.

"They say they'll sell him to cut sugarcane," Polly said. "A black man from Illinois can't last long in no sugarcane field."

She untied a little pouch and unfolded a few dirty, creased bank notes.

"I don't have much."

"Put those away," Abraham told her. "I don't want to see them again."

"I ain't looking for charity, Mr. Lincoln."

"It's not a case of charity. It's a case of doing what's right. I can't promise anything. But we'll see what we can do."

She rose, and he walked her to the door.

"My son's little boy, he blind from disease in his eyes when he was born. He don't complain about it. He can't remember what seeing is. But every day he ask when he going to see his daddy again."

She made her way down the stairs. From a window he watched her cross the street in her Sunday dress.

"If this isn't wrong, nothing is wrong," he told Billy.

They went to see the governor, William Henry Bissell. He leaned back in his chair, looked sad, and shook his head.

"It's an unfortunate case," he said. "But I don't see that there's much I can do about it."

"You can write the governor of Louisiana and tell him they had no right to lock Shelby up," Abraham said.

"That's not exactly true. If the fellow didn't have his free papers, their laws give them standing to arrest him. You know what the black code is like down there, Lincoln."

"We can send them his papers."

"He still owes the fine. There's no legal ground for me to challenge his imprisonment. I'm sorry, but I've got no power to interfere."

Abraham's brow flushed. "The lock of a hundred keys," he muttered.

"Pardon me?"

"By God, governor, I'll make the ground in this country too hot for the foot of a slave, whether you have the legal power to secure this boy's release or not!"

"You'll just have to do that, then." Bissell smiled.

Abraham contacted the governor of Louisiana through lawyers he knew in New Orleans but got the same response. No one cared to put himself out of the way for a poor, hapless Negro.

"We'll have to use a different blade to skin this bear," he sighed.

"How's that?" Billy asked.

"I hate to do it, but we'd better pay the fine and secure his freedom before it's too late. I'll draw up a subscription list. Judge Davis will contribute. So will a good many of our Republican friends."

They sent the funds to New Orleans to purchase the prisoner's liberty. Shelby made his way back north the same way he had gone south, working on a steamer.

Aunt Polly reappeared at the office with a large basket on her arm. She set it on Abraham's desk.

"What's this? I told you I don't want any pay."

"It ain't pay. It's a gift."

She lifted a scrap of burlap draped over the basket. A rust-colored chicken with red-orange eyes poked its head out.

"Tell Mrs. Lincoln this hen is my best layer."

"You don't need to do this, Polly."

"It's a gift," she said again.

He extended his arm, and together they walked slowly down the stairs to the street, talking of her little blind grandson as they went.

"God bless you, Mr. Lincoln," she said.

He climbed back up the stairs, stood at the window again, and watched her pull her little wagon down the road.

"At least that's one lock we managed to pry open," he told Billy.

CHAPTER 51

Autumn 1857 to Spring 1858

Jack Armstrong was dead. It was hard to believe. A letter from Hannah Armstrong brought the sad news. Years of hard drinking and brawling had finally caught up with him. His last days were filled with hard ailing in bed. Hannah, who had spent much of her life nursing his bruises, stitching up his wounds, and laughing off his sprees, nursed him one last time, and then her nursing of Jack came to an end.

She had other worries she put in the letter. Their son Duff and two other fellows had gotten into a fight near Virgin's Grove in Mason County. One was dead, and Duff was in jail, charged with taking part in the killing. The other defendant had already been sentenced to eight years of hard labor for manslaughter. Now it was Duff's turn for trial.

Jack had spent his last days worrying over his boy. From his sickbed, he had told Hannah, "Sell everything we have and clear Duff." He made her promise to write Abe Lincoln and ask for help.

As Abraham read the letter in his office, old images of New Salem flashed through his mind, including the day the militia had mustered to fight Black Hawk, and Jack had clapped him on the arm and drawled, "Abe, we want you to be our captain."

He laid the letter on his desk, pushed his spectacles off his nose up into his hair, and looked at the floor.

"Billy, I'll need to drop everything for a few days," he said.

Hannah came to Springfield to sit in his office and talk it over. Her fingers, knotty from years of corn husking and pot stirring, traveled up and down the buttons of her dress as she talked.

"I didn't know if I should write you," she said. "I thought you might be busy."

"I would have been angry if you didn't write."

He thought of the time he had shown Hannah two buckskins he'd earned for surveying work, and she had sewn them onto the legs of his trousers for protection from heavy brush. Duff couldn't have been more than a year old. Abraham had lain on the floor of the Armstrong cabin, tossing the boy in the air while Hannah foxed his pants.

"Duff has too much of his father's wild blood in him," she said. "But he's a good son."

"What has he told you?"

"He says there was a fight, but not the way they make it out. He says he was provoked."

"We'll get to the bottom of it."

"They say if he's convicted of murder, he could face the gallows."

"We won't let that happen."

She hesitated, then asked the question painful to them both.

"What will the cost be? I'm afraid I'm poor, Abe."

"It won't cost you a cent. Anything I can do for you, I'll do freely, without charge."

"I could deed you our farm."

"Now, Hannah, you are going to make me angry if you keep talking like that."

The indictment gave him the state's side of the case. Duff Armstrong and James Norris had attacked James Preston Metzker on a Saturday night after all three had been drinking at a makeshift saloon near a camp revival meeting. Norris clubbed Metzker on the back of the head with a piece of wood. Duff smashed his right eye with a slungshot, a metal ball wrapped in leather and fastened to a cord for swinging. Metzker managed to get on his horse and ride home, where he collapsed into bed with a cracked skull. Three days later, he died.

Abraham went to the Beardstown jail to get Duff's side of the story. The young man was scared but adamant about his innocence.

"I hit him with my fists, but only after he provoked me. I never used a slungshot."

"The sheriff found a slungshot there."

"It's not mine. It belongs to Nelson Watkins. You go ask him."

"Why don't you tell me what happened."

"I was stretched out on a big dry goods box near one of the little whiskey stands, sleeping off a drunk. Pres Metzker came along. He pulled me off and yelled, 'Damn you, get up!' I said, 'Let me alone, Pres. I'm sleepy.' He wouldn't let me alone. He threw my hat on the ground and stomped it. I walked over to the bar to get another drink, and he caught me by the throat and spilled the whiskey.

"I told him, 'Pres, if you do that again, I'll knock you down, even if you are bigger than I am.' He came at me again, so I hit him a terrible blow. We clinched and fought like tigers. Some of the boys pulled us apart. Then I went back to sleep."

"And you never hit him with a slungshot?"

"No, I swear."

There was something about the way he said it that wasn't quite convincing. Abraham did his best to buck him up and left him sitting in jail with his head in his hands. This was going to be difficult.

He chased after the details of the case. He stopped by Virgin's Grove to walk over the scene of the crime; interviewed Nelson Watkins to confirm that the slungshot was his; read the court papers from the Norris trial. It seemed that after the fight, Pres Metzker had fallen out of the saddle a couple of times on his way home. That might be made into something.

Several bystanders had witnessed the brawl. They agreed it happened about eleven o'clock that night. Charles Allen, the state's principal witness, swore he saw the attack by the bright light of a near-full moon shining almost overhead.

At Clark Smith's store, on the south side of Springfield's square, Abraham rummaged through a small bookcase and pulled a slim, dusty volume from the bottom shelf. Flipping to the page he wanted, he ran his finger down a column of figures. It rested at the bottom of the page for a moment.

He lifted his finger and closed the book. His spectacles slipped to the end of his nose as he examined the cover closely, tapped it slowly three times.

He smiled.

The trial commenced on a sultry May morning in the second-floor courtroom of the Cass County courthouse, a simple redbrick building at Third and State Streets in Beardstown, not far from the Illinois River. Hannah sat behind the defense table, surrounded by friends and Armstrong kin, including the aging remnants of the Clary's Grove Boys. She wore a big sunbonnet that obscured most of her face when she lowered her head to dab her eyes. The jury, which Abraham managed to fill with young men, sat in two rows of raised wooden chairs, looking interested, bored, awake, and sleepy all at the same time. Abraham wore a white suit with a black necktie. He hated to wear white at trial, but his other suits were dirty.

A parade of witnesses and medical experts passed before the bench. The jurors heard descriptions of the fight, watched demonstrations of the death blows. For most of the prosecution's case, Abraham sat with his head thrown back, his gaze fixed on a spot of blank ceiling. Then he scraped back his chair, hooked his thumbs behind his suspenders, and went to work saving Duff.

Nelson Watkins came to the stand and swore that the slungshot was his, that he'd made the heavy ball himself out of melted copper and lead, then sewed a calfskin cover on it using squirrel-skin string. Abraham took his knife, cut open the leather cover to expose the metal innards, and handed it to the jury so that each of the twelve could see. Watkins claimed he had brought the slungshot to Virgin's Grove the night in question. He had crawled under a wagon to get some sleep and placed the weapon on part of the wagon's frame, then forgot all about it when he woke up. He must have left it behind. Perhaps it fell on the ground, in the place the sheriff found it, when the wagon was driven away the next morning. To his knowledge, Duff had never hit anyone with it or even had the slungshot in his hands.

Dr. Charles Parker approached the witness stand, took the oath, and explained that in his professional opinion, the blow Jim Norris delivered to the back of Metzker's head certainly could have caused his death. Dr. Parker used a human skull he had brought with him to illustrate. He explained that Mr. Metzker possibly sustained the worst of his injuries when he fell off his horse on the way home, assuming his head struck the ground. There was no way to know, given the physical evidence, if a blow from a slungshot did in fact kill him.

Charles Allen told the court he had seen Duff hit Pres in the eye with the slungshot.

"How far away were you?" Abraham asked.

"About twenty yards."

"Are you sure the dark wasn't playing tricks on you?"

"There was plenty of moonlight."

"Where was the moon?"

"Up high overhead."

"Exactly overhead?"

"Almost. About where the sun would be a little past noon in the daytime."

"You're certain you saw a slungshot in Armstrong's hand?"

"Yes."

"Saw it in the moonlight?"

"Yes."

"And you say the moon was very bright?"

"Yes, that's right."

"Where did you say it was in the sky?"

"I told you, just about right overhead."

As the witness was swearing to the position of the moon, Abraham pulled out a copy of *Jayne's Almanac* to show him that on the night in question, at the time of the fight, the moon was low on the horizon, down behind the trees, within an hour of setting. The jury laughed aloud while the judge examined the almanac. The witness wriggled and looked dashed.

In closing his case, Abraham told the jury that if Allen was mistaken about the moon, he was surely mistaken about other things. As he talked, he took off his white coat and vest and his black necktie. One suspender slipped from his shoulder.

He spoke of old times in New Salem, and how he knew the Armstrongs to be good, plain folk. Jack Armstrong had wrestled him hard and then stood beside him the rest of his life. He used to stay at Jack's cabin for days, and many a time he had rocked Duff to sleep in his cradle. Hannah had always been kind to him when he was young and alone, had washed and mended his shirts when he was too poor to pay her. He stood before them, he said, partly to pay the debt of gratitude he owed her.

The judge gave the jurors their instructions, and they filed out of the room. Abraham pulled Hannah aside and whispered in her ear.

"Don't worry, your boy will be cleared before sundown."

An hour later the jurors filed back in, looking stony faced to show they had done their jobs, and announced a verdict of not guilty. Hannah threw herself into Abraham's arms. Duff, pale but grinning, pumped his hand. The old Clary's Grove Boys clapped each other on the back and went off for drinks.

"Now, Duff, be a good boy and don't get into any more scrapes," Abraham said.

He stepped out of the courthouse and walked slowly down the street toward his room at the Dunbaugh House. Dusk was falling. Red and gold streaks lay on a varnished sky. His chest felt warm and full for the memory of Jack and for being able to help his widow.

There was a small nagging spot inside him as well. All in all, given the witnesses and evidence, he wondered if Duff really did kill Pres Metzker with that slungshot.

CHAPTER 52

SPRING AND SUMMER 1858

Then it was back into the brawl of politics. Stephen Douglas was up for reelection to the United States Senate.

"I'd say this to no one else," Abraham told Mary, "but I'd fight a bear blindfolded to take that seat from him."

"I'd turn a bear loose on Steve Douglas, if that's what it took. Do you think you can beat him?"

"I think there's a chance."

"Then we must take it."

Willie and Tad came scampering through the sitting room in pursuit of Fido, their yellow mutt, Tad yelling "G'ab him, Papa-day, g'ab him!" as they raced by.

"I'd have to be gone quite a bit," Abraham said, watching them tumble into the dining room.

"If you weren't campaigning, you'd be out on the circuit. At any rate, the prize is worth it."

As much as she hated his being away so much, in the end, he could always count on her to hold the house together. He was grateful for that.

"Well then, Mother, fill your shot pouch and powder horn. We're going on a bear hunt. Or a Little Giant hunt."

"Mr. Douglas will turn out to be a *very* little giant by the side of my tall Kentuckian," she said happily.

They began the task of piecing together another campaign. Abraham reached out to loyal and savvy advisors—men like Billy Herndon and Jesse Dubois in Springfield; Judge Davis, Hill Lamon, and Leonard Swett in the north central part of the state; Norman Judd up in Chicago; and Joseph Gillespie in southern Illinois. Supporters at Republican county conventions passed resolutions endorsing him for the Senate. The party faithful in Illinois agreed he had earned the right to face Douglas.

As it grew apparent that he would get the Republican nomination, he went to work on a speech setting out his principles. Scribbled thoughts went onto scraps of paper, then into his tall hat, to be carried around on top of his head so the best ideas and phrases could filter down to his brain. He wrote them out in a draft, revised it line by line, rewrote it to get it right.

It was plain to him that forces were working to make it a right to own human beings in every state in the Union. The nation was coming fast to a stark moral choice between slavery and freedom. Stephen Douglas stood for one side of the argument, and he must stand firm for the other.

The Republican state convention met in the capitol building in Springfield, and its delegates unanimously declared that "Abraham Lincoln is the first and only choice of the Republicans of Illinois for the United States Senate." He stepped forward, bowed to an explosion of cheers, and delivered his address, quoting from the Gospels.

"A house divided against itself cannot stand."

I believe this government cannot endure permanently half slave and half free.

I do not expect the Union to be dissolved—I do not expect the house to fall—but I do expect it will cease to be divided.

It will become all one thing or all the other.

Either the opponents of slavery will arrest the further spread of it, and place it where the public mind shall rest in the belief that it is in the course of ultimate extinction; or its advocates will push it forward, till it shall become alike lawful in all the states, old as well as new—North as well as South.

His friends worried the speech went too far and would lose him votes, that it would be regarded as a Republican threat to take slaves away from Southern planters.

"No, it means just what it says, and nothing more," he grumbled back. "It's the wisest thing I ever said. I'd rather go down to defeat with this statement than to victory without it."

Over in Washington, word reached Stephen Douglas that Abraham Lincoln would contest his seat.

"I shall have my hands full," he was telling friends and reporters. "He's as honest as he is shrewd, and if I beat him, my victory will be hardly won."

Douglas came back to Illinois to campaign for reelection. People either loved him or hated him. Everywhere he went, huge crowds turned out to listen, hurrah, and jeer. Abraham took out after him, trailing him from town to town with his carpetbag, dusty frock coat, and worn silk hat. Wherever Douglas spoke, in courthouse squares or picnic groves, Abraham was in the audience, and when the Little Giant finished, he stepped onto the platform to issue his own invitation.

"My friends, you've heard what Judge Douglas has to say on these matters. I suppose he did his best to excite enthusiasm against me. And as I find he was tolerably successful, I don't suppose he will mind one bit if I say a few words in reply. Come back tomorrow evening if you care to hear them." His supporters passed out handbills giving details of the time and place.

Democratic newspapers ridiculed him for horning in on Douglas's crowds. "Poor, desperate creature, he wants an audience," the *Chicago Times* taunted. "Perhaps he should join one of the two very good circuses and menageries traveling through the state, for they always bring out a considerable audience."

His own advisors soured on the strategy.

"Your crowds are small compared to his," Norman Judd, a Chicago lawyer and member of the Republican National Committee, observed.

"That's because most of these farmers can't afford to take off two days in a row just to listen to politics," Abraham shot back. He realized he sounded defensive about it.

"It looks bad. He takes the crowd, and you get the leavings. You should challenge him to head-on-head debates."

"He's got nothing to gain by debating me. It would just bring me attention he already has."

"If you make your challenge public, he'll have to agree. Otherwise, he'd look like a coward."

The challenge went out. Douglas, after grumbling about it for a while, gave his consent on his terms. There would be seven debates in seven towns around the state. Each debate would last three hours, with equal time for each candidate, and prescribed times for opening speeches, replies, and rebuttals.

"The eyes of the nation will be on you, Mr. Lincoln," Billy gloated. "It's a chance to debate the question of the age."

"I'll need to be ready. No one is better than Douglas at this sort of thing."

"He's the greatest liar in all America! He'll tell one thing to five thousand people on Monday and the opposite to ten thousand on Tuesday!"

"You're too rampant, Billy," Abraham chuckled. "Though I'll admit, there's some truth to that."

This will be harder than fighting two Jack Armstrongs at once, he thought. But that contest had been thrust upon him. This was different. This one he wanted more than anything.

CHAPTER 53

August to November 1858

They came by the hundreds and by the thousands. They came in rickety wagons that looked to be one part wood and three parts dirt, rags, and twine. They came on special excursion trains so crowded that men climbed onto the car roofs and rode hunched like turtles on logs. The ones who came on foot scratched up clouds of dust that hung for miles along country roads and settled in a thin, gray layer on shoulders, corn leaves, fence rails.

Seven debates in eight weeks. Ottawa, Freeport, Jonesboro, Charleston, Galesburg, Quincy, Alton. Seven chances to stand up with his old rival to trade their best arguments. Douglas had all the luck a man could ask for in politics, had risen faster than just about any other man in the West. But he was wrong about slavery and giving it a chance to spread. That would kill American democracy. Abraham knew it in his heart.

If he could make people understand, make them see that Douglas was wrong, perhaps it would be his turn for rank and glory. If not, then perhaps he really would be through with politics for good.

Douglas traveled in a private car supplied by Captain George B. McClellan, vice president of the Illinois Central Railroad and a Democrat. With him traveled his wife, the beautiful Adele Cutts Douglas, along with hordes of admirers, chests of brandy, and boxes of fine cigars. A platform car at the rear of the train carried a small cannon that boomed the news of the Little Giant's arrival. Brass bands waiting at stations struck up victorious tunes.

Abraham traveled as a regular passenger, sometimes alone, sometimes with friends. With him he carried a leather-bound notebook in which he pasted material to study and commit to memory: newspaper clippings, the Declaration of Independence, favorite passages from Henry Clay's speeches. Occasionally he took out a little harmonica and wheezed away at it, not very well.

"This is my band," he laughed. "Douglas has his brass band, but this will do for me."

As his train pulled into Ottawa for the first debate, he looked out the window and was stunned to see a Mississippi River of people flowing at him. A welcome committee, led by marshals wearing bright sashes, bustled forward. Courthouse bells rang, guns fired, men hurrahed. Banners with slogans like "Old Abe, the Giant Killer" and "Stephen A. Douglas, the People's Choice" hung over streets. Processions formed to greet both speakers: fife and drum corps, military companies, carriages covered with bunting. A wagon with thirty-two young ladies dressed in white, each representing a state in the Union, looked like a basket of flowers. The parade stretched so far that clever fellows said it was long enough to reach around town and tie into a bowknot.

The public square swarmed with spectators. Peddlers hawked flags, candied peaches, and beef jerky. The marshals had to throw elbows to clear a path for the dignitaries. Several rowdies climbed onto the roof of the speakers' stand until the flimsy boards gave way and fell into the laps of the reception committee.

Douglas took to the podium first, dressed in a stylish blue coat with shiny silver buttons, a ruffled shirt, and a wide-brimmed white hat atop his groomed mane. He attacked hard and fast in his booming, deep voice, stamping his feet and waving clenched fists. He charged Abraham with promoting abolitionism and said his "House Divided" speech was the kind of talk that could incite civil war.

"Are you in favor of conferring upon the Negro the rights and privileges of citizenship?" he roared at the crowd. "If you desire free Negro citizenship—if you desire to let them vote on an equality with yourselves—if you desire to make them eligible to office—to have them serve on juries and judge of your rights—then go with Mr. Lincoln and the Black Republicans in favor of Negro citizenship!"

He tugged at ancient prejudices.

"I do not question Mr. Lincoln's conscientious belief that the Negro was made his equal, and hence is his brother. But for my own part, I do not regard the Negro as my equal, and I positively deny that he is my brother, or any kin to me whatever! The fact is, he belongs to an inferior race and must occupy an inferior position."

Abraham's turn came. He stepped forward in his worn black frock coat with sleeves too short. His first instinct was to turn back Douglas's assault. He explained that he was no abolitionist, that he had never suggested interfering with slavery in the states where it already existed. Nor had he ever called for political and social equality between the races—in fact, he never expected to see them living together on a footing of perfect equality.

"Notwithstanding all this, there is no reason in the world why the Negro is not entitled to all the natural rights enumerated in the Declaration of Independence, the right to life, liberty, and the pursuit of happiness. I hold that he is as much entitled to these as the white man. I agree with Judge Douglas that he is not my equal in many respects—certainly not in color, perhaps not in moral or intellectual endowment. But in the right to eat the bread, without the leave of anybody else, which his own hand earns, he is my equal and the equal of Judge Douglas and the equal of every living man."

They went at it for three hours under the late August sun. The surface of the crowd fluttered with hands mopping big handkerchiefs across brows. More than once, when Abraham put on his spectacles to refer to notes, he paused to wipe sweat from the lenses. When it was over, supporters rushed the platform to congratulate both speakers. Republicans grabbed Abraham, lifted him into the air, dropped him onto shoulders that lurched toward the mayor's house. The men carrying him were on the short side, and his feet dragged the ground.

Exhilaration and disappointment mixed in him as he jostled along. Part of him felt that he had not been persuasive, that he had let Douglas throw him too much on the defensive. But the first round was sure to be the hardest, and at least it was over.

"I'm glad to know I'm yet alive," he told them when they let him down.

They came in one town after another, standing in the broiling summer heat or raw autumn winds to listen. Gusts whipped at banners proclaiming "All Men Are Created Equal" and "No Nigger Equality." More bands played while cannons fired and flags waved. When taverns got full, people made tent cities on the outskirts of town. It seemed that every farmer in Illinois was willing to forsake the plow to watch the Little Giant and the Tall Sucker stand on a platform and go at it under the prairie sky.

Douglas spoke for many when he said that in his opinion, the signers of the Declaration of Independence were not thinking of the Negro in declaring that all men are created equal. "The signers of the Declaration were white men, of European birth and European descent, and had no reference either to the Negro or to savage Indians, or the Fiji, or the Malay, or any other inferior or degraded race, when they spoke of the equality of men." The plain truth was that "this government was created on the white basis by white men for white men and their posterity forever."

Abraham spoke for many as well when he insisted that "the entire records of the world, from the date of the Declaration of Independence up to within three years ago, may be searched in vain for one single affirmation, from one single man, that the Negro was not included in the Declaration of Independence." Its authors had looked forward to the day when slavery would be only a sad memory. "I say the way in which our fathers left this subject was in the course of ultimate extinction." To teach that the black man had no share in the Declaration was to muzzle the cannon that thundered liberty every Fourth of July.

An incarnation of the American spirit lay in Douglas's utterance that he looked forward to the day when each state would be allowed to do as it pleased. If a state chose to keep slavery or to abolish it, very good. He was for the right of the people to rule. "Let each state mind its own business and let its neighbors alone! If we will stand by that principle, then Mr. Lincoln will find that this great republic can exist forever divided into free and slave states. . . . Stand by that great principle, and we can go on as we have done, increasing in wealth, in population, in power, in all the elements of greatness."

There were other sparks and flares of 1776 when Abraham pointed out that to speak of a man ruling himself was one thing, to speak of a man ruling another without his consent quite another. Douglas was blowing out the moral lights around them, he told the crowds. "The real issue in this controversy—the one pressing upon every mind—is the sentiment on the part of one class that looks upon the institution of slavery as a wrong, and of another class that does not look upon it as a wrong."

Shorthand reporters followed the candidates to capture their words. Newspapers across the country covered the debates. There was something important going on in Illinois. Editors sensed it. The visions and passions of these two men of the West were diverging currents in the stream of the national conscience. Horace Greeley, publisher of the *New York Tribune*, consecrated the meetings as "a contest for the Kingdom of Heaven or the Kingdom of Satan—a contest for advance or retrograde in civilization."

The seventh and final debate was in the town of Alton on bluffs overlooking the Mississippi River in southwestern Illinois. Mary and Bob came down on a train from Springfield to hear it. Bob had joined the Springfield Cadets, a company of boys who marched at parades and rallies. He threw back his shoulders and tried to look dashing in the dark blue coat and gold braid of his Fourth Corporal uniform. Abraham and Mary winked at each other behind his back, but they were at least as proud as he was.

Douglas's voice was used up from campaigning and whiskey. The audience strained to catch his words. But Abraham's voice was still strong. It had been getting stronger throughout the campaign. In this final debate, he tried to make people understand, with all the skill he had attained over the years, that morality was the nub of the matter.

"That is the real issue. That is the issue that will continue in this country when these poor tongues of Judge Douglas and myself shall be silent. It is the eternal struggle between these two principles—right and wrong—throughout the world. They are the two principles that have stood face to face from the beginning of time and will ever continue to struggle. The one is the common right of humanity, and the other the divine right of kings. It is the same principle in whatever shape it develops itself. It is the same spirit that says, 'You work and toil and earn bread, and I'll eat it.' No matter in what shape it comes, whether from the mouth of a king who seeks to bestride the people of his own nation and live by the fruit of their labor, or from one race of men as an apology for enslaving another race, it is the same tyrannical principle."

Then it was all over—the debates, the parades, the rallies, and the barbecues. He had given sixty-three speeches and traveled more than forty-three hundred miles during the campaign. He went back to Springfield, collapsed into his sitting room rocker, pulled off his boots and socks, and stared at his bare feet. They were swollen and sore.

Mary came in and sat beside him. For a while neither spoke.

"We're going to lose—again," she finally said.

Her face showed the weariness that comes with bracing oneself for disappointment. There was no point in sugarcoating it. She was too good at reading the moods of the electorate.

"I expect we'll win the popular vote," he said. "But it won't be enough to take the legislature away from the Democrats. Douglas will keep his place in the Senate."

"And go on bamboozling millions with his sophistry!"

"We've done some good," he said philosophically. "We've given slavery a thorough discussion and taught thousands who never gave it much thought to hate it. An evil can't stand discussion. It's like a skunk. What kills the skunk is the publicity it gives itself. What a skunk wants to do is keep snug under the barn in daytime, when men are around with shotguns."

Election day arrived, cold and rainy. As he had predicted, Republicans won more votes, but the vagaries of apportionment laws left the Democrats in control of the legislature, which would no doubt send Douglas back to Washington.

Abraham stayed in his office that evening as the returns came in, watching raindrops tremble down a windowpane and accepting the condolences of friends who dropped by. Darkness fell, and he and Billy were left to commiserate alone.

"I feel like the boy who stubbed his toe," he said. "It hurt too bad to laugh, and he was too big to cry."

"It's the Irish, Mr. Lincoln! The wild, roving Irish!" Billy was convinced that the Democrats had shipped trainloads of Irish immigrants into hotly contested regions to cast illegal votes. "It's the only way they could whip us. Fraud, bribery, and corruption—that's the grease on the wheels of the Douglas Democracy."

"There's probably some truth in that," Abraham sighed.

"I feel like hell."

"We'll both feel better soon. Another blowup is coming, and then we'll have fun again."

Billy put on his coat and went out. Abraham sat with his thoughts and the rain, wondering if this was the end. It was probably his last chance for the Senate. He was glad he had run. He had put up a good fight and given Douglas a few good bruises. But there was no reason for Republican voters to keep placing their hopes with someone in the habit of losing. His one term in Congress was as far as he'd go. Most likely he'd now sink out of view.

He blew out the lamp, locked the door, and started for home.

The paths near the square, worn hog-backed from usage, were dark and slick in the rain. As he rounded a corner, one foot slipped, and he felt himself going down.

He threw out his arms, made a quick little stutter-step dance in the mud, and managed to catch himself before he went all the way over.

A slip, not a fall, he told himself. Landing on my face would have been a fitting end to this day. At least I've had that much luck.

His superstitious side was aroused. Perhaps there was something in a near tumble. He hooked his index fingers together, gave a pull, and said it aloud to be sure.

"A slip and not a fall."

CHAPTER 54

DECEMBER 1859

He was coming out of the Bloomington courthouse one December evening when Jesse Fell, a local attorney, hailed him.

"Lincoln! We need to talk."

Fell took him by the arm and steered him through the twilight to the law office of his brother, Kersey Fell. The chambers were deserted. They lit a lamp to talk in private as dark arrived.

"Lincoln, I've been traveling back East, from Pennsylvania to New York to New England. Everywhere I went, I heard people talking about you. They kept asking, 'Who is this man Lincoln who canvassed against Douglas?' I told them we have two giants in Illinois, and that Douglas is the little one, and you're the big one."

Fell was a locomotive on two legs, always pulling a trainload of schemes and ideas. He was a lawyer, a land speculator and railroad developer, a planter of trees and harvester of timber. Folks in Bloomington, where he lived, trusted him. An ardent Republican, he dabbled in journalism and politics. Abraham let him talk.

"You know that newspapers all over the East have published your debates. They've brought you quite a reputation. A lot of smart people think you're more than a match for Douglas."

Fell's plain, clean-shaven face glowed with enthusiasm. He leaned forward and clasped his hands.

"The truth is, I think that if we can make enough people aware of your background and opinions on the slavery question, you'd make a formidable candidate for president."

"Fell, you've gone crazy," Abraham snorted.

"Humor me for a minute."

"What's the use of talking about me for the presidency when we've got men like William Henry Seward and Salmon Chase in the running? They've got deep connections in the Republican Party."

"They're both good Republicans, no doubt."

"And they're much better known to voters than me."

"That's what I aim to fix."

"Besides, they've been leaders for Republican principles from the beginning, in spite of the personal abuse they've taken. The nomination should go to one of them, as a matter of fairness."

"Service to party doesn't make a good candidate. The truth is, Seward and Chase may have rendered too much service to win. They've said some controversial things about slavery. If nominated, I doubt either could be elected."

"And you think I could?"

"I think it's possible. What the Republican Party needs in 1860 is a man of the people, someone who opposes the spread of slavery but who hasn't uttered radical statements that will drive away votes. Your debates with Douglas have proved your commitment to freedom. You have no embarrassing record. You've sprung from the humble walks of life and shared its toils. If we can get these facts before the people, depend on it: there's a chance for you."

Abraham sat back and waited. Let's hear him out, he thought.

"Now I come to the business part of this interview," Fell pressed. "I want to get some well-considered, well-written articles published in Eastern newspapers, telling people who you are and what you've done. I can furnish information about your public life. But I don't know much about your private history—when you were born, and where, the names and origins of your parents, what you did in early life. Details like that. I want you to write them down for me. Will you do that?"

Abraham smiled.

"Fell, I admit the force of much of what you say. I admit I'm ambitious, and that I'd like to hold high office. And I appreciate the compliment you're paying me."

Fell, seeing the direction he was going, started to object. Abraham shook his head.

"But there's no such good luck in store for me as the presidency of these United States. Besides, there's nothing in my early history that would interest you or anybody else. There's not much to it, I suppose, because there's not much to me."

He rose and wrapped his shawl around his shoulders.

"As our friend Judge Davis says, the jury won't buy it. Good night, Fell."

He went outside and started down the street. Fell called after him. "You haven't heard the last of this, Lincoln! You'll come around!"

Mary looked at him in disbelief when he got home to Springfield and told her he had turned Fell down.

"What harm would it do to let him get up an article?" she cried.

"There's no point in entering a race I can't win."

"Mr. Fell is an astute man. If he thinks you have a chance, then surely you do."

"To tell you the truth, I don't really think I'm fit for the presidency."

"I can't believe I'm hearing you say that, Mr. Lincoln."

"I've got no executive experience. I haven't even held public office in the last ten years."

"If James Buchanan can be president, you certainly can. You're ten times more able than he is!"

"Mother, if I had a million voters like you, I believe I actually could win that race," he said.

"Steve Douglas won't be content to stay in the Senate," she insisted. "He wants the presidency. You've said yourself that he stands a good chance of getting the Democrats' nomination. Wouldn't you relish grappling with him again on a grander stage?"

"When you put it that way, I have to confess the taste is in my mouth a little."

The next day, he took a long stroll to think it out. The sky was a mix of changes, warm blue in the east and leaden clouds in the west, with a threat of cold. Light gusts whirled brown leaves that yesterday had shone red and gold. He walked with arms folded behind his back and his gaze on the dust in the street, where the fortunes of any man might be written.

The presidency of all the United States. The highest rank in the land, a place on the honor roll of history. It was absurd that his name should be connected to such an office. Did Fell realize that he had less than a year of schooling? That he had lost two Senate elections in a row?

Mary would say that losing is part of politics, that voters admire a man who keeps picking himself up to try again. True enough.

Even if by some wild chance he was elected, he had to ask himself if he could really be a capable chief executive. He had never served as governor, like William Henry Seward and Salmon Chase. A single term in Congress was hardly sufficient training for the White House. He couldn't even keep his own office organized. Not long ago, an energetic young fellow clerking for the firm decided to do some cleaning and found seeds sprouting from piles of dirt in the corners. How in the world could a man with a bundle of papers marked "When you can't find it anywhere else, look in this" on the floor beside his desk keep a whole branch of the federal government running?

No, he'd rather be in the Senate. His talents pointed in that direction. There a man could win distinction with his oratory. That was the place of highest reverence for the Constitution and laws. If he were to run for office, he would want to challenge Douglas again for that Senate seat.

But that would have to wait several years. In the meantime, perhaps a run for the presidency would raise his standing with the people and do his Senate hopes some good. And who knew—maybe Fell was right. Stranger things had happened.

Just think of a sucker like me being president, he thought.

His memory ran back to his youth in Indiana, back to days when he had walked miles through woods to lay his hands on books about men like Washington, Jefferson, and Adams. Iron men who had endured great hardships, who had themselves become presidents.

There must have been something more than common they struggled for, something holding out a great promise for all people. Something in that Declaration of 1776 giving not just liberty to the people of the United States but hope to the world for all time.

Now, eighty-three years later, that struggle was in danger of going badly wrong. The promise that in due time weights should be lifted from all shoulders, that all should have an equal chance, was still unfulfilled.

Little by little, but as steadily as man's march to the grave, we've been giving up the old faith for a new one, he thought. We began by declaring that all men are created equal, but now we've run down to another declaration, one that says it's a sacred right for some men to enslave others.

Those two principles could not stand together. The spirit of '76 and the spirit of slavery were as opposite as God and mammon. Whoever held to the one must despise the other.

We've got to stand up for that old Declaration, he told himself. We've got to do it to save the Union and keep it worthy of saving.

Something knocked into his stovepipe hat. It went flying off his head, spilling some letters he'd tucked inside the lining. He stooped to grab them before they scattered with the leaves.

Laughter erupted on the other side of a fence. Someone had tied a string hat-high over the sidewalk between the fence and an elm tree, and he had walked right into it. He had a pretty good idea who that someone was.

Willie, Tad, and a gang of friends came charging around a corner, floppy-eared Fido racing behind.

"We caught you in ou' t'ap, Papa-day!" Tad yelled.

They climbed all over him, shouting for joy while he picked up his hat and letters.

"You rascals ought to be ashamed of yourselves for imposing on an old man," he chuckled. They clung to him, whooping and giggling as he herded them up the street toward Webster's grocery store to buy them some nuts and cakes.

When their stomachs were full, he patted their heads, sent them away to un-hat their next victim, and walked to his office.

All was quiet there. Billy was off at the Illinois Supreme Court library, hunting up precedents for a slander case. Mild early winter light streamed through the window and mixed with cool shadows.

He sat at his desk, took up his pen, and began to write.

I was born Feb. 12, 1809, in Hardin County, Kentucky. My parents were both born in Virginia, of undistinguished families. . . .

CONTINUED IN *OLD ABE* BY JOHN CRIBB

ACKNOWLEDGMENTS

Generations of historians, some professional and some amateur, have toiled in the field of Lincoln studies. They have amassed an incredible amount of information, in books and online. This novel would not exist without their work, and I am indebted to them.

For a bibliography of works I consulted, please visit my website at www.johncribbauthor.com.

While researching and writing this book, as well as *Old Abe*, I visited many Lincoln sites, such as the Abraham Lincoln Birthplace National Historic Park; the Lincoln Boyhood National Memorial; Lincoln's New Salem State Historic Site; the Lincoln Home National Historic Site; and the Abraham Lincoln Presidential Library and Museum, to name a few. Walking the ground Lincoln walked was indispensable. The staff members and volunteers at all the sites I visited were always eager to help bring Lincoln alive.

Eric Kampmann, Al Regnery, and and everyone at Republic Book Publishers are an amazing team. They are dedicated to publishing books that uplift readers. I'm honored to be counted as one of their authors.

Marly Rusoff is much loved in the literary world for many reasons, including that she is one of the world's finest agents. She cares deeply about books and writers. She has helped many people, including me, and I'm grateful for her friendship.

Kathie Bennett, founder of Magic Time Literary Publicity, is also an amazing friend. Her ability to promote books and encourage writers truly is magic. Thank you again, Kathie.

Likewise, Antoinette Kuritz of AK Literary is a wiz at getting books out into the world. She does it with great judgment and is a joy to work with.

From the first day, years ago, that I got it into my head to write a novel about Lincoln, my dear friend Bill Bennett encouraged me. I first met him when I was a young greenhorn in Washington, DC, and as he has done for so many, he not only gave me a job; he helped set the course of my career. He also helped deepen my love of Lincoln.

Several people read portions of this novel and provided invaluable feedback as it moved through various drafts. Bill Bennett, Marshall Evans, Mary Beth Klee, and Dave Lambert helped shape the book by reading early drafts. Bill Bartelt, whose knowledge of Lincoln's youth in Indiana is unsurpassed, helped weed out errors. Ian Hunt at the Abraham Lincoln Presidential Library and Museum did the same, as did Trevor Thompson and Jane Carrington at Lincoln's New Salem State Historic Site. Alan Guelzo, one of the foremost Lincoln historians of our time, kindly read the chapter on the Lincoln-Douglas debates and gave me several penetrating insights. Gene Scalia, the best friend anyone could have, gave counsel on chapters pertaining to Lincoln the lawyer. Kay Smith at the Abraham Lincoln Association graciously steered me toward some of these expert eyes.

Laura Klynstra, who designed such a gorgeous cover for *Old Abe*, worked her magic again for *The Rail Splitter*. Mark Karis again designed an interior that perfectly fits Lincoln's story.

Carroll Foster of Hot Eye Photography took a great cover shot of Jacob Smith, who was very good-natured about donning a hat and suspenders to stand in for young Abe Lincoln.

Renée Chavez, Jacque Lancaster, and Alicia Manning trained their eagle eyes on the manuscript to help make it a smoother read.

Jeremy Powers of Sky Shutter Media, who is full of creativity and technology know-how, produced a great website, videos, and more.

Noreen Burns helped me in my Lincoln endeavors with great advice and ideas, as she always does. She is a wonderful friend.

The Spartanburg County Public Libraries system is an amazing place full of not only great books but wonderful people. I've mined its collection since I was a boy, and work on this book was no exception.

The Hub City Writers Project in Spartanburg, South Carolina, is a wonderful home for book lovers and writers. The staff and board members there have helped me in many ways.

Writing this book was a labor of love, and a loving family made it possible. My wife, Kirsten, read early drafts and cheered it on. Our daughters, Molly and Sarah, gave their dad much-needed encouragement. My family is my greatest blessing.